Kirov II

Cauldron of Fire

By

John Schettler

A publication of:

The Writing Shop Press

Kirov II – Cauldron of Fire, Copyright©2012, John A. Schettler

Discover other titles by John Schettler:

Kirov II

Cauldron of Fire

By

John Schettler

*"On the sea the boldest steer but where their ports invite;
But there are wanderers o'er Eternity
Whose bark drives on and on,
and anchor'd ne'er shall be."*

—Byron: Childe Harold III.lxx.

Kirov II ~ Cauldron Of Fire

By
John Schettler

Prologue
Part I – *First Blood*
Part II – *The Operation*
Part III – *Redemption*
Part IV – *Geronimo*
Part V – *The First Gate*
Part VI – *Decisions*
Part VII – *The Enemy Below*
Part VIII – *The Best Laid Plans*
Part IX – *Desertion*
Part X – *The Gauntlet*
Part XI – *The Eleventh Hour*
Epilogue

Author's Note:

*This book is about war, and as such it will present some of the
dilemmas, uncertainty, brash cruelty and senseless insanity of war. In
this cauldron every man reacts differently, some finding the full
measure of their courage and compassion, others finding the depths of
their cowardice and depravity. One should never be surprised that a
loaded gun fires a bullet, and that a bullet kills with no thought given
to things like courage and compassion. Given the record of history one
thing is wholly apparent: the only way a man can ever truly prevent
that loaded gun from firing
is to never make one.*

*As to the ships, planes and men depicted in this novel, while the ship
and crew of the Russian battlecruiser Kirov are of my own making,
every other ship and character mentioned, from the highest officers on
down to the lowest able seaman or pilot, is a historical figure, placed
exactly in the roles and locations where they served during the action
described.*

Prologue

Argentia Bay ~ August 9, 1941

"Are you certain you wish to be so forthcoming about Japanese intentions sir?" Field Marshal Sir John Greer Dill, Chief of the Imperial General Staff gave Churchill a look that spoke volumes. "It will reveal more than you might expect at first blush."

"What is it you mean, General? This is the blow we've been waiting for. This attack on the American task force was a godsend. There's simply no way the American public will let it stand unchallenged. Roosevelt will have no difficulty now insofar as the anti-war lobby goes. This has changed everything."

"Indeed, sir, but as to Japan, and particularly the plans involving Pearl Harbor, too frank a discussion will clue the Americans in on just how much of the Japanese JN25 Naval code we've been reading. It could prove to be an uncomfortable subject."

"Here, here now Sir John," Churchill waved a dismissive hand. "We can now speak more robustly. We only had to use that kind of language when we were wooing the Americans. Now she is in the harem with us, and more than willing, I might add." He gave his Chief of Staff a sidelong glance. "Leave the employment of any discretion in this matter to me. I believe I can navigate the waters well enough."

"Oh, I have little doubt there, Sir Winston," Dill smiled. He checked the time and then gestured to the door. "I believe Mr. Roosevelt is waiting then." Churchill could not be more eager to oblige. An hour later, after the grand first handshake and all the posing for the cameras, he was delighted to have the American President with him at long last, for a private chat about the course of events that were now certain to unfold. A few pleasantries and they would get to the heart of the matter—how to survive, and then prevail in the long conflict that lay before them.

"We had several thousand gift boxes with a few tasty tidbits from the ladies back home," said Churchill. "All for your crew here, but I'm afraid they were aboard *Prince of Wales*, and she took a couple of nasty hits from these new German rocket weapons. We managed to keep her afloat and seaworthy, but they tell me I might not have had the pleasure of this meeting if I had stayed in my cabin there."

"Shocking," said Roosevelt. "How the Germans could have developed these weapons without us knowing about it is astonishing."

"Yet to this day Berlin is mute regarding any involvement in this affair. They claim that they have no surface raiders at sea at this time, though I can hardly give credence to anything Herr Hitler would say on the matter."

"I would not expect them to be forthcoming," said Roosevelt. "Well, sir, I'll get right to the heart of it. If there was any doubt in your mind as to where the United States stands in this conflict, let me dispel it forthwith. I intend to seek an immediate declaration of war against Germany, and follow it with the same against any nation who stands with her. And I intend to get what I ask for, so let there be no doubt that we are both in this together, from this moment forward. Congress is just a formality now. After this attack on our naval forces comes to light in the news media, the nation will be enraged. So we are with you, sir…the only question now is how we best prosecute this war against an enemy who has developed a weapon as fearsome as the one unleashed upon our ships at sea."

"They tell me, all my able generals and admirals, that this was unlike any normal explosion," said Churchill. "It was supposedly an atomic weapon, and one of considerable magnitude and power. I'll not bandy about, sir. We are aware of the fact that the United States has a program underway to develop such a weapon. We knew the Germans as well as the Russians were also thinking along these lines, but the shock was to learn just how advanced the enemy plans have become. The only question we have now is in regards to the extent of their weaponization programs. How many of these new bombs might they have? This we wonder."

"My generals have asked the very same questions. I'll be frank and confirm that we do have such a program in the early stages of development. I'm told it is still largely theoretical, and not nearly ready for any serious deployment as a weapon."

"Our Mister Oliphant will want to discuss the matter with your technicians. We would willingly share any and all our information on the subject. We knew the Germans were on this same track when they first tried to purchase the whole stock of Norwegian Heavy Water from the hydroelectric station at Norsk, but we managed to spirit that all off through the French Secret Service and had it delivered to merry old England."

"As part of your Tube Alloy program?" Roosevelt smiled. He was referring to the top secret code name for the program already underway in Britain, also aiming to develop an atomic bomb.

"It seems that there are no secrets between us, Franklin. My only fear is that the Germans appear to have stolen a march on us in spite of our every effort to frustrate them. We got this Heavy Water out of Norway just before the Germans invaded there, and had it safely hidden away with the Crown Jewels in the Tower of London. We first thought these experiments with Heavy Water would come to naught, then my scientists told me that they had identified a new element, and subsequently we came to believe that the development of an atomic bomb was not merely feasible, but inevitable."

"It appears that the Germans have proven that point," said Roosevelt. "The only question now is this—how do we survive until we can do the same?"

"Quite so," said Churchill. "We know what to do, and how to go about it, but this program will take time. How long can we hold out? Can you imagine such a weapon unleashed on a massed army or fleet intending to land on the shores of France? And what if the Germans deploy this weapon next against the Soviets? They could knock Russia out of the war before we get our trousers on. Then where would we be when Germany turns the full force of her ire towards the West? Make no mistake about this, sir. Germany has only flexed a finger of her armed might against us thus far. She's hit us with Goering's Luftwaffe, but we endured and beat them off with our Spitfires. Most of the

Wehrmacht is in Russia, where I hope to keep it for some time. They have only two or three divisions deployed against us in North Africa. The rest are just garrisons in France, Denmark and Norway. She's flung the heart of the Kriegsmarine at us, and our Royal Navy was master of the situation, until this most recent sortie and the advent of these terrible new rocket weapons. Up until now it's been all feint and jab at sea, what with this *Bismarck* business recently concluded. They said they would even the score, but heavens above, who would have thought they could do this? A lone raider has damaged two of our newest battleships, sunk the battlecruiser *Repulse*, and gutted a carrier. A few of our lighter ships were damaged as well. I'm afraid you suffered even more grievous harm."

"That's an understatement, to be sure," said Roosevelt. "We've lost the *Wasp*, three cruisers, twelve destroyers, and the battleship *Mississippi*. Thousands died. A group of our destroyers got close enough to spot this demon ship, and they engaged her in a firefight, then came this new terror bomb. Our Task Force 16 was completely destroyed, and only a few of the ships that managed to get in close to the enemy have been accounted for. The others simply vanished. We presume they may have been swamped by the blast wave the weapon generated. Perhaps it got the enemy ship as well, though we haven't found any wreckage."

"The ocean is very deep there," said Churchill. "If this ship has gone to the bottom, all the better. Odd that the Germans would use a weapon of this magnitude and power as they did, deploying it on a sea raider. We thought an aircraft would be the only way to deliver it on a target."

"Clearly this was meant as a demonstration, Winston. They may have intended it to frighten us into capitulation, or perhaps even to prevent our union. Apparently they got wind of our planned meeting and thought to arrange a little welcoming committee. They could see what was happening in the growing alliance between our nations. I suppose they believed our union as one implacable foe was inevitable as well."

"This ship may have had a darker mission," Churchill suggested. "It may have been bound for your east coast, intending to put one of these rockets onto New York, or even Washington. They had no qualms about firebombing London last December. Having no bombers that can reach your shores, the only way they could deliver such a weapon would be by sea, on a U-boat, or one of the surface raiders. And these new rockets allow them to fire at ranges well beyond the guns of our ships. Our battle fleets never even set eyes on this new German ship, whatever it was. We thought it was *Tirpitz*, then *Admiral Scheer*, then *Graf Zeppelin*, but all those ships have been accounted for. So we're naming this one *Geronimo*, a renegade from your own wild west for an easy handle, and we think the Germans were planning to strike you while you slept, perhaps even intending to coordinate this attack with the Japanese."

"God forbid that," said Roosevelt. "Yet what is the status of this ship? Has it sunk? My admirals seem somewhat flummoxed. They still have our cruisers and a few destroyers out hunting for this German raider, in widely dispersed groups now, so as not to present too inviting a target."

"Quite right," said Churchill. "Everything we know about this ship is a mystery. While it looks threatening in the photo images your PBY was kind enough to fetch for us, it hasn't guns worth mentioning—doesn't need them given what we have seen with these rockets."

"Our destroyers were taking quite a pounding before that terror weapon struck."

"Yes, but those guns wouldn't bother our battleships. We've even shrugged off the damage from their rockets. Both *King George V* and *Prince of Wales* are still out there in the hunt as well, the latter a bit woozy, but still on her feet. Yet the enemy has vanished. We lost contact with her shortly after that last outrageous attack upon your Task Force 16, and we've seen nothing of her since. Planes from our carrier *Ark Royal* have scoured the sea as well, and seen nothing.

Maybe she did fall upon her own sword and go down with your destroyer group."

Roosevelt leaned in, tapping the table as he spoke. "I'd like to think one of our destroyers put a few torpedoes into the monster. My admirals would like to think it too, but they tell me the Germans might have run out of rockets and turned north again at high speed. Yet we've had planes out of Iceland searching as well, and seen nothing—no sign of the beast."

"That is our only consolation then," said Churchill. "Even if they have these weapons, they may as yet be few in number. If we've sunk this ship it will give them something to think about. We've also seen no sign of these rockets deployed on any other front. The Russian intelligence reports the same. So we are led to believe this was a prototype, a first deployment, and possibly a test. It has even been suggested, as you say, that the Germans learned of this very meeting, and intended to deliver that last awful rocket which struck your ships right here, on our thinning hair, to kill two birds with one proverbial stone."

"Quite a stone," said Roosevelt. "My people concur. They think this ship, its rockets and this bomb, to be a rarity. But that will change, Sir Winston. Now that its effectiveness has been proven, the Germans will ramp up production and we could be facing these weapons again in a matter of months, perhaps weeks if they have enough material in hand for extended production."

"I doubt that, but what you say is all the more reason for us to forge ahead in the strongest possible way," said Churchill.

"Yet how, Winston?" Roosevelt held out an empty open hand to make his point. "You said it yourself. We could assemble our armies, and then what? Would the Germans simply extinguish them in one blow with another of these rocket bombs? And what if they revisit London to finish what they started with the Blitz? As you say, these weapons could easily be delivered by aircraft as well."

"We are already taking precautions. The government is dispersing to hardened bunkers all over the kingdom. What you say is correct. Our normal method of war will not do. We cannot concentrate mass in men or steel lest we simply present the enemy with a most inviting target. Our cities are vulnerable. But our military must operate by other means now, just as our ships determined they had to sail in a net of smaller dispersed groups instead of one centralized fleet. Something tells me that ships, planes and these rockets will be the means of waging this war now, and not massed armies arrayed in fronts on the continent. Yet one day, if we should prevail, we must eventually go to Berlin."

"One day," said Roosevelt, "and let us hope we both live to see it."

The two men were silent for a moment, as if sitting with that thought, realizing their own mortality, as well as the vulnerability of their nations now in the face of this awesome German wonder weapon. Then Roosevelt spoke, his voice level and serious, and edged with steel.

"Let me be plain about this, Mister Prime Minister. We will in no way be intimidated by the Germans, not for one single minute. We have a big country. If need be we can move our factories to the heartland, or the Rocky Mountains, and no rocket could fire that distance to harm them in any way. We will build an arsenal the like of which the world has never seen. We'll start with planes and ships, just as you suggest. I intend to get at Germany's throat in due course, but before we do I'll have her bombed from every airfield within range, rockets or no rockets. We'll build three bombers for every rocket they turn out if we have to, and we'll get the job done, so help me God."

"Here, here," Churchill concurred, slapping the conference table with his open palm.

"As for the Navy, I don't think Germany can bother us on our Pacific coast, but we'll more than likely have the Japanese to deal with there. Do you think Hitler would share this technology with Japan?"

"Never," Churchill said confidently.

"That being the case, then I think we'll handle the Japanese if they decide to get into it, and with little more than a third of our war effort. Germany first. We can hold Japan at bay for a time if they think we are alert and ready in our Pacific bases. I must tell you that Admiral Kimmel has put the Pacific Fleet on full alert, and MacArthur is putting his forces in the Philippines on a wartime footing as well. If the Japanese want to tangle with us, we'll make them sorry for it."

"Your determination and confidence are encouraging, sir. Let me be frank and tell you that we believe the Japanese *are* up to no good at this very minute. They have a definite plan to attack your pacific fleet at Pearl Harbor, though these events may forestall the operation, and perhaps the loss of your ships here in the Atlantic may have saved a great deal of trouble in the Pacific. That being the case, Japan's intention is most certainly war, sir. And you must know it in no uncertain terms."

"Yes…" said Roosevelt, reaching for the long cigarette holder he was fond of. "Well, you just leave the Japanese to us, Winston." He tapped his cigarette holder on the table.

"Let us know if there is anything the Royal Navy might do for you," said Churchill. "On this end, I can assure you that Great Britain will do everything in her power to drive a stake into Herr Hitler's heart and end this misguided and obscene dream of his Third Reich. You may consider the whole of our island to be an unsinkable aircraft carrier. I suggest we also develop bases in Iceland as a logistical support for your planes as they transit the Atlantic. We're likely to take the brunt of whatever the Germans have left in the cupboard to throw at us. It will certainly be another ordeal, and God help us if they unleash one of these rocket bombs on London. I have sent a formal warning to the Germans telling them that we also have these weapons in development, and that I will destroy Berlin, Hamburg or any other city, tit for tat, should they revisit us with their new wonder weapon. Let us see if they believe it, but I should be grateful to have something more than my squadrons of Wellingtons in the event they call my bluff."

"You'll have them, Winston. We're going to put everything we have into air and sea power at the outset. And my admirals tell me a large, effective submarine fleet could be useful as well. With these weapons we believe we can keep the Germans at arm's length while we build up strength and supercharge the development of this new atomic weaponry. I can't tell you how long all this will take, as my generals and admirals cannot yet tell me. But it will happen, Winston. I give you my pledge. And by God, we'll stand with England to the bitter end. There will be no separate peace, if you agree, and we'll prosecute this war until Germany is a cinder heap."

"That is exactly what I have longed to hear from you, sir. I have little doubt that we will prevail. Yet we must also give some thought to the Russians. The Germans are likely to go for Moscow this summer. Russia is a big country as well. Perhaps they can hold out, but considering these developments, we cannot count on that. What if they capitulate? In that event we could see the Germans taking a second look at invading our islands next year as well."

"Winston, don't you worry about that for one minute. I can put fifty divisions on English soil if you invite me to do so."

Churchill smiled, raising an eyebrow. "But Franklin, the boys at Bletchley Park say you haven't got nearly that many in hand."

"At the moment," said Roosevelt. "We do things quickly when we have made up our minds. The main thing is this: the United States will never accept the occupation or capitulation of England. We will fight to secure your freedom with everything we have."

Churchill smiled broadly. "Mister President," he said. "I think I should like to try one of those Cuban cigars, if you don't mind. And perhaps you and I could drink to all this over a brandy."

"We'll shake on it first," said Roosevelt, and he took Churchill's hand in a firm handshake.

"I suppose we should draw up some mutual declaration concerning these matters," said Churchill.

"Why not call it the Atlantic Charter. We have long been one people separated by that ocean, and a common language," Roosevelt smiled. "Let the ocean be a bridge between us now, and by God, I don't care how many of these new raiding ships the Germans have. I'll fill that ocean with fire and steel in due course. It's ours, Winston, all ours. We'll stomp on these U-Boats and bottle up the German fleet in the Baltic. I think our first order of business will be to secure the Azores and Canary islands and build up long range bomber bases there, then on to North Africa to do the same. I want a ring of flying steel around Germans by the end of next year. We'll bomb them day and night. They'll need a thousand of those new weapons to stop us, and I don't think they have more than a handful now, if even that many. This may have been their only existing warhead."

Churchill took a deep breath, nodding his head. "The Atlantic Charter. It has I nice ring to it. And I agree with everything you have said. We'll win through, I have no doubt. It is just a matter of time."

Part I

First Blood

"So long the path; so hard the journey,
When I will return, I cannot say for sure,
Until then the nights will be longer.
Sleep will be full of dark dreams and sorrow,
But do not weep for me..."

- Russian Naval Hymn

Chapter 1

20 August, Year Unknown

Admiral Leonid Volsky slowly climbed last stairway leading to the main deck, emerging on the aft quarter of the ship on a clear, starry night. The warm breeze of the Mediterranean was welcome compared to the harsh winds he was used to in the north, and he breathed deeply, taking in the sweetness of the night air, and the all embracing calm of the quiet sea.

They had been sailing east now for all of ten days, crossing the Atlantic for European waters, intent on learning more about the strange circumstances of their voyage. As his mind wandered through the memories of these last few weeks he could scarcely believe the images that came to him—of the accident that sent the ship into the icy fog of infinity and the amazing and confounding dilemma that followed. A chance encounter with an old fighter plane had led them into the cauldron of the Second World War, as astounding as it still seemed. Within days his ship and crew were locked in a life and death struggle against the rapidly mustered strength of the Royal Navy and then her American allies as well. His illness, the stubborn headache and that odd spell of vertigo that had sent him into the infirmary with Dr. Zolkin, had allowed his truculent subordinate, Captain Karpov, to embroil the ship in heated combat. By the time he had awakened from his fit, *Kirov* was at war and, sadly, thousands would die when her arsenal of lethal modern weaponry was set loose in the fray.

Karpov....

The Admiral still shook his head to think on the man, hoping that he had finally managed to reach him when he visited him, just days ago, a thousand questions in his mind and heart. He remembered it now as he walked the deck, ambling slowly toward the aft helo bay.

"Why, Karpov?" he had said right out, his eyes lined with pain and the awful sense of betrayal he felt.

The brooding Captain remained silent, eyes averted, arms folded over his service jacket, an expression of restrained anger still apparent on his face.

Volsky leaned forward, waiting, like a wounded father scolding a wayward son. "None of the others were involved in this," he said evenly. "Tasarov, Samsonov, Rodenko—they were all blameless. Orlov I can understand," he said slowly. "Orlov is a dullard when it comes right down to it. How he rose to Chief of the Boat still befuddles me. I certainly had nothing to do with his promotions, but here he was, ready to follow any man's lead that seemed sensible to him in the heat of action, and given more to muscle than mind when any obstacle presented itself. Yes, he's a hard man, Orlov, but not one with guile. He would never have dreamed or dared what you did. No, Karpov. It was all *your* doing, yes? Orlov was nothing more than an witless collaborator, and I am willing to bet that you had to pressure him to complicity in this mutiny." He ended with a hard fat finger on the table between them.

They were in the Captain's personal day-cabin where Volsky had summoned his wayward officer from the brig, marched under guard here for this meeting as *Kirov* sailed east, away from the black horror of Halifax.

Karpov gave the Admiral a sharp glance, averting his eyes again, still sullen and unresponsive, folded in on himself and beset with a mix of emotions—anger, frustration, outrage and beneath them all the bile of shame that seemed to choke him now, stilling his voice and darkening his mind as never before.

"That's what I must call it—mutiny," said Volsky, "for there is no other word for it. And for a flag officer of the fleet with such a bright future before you, it is almost beyond belief."

"Future?" Karpov's voice was low and barely restrained. "What future are you talking about, old man?"

Volsky brought his fist down hard on the thin wood of the table, and the sullen Captain started with the unexpected blow. "Address me by name and rank, Captain! You are talking to the Admiral of the Northern Fleet!"

"Admiral of the fleet? What fleet is this you presume to command now, comrade? We are one ship, lost at sea, and lost in eternity. God only knows where we are now, but I can assure you, the fleet is long gone, and there is no one back home in Severomorsk waiting for us to return either. It's all *gone*, Volsky. Gone! Understand that and you have your fat fist around the heart of it. If you want to understand what I did you need only open your hand and look at it. All we had left was this ship, Admiral, and no one else seemed to have backbone enough to defend her. If I had not taken command it is very likely that we would all be at the bottom of the sea now—have you considered that? So do what you will. Choke me. Shoot me! Lock me away in the brig!"

He gestured painfully at the door where a guard stood stiffly at attention, pretending to see and hear nothing, a steel mannequin that nonetheless represented the business end of the Admiral's authority here—for that is what it had all come down to in the end, a contest of authority between these two men, the aging Fleet Admiral longing for the peace and quiet of retirement, and the hungry and assertive scheming of his Captain, pushing always to reach that next rung on the ladder of advancement.

Karpov had wrestled for control of the ship, and he had nearly succeed. Had it not been for the timely arrival of Fedorov, coming as he did to the sick bay to find it secured by padlock from the outside, the Captain's plan may well have caused even more havoc. In the brief interval while the Admiral had struggled to regain his freedom and restore his authority on the ship, the Captain had unleashed hell on the Allied navies that were closing in on them from every side. And now they were living in some distant quarter of that hell, a region of silence and eerie calm, where every shore they had come upon seemed blackened with the cinders of war.

The Admiral looked away, still pained, his eyes unsatisfied. He stood up and stepped over to the guard, speaking to him softly.

"Right away, sir," the man said smartly, and then quickly let himself out of the door to leave the two officers alone.

Volsky looked at Karpov where he sulked, head lowered, his elbows leaning heavily on the table. Slowly, deliberately he pulled the chair back and stat down again. He regarded his Captain with that same pained expression, waiting, but Karpov seemed apathetic and indifferent to the whole situation now, resigned within himself to any fate that awaited him. He had mustered all the courage at his disposal in that heady moment when he first slipped the padlock on the outer hatch of the infirmary, locking both Zolkin and the Admiral inside. Now he was spent, empty, and there was nothing more than a dull ache in his head and an awful sense of emptiness in his gut. A much younger man, the ordeal seemed to have aged him, and his eyes were dark and deeply lined, so tired and listless now as he stared at the empty table.

"I don't mince words here," said Volsky, "nor do I come here to shame you any more than you have already shamed yourself. But mutiny is the word for it, and you must stand accountable—as any man must—for what you have done. No... I will not choke you, Captain, nor will I shoot you. Yet a good long visit to the brig is in order, yes? It is clear that I cannot simply set you loose on the ship again after this. What would the men think? I could confine you to quarters, but first, the brig. Yes, the brig. You will sit there and contemplate, no doubt for some time before you catch a glimpse of the fact that you *are* a man, Karpov, and then perhaps you can begin to regain some sense of self-respect again, and remorse over what you have done."

"For what?" said Karpov dully. "So that I can look forward to swabbing the deck, and then join the ranks as a common seaman with the hope of someday making rank again? Don't you see how stupidly pointless that all is to me now? I had my hand on the throat of time itself and I let it slip from my grasp." He made a fist as he spoke now, his eyes hard and cold. "Don't you understand what we could have done with this ship?"

"I am still trying to understand what we *did* do," Volsky said quickly. "You were locked up in the brig when we made port at Halifax, and I had little mind to deal with you then. The men needed me on the bridge—and thank God for Fedorov. I had at least one other head I could count on in the midst of all this insanity. Fedorov and Zolkin—yes, thank God for them both."

"You forget Troyak," said Karpov, an edge of sarcasm in his voice. "Without him I might still be sitting in your chair up there, Admiral." He tersely thumbed to the unseen citadel of the bridge, somewhere above them on the upper decks.

"That is what it came to," said Volsky. "You with your key and a finger on the trigger, me with mine, and Troyak in the middle of it all. At least he knows what the word duty means, yes? At least he had the good sense to discern a madman when he saw one—for that's what you were, Karpov—a madman. Do you have any idea how many men you killed in these engagements you were so keen to fight? That is the least of it..." The Admiral breathed heavily, and turned when he heard a quiet knock on the door.

"Come." He waited while the guard stepped into the room again, a bottle of Vodka and two small shot glasses in hand. Volsky gestured to the table and the man placed them there and then stood quietly by.

"That will be all. You may wait outside."

"Sir!" The man saluted, and stepped crisply out through the hatch, closing it with a thud.

Volsky eyed the bottle and glasses, his gaze shifting to Karpov. Then he slowly reached for the vodka, twisting off the cap and pouring them both a shot glass of the clear liquor. He pushed the small glass across the table to Karpov, who gave it a sidelong look as he did so.

"Go ahead," he said. "It will do us both some good."

He raised the shot glass to his lips and drank, exhaling with the sting of the liquor on his throat, and with a certain satisfaction that only a Russian could really understand. Karpov watched him drink, then sighed deeply and reached for the shot glass himself. He downed it quickly, saying nothing. Volsky was silent as well, and poured them both a second shot.

Something in that simple act of sharing a drink together changed the whole atmosphere of the room. The two men sat in that small interval of silence, each lost in their own inner muse for the moment, lost in their own *toska*, as the Russians might say it, that sad inward-looking reflection tinged with melancholia and the quiet ache of yearning.

At length Volsky spoke again, his voice softer, flatter, with no edge of recrimination. "I understand what you did, Karpov. Though I cannot condone it, or even explain it away, I at least understand. But that changes little here today. We have sailed across the whole of the Atlantic because I thought to get the ship away from those unfriendly waters as soon as possible, and perhaps away from the shadow of guilt we all must shoulder equally after what we saw at Halifax. What was it we did, I wonder? Fedorov thinks they thought we were Germans, and that the war started too early for the Americans. He believes our use of atomic weapons put such hot fear into the Allies that they moved heaven and earth to get the bomb for themselves. Perhaps they succeeded and the war ended differently. We do not know. Yet one thing we do know: this ship fired no weapon at Halifax Harbor."

He paused, filling his shot glass and that of the Captain one more time. "We stopped at the Azores on the way over... Madalena Harbor was destroyed as well, and I think by a very low yield weapon. I put men ashore on Pico Island for fresh water, but we found little else. Some of the buildings were still sitting there untouched by any sign of war. But there were no people—just bones where they should have been. Just bones..."

He drank.

"So I thought we would have a look at the Med. Yes, I know there are too many targets there to think anything survived if they were willing to spend a missile on a distant island outpost like Madalena

Harbor, but one gets curious, yes? You were below decks, and did not see much of this, but as we approached the Straits of Gibraltar I thought, or perhaps I hoped we might see the lights of Tangier glittering on the coastline, yet it was black as coal. Once we got closer we encountered a heavy fog, thick as good borscht, and it was deathly quiet through the strait. Gibraltar was burned and smashed—almost beyond recognition. We sailed on all night, but the fog was still on the sea when dawn came, dull and gray. We skirted the North African coast for a while. Oran and Algiers were devastated—who knows why?" He held up a hand, inexplicably.

"I turned north and sailed up into the Balearic Sea. I don't know what I thought to see there after what we had already encountered. Perhaps it was only to confirm my worst misgivings....Then again, I have always been fond of the south coast of France. I thought, one day, that I might buy a cottage there and grow grapes for wine. But no more. Nothing is growing there now..." His voice trailed off, and he tightened his lips on the edge of the shot glass. The Captain drank with him, slower now, to savor the lingering taste of the vodka and chase the bile from his throat.

"Did we do all this?" Volsky waved his arm at unseen shores as he spoke. "No. We did not. We only made it possible for *them* to do it—all the other generals and admirals and prime ministers and presidents. We showed them what power was, and they wanted it for themselves as badly as you wanted it, Karpov. So now we see the result. In truth, I cannot blame you any more than I blame myself, and all we have before us now is simply a matter of survival."

Karpov nodded, and the two men sat in the quiet for a time. Then he looked up at the Admiral, and blinked. Something in his face spoke more than he was capable of at that moment, and Volsky was wise enough to see it—the sorrow, the anguish, and the shame.

"I want to have a look at Rome before we turn and head back out into the Atlantic," said Volsky. "I thought we might transit the Aegean and head for Sevastopol, but I see no point in that now. If there is still anything living on this earth it will likely be in the southern latitudes.

We'll skirt the Italian coast, then head west again through the Tyrrhenian Sea. After that, who knows."

"That island, Admiral?" Karpov managed a wan smile.

"That island."

Volsky stood and went to the door, looking over his shoulder as he went with one last word. "I'll have the guard escort you back to the brig now. It's best that the men see the consequences of what you have done, and it's also best if you bear it like a man. In due course I'll have you transferred to your quarters, and from there I suppose the rest is up to you."

Before he left he poured his Captain one last shot of Vodka. Then he tipped his hat lightly and reached for the door.

"Admiral…."

Volsky looked over his shoulder again.

"I was wrong… I… I made a stupid mistake."

Volsky nodded gravely. It was probably as close as Karpov could come at the moment to a genuine realization of his wrongdoing, and an apology, but the Admiral said nothing more.

Chapter 2

Now the Admiral was on the aft quarter, walking with memories of his discussion with Karpov and the still heavy sense of guilt he harbored for not seeing things more clearly.

I should have seen it coming, he thought. Karpov was too wound up, too argumentative and combative—and too hungry for advancement. At the time I was preoccupied with trying to get my mind around the insanity of our situation, but I should have seen what he was planning, what he would do if given the chance. Too late now, he concluded. The man may recover himself and prove to be of some use in the days ahead. But for now he's better off in the brig where he can come to that conclusion himself.

He walked with little enthusiasm this night. They had scouted down the north Italian coast and come at last to the fabled city on seven hills—Rome. There he gazed on Esquiline, the largest of the seven, where the Emperor Nero had built his 'golden house,' at one end, with the other end blighted by the charnel pits where criminals would be buried or their carcasses left for the birds. It was a fitting metaphor for the human endeavor, he thought grimly, that the same hill should be put to these disparate uses. Once the Gardens of Maecenas bloomed there to hide the remains of the dead, but no longer. He had resisted the urge to put men ashore, unwilling to hear the reports or view the evidence they would bring back to him. It was all gone, he knew, the city, the architecture, the amphitheaters, the cathedrals, paintings, statues, the Vatican and the long history behind it all, not the mention the lives of so many who lived there.

With a heavy heart he had given the order to move on, down past Naples, which was equally devastated, and then he gave up and simply turned the ship west. *Kirov* was now cruising roughly two hundred miles southwest of Naples in the Tyrrhenian Sea as Volsky walked, and that vague sense of disquiet became something more in the back of his mind. He stopped by the edge of the deck, holding on to a gunwale, strangely alert, his ears straining to hear something in the distance. Then he felt it, an odd vibration in the ship beneath his feet and, without really thinking, he was moving toward a nearby bulkhead to look for a call phone up to the bridge.

Volsky opened the latched door and picked up the handset, thumbing the comm-link button for the citadel above. "Admiral Volsky to bridge."

The voice of Anton Fedorov, his acting Executive Officer was quick to return. *"Aye, sir. Fedorov here."*

"Any developments I should be aware of?"

"Strange that you should call, sir. We just got a message from Dobrynin in Engineering. It seems the reactors are acting up again."

"Acting up?"

"That same odd vibration, sir."

"Yes, I felt it myself here on the aft deck."

"I'm holding at twenty knots unless you advise otherwise, sir."

"Hold speed for the moment, unless Dobrynin requests slower rotations on the turbines. You might call him and ask if that might help the situation. Anything more, Captain?" He had promoted his young Lieutenant to Captain Lieutenant and *Starpom* after the Karpov incident, not two weeks past, and the young man was working into the position with real energy now, gaining experience and competence, and more confident in his abilities with each day.

"Well, sir…" Fedorov hesitated slightly, then went on. *"Signals are showing some interference as well. Both Rodenko and Tasarov have picked up on low level background noise. They…well they look worried about it, sir. Perhaps you should come to the bridge, Admiral."*

"Very well," said Volsky. "Keep monitoring the situation, Captain, I'm on my way."

Volsky hung up the receiver, latched the call box door shut and turned forward, heading for the nearest stairway up. He walked past the life boats, glad they had no occasion to use them in spite of the ordeal they had been through these last weeks. Reaching the center of the ship he now had several levels to climb, and thought again how nice it would be to have elevators put in to relieve his thick but tired old legs of the burden of carrying his considerable weight. He was up his second flight on the upper aft deck near the outer hatch when he perceived what looked like an odd discoloration on the sea around them. He stopped, sensing something very wrong, and feeling again the same thrumming vibration that seemed to emanate from the bowels of the ship.

His mind raced over the last reports he had taken in before he left the bridge. Weather outlook was good, with no fronts or impending squalls, and calm seas. Yet the night seemed to thin out around him and he perceived a light glow all around the ship that seemed oddly out of place. It should be pitch black at this hour.

As he gazed at the sea, the peculiar discoloration grew more intense, an odd milky green, and he was stricken with the fear that something was again terribly wrong. Rather than navigating his way through the labyrinthine inner passages of the ship, he decided to climb the long vertical ladder on the main tower, and enter through the first maintenance entrance, coming to the citadel through the upper side hatch on the command deck. As he started to climb, another odd sound came to him, breaking the long silence of calm sea and sky they had been sailing in. He stopped, as if frozen in place, his senses keenly alert as he listened, eyes instinctively searching the rapidly lightening skies beneath his heavy brows. What was happening? The sound filled him with both excitement and dread, for he immediately knew what he was listening to—the drone of a low flying aircraft!

Who was out there? By God, something *survived* this hell of a war after all! But who? And what was bearing down on them now in the grey skies above. Grey skies? Where has the night gone? He looked out to the horizon, astounded to see it brightening with each passing second. It was just past one in the morning when he rose from his bunk to clear his mind and take this walk on the aft deck. Could he have idled here for four hours? It seemed like minutes to him. Then all these questions suddenly coalesced into a dark shape in the sky, bearing down on the ship from the aft quarter. He reached for the next rung on the ladder, breath coming fast now, and his heart racing more with anxiety than anything else. Every instinct in his body screamed danger, and the adrenaline rushed through his system, giving him renewed strength to climb.

What now, he thought, his mind racing ahead of him to the bridge. Did Fedorov see it? Would he know what to do? Thankfully, the sound of a warning claxon signaling battle stations was a relief.

The drone of the engines was very loud now, so much so that Volsky stopped and craned his next to look behind and above where the ominous winged shadow loomed in the glowering sky. Then it suddenly seemed to come alive with white fire, and he could clearly see the hot streak of tracer rounds coming towards the ship, followed at once by the harsh rattle of what sounded like heavy caliber machine guns. They were under attack!

August 11, 1942 – Tyrrhenian Sea East of Sardinia

Flight Officer George-Melville-Jackson was up in his twin engine Bristol Beaufighter VIC for a reconnaissance run. Assigned to the newly arrived 248 Squadron, he had landed on Malta the previous day from Gibraltar where the squadron had been flying missions for Coastal Command. Now the flight of six Beaufighters was to support the crucial effort at hand as Britain struggled to push yet another convoy through the dangerous waters of the Mediterranean to send much needed supplies of food, munitions and most importantly, oil to the beleaguered island outpost.

He had flown northwest over the dangerous waters of the Sicilian Narrows, and then turned north towards the Tyrrhenian Sea until he reached a position about 300 nautical miles out where he made a graceful turn as he began to scour the sea for signs of enemy shipping. With the convoy due in just a few days time, it was imperative that the fighters and bombers on Malta keep the seas clear of heavy enemy units, and Melville-Jackson did not have to wait long before he made his first contact. Squinting through his forward windshield, his eye was pulled to a strange glow on the sea below. He nudged the stick and eased his plane down a few degrees for a better look .

"What's this, Lizzy?" he said aloud, invoking the name of his sweetheart and wife back home. "What have we got here?"

He spoke into his face mask, somewhat annoyed that he had not been advised of the contact sooner. "Sleeping are you, Tommy? What's that down there at three o-clock? Not much good having these new radars in the nose if you're not going to use them, eh?" He squinted at the strange glow below them, as if the water was upwelling from bottom and churning the surface of a quarter mile swath of the sea. There he could now vaguely discern a dark shadow in the center of the disturbance. Was it a submarine coming up from below? Impossible. This was much too big for a U-Boat.

Designed as a night fighter, his Beaufighter was also equipped with Britain's latest airborne intercept radar set in its nose, the Mark VIII unit with one of the newest concentric screens, and he wanted to know if it had the contact as well on this initial dry run. All the other Beaus had the older AI Mark IV radars, and the Germans had found its bandwidth and were doing a good job of jamming it in recent weeks. It was hoped his new set would solve the problem.

"Not a whisper of anything on my screen the whole way out," said Thomason on radar, "but right you are now... reading something at five miles—very odd though."

"It looks big! I suppose we had best get down and have a look."

Melville-Jackson put the plane into a fast descent, racing down through the pre-dawn sky with his two powerful supercharged radial engines roaring as he went. His navigator and radar man snapped alert now in the rear cupola when the plane went into action.

As he dove on the contact Jackson tightened his jaw, lips pursed beneath his sandy mustache, expecting the skies to light up with flak at any moment, but none came. A moment later the shadow on the sea took on the ominous shape of a warship, its superstructure and battlements now quite evident as he closed the distance.

"What, have we caught the Macaronis flat footed this time?" He smiled, sure he had come upon a big Italian cruiser positioning itself to lay in wait for the convoy. "Let's announce ourselves, Tommy," he shouted through the headset.

The Beaufighter was one of the most powerful long range fighters in the RAF inventory. It's bomb bays on the lower fuselage had been removed to mount four 20mm cannon there, and this was augmented by six Browning .303 machineguns in the wings, more firepower than any smaller fighter, and even more than many heavier bombers might muster.

As the plane descended he could see no markings or service flags, but he was certain from flight briefings that there would be no friendly ships in these waters if he encountered anything. On another day he might have made one high altitude flyby for an IFF run before he made a strafing attack, but not today, not with hostilities impending and the noose tightening on the island fortress as never before. Rommel had pushed damn near all the way to the Nile and Jerry was keen on smashing what was left of resistance on Malta so they could get him the supplies he needed for one last big push. If this new General Montgomery was to have any chance of stopping him short of Alexandria, they would have to make sure the sea lanes remained a hostile environment for Axis supply ships. Malta was the key to that effort—Malta and men like Melville-Jackson in his Bristol Beau. He tightened his finger on the gun triggers as he aimed the plane at the ship below, amazed to see a pulsing light surround the shadow on the sea.

"Get a message off," he called back to his navigator. "Sighted one hell of a big cruiser, these coordinates. Saying hello before we return home." He was in no hurry to get back to Takali airfield on Malta, but switched on his gun cameras as he dove, mindful that intelligence would want more than his word on the sighting. Pity we didn't have a torpedo at hand for a moment like this, he thought. Perhaps another time.

Then he fired, and the powerful 20mm cannons snarled in anger, joined by the fitful chatter of his Browning .303s. The guns sent a hail of iron at the center of the ship, raking the sea in a wild rain of fire and water and smashing into the superstructure in a storm of fire and smoke.

Volsky heard the guns firing, then the terrible howl of the plane's engines as it flashed by overhead. The sea was awash with spray where the leading rounds fell short, but they raked across the center of the ship, shuddering into her superstructure and sending a scatter of flayed aluminum shrapnel and hot white sparks flying in all directions as the heavy rounds slammed into *Kirov* with deadly effect. Admiral Volsky felt a searing hot pain as something struck his side and leg, and he was flung from his perch on the ladder, falling all of eight feet with a hard thud as his head struck a hand rail below. He was lucky he had not climbed higher, as the fall itself could have killed him. As it was, he lay unconscious and bleeding from shrapnel wounds on the deck below, and did not hear the shrill panic that wailed through the ship as heavy booted men were running in all directions, shouting and donning life preservers and helmets as they manned their battle stations.

On the bridge, acting *Starpom*, Anton Fedorov heard the awful drone of the plane as it dove to attack, hastening to the port viewport in a state of surprise and shock. Rodenko had been complaining of a strange interference on his sensor screens—Tasarov as well, but they had seen and heard nothing until the distant sound of an aircraft emerged from the thick cottony silence of the night, strangely attenuated, now loud and threatening, and then hollow and forlorn. The air seemed suddenly charged with heavy static, and a throbbing pulsation seemed to quaver all around them. Fedorov took in the scene outside the ship with wild surmise. The sea was aglow with undulating light, and the skies were brightening with an impossible luminescence. He glanced quickly at his chronometer and read the time. It was 1:37 in the morning, and the night had been clear and dark just a few moments ago, the new moon not yet risen. What was happening?

Then the sound of the aircraft seemed an angry roar, and Fedorov's better instincts for survival prompted him to wheel about. "Sound alarm," he shouted. "Battle Stations!"

A split second later the night sky seemed to erupt with light and fire, something came flashing down from above in terrible rage, and white hot shafts of light seemed to pass in through the view panes and bulkheads, like lasers, vanishing into the guts of the ship. The sound that followed was clear and unmistakable, a rattling grind of metal on metal. It was as if the light had suddenly found shape and form, and become a liquid fire, then hard iron as it finally bit into the ship.

They felt heavy rounds shudder against the armored citadel and sheer through the lattice of more delicate antenna domes above them. Then the deep growl of the plane's engines diminished, fading off the starboard side of the ship. Fedorov turned and saw everyone on the bridge staring at him, some with expressions of shock and others with fear and amazement. His mind was racing as he struggled to make sense of what he had just experienced.

"Did you see that?" Tasarov was pointing to the spot where the searing light had lanced through the bridge and vanished into the deck plates, but there was no sign of damage there at all.

Fedorov could not answer him. He knew he had to do something, take military action to secure the safety of the ship, but what should he do? He was trained as a navigator. He had never gone to combat schools, though his instincts were good and his judgment usually sound, he had no real reflex for battle at sea. He removed his cap for a moment, running the sleeve of his jacket over his brow where a cold sweat had settled. They were all waiting, watching him now, and he struggled to remember how Admiral Volsky would act in a similar situation, and how Karpov would maneuver the ship in the heat of an engagement.

"Rodenko," he said haltingly. "Look to your screen. Are we tracking that aircraft?"

"There was nothing on my readout earlier, sir, but yes, I can see him now, just barely. The signal is very weak and I still have a lot of clutter, but he's moving off to the south—fading in and out. I don't think he's coming around again."

"Tasarov—anything?" Fedorov wanted to know what was happening beneath them as well. The first rule, he remembered, was to assess their immediate situation and get as clear a picture as possible of the battle space around them. He had seen Karpov do this on exercise many times, and so he did the same, checking the ship's eyes and ears, and letting the unanswerable questions go for the moment.

Tasarov fitted his headset more snuggly, closing his eyes. Then he blinked and checked his sensor screens as well. "Nothing sir," he said. "The sea is calm. I have no transients—but I have no range either. Something is wrong, sir."

"Helm, come around. Fifteen degrees to port."

"Port fifteen, sir and coming about on a heading of 210."

Change your heading, he thought. Good. He had seen Karpov do this as well to throw any stalking enemy off the scent, the most rudimentary of evasive maneuvers. As the ship came around on the new heading the tension subsided somewhat, and then Fedorov looked to his radio man. "Mr. Nikolin," he said calmly. "Please activate the Tin Man display and do a full pan of our forward and rear arcs." If the sensors had not seen the plane, he thought, what else might they have missed?

"Aye, sir." Nikolin toggled his display to activate HD video camera systems for optical data feed to a hi-res flat panel monitor on the bridge. These systems stood on the forward and aft towers to give the bridge a real time 360 degree video view of the surrounding area. The feed came in, with mild breakup due to the residual static that still seemed to be affecting all the equipment on the bridge, but Fedorov could see that the image showed a clear, calm sea, with no sign of any visual contact on any heading. Yet it was broad daylight now! The scene seemed to astound the junior bridge crew members, who watched the screen with large round eyes, looking at the images and then at Fedorov to note his reaction. Light streamed in through their forward view panes, chasing the soft glow of their night lighting away. Fedorov blinked, amazed, but composed himself to try and set an example for the men.

"You've had an easy life these last ten days or so, Mr. Nikolin," said Fedorov. "Now would you kindly do a full search of the entire radio band. Scan everything, AM, FM, wireless and short wave bands as well, and please notify me of anything you receive."

"Aye, sir." The young *mishman* was soon busy at his radio set, and then Fedorov turned to his last senior midshipman on the watch, Victor Samsonov, his strong right arm at the Combat Information Center.

"Mr. Samsonov," he said coolly. "Your report, please."

Samsonov swallowed hard, his thick features uncertain for a moment, then launched himself into a standard status check report, his voice deep and clear. "Sir," he began, "I have nothing on my board by way of an active contact, and no systems are engaged at this time. The aircraft which made that strafing run has vanished, as least that is what my systems indicate. My board notes two fire control radar systems reporting red with full malfunction—both on the forward MR-90 systems, and I have one yellow light on the S-300 system as well."

There was damage to the ship's medium range air defense guidance radar sets for the "Klinok" (Blade) surface to air missile package, the ship's primary AA defense for threats at medium ranges between thirty and 90 kilometers. NATO planners once referred to it as the "Gauntlet" system due to its lethal efficiency, and the system aboard *Kirov* had seen many improvements since that time. The yellow light on the S-300s referred to the longer range vertically mounted SAMs on the far forward deck, a separate system, but equally lethal. They had used it weeks ago to devastate the carrier air flights off *Victorious* and *Furious*, and the thought that it might be compromised in any way filled Fedorov with misgivings.

"Anything more?"

"All three main SSM systems report green sir. We have full fire control and I have spun up one silo to full battle readiness for each system." The ship's real teeth, the lethal ship to ship missile batteries beneath their hatches on the long foredeck, were as sharp as ever.

"Very well," Fedorov nodded, remembering that the Admiral would often use that same expression after receiving a report. And for that matter he assumed as well the familiar stance that Volsky would adopt while he took stock of a tactical situation on the bridge, arms clasped behind him, chin high and a observant eye to the seas around them—mid-day seas, with the sun glistening of the low wave caps and high in the sky. He had watched the old man with much admiration many times from his former post at the navigation station, and he took heart to know that the Admiral was on his way at this very moment, collecting his thoughts for the report he would soon be asked to give himself. But minutes passed and Volsky did not appear. Time stretched on and he stood there, not knowing what to do next.

A low tone sounded and Fedorov walked quickly to the comm-receiver near the Admiral's chair to answer. "Executive Officer Fedorov here," he said, eager to hear the voice of Admiral Volsky again in return, but instead it was Dr. Zolkin in the infirmary.

"I'm afraid we have casualties, Mr. Fedorov," the voice said in a low and serious tone. *"If the situation allows, could you please come to sick bay?"*

Fedorov hesitated briefly, wondering. Then he marshaled his courage and spoke up, trying to keep his voice clear and level. "Very well, Doctor. I need to run down damage reports, but I'll see what I can do."

As he slipped the receiver back into its holder he had a sinking feeling that he knew why the Admiral had not yet reached the bridge.

Chapter 3

Lingering near the Admiral's chair Fedorov realized that he might soon be sitting there in a way he had never fully imagined, or even desired. Yet the urgency of the moment pulled at him. He could still hear claxons sounding and knew there was a fire below decks. The damage control parties were scrambling to douse the flames, and when he looked out the forward view pane he could see a column of thick black smoke rising past *Kirov's* tall central tower, up past the main mast where it darkened the rotating radar antennae with soot.

Chief Byko called up to the bridge to report the full extent of the damage, which seemed remarkably light given the sound and fury of the attack they had just endured. One of the lifeboats on the port side had been riddled with machinegun fire and set ablaze. Heavier rounds had piled into the main superstructure, some penetrating to the outermost compartments in the interior of the ship, where three seamen lost their lives and seven more were wounded by shrapnel. An examination of the damage showed that the worst of the attack had been aimed at the command citadel, though remarkably little harm was done there. The 200mm armor plating surrounding the critical systems and personnel in this area had deflected most of the heavier rounds, but some of the more sensitive radar and electronics components above suffered serious damage. The port side radar control for the Klinok (SA-N-92) Missile system was shot completely through and virtually shattered. Byko had engineers up on the roof of the citadel removing the unit and gauging their chances of replacing it with reserve components from the engineering bay.

Rodenko finally seemed to get his primary search radars clear of interference and was getting a good picture of the area around the ship, though his range seemed limited. "All clear for the moment," he said to the Executive Officer. "I suppose we can count ourselves lucky that they didn't hit the main search radars. Our Voskhod MR-900 system is green and the 3D Fregat MR-910 on the aft mast is fully operational. Not sure why our signal range is so attenuated at the moment, but it was not from any damage sustained in that attack."

"We had the same situation with signal range the last time," said Fedorov. My Navigation Radars were at 50% of capacity for several hours."

"The last time?" Rodenko looked at him. "You mean to say—"

"That was no modern aircraft that just hit us," said Fedorov. "In the heat of the moment I could not get a clear look at the plane, but I did see enough to know it was a twin engine fighter—probably a Beaufort or perhaps even a BF -110."

Samsonov frowned. He had never heard of either aircraft, and realized things were skewing off in an impossible direction again. "Then we are still back to the Second World War? This is crazy! What is going on?"

Fedorov looked at him, thinking, but said nothing for a moment. Remembering the attack, he recalled the piercing lights that lanced through the bridge compartment. Rodenko had seen them as well, and he questioned him about it.

"Those lights, Rodenko. Do you remember what happened?"

"I thought it was a laser," said Rodenko. "Came right through the main bulkhead of the citadel and hit the decks. But, as you can see, there is no damage at all." He scratched his head, clearly flummoxed by the attack.

"It was probably rounds from the main cannon on that aircraft," said Fedorov.

"Impossible," Samsonov complained. "Right through our armor? Then where are the holes?"

"I don't think they really hit us," Fedorov began, still feeling his way through the explanation himself, trying to get his mind around it even as he spoke. "This trouble with the ship's reactor Dobrynin reported… and strange light on the sea just before the attack, the odd pulsation in the air—it was all just as we experienced it before. I think we may have slipped again, moved in time again."

"But how?" Rodenko and Tasarov both turned in their chairs now, keenly attentive to what Fedorov was saying. The other crew members were listening, though Rodenko waved a hand at one, a look of annoyance on his face that set the man back to his watch on the radar.

Fedorov stepped closer and the four men seemed to form a circle, the senior officers on the bridge now, Fedorov as the acting *Starpom*, or First Officer, and his senior Lieutenants, Rodenko, Tasarov and Samsonov. He went on, still trying to sort through the situation in his mind as he spoke.

"Suppose we moved again," he began. "God only knows where now, but it was clearly not forward in time. We've slipped *back* again—or we were pulled back again. Who knows why? But it was as if we were not quite all here when that plane came in on us. Some of those rounds seemed to pass right through the bridge, just as you say Rodenko, like a laser. Then, as we solidified in this moment, the shells began to bite against the citadel's armor. We got off rather easy with this attack. Those cannons could have done a lot more harm if they had hit more critical systems, but I think most of the rounds passed right through us...because we weren't really *here* yet—we were still manifesting in this new time."

He realized how crazy his words must sound, but by now the crew had come to accept the impossible circumstances of their situation. "Look at the time," Fedorov pointed to the chronometer. "It is two in the morning, and we should be in the thick of night. Please correct me if I am wrong, but it is broad daylight now. Where has the night gone? Unless the earth's rotation has suddenly changed, we have obviously moved in time."

"But there was no nuclear detonation," said Rodenko. "How did it happen this time? How could we move again like this?"

"I don't know..." Fedorov was quick to admit his own ignorance. "We may never know. It could be that we have never really settled in time again after that first accident that sent us reeling into the past. Ever skip a rock on a pond? Perhaps we are skipping along in time like a stone skips on the water. We landed in 1941, and then skipped off the water into that nightmare world of the future, only to fall back into the drink again. We just sailed across the Atlantic, so we have deliberately moved in space."

"That I understand," Rodenko argued. "But I see no controls at the helm for time displacement! How is it possible?"

"I said I don't know," said Fedorov. "Look—we won't be able to sort through all of this any time soon. It took us days to realize what had happened the first time, but we may not have the luxury of time like that again. We need to be alert and ready, and must assume we are still not where we belong. If we *have* moved again, we need to find out where we are, because if we've landed back in the 1940s as before, then this could be a very dangerous place." He pointed to the forward view pane. "Don't be lulled by those nice calm seas and clear blue skies. The Mediterranean was a cauldron of fire during the Second World War, and we've sailed right into the middle of it. If I could only figure out the date and time…" He remembered his radio man and turned to that station, his eyes alight.

"Anything to report, Mr. Nikolin?"

"Nothing yet, sir. The band is all clouded over. I think I'm starting to get a signal, then I lose it. It comes and goes like that, but I get nothing clear enough to record."

"Well, keep at it." He surveyed the bridge, thinking what to do next. The situation had calmed for the moment, and he wanted to get below and see the damage first hand, but even more to get to the infirmary and see what the Doctor was calling about.

"We'll sort out what has happened soon enough," he concluded. "In the meantime I need to find the Admiral and give my report. Stay on that scope, Rodenko—all of you—be keenly alert now. And Mister Samsonov," he warned, "we cannot afford to be caught by surprise again. I assess no blame here. None of us saw that plane until it was right on top of us. But don't let another aircraft get within striking range of this ship, eh? If Rodenko finds anything and feeds you a contact, you have my permission to fire at will and shoot it down. I'm afraid the circumstances compel us to shoot first and ask questions later until we know what has happened and where we are." He straightened his cap, resolved.

"And now, gentlemen, I must go below. Mister Rodenko—you have the bridge."

"Aye, sir."

He made his way out the hatch and down the stairway to the decks below. Men saluted as he passed, to his uniform and rank if nothing else. They knew him as Fedorov, the young dreamer at navigation, lost always in his books when he wasn't on duty, and always ruminating on the dusty pages of history past. Yet, with the rumors that had been circulating about the Admiral, they were glad, at least, to see a ranking officer in their midst. Karpov and Orlov were still locked up in the brig, and most of the other senior officers were on the bridge. Though many of the junior officers still thought of Fedorov as one of their own, the fact remained that he was now wearing three stripes and two pips of a Captain Lieutenant, and was designated *Starpom*, the First Officer of the Boat in authority beneath Admiral Volsky.

Down in the lower decks, the chief warrant officers, or *mishmanyy*, held sway, commanding the ranks of *starshini* below them, Chiefs and Petty Officers of various classes, down through Senior Seamen, though the bulk of the 750 man crew were still at the lowest navy rank, the *matpoc* who carried out all the daily tasks required to keep the ship running in good order. The men still had on their bright orange and yellow life vests and helmets, already hosing down and swabbing the decks where residual fire damage had occurred.

Fedorov saw where the worst of the attack had riddled an outer hatch with sharp punctures, the metal spraying inward as shrapnel to kill and wound several men in this compartment. Some of the overhead insulated piping and wire conduits that ran in cluttered runs along the roof had also been sheered to ribbons, and technicians were already at work there, cutting and replacing wire and nosing about in an electrical panel fuse box that was blackened with recent fire.

"How bad was it?" he asked a seaman where he worked.

The young man looked up at him, saluting when he saw Fedorov's cap and shoulder insignia. Then he recognized the face, and half smiled in recognition. His eyes clouded over soon after. "There was a lot of shrapnel. We lost three men here," he said: "Gorokhov, Kalinin and Pushkin. The rest weren't too bad off. The *starshina* sent them to the sick bay twenty minutes ago."

Fedorov knew one of the men well enough to take the news with a bit of a sting. He nodded, his features taut but controlled. "I'm off to see about them then," he said.

"What was it, sir?" the seaman asked, his eyes wide.

"An aircraft of some sort. We haven't sorted it out yet, but stand easy. Rodenko is on the watch and we are in no further jeopardy at the moment."

"But what about the Admiral, sir? Is it true he was killed in the attack as they say?"

"Killed?" Fedorov tried to sound as if he knew what he was about, but the news shook him, and the look on his face could not conceal the emotion. "We have not heard that, seaman," he said in a low voice, "but I will keep the ship informed. For now we can only carry on. As you were."

Fedorov edged past the man into a long corridor and made his way quickly through the ranks toward sick bay. Along the way many men pressed him with questions, but he bid them to attend to their duties and hurried on, which did little to quell the anxiety that seemed to jangle the nerves of the whole ship's crew now.

Killed? The thought of Volsky dead was leaden on him now. If that were so then it would all fall on his shoulders, the responsibility for commanding the entire ship and crew. In truth, he never wanted a command position, being content with his status as the ship's navigator. Admiral Volsky had been a mentor, and almost a father to him. He listened to him, guided him, and was slowly easing him into his new role as *Starpom* these last days. He can't be gone, thought Fedorov. He can't! But if it were so he knew he would have to set an example for the others now. Volsky was the one great link that seemed to bind this crew together. They loved the man and would do anything for him, which is why Karpov's betrayal and mutiny was doomed to fail from the moment he first planned it. But now…if the Admiral was gone…

What would the men think? They had been through a great deal these last days. Even the long, uneventful cruise across the Atlantic had filled them all with a sense of foreboding ever since they first made landfall on the Azores. Rumors quickly circulated that everyone was dead and there was nothing but burned out wreckage and fire scored bones left on the islands. When they finally entered the Mediterranean Sea and scouted north to Toulon and then down the coast of Italy, the men could finally see for themselves that the rumors were true. They had gathered in groups on the outer decks, clustering near the gunwales and railings to gawk at the destruction of Rome and Naples. It did little to improve morale. Were they the last survivors of a terrible war, they wondered? And what would become of them now?

At length Fedorov reached the sick bay, seeing two first class seamen leaving with a salute just as he arrived. One had a bandaged head and the other had his arm in a sling, but neither man looked seriously injured. He slipped through the hatch, catching a glimpse of three bodies shrouded in white sheets on the tables at the far end of the room. His heart leapt when he thought he might see the Admiral lying there but then Zolkin appeared from the next room with a wan smile. The bearded, bespectacled senior medical officer was a Captain of the second rank after his long career in the Russian Navy. He was, in fact, two ranks above Fedorov, though the medical branch was not in the operational arm of the service.

"Ah, Mister Fedorov. I was hoping to see you soon. They tell me that a plane strafed the ship? Is this so? I hope there was not any serious damage. As you can see we have already lost enough." He gestured grimly to the three bodies.

"All is well—for the moment," said Fedorov. "But what about the Admiral, doctor? The men tell me—"

"Don't bother with what the men are saying," said Zolkin. "Here I was just lecturing these last two to keep their composure and stop with all these preposterous rumors. One man says this, another one says that, and the next thing you know the *Titanic* is sinking off our starboard bow." He was drying his hands with a clean white towel as he spoke, and Fedorov could not help but notice the blood stains on his medical apron.

First blood, he thought. The enemy, whoever they were this time, had finally put claws into the ship, and hurt us with an attack.

"Then the Admiral is alive?"

"Of course he's alive—at least he was five minutes ago—but he'll have one hell of a headache when he wakes up. He was struck by shrapnel when that plane came in on us. What in the world is going on, Fedorov? I thought we were clear of danger, floating around in some new nightmare of our own making. Now this! What has happened?"

"Admiral Volsky will recover?"

"Yes, he's just in the next room. Leg wound and a superficial side wound, but he was trying to climb the long maintenance ladder on the main tower and fell when we were fired on. What was that old man thinking by trying to climb that ladder at his age? The Admiral has been in fairly good health, but he is no spring chicken. Now he has a nasty weal on the side of his head, and probably a nice concussion for his trouble as well. But I've patched him up and he'll be well enough in a few days."

"We lost three men?"

"I'm afraid so. There was nothing I could do for them. They were dead before the rescue crews got them to me. Lucky for Volsky that a fire crew fetched a stretcher and got him in here safely. But what about my question. What's going on out there?"

"We don't know just yet."

Fedorov was going to say he was as much in the dark as anyone else, but an inner voice reminded him that he needed to show more resolve now, and muster all the strength at his disposal. At that moment, the comm unit buzzed and Zolkin glanced at it over the rim of his round silver spectacles.

"Be my guest," he gestured as he finished drying his hands. "It's probably for you in any case, yes? I'll get rid of this apron and tidy up."

Fedorov reached for the handset and answered. It was Issak Nikolin, his radio man reporting on a signal. *"It came in on the wireless bands, fairly weak but audible. Sounded like ship to ship traffic, sir. I recorded it, but it is in English. Something about an eagle."*

"An eagle?"

"Yes sir, but I think it's something about a ship—they say it's the fifth of the war now, at least I was able to hear that much. Then the signal cut loose and I lost it again."

Fedorov thought hard for a moment. An eagle…a ship…the fifth of the war… Then his mind suddenly joined the three odd clues and he knew like a thunderclap what it was about, and where they were!

"Keep listening, Mister Nikolin. I'll be on the bridge again shortly."

Fedorov's mind reeled with the sudden realization that had come to him. How could he be sure? How could he get confirmation?

"More bad news?" asked Zolkin as he tossed his soiled medical apron into a hamper. "You look like you've just seen a ghost. Here, why don't you sit down for a moment, Fedorov."

"No time, Doctor. I've got too much on my back just now."

Zolkin gave him an understanding look, and clasped him by the shoulder. "Yes, I can feel it," he said with a wry smile. "Take your time, young Captain Lieutenant. Catch your breath and give yourself a moment. You've been under the spotlight all these last days in your new post, and that's enough to unsettle most any man."

"Thank you, Doctor," Fedorov nodded, and then lowered his voice. "I think something has slipped again. That was Nikolin with a fragment of radio traffic. I think I may know what has happened—where we are—and it gives me no cause for comfort. How soon before the Admiral might recover?"

"Hard to say. He'll need at least a day before I allow you to pile your load on to his belly again. I'm afraid you'll have to carry things for a while longer. Go and see to your business on the bridge, and if you can manage to get some sleep, that would be good as well. I see we have an unaccountable day, and my night's sleep is gone as well, but I take it to have something to do with all the other scenes in this nightmare we've been living these last weeks. Come back when you know more and we'll all have a chance to sort it through—you, me and the Admiral."

"Probably best," said Fedorov. "I'll get up to the bridge then—oh yes—do you remember that book I brought with me and gave to the Admiral? The Chronology of the War at Sea?"

"Need to do some more reading? What are you fishing out now, Fedorov?"

"I need to check some dates and times."

Zolkin folded his arms, rubbing his thick beard as he thought. "Well I think the Admiral had that book in his quarters. After this Karpov business was finished it kept him up reading a good many nights."

"Thank you, Doctor. I'll be off now." He looked at the three men lying under those sheets. "What should we do about them? I suppose a burial at sea would be appropriate."

"I'll handle that," said Zolkin. "You've enough to worry about as things stand now. Go and find your book."

Fedorov tipped his hat with grim nod as he left, and Zolkin shook his head after him.

Yes, there was a great deal on his shoulders now, thought Fedorov. More than he had ever tried to carry in his life. He wondered if it would break his back, or if his legs would give out from under him in a crucial moment that would cost them all much more than the lives of those three men.

As he walked on down the long corridor to the ship's officer's quarters a fragment of a poem came to him when he thought about the men he had seen there in sick bay.

> *No heroes death for those who die*
> *in boats where none can see.*
> *no wreaths, no flags, no bugle calls -*
> *just peace, beneath the sea...*

Part II

The Operation

"It will be necessary to make another attempt to run a convoy into Malta. The fate of the island is at stake, and if the effort to relieve it is worth making, it is worth making on a great scale. Strong battleship escort capable of fighting the Italian battle squadron and strong Aircraft Carrier support would seem to be required. Also at least a dozen fast supply ships, for which super-priority over all civil requirements must be given. I shall be glad to know in the course of the day what proposals can be made, as it will be right to telegraph to Lord Gort thus preventing despair in the population. He must be able to tell them: "The Navy will never abandon Malta."

- Prime Minister, Sir Winston Churchill
Most Secret memo to the first lord of the Admiralty, the First Sea Lord, and his Chief Of Staff, Gen. H. L. "Pug" Ismay.

Chapter 4

Fedorov flipped through the pages of his book, intent on running down Nikolin's clues in the history. His first thought was that the ship had rebounded in time, and had returned to the year 1941, but as he read the entries for activity in the Mediterranean, he could see nothing that mated with the cryptic message his radio man had received. He was sitting in the quiet of the Admiral's cabin, where he had found the book there on the nightstand, just as Zolkin had advised him.

"An eagle, a ship, the fifth of the war," he muttered aloud. He was sure of his hunch now. HMS *Eagle* was the name of a British aircraft carrier operating in the Med during 1941 and 1942. She was found by a German U-boat that slipped inside her destroyer screen and the carrier was hit by four torpedoes broadside, keeling over and sinking in a matter of minutes. There! He had the reference now, and he had slipped in a photograph of the from page of the Daily Telegraph when the story broke in England under the glaring headline: "Fifth Aircraft Carrier Lost." He squinted at the blurry text, reading:

"Admiralty communiqué this afternoon announced that the aircraft carrier H. M. S. *Eagle* has been sunk by a U-boat in the Mediterranean. A large number of the ship's company are safe. Next of kin will be informed as soon as details are received.

H M S *Eagle*, 22,600 tons was commanded by Captain L. D. Mackintosh. She was begun by Armstrong Whitworth as a battleship for the Chilean Navy in 1913, but in 1917 Britain purchased her for 1,334,358 pounds and she was commissioned for trials as an aircraft carrier on April 13, 1920.

The last British aircraft carrier to be lost was *Hermes*, which went down last April in sight of Ceylon, sunk by Japanese bombing. Since the outbreak of war three others have been lost. The first was *Courageous*, torpedoed in September, 1939. *Glorious* was lost in 1940 after an action with the *Scharnhorst* and *Gneisenau* off Norway, and the third was *Ark Royal*."

Eagle was the fifth carrier lost in the war, thought Fedorov. He had been correct! But oddly, when he checked the date of the article it read August 12, 1942, a full year after their last dreadful ordeal in the North Atlantic. Since then they had vanished into to some unknown future time where blackened cinders seemed to be all that remained of the world. They had cruised across the whole of the Atlantic and Mediterranean Sea, and their chronometer now read August 20. Yet checking his references it was clear that the *Eagle* had been sunk August 11, 1942 at 1:15PM, and that story in the *Daily Telegraph* had come out a day later. The dates did not match up, and he was suddenly confused.

The attack by that plane, clearly not a modern aircraft of any sort, and the sudden change from darkest night to mid-day sunshine convinced him that they were indeed outcasts in another time again. Was Nikolin receiving a radio story about an event that happened weeks ago? Or was the event current, happening now, and a clear signpost to their present position in time? He needed more information, and he looked to his radioman eagerly for any further news.

He stood up, feeling the urgency of the moment and nagged by the realization that he should be on the bridge. As he did so he noticed a photo of the Admiral and his wife together there on the nightstand, and the thin tracings of pen on paper. The Admiral had been writing a letter, it seemed, and Fedorov had been so intent on getting his hands on the *Chronology of the War at Sea* that he did not even notice it until he stood to leave. He passed a brief moment tussling with the temptation to read the letter. The clear salutation was written at the top in a firm hand, *"My Darling Wife...."*

He smiled to think that if the Admiral had begun this letter earlier, when they were in the heat of action in the Denmark Strait, the woman had not even been born yet! And if he composed it in recent days it was clear that she could not have survived the devastation they had seen as they cruised from one blackened shore to another.

He was touched by the moment, but his thoughts suddenly left him feeling very alone. Every man finds his comfort somewhere within, he realized. Even the Admiral needed someone to hear him out on the long, empty nights aboard ship, lost as they were in this impossible dilemma, so he wrote to his unseen wife. Every man held on to something—memories, places, people he had known and loved, all wrapped up in that nurturing inner place he called "home."

Is there any place in this world where my heart can be at ease, he wondered? He had left no sweetheart behind when he sailed. His books and his history were his only true companions—the faces and haunting echoes of men, all long dead. He knew them so well that they often seemed more real and vital to him than his shipmates, and now here he was, thrown like a teabag into this hot water of time and in their very midst! At this moment, he realized with his sharp grasp of the history, Churchill was probably sitting down with Stalin in Moscow, and ready to break the news to him that there would be no second front in the west any time soon—if this *was* the year and month he now suspected.

The *Eagle* had been sunk on August 11, 1942. He had to be sure, and that pulsing urgency snapped his reverie and set him moving again, out the door and on his way to the bridge.

An hour later Fedorov had the answer to the many questions circling in his mind. Nikolin had been monitoring radio traffic closely, and the bands were slowly clearing up. He got hold of snippets of new broadcasts, and segments from the BBC. One after another they began to paint the gruesome new picture that *Kirov* now found herself in. The German 6th Army had just crossed the Don and captured the town of Kalach as they drove for their ill-fated attack on Stalingrad. Further south Operation Edelweiss was in full swing as well, and the Russians had lost the oil fields of Maykop as they fell back on the Black Sea coastal ports in considerable disorder.

There were other gleanings, smaller engagements that were given passing mention in the news stream. In the South Atlantic a U-boat attack sunk Norwegian SS *Mirlo* and all 37 crew members abandoned ship in 3 lifeboats to be picked up by the British sloop HMS *Banff*. Fedorov was able to hone in on the exact time and place of that attack in his research library: 2:27 PM, some 870 miles west of Freetown, Sierra Leone—the work of U-130. The night raid on Mainz by 154 RAF bombers was also reported, all events that had occurred on Aug 11, 1942. The evidence mounted to the conclusion that *Kirov* had slipped into the cauldron of fire once again.

Yes, thought Fedorov, out of the frying pan of the North Atlantic and into the fire of the Med! But they had lost all the days they had sailed in that black oblivion of the future. They had never really determined what year they had been in when Volsky set the ship on a course across the Atlantic, but now they were back, just a few days after they had disappeared in that first engagement with the Royal Navy, but a full year had passed in the war while they were gone. And this time there was no easy option to turn off into the wide expanse of the Atlantic and avoid conflict. This time they had sailed right into the bottle. There were only three ways out of the Mediterranean Sea: Suez, the Bosporus, and Gibraltar, and none of the three would be easy sailing. They had been sighted and attacked in the very first seconds when they emerged in this new time frame, and Fedorov had little doubt that they would soon be facing the most difficult decisions of their lives.

The young Executive Officer was finally convinced of the where and when of their present fate. That had been the easy part for him. He was a willing believer after all they had been through, and there was no Karpov on the bridge to oppose his speculation this time. Now he had to decide what to do about it, and more than ever he wished Admiral Volsky was sitting there in the command chair. What should he do?

The other men on the bridge were watching him, their attention moving from their radar screens and equipment to his own fitful activity near the navigation station. They could see the furrowed brow and dark eyes as he flipped through reference books, and peered at data stored on his pad. The more they watched, the more it became evident that Fedorov was very worried about something.

"Well Captain Lieutenant?" Rodenko finally came out with it. "What have you been digging up this last hour and a half—another bad dream?"

"Bad dream?" Fedorov looked over at his sensor chief. "You've said it well enough, Rodenko. If I'm correct, and these reports Nikolin has intercepted are accurate, then we've a real nightmare on our hands this time, and the only question in my mind now is what to do about it."

"Don't worry, Fedorov," said Rodenko. "My systems are beginning to clear up now. I'm getting coastal returns from both Sicily and Sardinia, and I can see air contacts over those islands, though nothing is headed our way. We won't be caught by surprise like that again, and we can blast anything we encounter out of the sea. So all you have to do is set our course. What are you worried about?"

"Well…If the date is what I think it is, then this is August 11, 1942, and we are very close to one of the largest naval operations of the war. What am I worried about?" Fedorov gave him a hard look, lowering his voice so the other men would not hear. "I can tell you that in one short word," he said darkly, "survival."

They had argued it for a very long time when the hatbands finally gathered at the Admiralty. PQ-17 had been a disaster when twenty-four of 39 merchant ships had been sunk in the ill fated attempt to run supplies up to Murmansk. Now the Prime Minister had insisted that they do the very same thing in the Mediterranean! The Admiralty had its reservations, to be sure. They were already stretched too thin in the Atlantic, and losses of both men and material had been rather severe. The German U-Boats had been having a field day feasting on convoys and sinking far too many ships, and there never seemed to be enough cruisers and destroyers to go around.

Now he was asking the navy to clench their fist with all of 50 warships to serve as escort for a convoy of only 14 transports to Malta! It seemed preposterous at first. The disaster on that last run to

Murmansk had forced the cancellation of all convoys to Russia for the moment, and now this? Yet with his usual forceful eloquence the Prime Minister has clarified the critical importance of the island to the whole war effort then underway in the west.

Things had not been going well for Britain that year. Rommel had landed in Africa and chased Auchinleck back to Gazala, then sent him packing again in May on a long retreat to the Nile Delta. Now the battle lines were no more than 60 miles west of Alexandria, and Tobruk sat in stubborn isolation for a time, invested by Italian troops well behind that battlefront, the sole remnant of the favorable positions the British 8th Army once commanded in North Africa. It had finally fallen on the 21st of June, leaving nothing for the British to do in their desert war but lick their wounds near El Alamein and ferry fighters to Malta's embattled garrison. The tide of Axis victory threatened to sweep their entire position away, and Malta was now the last, solitary rock in the stream.

If there was anyone who could sketch out the dire nature of the situation, it was Churchill, and he had done so, convincing his Admirals that the defense of Malta was of utmost importance. "We may lose our ships at sea in this struggle," he argued "but Malta is an unsinkable aircraft carrier, sitting right astride the supply convoy lanes the enemy needs to use to reinforce Rommel." From Malta the RAF could send out far ranging patrols to spy out the enemy supply ships and vector in their strike aircraft. After their disaster at Crete, the German Army was not likely to attempt another parachute assault on the tiny island, and the Italian Navy had not demonstrated either the resolve or the ability to cover an invasion by sea.

So Malta had become an echo of the fabled Battle of Britain, bombed day by day from airfields on Sicily and Sardinia, and defended by flights of Spitfires ferried in by Royal Navy carriers. The Germans could swarm the whole of North Africa, Churchill argued, but the British needed to hold only three places to ensure eventual victory: Gibraltar at one end, the Suez Canal at the other, and Malta in the middle of that cauldron of fire and steel. The island was a rock in the enemy's soup, and as long as it could be held Rommel's supply lines could never be fully secured.

So it was that the "Operation," as it came to be called in the discussion, was deemed so vital that the Royal Navy would be asked to send fully half of its available escort fleet to secure it. Churchill's eloquent arguments, shouted from the pedestal of his commanding position as Prime Minister, could not be dismissed, and so there would be another convoy—another "Winston Special" to be designated WS-21S. Its mission was the delivery of vital food and oil to Malta, and it was to be given the most powerful escort of any convoy in the war to date.

No less than five aircraft carriers would support various aspects of the operation, to muster as much seaborne air power as possible. The two grand old battleships of the interwar period, *Nelson* and *Rodney*, would both be assigned at the heart of the main escort. Identical in design, and representing the whole of their class, there were no others like them, with the biggest guns in the Royal Navy at 16 inches. Ponderous and slow at a top speed of just 21 to 23 knots on a good day, they were nonetheless well armored and perfect in this role of escorting slower merchant ship traffic. Both had served well in guarding the Atlantic convoys from German surface raiders, and one, HMS *Rodney*, had been instrumental in the hunt for the *Bismarck* a little over a year earlier.

Nine other cruisers and some thirty destroyers, including forces from the Eastern Med as well, would combine in one of the largest sea operations ever attempted. All these warships had been gathered to the defense of just fourteen precious merchant ships, including the vital fast oil tanker *Ohio* that Churchill had wrangled from the Americans after much exertion of his unique powers of persuasion.

The five carriers bore exalted names born of empire: *Indomitable, Victorious, Eagle.* Two others would join as well, the *Argus* and *Furious*, the latter with a special assignment in ferrying thirty-eight Spitfires to Malta's hard pressed air squadrons. The cruisers were named for provinces and outposts of that empire: *Nigeria, Kenya,*

Manchester, Cairo, and others bore names of the same ancient Greek Gods who had presided over the fate of men on these waters in ages past: *Charybdis, Sirius,* and *Phoebe.*

This massive force had sailed from home waters down to the Bay of Biscay where the carriers had drilled their planned operations, scrambling fighters and staging fly bys over the convoy for plane recognition drills. For their own part, the fourteen ships practiced high speed emergency turns, and movement from the open sea four column formation to a tighter two column sailing order that they would use in more constricted waters. They sailed through the Pillars of Hercules, passing the mighty Rock of Gibraltar on a grey, moonless night enshrouded in fog, August 10, 1942. The very next day the five carriers went into action, their new Sea Hurricanes replacing the older Fulmar fighter squadrons to provide air cover over the convoy. HMS *Furious* was living her third life, rebuilt from near scrap metal after her harrowing encounter with a strange German raider a year ago in the North Atlantic and pressed again into service on her ferry mission, flying off her Spitfires that same day.

All seemed to be going according to plan in those first hours, until disaster struck the convoy an hour after mid day on the 11th of August when a stealthy and experience German U-Boat commander, Kapitän Rosenbaum, slipped past the fitful escort of destroyers and sent a fan of four torpedoes into HMS *Eagle.* All the torpedoes hit home in four shuddering explosions, one after another. The ship was ripped open and water surged into her gutted bowels sending the carrier into an immediate and unrecoverable list. In the next few minutes men rushed about for their lives, leaping in to the sea to grasp anything around them that seemed to float. One man flailed over to a comrade, recognizing his ashen face, only to find that the man had been ripped in two, his lower torso and legs sheared off in the initial explosions.

After twelve successful missions in those same waters, and a long, distinguished career, HMS *Eagle* keeled over and sank in a matter of minutes. Thankfully the bulk of her crew was saved and plucked from the sea by nearby destroyers. It was the fifth carrier lost in the war to date by the Royal Navy, and twelve Sea Hurricanes went into the sea with her, the bulk of 801 Squadron and all four planes comprising 813 Squadron were lost. Only four planes in her 801 Squadron survived, as they were already in the air and were able to land on the carrier *Indomitable.*

The plan, like all plans before it, was beginning to fray right at the outset. It was hoped that the heavy escorts would guarantee a safe passage at least as far as Bizerte, but HMS *Eagle* was sunk hundreds of miles to the west, due north of Algiers. The suddenness and shock of the attack was an awful harbinger of what was yet to come on this adventure—"Operation Pedestal" as it came to be called. It told the Admirals and Captains that their enemies were well aware of their plans and had assembled a considerable force in opposition. Kesselring boasted that, after recent reinforcements from other theaters, he could fling upwards of 700 planes at the British fleet. Beyond this there were U-Boats and Italian Subs in the Med, and near the islets of Pantelleria and Lampedusa, the Italians also had a hornet's nest of fast attack torpedo boats to strike at any ships that made it past Cape Bon at the northernmost tip of Tunisia to begin the last desperate run for Malta. In those narrow, mine infested waters, a place where the more powerful British battleships could not go, the small, fast craft were the ideal defenders.

Yet there was one other element the Admiralty had not planned for—could never have planned for, in spite of their harrowing encounter with the same dreadful raider a year ago—*Kirov.*

Chapter 5

Melville-Jackson strode through the outer entrance to the flight officer's room at Takali airfield on Malta, ready for debriefing, and with quite a story to relate. Wing Commander David Cartridge was there along with another pilot out that morning for reconnaissance, George Stanton, and for this occasion Air Vice Marshall Keith Park, chief of the Malta Air Defense effort was also waiting when he entered. Jackson saluted crisply and took his chair.

"Good afternoon gentlemen," said Park with an amiable smile. "How's the new radar kit?"

"Well enough, sir," said Stanton, "A bit limited in range but more than suitable for low level sea search."

"I must say we had rather a different experience on our flight," said Melville-Jackson. "I made a visual sighting of my target before we ever got a peep on the radar. Thought my mate was sleeping at first, but he swears his scope was clear until we were right on top of the damn thing."

"Ah, yes," said Park. "This big Italian cruiser you reported... Latitude 39.00, Longitude 11.16 from your report. Some two hundred miles east of the Cagliari, on a heading of 225 south by southwest."

"Yes sir. Came up on it all of a sudden. Odd disturbance in the sea as well. Thought it was a submarine blowing tanks until I saw the disturbance was much too big, and the contact as well. It was definitely a warship, sir, though I must say we haven't had much of a look at the Italian Navy just yet, so I can't be more specific other than to say this was at least a cruiser—most likely a heavy cruiser at that."

Park was a crisp and thorough officer, with a penchant for details and a good understanding of all the new technology that was impacting the war effort, particularly the new radar sets. "Well

Jackson, you've only arrived yesterday from Coastal Command, and yes I dare say the Italians are not too fond of sailing that far west, but do have a look at ship silhouettes before you fly out again this afternoon. The waters in these regions get fairly busy, and you'll want to know exactly what you are shooting at next time around."

For his part, Park knew well what he was talking about when it came to air operations. A New Zealander and First World War flying ace, he soon rose through the ranks to become a commander in the RAF. He was also well versed in naval matters, having gone to sea at the early age of nineteen on a steamship where he earned the nickname "skipper." He later fought at Gallipoli, and the battle of the Somme where he learned firsthand how valuable good aerial reconnaissance could be to the outcome of any military conflict. In fact, he had flown old Bristol fighter recon planes in the First World War, biplanes then, and had many kills against German fighters for his effort. When the second war came Park was an air vice Marshal taking part in the defense of London with Number 11 Group, RAF. He had fought in the skies over the city, and taken part in the planning and briefing in the Battle of Britain bunker at RAF Uxbridge. After a stint in Egypt, Malta seemed the perfect place to post a man like Park, for it was enduring its own daily struggle with the Luftwaffe and his experience fit hand in glove.

"You say you took gun camera footage of this ship?"

"Yes, sir," Jackson replied. "Gave them a taste of my cannon as well. Caught them flat footed, it seems. They never fired a shot before I was over them and gone. Yet I thought the better of trying to come round for a second pass after waking them up. A cruiser that size is a job for the full squadron."

"Indeed," said Park. "Well, we'll have a good deal to do over in the Ditch these next few days." He was referring to the underground cave sites beneath the city of Valletta where the island's fighter defense was coordinated. "I was going to send you out to hit Comiso on Sicily this afternoon. We need to pound their airfields there as well before things get so hot with this convoy that we're thrown completely on the defense. But seeing that you've jumped on something here, we'll give that mission to 235 Squadron with the Mark I Beaus. You've a couple newer planes in 248 Squadron, and two with these new radar sets. So it looks like your job will be to hunt north for this contact and ascertain her position and intentions. Admiralty indicated that the Italians have their 3rd and 7th Cruiser Divisions operating in the Tyrrhenian Sea, and they will definitely be up to no good insofar as this convoy is concerned."

"Right enough, sir." Jackson was game for any sortie they would put his name to, and the four men spent the next several minutes going over the briefing for the Comiso air strike mission for 235 Squadron before the technicians brought in his gun camera footage and began to mount it on the projector.

"These other two gentlemen have had a look or two at Italian cruisers," said Park. "And I daresay I've a fair amount of experience in the matter as well." They looked at the film with interest and, as the footage ran, Park found himself edging forward, hands clasped behind his back, leaning in slightly to get a better look. The opening frames were clearer, though the range was farther away and the contact seemed shrouded in shadow. When Jackson began firing in earnest the shells sent a wild forest of thin geysers spraying up all around the ship, which was struck amidships near the main superstructure where a fire soon started and began to obscure the images with smoke.

"Can you run that back to the start and hold a few stills?" said Park over his shoulder. "Yes... There now... Have a look at that gentlemen. What do you make of if, Mr. Cartridge?"

The wing commander was quick to reply. "Not an Italian cruiser sir, where are the stacks?" He pointed at the screen. "That tall mainmast area there where most of the fire was concentrated—I don't see a stack. It should be about here on most Italian cruisers, and angled slightly back, with one more smaller stack located aft. That could be this feature here," he pointed again, "but this main superstructure area is all wrong for an Italian ship in my view—at least for their cruiser designs. And it looks too big, sir."

"Yes, quite a monster this one," said Park. "Look at that shadow on her aft deck. Is that a float plane? Could it be a battleship?"

"Can't see much in the way of big guns from this angle. The forward deck seems rather empty, but these images aren't very clear, sir. Odd shadows and light, and too much smoke when you get in close."

"All the same, I'm glad you took your shot Jackson." Park folded his arms, a glint in his eye as it lingered on the images.

"If that's the case, sir, they'll need a whole squadron to deal with a battleship—a flight of six planes at a bare minimum. But I thought fuel shortages are keeping most of their big ships in port."

"Yes, they've been using them to refuel their destroyers and lighter escort ships, but if they've gotten wind of this operation they may be pulling out all the stops and sending out heavy units."

"Doesn't sound much like the Italian Navy I know, sir," said Cartridge. "They'll fight when they have to, but more often than not they think twice about that, particularly if they can't provide adequate air cover, or if we've got heavy units in the vicinity. For that matter, I can't imagine a battleship would be there all by itself, sir. It might be a big freighter, but that would surprise me as well with no escort."

Park raised his eyebrows in agreement. "Let's send this along to Intelligence and see if we can find this fellow again later today for confirmation. For the moment, however, I don't think there's much else we can do about it. Good job, Jackson. You may have put us on to something here. Get some rest and be ready for another sortie in short order. In the meantime we'll get a Maryland from 69 Recce Squadron over at Luqa Field to fly reconnaissance and make sure this ship isn't heading our way. Carry on, gentlemen."

Aboard *Kirov* Fedorov was convening his own briefing in the sick bay with Rodenko, Tasarov and a very woozy Admiral Volsky who had awakened with a raging headache, just as Zolkin had predicted. He was stabilized, and the shrapnel wounds had been thankfully minor. Still, he was not clear headed, and the pain killers Zolkin gave him made him somewhat drowsy.

Is this what it is to sit at death's door, he thought to himself. Memories of that awful sound of the chattering machine guns, then the sharp bite of metal on metal, the whine of ricochet, the hot fire of the pain in his leg and side as he slipped from his perch on the ladder and made that headlong fall. Then he felt the hard thump on his head, a flash of white light, sharp pain and darkness as his awareness seemed to collapse inward on itself like a black hole.

Now he longed for sleep, and just a moment's rest without the burden of command, but here was Fedorov, with another impossible story that he must certainly believe. His voice seemed to echo in his mind, and he struggled to focus his attention. The young officer had been right at every step in their first encounter in the dangerous waters of WWII, and there was no reason to believe otherwise now.

"Operation Pedestal," he said slowly after his First Officer had finished speaking. "Yes, I studied this battle in the academy, but that was too long ago to remember the details. Something tells me you have that well in hand, Mr. Fedorov, and I can give my aching head a rest. Yes?"

"I have a 50 page paper from the American Naval War College on the campaign, sir. It will tell us everything we need to know—down to the last details: dates, times, orders of battle—everything."

"Where are we now?" asked Volsky.

"Sir, I changed our heading to 210 right after the attack, and we held that course for two hours at twenty knots. But we are about to exit the Tyrrhenian Sea, and I believe that course will be very dangerous for us now. I have just come about to head northeast again on a heading of 45 degrees. We are making our way back into the Tyrrhenian Sea, which could provide us a little maneuvering room away from the major action getting underway now while we catch our breath."

"And you tell me you believe the current date and time is August 11, 1942 at sixteen hundred hours—give or take a few minutes I suppose." Volsky managed a wan smile, though it was clear to them all that he was still in considerable pain. "Not August 20th?"

"Yes, sir. I can only go by radio intercepts we've made, but events reported would seem to indicate that HMS *Eagle* was sunk today at mid-day, at 13:10 hours. Nikolin says he is still getting residual radio traffic on that event regarding the movement of survivors to Gibraltar. We would not be hearing that traffic a week later if it was August 20th."

"So what happened to those days we were sailing across the Atlantic?"

"I cannot say, sir. I can only make my best estimate of our current time."

"Of course…Well done, Mister Fedorov, as always. Your prompt action may have saved the ship from blundering into the middle of something we would come to greatly regret. It is imperative that we steer well away from this operation. The only question now is what course to set in our present circumstances? But before we begin, I would like to ask that one more officer be included in this briefing." The Admiral looked at his good friend Dr. Zolkin. "Would you kindly summon Mister Karpov, Doctor?"

"Karpov?" Zolkin was quick to express the reaction they all had, his face clearly registering displeasure.

"Yes, yes, I know how we all still feel about the man given what happened. But he is a highly trained officer, one of the best combat officers in the fleet. I would like him to hear this briefing so that we might have the benefit of his opinion from a military perspective."

The Doctor folded his arms, frowning."Well if you want my opinion, there was nothing admirable in the tactics he displayed in the North Atlantic. He sailed directly into the teeth of strong enemy forces and engaged them with no regard to life, principle or anything else beyond his own personal ambition. God only knows what he was planning to do at Argentia Bay, set another nuclear missile loose on Churchill and Roosevelt?"

"I understand, Dmitri," said Volsky, addressing his friend in a more personal manner. "But you are the psychologist here. What will we do with this man? Do we leave him rotting in the brig for the duration of this business? Who knows how long we will be at sea, perhaps indefinitely, yes? I agree that Karpov made serious mistakes. His judgment was clouded by his own desire to make some decisive intervention, and perhaps by something darker. He will be the first to know this. Yet he is a serving officer in the Northern Fleet, or at least he once was. Perhaps we see what he did as the work of a madman, or worse, an animal. But if he is ever to have the chance to redeem himself and become a man again, in his eyes and in ours, then we must find a way to give that opportunity to him. Don't you agree?"

Zolkin started to say something, then checked himself, thinking for a moment. He rubbed his dark beard and nodded. "Perhaps you are right, Admiral. We may not like the man—even despise what he did—but yes, he is a man nonetheless, and one of our own. Would I be pleased to see him become something more than we all may think of him now? Yes, of course. But I must tell you that I have real misgivings at this stage."

"As do I," Volsky agreed. "But we must begin somewhere—*he* must begin. Send for him…Unless I hear further objection from these young officers?" He looked first at Fedorov, then Rodenko and Tasarov. They all took the situation with the seriousness it deserved, but none voiced an objection, and the Admiral sent a guard to fetch Karpov while they discussed the recent air attack and damage sustained by the ship. Rodenko reported that he had good response from the main search arrays, though he was somewhat concerned over the condition of the medium range tracking radars for the ship's missile defenses. Tasarov said he had no problems with subsea sensory capabilities, and also noted that he was very pleased with young Velichko's improving abilities on sonar.

Zolkin threw one more comment in while they waited. "What about Orlov? He's down in the brig as well—in a separate cell I hope.

The last thing we need is for the two of them to be commiserating together."

"I have given him some serious thought as well," said Volsky. "Orlov did not come up through the naval schools like Karpov. He was a *mishman* and advanced to his position the old fashioned way, by waiting it out and working his way up the ranks. I accepted him as Chief of Operations, as that is where I found him when I came aboard for these maneuvers, if we can use such a word for this ordeal. Yet I have never been fond of the way he handled the men. Beyond that, Orlov has no combat naval training to speak of, and I doubt he has the brains for it in any case. No—he was clearly subverted by Karpov in the events that transpired days ago. Karpov needed his authority, and I think his muscle in many respects, before he would dare what he attempted. I do not hold Orlov blameless—not by any means. But I do not think he had anything to do with initiating this mutiny."

"I'm glad you have called it that," said Zolkin. "Because that is exactly what it was."

Volsky nodded, but continued with one last thought. "Perhaps one day we will hold a proper hearing and court martial for them both. But for now we do not have the time to bother with that. As to Orlov, I assigned him to Troyak's team yesterday. He's a bull out of his pen for the moment, and too accustomed to bullying anyone who opposes him. But Troyak—" Volsky smiled. "Troyak is the one man on this ship that can back Orlov down if he has to, from a physical standpoint and also considering the temperament of the man."

"Yes, thank God for Troyak," Zolkin was quick to agree.

"He knew his duty when he saw it. Such men are natural leaders. So sending Orlov to join the ship's commandos where Troyak can smooth out a few of the rough edges seemed like a good idea. That is exactly the sort of situation that will benefit a man like Orlov, do you agree?"

"A good plan," said Zolkin, and the other men nodded.

"Very well," said Volsky, turning his head when a knock came on the outer hatch. "I believe that will be Mister Karpov under escort from the brig. Let him in, gentlemen. And then let us see if we can sort out this mess and decide what best to do."

Chapter 6

Karpov entered the room, eying the others with a guarded expression, but saying nothing. He had expected this, a kangaroo court where the others would flay him and decide his punishment, and he had already resigned himself to the fact that he would likely be busted down to Able Seaman, and rot in the ranks aboard this doomed ship for years. It came as some surprise then when Admiral Volsky indicated this was to be a tactical briefing, gesturing that they should all have a seat around Zolkin's desk. He endured the edgy glances and looks from the others, but seated himself next to Tasarov in sullen silence, waiting.

"Very well," Volsky began from his recovery cot. "I will give the floor to my First Officer, Mister Fedorov."

Karpov suppressed a wince at that, realizing again what he had risked, and done, and lost. He fixed his gaze on the desktop, not meeting the eyes of the others, ashamed on one level, and angry on another at his own stupidity. Here was a young *Starshina*, still wet behind the ears and three ranks beneath him now elevated to First Officer of the ship. But when Fedorov began to speak he was again shocked at what he heard.

"To bring you abreast of our earlier, discussion, Captain," Fedorov began by addressing Karpov, who did not fail to notice he was referred to by his proper rank, which he appreciated. One thing about Fedorov—he was always respectful, even if Karpov no longer believed he deserved that respect. "…the attack three hours ago was made by a twin engine fighter aircraft, possible a British plane out of Malta, or even a German long range fighter off Sicily or Sardinia. I did not get a good look at it, but I'm inclined to believe the former. Its sudden appearance led me to research that has since indicated we have slipped backward in time again and remain involved in the Second World War. I don't know how it has happened, but Dobrynin reported that same odd reactor flux just before the event, and …well…here we are, strafed by a twin prop fighter aircraft. To be as specific as I can at this point, I believe the present day and time to be August 11, 1942, at 16:20 hours." He glanced at the wall clock, which Zolkin had reset earlier to account for the time shift they experienced."

Karpov's eyes widened as he heard the unbelievable yet once more, but there was no way he could argue otherwise, and he had come to accept the impossible as a matter of daily occurrence on this ship by now, so he waited to hear more.

"We are now in considerable danger, bottled up in the Mediterranean Sea, and very close to a major air-naval campaign that was fought as the British attempted to relieve Malta by sending a convoy of much needed supplies and oil. The next three days will see major combat operations to the southwest of our current position, which is presently here." He stood up and indicated a position on the wall map in the infirmary. "Our present course is 45 degrees and we are making twenty knots. We have minor damage, but most critical systems are functional, and Chief Engineer Dobrynin tells me that the reactors are now stable and in good operating order."

"Operation Pedestal, Karpov," said Volsky looking at his ex-Captain. "You recall it from the academy?" Karpov thought for a moment, and then nodded in the affirmative and Fedorov continued his briefing.

"The action has begun," he said. "The convoy reached the first Axis submarine picket line north of Algiers at mid-day and, true to the recorded history, the British light carrier HMS *Eagle* was sunk by torpedoes. They are continuing east and will not be engaged again until 20:00 hours, near dusk this evening—a probing attack by some 36 planes off of Sardinia. There will be two more attacks until the convoy reaches the Skerki Bank northeast of Bizerte. At that point, if the history repeats itself, the heavy escorts will turn back while a force of lighter cruisers and destroyers attempts to ram the convoy home, around Cape Bon, down through the Sicilian Narrows, and then to Malta. They will endure heavy attacks by fast torpedo boats from units based at Pantelleria near Cape Bon, and as they approach Malta by renewed air attacks from Comiso and other airfields on Sicily. This convoy was the most heavily escorted of the war to date, with some 50 British warships, including two heavy battleships and five…now four aircraft carriers, all trying to secure the safety of just fourteen merchant ships. That said, only five supply ships got through to Malta, and one, the tanker *Ohio*, was barely afloat and had to be sandwiched by two destroyers under tow to get her there. Beyond that, the British are going to lose several valuable cruisers and a few destroyers as well."

"To make it simple," said Volsky, "it is a hornet's nest of fire, right astride our most logical route of escape. If we head for the Atlantic as planned now, we will most certainly become embroiled in this operation, and I do not think the British will welcome us at the Suez Canal, or facilitate our transit there, so we have quite a problem on our hands here. Now I want the best opinions from each of you— particularly from you, Captain Karpov, as you are one of the finest tactical officers in the fleet."

Karpov heard the admiral's praise and it seemed to bolster his flagging spirits, particularly in front of the other men, making the mantle of his shame a little easier to bear. He glanced at Volsky appreciatively, and sat just a little straighter in his chair, no longer slouching with averted eyes, but now stealing sidelong glances at the others to gauge their response to his presence.

"Our present course will lead us into the Tyrrhenian Sea again," said Fedorov. "That area was not much involved in the action, as both sides were focusing their efforts more on the triangle formed by the Cape of Tunisia, Sardinia and Palermo on Sicily. That said, the Italians had several cruiser divisions planning to rendezvous off Palermo for a possible run at the convoy when it attempts to transit the Sicilian Narrows. Our radars are clearing up, and we may soon have a fix on their positions. But we have been spotted, and I have little doubt that whoever fired on us will be looking to confirm the sighting, and may have planes in the air at this very moment searching for us. If British, they will most likely assume we are one of these Italian cruisers, but they also arranged regular reconnaissance runs over Italian ports in the vicinity, and in time they will make an accounting of all ships in the Italian inventory. Then the real game begins for them, and they will wonder who and what we are, just as before."

"And if it was an Italian or German plane that attacked us?" Volsky asked.

"Then they will have to assume we are part of the Allied operation, perhaps a fast cruiser intending to mount a raid on coastal facilities. That would be rather risky, but it is possible. The danger for us now is therefore acute. On 11 August, there were upwards of 780 Axis aircraft in the region, 328 Italian and 456 German if the history echoes true. The Allies had 140 aircraft on Malta spread over nine fighter squadrons, three torpedo squadrons, four bomber squadrons, and two more for dedicated reconnaissance. They were just reinforced by 37 more Spitfires flown off HMS *Furious* at about the same time the *Eagle* was torpedoed."

"*Furious?*" Karpov finally said something, somewhat surprised to hear the name of an aircraft carrier he had made a point of attacking just days ago—a year ago now, as astounding as the prospect seemed.

"Apparently the ship survived," said Fedorov. "Probably towed to Iceland and then back to Scapa or the Clyde. In any case, they've repaired her and put her back in service if she's here—though we have no real confirmation of that yet. She is mainly used for these ferry operations, just as CV *Wasp* was first used to send those fighters to Iceland…"

The men shifted uncomfortably. It was as close as Fedorov wanted to come to any recrimination for Karpov here, but it needed to be said. Karpov stewed, but said nothing, though his posture was more closed now, arms folded, and just a touch of anger in his eyes.

"The British managed to keep fighter strength on Malta high, and will bring even more to the fight on their carriers. Needless to say, we do not have that many air defense missiles aboard." His point was obvious, and Rodenko spoke up on that note about the damage to the Klinok system tracking radars.

"We can replace one system within twenty-four hours," he advised, "and probably rebuild the second from spare components, but that will take much more time. The long range S-300 system is viable, and there was no damage to our close in defense systems, but the First Officer makes a good point—780 or more Axis aircraft, 140 or more on Malta and then their carriers. How many there, Fedorov?"

"Forty-six on *Indomitable*, including four recovered from *Eagle*, another thirty-eight on *Victorious*—yes, we fought that ship as well in our first encounter, Captain Karpov. The old carrier *Argus* was present, but no real threat with a flight of just six Sea Harriers, and there would be four more Albacores on *Furious* after her Spitfire deliveries, though she is heading west for Gibraltar and out of the immediate combat zone. So let us call it about ninety carrier borne aircraft escorting the convoy at this point."

Rodenko nodded his head, raising an eyebrow. "That makes over a thousand aircraft in the region. Well, we have ninety-six Klinok medium range SAMs still available in inventory, and forty-seven of the longer range S-300s." If my arithmetic is correct, then we have about one missile for every seven planes out there in theater."

"Not a very good equation," said Admiral Volsky. "The attack just hours ago showed us how vulnerable we are should even one enemy plane get through our defense umbrella."

"At the moment we are perhaps in more danger from Axis aircraft than from the British," said Fedorov. "Kesselring has ordered numerous squadrons of II Air Corps in Italy, and also units that were based at Sicily, to airfields on Sardinia for the first phase of the gauntlet they are setting up for the British. So the center of gravity is moving west at the moment. There may be flights up this minute and we could be called to battle stations again at any moment. The only good thing about our position here is that we would probably be presumed to be Italian—by both sides. We must decide what course to set, and that quickly, before we are spotted again and that presumption changes."

"What about submarines," said Karpov, and with an audible tinge of foreboding in his voice.

Fedorov was quick with an answer. "The initial Axis picket line is much farther west, but they had seventeen Italian subs and two German U-Boats available for the operation. Here, I have the reference from my paper… Seven Italian and two German U-boats deployed north of Algeria. Ten more Italian submarines between Fratelli Rocks just west of Bizerte and the northern entrance to the Skerki Bank closer to Sardinia. This is their second picket line, and some of these submarines will move northwest off Cape Bon to operate in cooperation with aircraft. In addition, an Italian submarine should be deployed just west of Malta, another off Navarino, and three boats about a hundred miles west-southwest of Crete." He put the document aside but pointed out these areas on the wall map. "As for the British, they'll have a couple subs watching the Strait of Messina, and then four more well west of Malta. Again, there shouldn't be anything near us now."

Tasarov confirmed that they had located no signals that might be hostile submarines thus far, and this seemed to ease the tension in Karpov's shoulders a bit. He shifted, leaning on his right arm where the elbow rested on the side of the desk.

"We would have to cross both those Axis submarine picket lines if we move west now by the most direct route," said Fedorov.

"Out of the question," Volsky replied quickly. "And I think we can thank our stars that we emerged where we did. A few more hours and we would have been right in the thick of things. Yet the question still remains: what course *should* we take in the long run, and where should we be in twenty-four to forty-eight hours at the height of the battle? Opinions gentlemen?"

Rodenko ventured to speak first "What about the Strait of Messina?"

"That will not be easy sailing for us, I can assure you," said Fedorov. "There's an Italian cruiser base there and two more British subs are lurking nearby as well."

"I can take out those British subs easily enough," said Tasarov.

"And we have sufficient missile inventory to deal with air strikes at the moment, and plenty of Moskit-IIs left for those cruisers if they bother us." Rodenko reinforced his idea, waiting.

"There will also be shore batteries, and the channel is very narrow. But suppose we do bull our way through as we surely can," said Fedorov. "Then where do we go? As you have said, the British will not welcome us at Suez. I suppose we could run through the Aegean and try to run the Dardanelles. After another transit of narrow and dangerous waters, we would then be master's of the Black Sea."

"We could smash Axis forces there and assist our comrades!" Tasarov smiled.

"Comments on this course?" asked Volsky, his bushy brows rising as he looked to the others, particularly Karpov, who spoke next.

"Heading for the Black Sea is a definite possibility," said Karpov. If we made it through the Bosporus then we might join in the fighting around Novorossiysk. For that matter, we might even be able to smash the German Sixth Army with our remaining nuclear weapons and prevent the misery and death of Stalingrad. That option could reverse the course of the war in the east much sooner. If we have to fight again, why not fight directly for Russia this time?"

Volsky frowned at the mention of nuclear weapons, the image of the massive explosion at sea all too fresh in his mind.

"Stalin would certainly appreciate that," said Volsky. "I had some time to consider such a course when we first began this misadventure. We also have information about the course of events that will be more valuable than the weapons we could use. We know the timing of every German offensive and its objective, correct Mr. Fedorov?"

"True, sir, but that is 1800 sea miles to the Black Sea, and through the Strait of Messina, past Crete and all the Axis bases in Greece, then into the Dardanelles for a 200 mile cruise in those restricted waters, through minefields, past shore batteries and also within range of German air power. And once we do fight through we'll still be bottled up in the Black Sea for the duration of the war, assuming we do not suddenly vanish again. Then what? How long before our own countrymen begin to insist on a little more than information from us? I have not forgotten what we all said about Stalin the first time we visited this question."

Volsky nodded, a grim expression on his face.

Fedorov continued. "Here is another alternative. I think we could get up north into the Ligurian Sea easily enough, or into the Northern Med south of Toulon. We could hover off the coast there and wait out the operation. Let the two adversaries slug it out as they did historically and interfere as little as possible. If we sail anywhere near the action now then we will eventually be discovered and engaged by one group of forces or another. Yes, we can probably prevail in these actions, but eventually word will get out and the concentration of Axis forces will begin to mass against us—or British. We could even be attacked by both sides at once in the confusion. We can't go west in the short run," he reasoned, "and if we go south east through the Strait of Messina we are committed to a long voyage through the Aegean, with enemy airfields on every side and then internment in the Black Sea."

"Then it looks like our only option is north away from the major fighting while we consider this question further," said Volsky.

"A good possibility," said Fedorov. "But it would mean we would have to run past these Italian cruiser patrols, and then surge north through the Tyrrhenian Sea again and either run north of Corsica, past the major Italian base at La Spezia and a lot of enemy aircraft, or else we must risk the narrows of the Bonifacio Strait and the Italian naval facility at La Maddalena there."

"And then what," said Volsky. "Suppose we do this and fight our way west of Sardinia and Corsica by one route or another. Suppose we work our way north of the Balearics, then what? We will be ready to run the final bottle-neck to Gibraltar, yes? And what will we find there?"

"The British," said Fedorov flatly. "Everything they have left after the battle will withdraw in that direction, and the heavy units will be there well before us, unless we move quickly. Battleships *Nelson* and *Rodney* for a start, and a swarm of destroyers and cruisers. Their carriers get beat up pretty badly if the action follows the history. They have already lost *Eagle*, and later on *Indomitable* will also be hit and damaged to a point where she can no longer operate effectively. *Argus* is of no concern, but they will still have our old friends *Victorious* and *Furious*, and all the air power they have left flying out of Gibraltar, another unsinkable aircraft carrier like Malta."

"Could we punch our way through, Karpov?" The Admiral wanted to bring the Captain into the discussion.

"Of course," Karpov said immediately. "You saw what we did when the full power of this ship was focused as it can be in dire need. I do not wish to say that the course I took was the wisest...." He paused, and Volsky could see that this was difficult for him. "...or even that my choice of tactics was correct in that regard. I was obsessed at the time with the possibility of striking a decisive political blow—one that would truly alter the course of events and leave the world a better place for the Russia we left back home, the country we all swore to protect and defend."

"True, but we have seen the result, Captain, and it was not pleasant. We found hell out there, or as close to it as any man can come while alive on this earth. We may all get there again on our own when we pass on," he smiled. "But I have little desire to go there again now."

"But that is what we must do if you sail west or east," said Karpov. "We must pass through the gates of hell—be it Messina, Bonifacio, the Bosporus or Gibraltar. The western course is also some 1800 miles of dangerous sailing, and a major battle at the end."

"Yet one you feel we can win?"

"Certainly, though much will depend on the status of our missile inventories when we reach that place. I know I invite your rebuke with this next remark, but I must tell you that where this ship sails, there are no unsinkable aircraft carriers." He put his fingertip flatly on the desk to emphasize his point. "We have the means to obliterate either Malta or Gibraltar if it comes to that, and wipe their air power off the map in one blow. And if there is still any stomach for the ideas we discussed before this whole thing began, then I must also say that by destroying either of these bases we would decisively effect the outcome of this war, particularly now, at this moment, August of 1942. The loss of either base would seriously tip the balance in favor of Rommel in North Africa. He may not prevail in the end, but there would be a strong chance that he pushes into Alexandria, or even to the Suez Canal itself. It could effectively knock Britain out of the land war, at least for a time."

Fedorov noted how each course eventually led to the deployment of nuclear weapons to make a decisive blow and alter the course of the war, at least in Karpov's mind. He was cautious about getting into a shooting match here with the Captain, but was not surprised to hear this hard line from him. He glanced at Volsky before he spoke, waiting to see if the Admiral had any remarks, then offered another point.

"What about Operation Torch. The Americans are about to enter the war in those landings, scheduled for November 8th. If Rommel manages to push the British back to Suez, he will still find the American Army behind him in due course. All things considered, the loss of Malta may make a considerable difference—and certainly Gibraltar, but I believe the Allies would still persist with the plan for an invasion at Casablanca, Oran and Algeria, and then drive east."

"We can guess and conjecture this all day," said Karpov. "I do not say you are wrong, Fedorov, but without Malta or Gibraltar, the Axis forces will easily supply Rommel with anything he needs, while their own supply lines to Egypt will stretch thousands of U-boat infested sea miles around the Cape of Good Hope. Suppose Rommel were to defeat the Americans as well?"

"A possibility, Captain."

"Yet how will we know?" The Admiral put his finger on the real problem. "That is our dilemma when we talk about decisive interventions. We can never really know what turn the history will take, and it may darken in ways we have already seen."

"I agree, Admiral," said Fedorov. "Suppose we leave off this line of argument and think to our more immediate needs—*survival.* Destroying Malta, Gibraltar or smashing the Sixth Army would certainly have a dramatic effect on the war, but haven't we seen enough death and destruction already on this cruise?"

Zolkin had been listening to everything intently. He was not a military man, and so did not entirely grasp the implications of what Karpov and Fedorov were discussing. Instead he was watching the men, gauging their emotions, and sounding out things on another level. Now he spoke with a pointed remark that changed the tone of the argument.

"You have all been discussing what we might do, what we are capable of doing, and yes, what the consequences may be in the end, but speak now to what we *should* do…" The implication of some moral element in the decision was obvious. "Yes, we can smash our way through these ships, and blacken Malta or Gibraltar if we so decide, but should we? Simply to secure our own lives and fate? How many will die if we attempt this?"

The sharp alarm of general quarters came in answer, long and strident in the still air. Karpov sat up stiffly, his reflex for battle immediately apparent and a new light in his eyes. "Listen, Zolkin," he said quickly, a finger pointing to the scrambling sound of booted feet on the decks above them. "Hear that? This is no longer a question of what we should do, but what we *must* do. It is either that, or we go to the bottom of the sea like so many before us."

"Mister Fedorov, I think you should get to the command bridge," said Volsky.

Fedorov was already up and heading for the hatch but Karpov pulled at him: "Fedorov," he said quickly. "You can cross circuit the Klinok SAM system with any other radar. Rodenko—bypass the damaged systems and target via your primary search array. After that the missiles can operate on their own!"

Volsky, nodded and then gave one final order. "Protect the ship, Mister Fedorov. Do what you must. Rodenko, Tasarov—get moving!"

Part III

Redemption

" I never worry about action, but only inaction... If you are going through hell, keep going...A pessimist sees the difficulty in every opportunity; an optimist sees the opportunity in every difficulty."

~ Prime Minister, Sir Winston Churchill

Chapter 7

By the time they reached the bridge the danger was acute. The younger officers there had picked up a single airborne contact that seemed to be passing astern, moving on a heading away from the ship. They watched it for ten minutes before Kalinichev on radar noticed a group of several planes coming on screen from the south. They were out over the sea, bypassing the Sicilian mainland and on a heading towards *Kirov*. They tracked the contact nervously for another ten minutes until, at a 130 miles out, they were convinced it was a threat and sounded battle stations.

Five minutes later Fedorov and the other senior officers rushed onto the bridge, and Rodenko assumed his station, immediately cross indexing the Klinok SAM system with their main Fregat 3D Search Radars as Karpov advised. It took him five minutes to bypass some damaged circuits and establish a link, and by the time he was ready to feed fire control data the contact was 80 miles out and closing at 300 miles per hour. It would reach them in fifteen minutes.

"We can use the S-300 system at once," he said. "It has the range to engage now."

Fedorov considered his options, wishing he knew more about the contact, but concluding it was most likely long range fighters or torpedo bombers off Malta. Its course made it obvious that it was vectoring in on a designated target. The ship was most likely spotted by the recon aircraft that was dismissed by the junior officers as no threat. It was obvious that *Kirov* had been spotted again, and was now targeted for a strike mission, yet he hesitated, realizing that he was now about to intervene in the history of this battle and possibly kill these planes and crews when they might have survived and made some significant contribution to the battle, or even the war at a later time. Volsky's last words came to him again, *"Protect the ship, Mister Fedorov. Do what you must..."* He could engage now with the longer range S-300s, or wait until the planes moved inside forty-five kilometers to use the medium range system. He did not have long to decide.

"We'll wait," he said at last. They had only forty-seven more S-300s in inventory, and twice that number of Klinok SA-N-92 missiles. "Activate our Klinok missile system, Mister Samsonov, and prepare to fire."

"Battery keyed and ready," said Samsonov.

The missiles were installed both forward and aft on the ship, available in batteries of eight with one missile firing every three seconds. They were deployed in vertical silos beneath the deck, and would eject by catapult and decline towards their aiming point by means of a dynamic gas jet before igniting their rocket engines.

As he waited, Fedorov realized he was now judge, jury and executioner sentencing men he could not see or ever know to death, along with everyone they might ever sire, for all generations to come. He felt a tremor in his hand as he reached to adjust the fit of his cap, and when he spoke his voice sounded thin and detached. He knew now how the Admiral must have felt when he first engaged the British, and also had a taste of Karpov's mindset when he stood in command of the battle.

"Fire at forty-five kilometers."

"Aye, sir."

The minutes seemed to extend interminably and tension elevated as they waited. Rodenko continued to call out range intervals on the contact, counting down audibly for Samsonov. At forty-five kilometers Samsonov acted reflexively, dispassionately, even as he had in previous engagements, and toggled the firing switch for launch. He was going to fire off a barrage of six missiles, holding the final two in the battery as a reserve should they be needed.

A claxon droned and warning lights flashed on the aft deck. Three seconds later the first missile ejected, declined, and ignited with a roar, streaking away with a long white exhaust in its wake. The next missile was up and away in seconds, then the third ejected—when disaster struck.

The dynamic gas system had been overcharged, the valve adjusted incorrectly, and it fired too hard and too long. The missile was tipped some forty-five degrees beyond its correct angle of fire when its rocket motor kicked in. Deployed just forward of the aft helicopter landing pad, it struck one of the rotors on the KA-40 there, and was deflected downward even more, careening into the stern of the ship and exploding right above the Polinom "Horse Tail" sonar system access panels. The rocket fuel ignited and there was a billowing explosion of flame and smoke.

As the fourth missile in the barrage popped up from its deck silo it was caught by the shock wave and was sent wildly off course when the rocket engine ignited, smashing into the sea where it fumed like a wild shark in a maddened rage. The fire quickly enveloped the nose of the KA-40 helo as desperate fire crews rushed to the scene even while missile five ejected, declined, and safely fired. As the shock of the explosion rippled through the ship, Samsonov realized something was seriously wrong and aborted the sixth missile. Now the stern of the ship was enveloped in an angry fire, and it looked impossible to save the KA-40. The frantic call came into the bridge, which had no direct view of the stern given its location forward of the ship's main mast.

"This is Engineer Byko—cease fire on the aft deck systems, we have a major fire on deck! I repeat, cease fire!"

Orlov heard the warning claxon and call to arms. He had been sulking in the ready area for the ship's commando unit, brooding over his fate and galled by the notion that he was now a common lieutenant again. Volsky had come to him the previous day and explained what he had decided, busting him three pegs and stripping him of his rank as Captain. At the same time he asked him to redeem himself and make the best of the new assignment. It was obvious to him that he could no longer maintain his post as Chief of Operations. Now everything he had worked for, and all the bruising and sweat of his climb up the ladder of command these last five years, was gone. At least he wasn't a ranker, he thought. It could have been worse.

Karpov, he thought. I should have never listened to that weasel. What was I thinking? He was afraid to do what he wanted on his own, and so he thought he would find a strong ally in me. Yet I was a fool to think we could take the ship—no—an idiot! Yes, Severomorsk is gone and power is now anyone's for the taking, but the collective of the ship, the ranks of officers and crew remained intact. I knew the men would follow Volsky. What was wrong with me? And Karpov, that bastard set me up with his sly arguments and clever reasons, and I was duped like a schoolboy…If I ever get my hands on that rat again—

The warning claxon cut his reverie short and he was immediately on his feet. Men reacted by reflex, and it was Orlov's to look about him for anyone not moving to his post and lash them with the whip of his authority. Yet now *he* was the one without a post. He had been escorted to Troyak's unit under guard, and released to his supervision. These were not the same ordinary crewmen he was so accustomed to bullying and cajoling with his brawn and bad attitude. They were highly trained combat veterans—Naval Marines, and Troyak was one of the best in the fleet. In fact, it was only because Karpov had indicated Troyak was going to support him that Orlov allowed himself to fall under the Captain's spell.

He stood there dumbly for a moment, watching men race to the weapon's bay to fetch their rifles and helmets, yet he had not been integrated into the unit yet, and had no locker of his own. Then he heard the word *fire,* heard the men running on the decks above, and he instinctively rushed to a ladder to get topside. When he emerged on the aft deck he was stunned to see it embroiled in a major fire. Three men were struggling to deploy a fire hose and he turned to see five more running to the scene and immediately took charge.

"You men—follow me!" he shouted, and seeing Orlov the men responded at once, in spite of their surprise that he would even be at large after what they had heard in the rumors that passed through the ship: that Orlov had tried to take command with Karpov and was now in the brig.

The former Chief of the boat was still acting like one, whether or not he held the rank. He ran towards the KA-40 helo, seeing the fire enveloping the nose of the craft, and immediately ascertained that it could not be saved. And when the fire reached the fuel tanks behind the main cabin there would be another explosion, and even more fire and damage could result. They had to get the helo off the ship!

"Come on!" he shouted. "Unlatch the securing cables!"

He was on his knees, feverishly working to loosen the nearest cable that held the helo in place on the landing pad. Other men rushed to assist, and Orlov knew they had to be quick. Already the heat and smoke were terrible, but one man had a pair of heavy duty cable cutters and, after releasing the two cables they could reach, Orlov seized the tool, dove beneath the Helo, and strained to extend the biting jaws of the cutter to sever the last cable. Smoke nearly blinded him and the heat was awful, singeing his exposed, gloveless hands as he strained with all his might, shouting with the pain. Thankfully the tool had a hydraulic assist and the jaws clamped tight with a vicious snap. The last cable had been cut.

Orlov pushed himself back from under the helo, realizing the whole thing could explode at any moment. He staggered to his feet, rubbing his eyes and coughing. *"Push!"* he bellowed, his voice gritty and hoarse.

Five men ran to help, then seven. They took hold of the chopper wherever they could and together they strained with all their might, joined by five others, to heave the aircraft off its landing pad in one mighty lurch. It scudded across the deck on its wheels, aided by a timely roll of the ship which tilted sharply over. It was this extra momentum that allowed the men to keep the helo moving until it crashed violently against the aft starboard gunwale with a hard thud, nearly lurching off the side, but perched now with one stubby wing grinding on the handrails.

Orlov had his big shoulder under the aft tail section, shouting. *"Heave!* Lift it and push for your lives! Tip it over the side!" The crewmen strained and exerted themselves mightily, slowly lifting the helicopter's tail end with their combined muscle and increasing the angle of its precarious tilt. The main cabin was now fully afire, and flames were licking at one of the overhead engines. They managed to move the helo again with one concerted shove and it finally tipped over the gunwale and reeled down into the sea. Seconds later there was another booming explosion when the engine fuel hose was licked by fire on the way down and ignited one of the fuel tanks. They staggered back from the gunwale and Orlov felt something graze his cheek, a fragment of shrapnel from the immolated helicopter. The ship shuddered again with the explosion, and several men were thrown off their feet to the deck, but their effort had saved *Kirov* from even worse damage if the helo had exploded on the landing pad.

Orlov was bent over, retching the smoke from his throat, his hands burned, face bleeding. He turned, a look of agonizing pain on his face, that soon gave way to an expression of relief. They had all come within seconds of losing their lives, but what in God's name was happening? What was the ship firing at?

Melville-Jackson soon knew the answer to that question. A little over an hour ago a flight briefing aide had rushed into his squadron ready room at Takali airfield on Malta and he was informed that a Maryland of 69 Recon Squadron had re-acquired what they believed to be an Italian cruiser. It was heading northwest this time, away from the planned convoy route, but Jackson's 248 Squadron was immediately activated with orders to fly a strike mission nonetheless. They were to intercept the contact, verify its identity and take hostile action if they deemed it an enemy ship. Word had come that elements of several Italian cruiser divisions had left their Mediterranean bases, and this ship was obviously part of that operation.

Six Beaufighters were soon aloft and heading northwest in a tight formation through the Sicilian Narrows as before. This time there were four Mark Is carrying torpedoes, and two newer Mark VI planes with the latest radar sets. Jackson was in one of these, and serving as acting flight leader.

They sped north, slowly closing the distance to the target. The plan was to split into two sub-flights and converge on the contact from two angles. Stanton would lead a group of three Mark I Beaus with torpedoes off the starboard side of the ship, and Jackson would take the last Mark I and the second Mark VI to attack the port side. The two sub-flight leaders signaled to one another, tightened their face masks and banked their planes away from one another, their mates following as planned. The flight split into two groups just as *Kirov* began to spin up her SAM barrage and fired.

The first two missiles were up, their integrated radars quickly acquiring the incoming planes, and both selected targets. When the flight split, they veered left to seek out, unknowingly, the group of Mark I beaus carrying torpedoes. Accelerating with their powerful rocket engines, they streaked out and lanced toward the oncoming planes. Staunton saw something odd in the sky. Blinking and leaning forward to squint through his cockpit, he first thought it to be a contrail from another plane rising to meet them. The enemy must have air cover, he reasoned.

He did not have long to wait before his mystery was solved. The first missile had acquired his sub-flight and was boring in. Seconds later he saw what looked like fireworks in the sky, and with a shuddering explosion a rocket obliterated his wingman to the right. Shocked, he hit the stick and rolled his plane, just as the second missile found and destroyed his last wing mate.

"God almighty!" he breathed as his plane dove for the cover of a low cloud bank.

Off to the east, it was only missile number five left from the initial planned barrage, and it was racing towards Melville-Jackson's group. He suddenly heard a frantic radio call from Stanton: *"Mayday! Mayday! We're under attack! Two planes gone and I'm diving."*

Under attack? What was Stanton talking about? He immediately craned his neck, looking this way and that for sign of any enemy fighters. Two planes down? There must have been a group of long range German fighters, perhaps BF-110s if they were out this far. That was a twin engine fighter like his own Beaufighter, fast and dangerous. Then he saw it, the number five missile streaking up through a white cloud and heading straight for his flight. He passed a moment of shock and surprise, then instinct took over and he shouted into his mask radio set.

"Roll out, we're under attack!"

His two mates reacted to the command and the sub-flight split in three, each plane angling off in an evasive maneuver. Jackson saw the awful streak turn suddenly to follow the plane on his left, and Billings was struck seconds later, his right wing blown clean off. The Beaufighter was sent cart wheeling down in flames, and Melville-Jackson gaped at the scene, his eyes quickly scanning the sky for sign of—of what? What in blazes had hit them? There was no sign of an enemy plane anywhere to be seen.

Chapter 8

Volsky heard the missiles firing, one—two—then he immediately knew that something had gone wrong. His eyes found Karpov's when they heard the explosion and felt the ship shudder in response.

"Missile failure!" Karpov said at once, resisting the urge to leap to his feet and run to the bridge.

The Admiral nodded in agreement, his face set, still in obvious pain but now more concerned for the wellbeing of the ship. What had happened? His damage control officer Byko would get news to them in time, but he would call the bridge first, then engineering, and a call to sick bay would not be on his list at the moment. But Karpov had put his finger on it immediately. The ship had been through a great deal these last weeks. He should have used the time to finish all the system checks, particularly on the reactors, as they seemed to be strongly connected to the strange conditions that moved the ship in time. It still sounded so impossible, but here they were, firing at something bearing down on the ship again, and now they had another accident in the mix to complicate matters.

Volsky shook his head, with both regret and displeasure. "We have been far too sloppy," he said. Then they heard the fire alarm and the commotion aft, men running, shouting, the hiss of a fire hose deploying.

"The aft missile bank," said Karpov, listening. "It was probably a misfire, or perhaps the missile engine exploded. We will know in time. I heard two missiles get off safely. It was the third."

The jarring sound of the alarms sent the Admiral's head to throbbing even worse. He looked at his Captain. "Damn you, Karpov," he breathed. "I *need* you! I need your experience, your skill at the helm, your battle sense and tactical awareness. Fedorov is a navigator! He's never seen combat, or even trained on maneuvers. But how can I send you up there now, eh? Tell me?"

A much louder explosion shook the ship now, prompting them to brace themselves.

"What was that?" said Doctor Zolkin? "Have we been hit?"

"I don't think so…" Karpov's dark eyes seemed to scan the ceiling, as though he was straining to see through the decks above them to discover what had happened. "If I know Rodenko, they would fire at about forty-five klicks out. If these are old planes from the Second World War, then they would not close that distance so quickly. It must be related to the fire aft. Possibly one of the Helos was involved—it's the only thing that makes sense at this point."

"A KA-40?" Volsky raised his heavy brows.

"That or the 226 model. What did you have on the pad?"

"I was just aft for a deck walk before that first attack caught us by surprise. There was a KA-40 on the pad. The bay doors were shut and the other two helos were below decks. I hope we haven't lost it."

"That sounded very bad," Karpov warned.

"Damn, I wish we could get a Tin Man video feed in here."

"I'm sorry, Leonid, but I'm not fond of watching battles," said Zolkin. "I'm like Byko. He picks up the pieces, I patch up the men— when I can." He looked over his shoulder at the three body bags. "I hope I will not have to fill very many more of those any time soon."

"As do I, Dmitri," said Volsky, "as do I."

Karpov looked down, rubbed the back of his neck, and took a deep breath. "What do you want me to say, Admiral?" he spoke quickly. "That I was wrong? Of course I was wrong. I was a fool, and I'll pay for that mistake, but if you need me, I can help you now, in any way you order."

The Admiral looked at him, then closed his eyes, rubbing his brow, so weary. He wanted nothing more than to sleep, and Zolkin gave him a concerned look, reaching to his medical stand and fetching a syringe.

"How can I send you back, Karpov?" Volsky said sadly.

"I *swear* to you—here and now—that I will serve this ship and obey your orders, or those of any man you place over me. Send a Marine with me to the bridge if you wish. I know what I did, and why, and that is over now. I know I deserve nothing but your contempt, but give me this chance and I will not fail you again—ever." He had a pleading expression on his face, eyes wet, lips tight as he held his emotions in check.

Zolkin was going to administer a sedative to the Admiral, but he paused, one hand holding a cotton swab, the other holding the syringe. The admiral opened his eyes and looked at his Captain.

"Very well," he said slowly. "If there is any shred of honor left in you, Karpov, I will give you this one chance to find it again. Fedorov is young, and yes, he is inexperienced at sea—particularly in battle. But I must tell you that his judgment is sound, his insight into what we have gone though exceptional. Without him I do not think this ship would have survived our last encounter with the combined British and American fleets. So Fedorov will remain senior officer in command, and I'll give him the leg up in rank to make that clear. He is the one who will order what we *should* do, Doctor Zolkin," he angled his head to his old friend now.

"But you, Karpov, you will do what we *must* do to accomplish his objectives. Assuming he accepts your presence on the bridge. And one more thing—leave off discussion of how we might best use our nuclear weapons, please. That question is mine to decide. Is that understood?"

"Yes, sir," said Karpov penitently. "I will serve as Fedorov's first officer if you wish, and support him with all the skill I have. I will state my opinions fairly if asked, but will not argue the matter in the face of the enemy, or in front of the other men. And if he gives me an order, I will follow it—I swear it."

"You are fortunate to be in sick bay," said Volsky, with a smile. "That's a lot of pride to swallow in one gulp, and you could choke." He laughed, feeling a great burden of worry taken from his shoulders.

Karpov smiled, appreciating the old Admiral in a way he never could before. Now, when he looked over his shoulder at the man he was before—always resenting Volsky's presence and authority over his ship, always scheming out ways to subvert him and oppose him, he felt nothing but shame. If Volsky gave him this chance, he could not let the man down—could not let himself down.

"Will the men accept his, Leonid?" said Zolkin.

"Perhaps," said Volsky. "Perhaps not, but they will do their duty nonetheless." Now he looked at Karpov, deciding. "This is a good ship, Captain, and a good crew. They deserve more than our lot now, and it is our job to save them, and preserve this ship. Very well... As punishment for your actions earlier, and the willful mutiny you instigated, you are hereby reduce in rank three marks to Captain Lieutenant. Fedorov I hereby promote one level to Captain of the third rank, and he and will assume the position of acting Captain of the ship until I can make a full recovery. You are hereby designated his first officer, *Starpom*, and immediately assigned to the current watch in that position. You will proceed to the bridge at once, and yes, I think I *will* send the Marine guard outside along with you, until you have proven the pledge you have made here today, to me, and to the other men on this ship."

Karpov's eyes were glassy as he nodded, grateful for the chance the Admiral was giving him now. "Rely on me to keep my word in this," he said. "To you and to the men…"

"Go then," said Volsky. "And Mister Karpov—when you get there, and inform Fedorov of his new rank and position, don't forget to salute."

Karpov smiled. "I will click my heels, sir."

Volsky laughed again, but it subsided with a wince of pain. "Can we still that claxon? My head is killing me. And Doctor, you may give me your shot now. If you have a few hours sleep for me in that syringe I will be a new man myself."

Fedorov was as surprised as anyone else when the citadel hatch opened and Karpov stepped onto the bridge, a Marine Guard in his wake. He had been staring up at the aft Tin Man video display, watching the chaotic effort to fight the fire there and seeing the desperate effort of the men as they heaved the KA-40 over the side just before it exploded. Now he and the other officers turned, equally surprised, and Karpov looked down, fighting his shame, then found resolve and straightened to attention in a way he had promised, literally clicking his heels as he saluted.

"Sir," he said formally. "I am ordered here by Admiral Volsky, and with the new rank of Captain Lieutenant. I am to inform you that you are hereby promoted to Captain of the Third Rank, and the Admiral wishes you to assume formal command of the ship until such time as he is fully recovered. I have asked him, and I now ask you, to accept me as your first officer, and I pledge that I will serve you to the best of my ability." He held his salute as he spoke.

Fedorov returned it, astonished, but inwardly relieved by this development. He had been distracted by the explosion aft and almost forgot that the ship was engaged. When he remembered the incoming aircraft he was thinking what to do next when Karpov appeared. The enormity of these events was a lot to process at once, but he maintained his composure and turned to Karpov, nodding.

"Very well," he said, imitating the Admiral again. "Now hear this," he said to the bridge crew. "I formally accept command of battlecruiser *Kirov* until such time as the Admiral returns to duty, and I hereby accept, and appoint, Captain Lieutenant Karpov as my First Officer. He will advise me and second my decisions according to protocol. Understood?"

The men nodded, particularly his senior officers, Rodenko, Tasarov, Samsonov. "Mister Karpov, please work with Rodenko to monitor the status of an incoming air contact and use your best judgment as to how to deal with it to ensure the safety of the ship. I must coordinate with Byko on the comm-link to assess what has happened aft."

"Sir!" Karpov saluted again, and went immediately to Rodenko's Fregat radar station to get on top of their present tactical situation. Rodenko felt his presence looming over him, but something seemed different in the man now. That edge of haughtiness was gone, and the arrogance. Instead he looked and saw Karpov scanning the readout with the quiet, cool assessment of a trained naval combat officer, and he was glad, relieved even, to have the burden taken from him. He had advised Fedorov as best he could, but in truth, his specialty was radar.

"Samsonov," said Karpov, "You used bank seven on the Klinok system?"

"Aye, sir," said Samsonov, and the mood of the bridge tamped down to business as usual. "We only got off three missiles before the misfire."

"All three hit, in spite of the damage to the main ship borne guidance radars. But we have lost time with this misfire and Rodenko is still showing three airborne contacts, very close now. We will have to switch to the Gatling guns, but they may need tracking assistance."

"Aye, sir. Activating close in defense system."

Melville-Jackson emerged from the bank of low flying clouds, his radar man shouting out the contact: "Three-o'clock, Jackie and Five miles out!"

"Roger that. Put your fish in the water now boys, and let's get moving. We've bitten off more than we can chew from the looks of things. This is no cruiser. It's a bleeding battleship! Look at the damn thing!"

Two of the three planes still had torpedoes, and there was no sense in trying a strafing run with his shattered flight now. He pulled the stick back, breaking round in a sharp turn. Then he caught a glimpse of the distant enemy ship as he emerged from a cloud, and could clearly see a fire aft. Perhaps one of his boys got a torpedo in the water after all! A moment later he heard Stanton calling "fish away," but no word from Dobbs in the other Mark I.

Stanton's shot was four kilometers out, just inside the maximum range for this torpedo, and then he turned on Jackson's heading. But Dobbs kept running on, bearing in on the target to get a better shot. Jackson saw something flash out of the corner of his eye and craned his neck to get a look behind him. The dark silhouette of a warship lit up with the firing of a single gun, a Bofors from the looks of the volume it poured out, but it was lethally accurate. A hail of fire swamped Dobbs plane and it was riddled and on fire in seconds. He quickly lost control and went into the sea.

"Damn!" said Jackson. His squadron was decimated—worse than decimated. What in hell were they shooting at us? He had his cameras running the whole while, and hoped the footage would be valuable if he could get it home safely. "Bad day's work", he said to Stanton on the radio.

"Bloody hell!" came the return. "Let's get out of here."

"Torpedo in the water!" Tasarov called out loudly. "Two signals, both running true!"

Karpov, turned to Fedorov near the comm-link. "Mister Fedorov," he asked. "Will these torpedoes home in on the ship's hull?"

"No," said Fedorov, "they will run true as aimed to their maximum range, and only detect the hull for purposes of detonation. They have no active tracking radar or sonar components. You can avoid them by maneuvering the ship."

"Helm, come hard to port and all ahead full!"

"Aye, sir," came the echo, "Hard to port and ahead full!"

The ship went into a high speed turn, leaning heavily in the sea and surging forward with renewed speed. Karpov wanted to get as far off the torpedo bearing as possible, and he was easily able to maneuver the ship out of harm's way. Then he went to the viewport, looking for his binoculars, pleased to find them hanging just where he had left them, so long ago it seemed now. A quick scan satisfied him that the evasive maneuver had worked. He saw the two torpedo wakes well off the starboard side of the ship and breathed a sigh of relief.

"Two airborne contacts withdrawing," said Rodenko. "I think they've had enough, sir."

Karpov nodded. "Let us hope this is the last we see of them for while." And then to Fedorov he said. "Captain, how is the situation on the aft deck?"

Fedorov had just finished being briefed and had a grim expression on his face. "Not good," he said. "The KA-40 caught fire when the missile failed and they had to jettison it over the side. I don't know how they managed that, but they did. That secondary explosion we heard was probably the fuel tanks going up. If the ship is in no further danger I suggested we slow to ten knots and get divers down to have a look. Byko tells me the aft Horse Tail sonar has been badly damaged and we may have sustained further harm from that explosion."

"I confirm that," said Tasarov. "I have a red light on the aft sonar system, but the forward bow dome is still returning good signals. It looks like we won't be able to deploy the Horse Tail variable depth sonar, but at least our jaw isn't broken. And if we still have the other two helicopters in working order we can use their dipping sonar as well."

The ship utilized a variant of the older Horse Jaw low-frequency hull sonar system, principally deployed in a prominent bow dome and along the forward segments of the hull. But the aft quarter also allowed for the deployment of additional sensors towed by a long cable which allowed them to move the devices to variable depths and listen through thermal layers when necessary.

Fedorov shrugged, stepping to the center of the command citadel and resting an arm on the Admiral's chair. Karpov drew near, and clasped him on the shoulder. "We are no longer in any immediate danger," he said.

"Glad to hear that," said Fedorov. "It seems like I've been on my feet for hours now."

Karpov smiled. "Get used to it, Captain." Then he looked at the Admiral's chair and gestured. "Have a seat, Fedorov. The ship is yours now."

"Thank you, Captain," said Fedorov, and he slipped quietly into the chair, realizing it was the first time he had ever sat there. Something about the moment stayed with him the rest of his life. He was commander of the most powerful ship in the world, at least for the moment.

Chapter 9

Three men showed up at sick bay, and Zolkin was surprised when he saw Orlov among them, his face black with soot, and bleeding. He also quickly noticed his hands, clenched and held tightly near his soiled sweatshirt, as if protecting them from further harm. His wool cap was still on, and pulled low on his forehead, and he looked every bit the threatening, brute of a man that he had been while serving as Chief of Operations.

But for Zolkin, a man in medical need was his charge and duty, and he put aside his ill feelings for Orlov and got him quickly onto a cot for some much needed first aid.

"Well, I hope you don't plan on getting into any boxing matches with those hands, Orlov. How did this happen?"

Orlov grimaced as the Doctor applied antiseptic and bandages, but the burns were not severe. He told Zolkin of the fire, and the effort to ditch the helicopter before it exploded. The other two men in for minor bruises and burns heaped praise on Orlov, and not because they feared any reprisal on his part if they failed to do so. In the heat of a dire emergency Orlov had instinctively acted to save the ship, risking his own life and the lives of all the men he called to action with him, but narrowly averting that fate by a matter of seconds. Yet the fact remained that he was seen as a hero by the men for what he did, and Zolkin thought this good for a change, and a positive first step for Orlov in his new post.

"In spite of what I might wish to say to you on other matters," he said, "I put that aside now and congratulate you for your courage. Two other men were here before you with tales of your herculean feat. The Admiral will be pleased when I tell him what you have done."

When the other two men had been dismissed Orlov pressed the Doctor with a question. "What has happened, Zolkin? I have heard nothing. What were we firing at?"

"Don't ask me. Yes, I was in the briefing and can tell you that the ship has moved again, backward, into this mess of a war that we blundered into. Fedorov was able to pinpoint the date as August 12, 1942, a full *year* after our first adventure, to put things lightly. Apparently there is a lot of shooting going on south of us, and he's maneuvered the boat into the Tyrrhenian Sea to avoid it. But, as you can see, we have been spotted. You are not the only officer wounded. Volsky is in the next room, sleeping at last again."

Orlov lowered his head.

"I was a fool, Zolkin," he said in a low voice. "Karpov duped me, that snake, and I fell for his *vranyo* hook, line and sinker. If I ever get my hands on him—"

"Now, now—that will do you no good either, Orlov!" Zolkin wagged a finger at him, admonishing.

"Let him rot in the brig, then. At least I have a post, and some measure of rank left."

"Don't become perturbed, but Karpov was sent to the bridge as acting First Officer to Fedorov. The Admiral may not recover for some days yet, and we were under attack. What does Fedorov know about naval combat? Nothing. Karpov pledged to serve faithfully if given a second chance, and the Admiral sent him up."

Orlov shook his head. "It was his doing!" he said. "All his doing!"

"Don't hold yourself blameless, Orlov. You had a choice to make and you chose wrongly. If it is any consolation to you, Karpov was also reduced in rank three levels. He is Captain Lieutenant now, under Fedorov. I expect they will make a formal announcement when this business settles down. For your part, you have done something right in that action just now. Good for you. Now don't let the bear in the kitchen over Karpov and keep your wits about you. You are a natural leader, Orlov, but you let your anger get the best of you all too often. Think about that—and don't get any more stupid ideas in your head about Karpov. There is a limit to Volsky's forbearance. He has given Karpov a chance to redeem himself. You now have yours."

He looked over the top of his glasses and smiled. "I'll tell Troyak that you are to rest those hands for at least 48 hours. In the mean time—find a good book, or better yet, a good meal. Your rank as

Lieutenant still gets you into the officer's mess. And while you are at it, mending a few fences with the men would be in order as well."

Orlov sighed, nodding his head. "Alright, Zolkin. What you say makes more sense than I have had in my head for a good long while. I'll mind my manners, and if no one bothers me there will be no trouble. But don't ask me to sit at Karpov's table just yet, eh?"

"It will be easy for you to blame Karpov for what you did," said Zolkin, "but not wise. Look to yourself, Orlov. Make your peace there first, and if you can do so, make your peace with the men. They are the ones you really let down. Now they look to you with some praise in their eyes instead of fear. That has to feel good for a change, and I hope it may open a new road for you."

They had no time to rest on the bridge. Rodenko's systems finally reached full range, with good, clear readings in all directions. His screen was suddenly alight with numerous contacts, on the sea and in the air. Fedorov interpreted one air contact moving from Sicily towards Sardinia as the movement of German reserve aircraft to Sardinian airfields for the major strike on the British convoy that would occur the following day. But a surface contact to their west, and closing on an apparent intercept course, was of some concern.

"I don't think the Germans are aware of our presence yet," he said to Karpov. "That surface contact, however, will be two light Italian cruisers—6 inch guns—and a couple of destroyers led by Admiral Da Zara. They are fast, and will be able to shadow us if they sight us. Though I am inclined to believe that they may think we are friendly at first blush. They were ordered to rendezvous with other cruiser divisions in this region, and will not expect any enemy ships this far north of the planned convoy route."

"Good," said Karpov. "May I suggest we run north for a time? We need waste no missiles on those ships. If they find us and seem hostile, we can just use our deck guns at superior range to drive them off."

"I agree," said Fedorov. "But their main force is coming from other bases, with more cruisers and destroyers. Two will be heavy cruisers *Bolzano* and *Gorizia*, moving up from Messina with five more destroyers to join them. They intend to rendezvous here, he pointed to a map on the clear Plexiglas of his old navigation station. "The island of Ustica. It's too bad that they lost their nerve and were ordered to stand down, this will mean that several of these ships will be lingering in the Tyrrhenian Sea, instead of heading southwest away from us. We must be cautious, and ready for the possibility that the Germans could also spot us at any time."

The ship was ordered on a heading just shy of true north and as they came about there was an audible groan, with some vibration. Karpov noticed it immediately, though Fedorov was frowning over his notes on Operation Pedestal.

"Did you hear that?" Karpov asked.

Fedorov looked up at him, clearly unaware of what had happened. He had been lost in the history of 1942, oblivious for the moment while he considered how their present course might best avoid further conflict.

"There was an odd sound, and some vibration when we turned," Karpov explained. As if on cue the comm-link phone rang and Fedorov answered. It was damage chief Byko, with a little more bad news for them.

"*I think we have some damage below the water line near the starboard propulsion shaft and rudder,*" he said, "*possibly from the explosion when they ditched the KA-40. Can you reduce power so I can put divers overboard. 10 knots would do it.*"

Fedorov looked at his chronometer, calculating mentally. "Very well, Byko. We'll slow to 10 knots. Keep me informed." He looked at Karpov, somewhat concerned. The last thing they needed now was any loss of speed and maneuverability. If they were sighted again, by air or sea, and became the object of enemy attention, it could quickly embroil them in a fight Fedorov dearly hoped to avoid for the moment.

"Byko is a competent man," said Karpov to give him heart. "Don't worry, he'll have us on our way in no time."

Some miles to the west the day faded towards dusk, the skies ripening to amber and rose as the sun fell lower on the horizon. Aboard the battleship HMS *Nelson*, Vice Admiral Edward Neville Syfret stood in overall command of the entire operation, and principally of the main covering "Force Z." Off his stern he was followed by *Nelson's* sister ship, HMS *Rodney*, the core of real naval muscle assigned to the operation, and more than enough to give the Italian Navy second thoughts about any sortie as long as these two powerful ships were on the scene.

After an uneventful passage of the Strait of Gibraltar on the previous day, the operation began in earnest on the 11th of August, and was soon well informed that the seas and skies they were sailing into would not be friendly. The loss of HMS *Eagle* at mid day had been jarring, with 260 men lost in spite of an outstanding effort made to save the bulk of her crew.

It was a day of terrible setbacks and thankful consolation. Syfret grimaced at the stinging loss of the venerable old carrier, along with sixteen much needed aircraft. The sight of those Seafires sliding off the steeply listing deck as *Eagle* keeled over was still dark in his mind. Yet he took some comfort in the rescue of over 900 crewmen. The oiling operation for his flock of thirsty destroyers had also gone off well enough, and he had all of twenty-four of these fast escorts at hand for this segment of the run. That said, a submarine had still managed to slip through and hurt them badly, and it gave him worries about what would lie ahead. This was only the enemy's outermost screen of undersea boats, he realized. The odds would be much worse later, when the bulk of his destroyer escorts would have to turn back with his heavier ships and carriers. Thus far they had only been bothered by a handful of enemy aircraft, shadowing the convoy from a safe distance, but this too would change as they drew nearer to the main enemy airfields on Sardinia and Sicily.

A careful and experienced man, he knew this was just the opening round of the battle ahead of them now, and the loss of the *Eagle* was a particularly telling blow. It was clear that the air and undersea threats would have orders to strike at his all important carriers as a priority. This was the first time the Royal Navy had ever operated with five at once, though that distinction was tragically short-lived now with the loss of *Eagle*.

Born in Cape Town South Africa in 1889, Syfret's career saw him hopping from battleship *Rodney*, to command of a cruiser squadron and now a post at Gibraltar's Force H. He had seen the fire and steel required to push through to Malta on previous convoys, and had no doubts about the difficulties ahead of them now. He had pushed 15 of 16 merchant ships safely through to Malta earlier while commanding HMS *Edinburgh*, a record that had not gone unnoticed at the Admiralty.

Tonight may be our last breath of calm for a while, he thought as he removed his admiral's cap and ran a hand through his fine wavy grey hair. Tall and trim, his face was lean and serious, his eyes harboring the wisdom of many decades at sea, in both good times and bad. It was going to get rather gritty, he thought, but grit was one element of his character that was never found wanting. He had sat at Churchill's right hand as his secretary when the redoubtable Prime Minister had served as First Sea Lord, and was soon sent back to real active service when the war came.

Now he led two of the Royal Navy's biggest battleships, 38,000 ton behemoths when fully loaded, with nine 16 inch guns each and a bristle of medium batteries and anti aircraft guns as well. It was just as he preferred it—to be at sea on a ship with some good brawn and armor, and the guns to sail where she pleased. There was only one segment of the run in to Malta that he would have to forsake this time out—the Sicilian Narrows—infested with U-boats and peppered with mines, the two ponderous battleships would not have the sea room they needed to sail on through the narrow gap in the Skerki Bank, a jagged series of limestone reefs at the mouth of those narrows. They would cover the convoy as far as the bank, and then turn back while lighter and more maneuverable cruisers under Vice Admiral Burrough took on the duty of final escort to Malta with Force X.

It was already time to deploy the paravanes, and he was watching the crews rigging the lines to the bow, his gaze reaching down *Nelson's* broad gun laden foredeck to the tip of the ship. Two paravanes would be deployed on each side of all the larger ships as night gathered its shadows before them. These were a kind of underwater glider, the general shape and appearance of a winged torpedo, yet shorter, and with stubby foils and a tail designed to maneuver it in the water. They would be towed by a heavy cable rigged to the ship's bow, and the wings would serve to keep the paravane well away from the hull as it trailed out to the side of the big ship. Their intent was to ensnare the anchoring cables of hidden mines, and by so doing it would break those lines and send the mines bobbing up to the surface where they could be spotted and detonated by machine gun fire.

The game had begun, he mused. No, not a game, but a grueling run of the gauntlet. Would they win through this time? He remembered his final urgent instructions to the convoy masters on his last run in to Malta at night... *"Don't make smoke or show any lights. Keep good station. Don't straggle. If your ship is damaged keep her going at the best possible speed..."* How many of the fourteen precious merchantmen would get through this time?

At 16:34 hrs a message came through from Flag Officer North Atlantic that was not unexpected. It warned of an imminent attack by enemy torpedo bombers, and the British fighters were soon scrambling from the decks of their remaining carrier escorts, *Indomitable* and *Victorious,* and climbing up into the salmon sky. When they came, the German Ju88s swooped low on the deck but were well harried by the fighters, who broke up their sub-flights and sent at least three into the water. Syfret gave the order to commence firing and the line of cruisers and battleships began filling the gloaming skies with puffs of broiling fire and grey smoke, laced with white tracers from the Bofors AA guns. He reckoned this to be nothing more than a probing attack, some thirty planes from the look of it. They would get much worse in the days ahead.

Now…what was this last bit in that signal warning: *"Malta reports large enemy ship sighted very near Sicilian Narrows. Sortie by this and enemy cruiser squadrons deemed very possible."*

Large enemy ship? A battleship? Couldn't they be more specific?

Kapitän Helmut Rosenbaum of U-73 received the message from Untermittlemeer Squadron headquarters at La Spezia with real satisfaction. *"Congratulations in order for our newest recipient of the Knight's cross."* All he had to do now was stay alive to collect his medal, and he was glad that he could soon make use of his new radar sets once he got clear of the main enemy convoy and found some open water.

U-73 was a very special boat, one of a very few to have the FuMO61 "Hohentwiel" radar installed. Named for a fortress constructed at the top of an extinct volcano in the year 914 by Burchard III, then Duke of Swabia, it became one of the most powerful fortresses in the duchy, and a watchful outpost on the mountain passes in the Baden-Wurttemberg region of Germany. The radar was perched atop the starboard side of the U-boat's conning tower, scanning the area around the boat while she was surfaced to keep watch for enemy aircraft and surface units.

Her Kapitän and commander, Helmut Rosenbaum, had put her to good use on seven sorties, sinking six merchant ships and causing the loss of two the smaller vessels that were being transported on one of these targets. The crew wanted to credit him with eight ships sunk for the feat, but he was reluctant to count those last two as kills.

"No boys," he told them. "I'm counting it at six, so now we go hunting for our lucky number seven." Most of his kills were obtained while operating out of St. Nazaire and Lorient on the Brittany coast, but on one occasion the boat was deep in the Atlantic operating with the Grönland Wolfpack when she sighted a very odd looking warship that seemed to be the focus of a major operation. Rosenbaum had no intelligence indicating that the enemy was running any convoy at that time, so what was underway here in the icy North Atlantic, he wondered? He knew there were no German surface raiders out to sea at that time, but here was a warship of considerable size, with a lot of Royal Navy units thrashing about in pursuit.

He peered through his periscope, noting how ominous and threatening her profile was, but perplexed by the lack of any big guns on the ship. Concluding that this must be an old British battleship that had been stripped of her guns and put to sea for maneuvers and drills, he decided to spoil the party and put the ship on the bottom of the sea. The ship accommodated him by sailing right into firing position as he hovered in the silent cold waters, and was preparing to set loose one of his last torpedoes when he suddenly saw the ship put on an amazing burst of speed and veer hard into a high speed evasive turn! He realized at once what had happened. One of the other boats in the wolfpack had seen the ship as well, and fired, probably U-563 operating on his right under Klaus Bargsten.

"What are you doing, Klaus?" he breathed. The shot was far too long to have any chance of success. It was not like Bargsten to make a mistake like that, but the reaction of the target ship made Rosenbaum realize that this was no old battleship. The speed and precision of the evasive maneuver took his breath away. Then he saw something flash from the side of the dark ship and streak off at an impossible speed. Moments later there was an explosion, and he pivoted his scope to see a geyser of water in the distance, right on U-563's line of fire. Something had lanced out and destroyed Bargsten's torpedo! He wanted nothing more to do with this ship, and immediately ordered an immediate dive to reach a cold thermal layer and slip away. His comrade was not so lucky. The ship found U-563 sometime later and Rosenbaum's boat and crew could feel the throbbing vibration in the sea when they killed the U-Boat.

The Kapitän remembered how he had turned to his First Officer of the Watch, Horst Deckert, amazed. "That was a battleship if I have ever seen one," he breathed. Or at least it was something easily that big. Yet the way it moved and turned, it was like a destroyer, and the damn thing…" He checked himself, unwilling to say more. "Get us out of here, Deckert. Get us out of here."

A year later, and now on her 8th sailing, U-73 would slip through the guarded gates of Gibraltar, her engines off, just drifting silently through the channel pushed by the swift ocean currents. She would join Unterseeboote Mittelmeer (Undersea Boat Group Med), with the 29th Flotilla, and make her way to a new operating base at La Spezia in Northern Italy. She had been out on patrol since August 4, this time in the Med, looking for another kill when Rosenbaum got word that a big British operation was underway and was vectored in as part of the initial U-Boat trip-wire defense north of Algeria. There he spotted the British convoy assembled for Operation Pedestal and slipped around to the rear to where the carriers were operating to provide air cover.

Rosenbaum skillfully escaped detection, in spite of a close escort of four British destroyers in his immediate vicinity, and worked his way stealthily into a perfect firing position on the old British carrier HMS *Eagle*, ripping her open with four hits and sending her to the bottom in a matter of minutes. In the ensuing chaos he eluded detection and withdrew from the slowly advancing Allied convoy. In time he would work his way north to hover off the Balearic Islands. For the sinking of HMS *Eagle* he soon learned that he was to be awarded the Knight's Cross and given a new assignment—command of the Black Sea U-Boat flotilla, Hitler's "lost fleet" in the inland waters of southern Europe.

In an ingenious and daring operation, the Germans had partially disassembled a flotilla of six Type IIB Coastal U-Boats at Kiel, removing their conning towers by oxyacetylene torches before they moved them overland on the most powerful land haulers and tractors in Germany. They eventually reached the Danube where they were packed in pontoon crates and then made their way slowly by barge to the Black Sea! Originally scheduled to arrive there in October of 1942, they were two months early, and the newly decorated Helmut

Rosenbaum would now take command as soon as he returned from his current mission.

He rubbed his hands together, grateful for the new assignment where he could now command a flotilla of six U-boats. Yet in a strange twist of fate, he would have one more chance encounter at sea before he made it home to collect his laurels, and one more chance to best his lucky number seven kill. U-73 seemed to have some strange magnetic attraction to the center stage of danger where *Kirov* was concerned, for she was to soon come once more within firing range of the very same ship Rosenbaum had seen a long year ago in the North Atlantic…

Part IV

Geronimo

"We took an oath not to do any wrong, nor to scheme against one another...I was no chief and never had been, but because I had been more deeply wronged than others, this honor was conferred upon me, and I resolved to prove worthy of the trust."

~ Geronimo

Chapter 10

Aboard *Kirov* Rodenko was watching his long range radar screens with some concern. A small flotilla of five contacts continued to move east from Cagliari, and with the ship now slowed to just 10 knots while the divers were working astern, this put the contact on a direct intercept course. Fedorov seemed lost in his research, trying to ferret out any information he could concerning the details of the Italian presence gathering in the Tyrrhenian Sea. He began to make notations on the Plexiglas at the Nav station, and Karpov watched him out of the corner of one eye while he received reports from Byko on the status of the damage control operation.

A sizable piece of the exploding KA-40 had been flung against the side of the ship, causing some minor buckling, though water tight integrity was not lost on the hull. *Kirov* had a shrapnel wound there as well, but the divers were able to seal it off, and also clear some debris that was dangerously near their starboard propulsion shaft and rudder. Two hours later Byko was pulling his men out of the water, and he called up to the bridge to report that he could certify normal cruising speed in ten minutes.

"As for the Horse Tail sonar unit," he said. "I will have to replace the retraction motors and a few cowling plates, but that will take another eight to twelve hours."

"Well put your grandpa on it! We'll need that system up as soon as possible." Karpov was referring to the ship's chief mechanic, often called the "Grandpa" when it came to all things mechanical. He passed the information on to Fedorov.

"Good enough," he said. "I think we will have no major concerns for the next several hours. That contact to the west out of Cagliari will continue to make a gradual approach, but if we take no overtly threatening action we may just be able to slip by. I expect visitors from the north and east as well, but not for some time. The men need rest. Can you stand a watch until midnight?"

Karpov gave him assurances, and so he went below with several members of the senior bridge crew. Dusk gave way to a clear, dark night, returned to them at last since it was so rudely stolen, and the time slipped towards midnight. Karpov was grateful that Fedorov had enough faith in him to let him stand a command watch, though the Marine guard still remained at his post as a precaution. Still, he had the bridge for the first time in a long while, and slipped into the Admiral's chair, remembering how it felt when he was the unchallenged master of the ship, and thinking how foolish he had been, how blinded by his own ambition.

He still struggled inwardly with it all, and his mind offered up arguments and justifications as it had so many times while he languished in the brig. But here he was given a second chance by the man he had betrayed, and that came to few men in the Russian Navy, particularly those charged with mutinous conduct. In any other circumstances he realized he would still be in the brig, and facing severe disciplinary action, or even a desultory court martial and possible death sentence.

Kalinichev was at radar when he noted that the contact he had been monitoring to their west, which had been steaming at fifteen knots, had suddenly increased speed. "It looks like that have increased to twenty knots, sir," he reported, "And they are now within 15 kilometers."

"Still bearing on an intercept course?"

"Yes, sir."

"Range to horizon?"

"From the top of one of those ships, sir?" Kalinichev made a hasty calculation. "I would say we are probably on their horizon now, sir, but it is very dark."

"Shut down all running lights," said Karpov, concerned. "Rig the bridge for black."

"Aye, sir."

He considered what to do as the night seemed to flow into the bridge, the phosphorescent glow of the radar and sonar screens the only illumination. He could put on speed and race north to outrun the contact. This is what Fedorov would advise, he knew. But something in his bones refused to give way to these ships, galling him. He decided, in the end, to advise Fedorov and avoid any suspicion or charge that he was again attempting to engage the ship in combat, even if that was what he might prefer. He had given his word to Volsky, a man who had little reason to grant him the grace of his present position, and so he would honor it.

Ten minutes later Fedorov returned to the bridge, still bedraggled with half-sewn sleep.

"Captain on the bridge!" a watch stander called, announcing his arrival. He took a moment, adjusting to the darkness, then found Karpov near the radar station. "I relieve you, sir," he said politely, taking formal command of the ship again.

"I stand relieved," Karpov repeated the forms, still fighting off his inner demons in having to relinquish command to a former navigator. Yet he stood to one side, waiting as Fedorov studied Kalinichev's screen.

The ship's new captain had expected the contact would occur right around midnight, and he was gratified that events seemed to be unfolding as the history was recorded, like the well oiled mechanism of a clock. He made the decision Karpov had predicted.

"Helm, maintain course and give me thirty knots."

A bell rang and the helmsman echoed the order. They could feel the powerful surge of the ships twin turbines as the *Kirov* forged ahead. Fedorov went to the forward view pane, noting Karpov's field glasses. "May I?" he asked gesturing to the binoculars.

"Of course," Karpov nodded.

Fedorov looked off their port quarter for a few moments, but was not satisfied. "The moon is still down," he said. "Not that there will be much of it when it arrives. It is very dark. Nikolin, please activate the port side Tin Man and scan the horizon at 315 degrees."

The Tin Man rotated and deployed its special night optical filter, with infrared capability, moments later they were staring at an enhanced HD video of a small task force to the northwest. The ships were right on schedule, cruisers *Savoia* and *Montecuccoli*, and destroyers *Oriani*, *Gioberte* and *Maestrale*.

"The contact is increasing speed to twenty five knots," said Kalinichev. "Thirty knots now, sir."

Karpov gave Fedorov a hard look. "They would not be making that speed for a casual rendezvous," he said. "I suggest we come to general quarters, Fedorov. I can smell trouble here."

"Anything else on the screen?" asked Fedorov. "Use your extended range systems."

"Sir, I have two contacts at 25 degrees northeast at a range of 62 kilometers and three contacts at 55 degrees northeast at a range of 120 kilometers." Kalinichev adjusted his screen, using their long range over the horizon radar system to report these additional sightings. Fedorov was suddenly concerned.

The numbers and bearings of the contacts did not surprise him, but their timing did. The first would be the heavy cruiser *Trieste* and a destroyer escort, the *Camica Nera*, the latter would be light cruiser *Muzio Attendolo* and two more destroyers, the *Aviere* and *Geniere*. They seemed to be early and he went to his old desk at the navigation station to study his notes again while Karpov fidgeted, his eyes watching the overhead Tin Man Display.

"Something is wrong," Fedorov muttered to himself, confirming his misgivings. "The *Muzio Attendolo* should not have received its orders to move this soon. Something has changed…"

Karpov overheard him, drifting in his direction. "Look to the screen Fedorov, not your history books. Something has changed? Most likely. Who knows what, eh? We lit up like a candle when that fire started earlier, and the British are obviously aware of our presence. Do not surprise yourself if the Italians have discovered us as well. All I can say is that the movement of those ships does not look friendly." He pointed at the Tin Man Display, which was now good enough to zoom and show that forward turrets were rotating on the lead cruiser and coming to bear on their heading.

Fedorov stared at the display, his heart beating faster. The history had changed! As much as he might want to slip quietly away, *Kirov's* presence was a shaft of fire and steel in the very heart of the Italian Navy's innermost exclusion zone—the Tyrrhenian Sea. Now he realized that the early arrival of these other contacts and the sudden movement of the nearest group had to be related to their presence here. To make matters worse, Kalinichev spoke up again, in a loud clear voice.

"Sir, I now have airborne contacts in a large group at 255 degrees southwest, range 92 kilometers. They just emerged from the landform clutter of Sardinia. I'm reading twenty discrete contacts."

Fedorov immediately knew those had to be Italian planes out of airfields around Cagliari. The situation was now spinning out of control and it was obvious to him that the ship was under coordinated attack. Karpov had been waiting impatiently, an exasperated look on his face. He was about to speak again when Fedorov cut in quickly with the words he hoped he would not have to speak this early in the campaign. "Battle stations! Sound general quarters!" The alarm was sounded, much to Karpov's relief, and he nodded his head in agreement.

"Mister Karpov," Fedorov turned to his *Starpom*, activate our 152 millimeter deck gun systems and prepare to engage the near contact on my order to fire."

"At once, sir!" And Karpov was quick to pass the order to Gromenko, who was now filling in for Samsonov in the Command Information Center. "Feed your targets to the CIC, Kalinichev!"

"Aye, sir. The data is active and we have radar lock."

Fedorov bit his lip, very disheartened now but committed. "Prepare to repel incoming aircraft," he said quickly. "Expect 20 planes for a low level torpedo attack."

Da Zara was also impatient tonight. The Italian Admiral squinted through his field glasses at the shadow on their horizon, wondering what he was getting himself into now. One of Italy's most capable fighting admirals, he set his flag on the light cruiser *Eugenio di Savoia*, and was out from the division base at Cagliari to rendezvous with numerous other ships in preparation for an attack on the British convoy near Pantelleria the following day. In fact, he had pulled off this very same maneuver against the last British attempt to relieve Malta, leading the charge in a fast air and sea action that sent the British destroyer *Bedouin* to the bottom and heaped misery on the decimated convoy just as it was within smelling distance of its objective. He planned to do the same this time, until a priority message from Regia Marina changed everything.

He was ordered to hold his course and search out a suspected British cruiser that had been sighted near dusk by the Italian submarine *Bronzo* limping back to port with a bad engine, unable to take up its post on the inner picket line. The report was very odd. For a British ship to boldly entered the Tyrrhenian Sea was one thing that immediately jarred naval authorities. When the sub sighted it there appeared to be a fire aft. Was it damaged somehow? Thinking that Naval Aeronatuica already had its teeth into the intruder, the sub captain simply wired in the sighting and continued on his way.

"One ship?" Da Zara had said in disbelief when he received the message. There must be an error, he thought. It could not have come from their main convoy escorts, or our submarines would have surely detected it long before now. What has Mussolini been drinking tonight? Could it have sortied from the east as a diversionary operation? If so, it would be a sly devil to get this far in without being sighted. But yes, a fast cruiser could do this, particularly since all our planes, have been piling up out west on Sardinia for the initial round of air strikes on this British convoy. Who would think to look right here in our own back yard?

He was soon encouraged to learn that two squadrons of SM-79 Sparviero "Sparrowhawks" were already in the air to coordinate with his attack, and that orders had been given to send out ships from Naples to join him, along with 7th Cruiser Division at Messina, which would also be leaving early for the planned rendezvous near Ustica Island. But first, he thought, we deal with this thief in the night, eh?

"Gobbo Maledetto!" he said to his gunnery officer. Where are those damned hunchbacks? We're too close! They'll see us any moment if they haven't already."

The 'damned hunchbacks' were the nickname many gave to the SM-79s, with their odd three engine design and high dorsal hump, it seemed a much more suitable name than 'Sparrowhawk.' An old plane that had first been conceived as a small passenger aircraft, it was converted to a bomber as the war loomed and had served alarmingly well in that capacity. It was fast for its age, durable in spite of its wood and metal amalgam frame, and lethal enough if it could get in close for a torpedo run.

Da Zara stepped out onto his weather deck, his heavy sea coat hood thrown back, his gold braided admiral's cap fitted smartly, gloved hands holding his field glasses. A handsome man, in his day he had been known to make more than a few prominent conquests, though now he set his mind on little more than his beloved light cruisers.

"Avanti!" He called over his shoulder. "Sparare!"

His command was answered immediately with the bright orange fire and sharp concussion of his forward deck guns. *Eugenio de Savoia* carried four turrets with two 152mm guns each, and his initial salvo streaked through the darkness toward the formless shadow on the horizon. His second cruiser *Raimondo Montecuccoli* followed suit and opened fire as well, and the three destroyers in the van began to fan out to make their torpedo run, accelerating to high speed and leaving white frothy wakes behind them as they charged ahead.

At that moment Da Zara heard the low drone of aircraft overhead, looking back to see flights of the ungainly Sparrowhawks roaring to join the fight in a well coordinated attack. The smell of the sea and gunfire excited the Admiral, who had boasted he was the only fighting commander in the Italian Navy who had bested the Royal

Navy at its own game. Now he was eager to make good his claim, and send this bold intruder to the bottom of the sea.

Fedorov saw the distant flashes on the horizon, too close to give him any comfort. His plan to slip past the unknowing Italians had been foiled. They must have been spotted, by one means or another, while Byko's engineers were putting out the fire and seeing to the damage below the waterline. The instant he saw the distant muzzle flashes he knew the ship was in real peril. *Kirov* was never built for close in action with well gunned adversaries. Even though these were only light cruisers, those six inch shells would cause serious harm anywhere they struck the ship. Only the command citadels had sufficient armor protection from them. No—the ship's power was in standing off and pummeling her enemies from long range, using the speed and lethality of her anti-ship missiles to decide the conflict before the enemy had even knew they were there. He had counted on the night, the darkness, and a witless opponent, and now found himself regretting the decision to wait so long. They had been spotted and were now under fire, a circumstance that never should have happened for a fighting ship like *Kirov*.

The first enemy salvos were short, and laterally wide off the mark, which did not surprise him. The Italian ships had no radar to speak of, relying on good night optics to site their guns. And this particular naval gun had a history of different problems. The lateral dispersion on salvos resulted from imprecise size and weight in both the main rounds and their propellant charges. Beyond that, the guns were prone to misfire, as much as 10 percent of the time, and mechanical faults or delays in loading, insecure breech closure, and problems with the shell hoists seriously reduced their rate of fire. The gun's designers had claimed three rounds per minute, but tonight Da Zara's ships would do no better than two.

Fedorov looked at Karpov, resigned to the fact that *Kirov* had to fight. "Mister Karpov," he said quietly. "Deal with those ships."

Karpov smiled. "My pleasure, sir." Then he turned to Gromenko and gave the order to fire. Now it was *Kirov's* turn with her three twin 152mm gun turrets, the same size in real weight as the enemy but with far more accurate fire control systems with precision round tracking, water cooled barrels, lightning fast loaders, and ammunition that was state-of-the-art. The guns fired with a sharp crack, both barrels recoiling to fire again and again. Gromenko had the interval set at three seconds, and in the long minute while Da Zara's force was struggling to load, sight and aim the four forward twin gun turrets on the two cruisers, *Kirov* unleashed all of twenty salvos, 120 rounds to the 16 shells the Italians finally managed to throw their way. And every round the big battlecruiser fired was radar guided, streaking across the sea in a violent storm of steel.

Chapter 11

Before Da Zara could get his field glasses focused on the target to spot his salvo geysers, his ship was rocked by three direct hits with one near miss, and he was nearly thrown off his feet.

"Madre de Dio!" he exclaimed, then he saw *Montecuccoli* erupt with fire and smoke, shuddering under two, then five jarring hits. Her forward turret exploded, sending one of the gun barrels cart-wheeling up and away from the ship like a hot lead pipe. Two of his three destroyers were riddled with fire as well. It was as if someone had crept up on his task force with a massive shotgun and blasted his ships at close range! He gave the order to come hard to port, hoping his aft batteries could get off at least one salvo, but his enthusiasm for this sea battle was suddenly gone.

As *Savoia* heeled over she was struck three more times, the final round very near the bridge quarterdeck, sending the admiral down onto the hard cold iron. He groaned, coughing with the smoke and feeling the heat of fire below. Then he gaped in awe at what he saw in the skies above him!

Flights of Sparrowhawks thundered amid a wild display of streaking light and violent explosions. Fiery trails of orange clawed the dark sky, like molten fire arrows flung at the bombers, and they were being picked off with lethal accuracy. Three, then five, then nine, the night shuddering under the intensity of the sound, the wine dark seas gleaming with reflected fire. He crossed himself, watching the carnage of his fellow countrymen as they died. Then he reached for the hand rail, clutching it with a bloody glove and dragging himself to his feet.

He cleared his voice and shouted one last command. "Avvenire! A tutta velocita. Andiamo via de qui!" And as his ship lurched about, her aft guns plaintively firing one last salvo, he shook his head, as much to gather his sensibilities as anything else. This was no mere cruiser, he thought. It's a battleship, and it blew my task force away with nothing more than its secondary batteries! But Madre de Dio! What was it firing at the hunchbacks? He looked at it one last time as the cruisers and destroyers made smoke to mask their retreat. The British have avenged their losses of a few months past, he thought. And now he knew how this one ship might be so bold as to sail here on its own. It was a behemoth of vengeance and a devil from hell!

They had inflicted heavy damage on Da Zara's squadron, but it gave Fedorov no real satisfaction when he saw the ships turn and run. Then the flights of low flying bombers arrived, and he watched how Karpov coolly ordered the use of the same Klinok medium range SAM system that had caused the accident earlier, only now he was utilizing silos mounted on the forward deck. There was no malfunction on this occasion. The missiles were smartly up from their silos at three second intervals and streaking away towards the incoming aircraft. Seconds later they heard saw the awesome display in the sky as missile after missile found targets and ignited in brilliant spheres of fiery orange on the horizon. It was as if a terrible thunder storm had broiled up over a dead calm sea.

Karpov had activated two batteries of eight missiles each, and true to protocol, he had Gromenko fire the first six missiles in each battery, holding two in reserve. All twelve missiles found targets, and the shock of the attack sent the remaining eight SM-79 Sparrowhawks into wild evasive maneuvers, insofar as they were able for a lumbering tri-engine plane. Four bugged out completely, turning and diving low on the deck to roar past Da Zara's burning cruisers while the Admiral shook his fist at them, the remaining four carried on bravely, three launching torpedoes and then quickly turning away, the last stubbornly bearing in on *Kirov*.

"What is the range of those torpedoes?" asked Karpov as he watched the planes on the Tin Man display.

"Don't worry about them," said Fedorov. They need to be inside two kilometers to have any chance of hitting us."

Karpov considered that, then gave the order to secure the Klinok system and activate the close in defense Gatling guns. The AK-760 gun system was the latest replacement for the navy's older AK-

630M1-2 system. It was housed in new stealth turrets, and still utilized the six barreled 30mm Gatling gun, though its rate of fire was an astounding 10,000 rounds per minute. Oddly, the under mount magazine held only 8000 rounds during normal operations, so it was rare that the gun would ever fire full out. Instead it would bark out short fiery bursts of HE fragmentation rounds that could shred an incoming missile at a range of four kilometers. With radar, optical sighting, TV control and laser lock systems, it was amazingly accurate, and Karpov waited confidently until the port side guns locked on and then fired two short bursts when the plane reached the 4000 meter mark.

The pilot of the last brave hunchback was clenching his stick and ready to pull the release on his torpedo when he felt his plane shake violently as the fragmentation rounds ripped off his right engine and half the wing. Low over the sea, his plane went into an immediate and unrecoverable dive, plunging into the water with a huge splash.

Up in the citadel they could hear the sound of the men cheering on the decks below as the last plane went down, and Karpov smiled, giving Fedorov a sidelong glance. "You may secure your gun system, Gromenko."

Fedorov breathed deeply, his lips tight. He had no real idea how to fight the ship as Karpov did, but he stowed the lesson away. Karpov stepped over to him and spoke quietly. "I know how you feel, Captain," he said in a low voice so that none of the other officers would hear. "What *must* be done is sometime very unpleasant. When it comes down to their ships and planes or the loss of ours, you will know what you must do."

Fedorov looked down, still unsatisfied within, but he nodded, acknowledging what Karpov was saying. Then he straightened up, turning Gromenko. "How many missiles remain for our Klinok system?"

"Sir, my board notes 17 missile fires in the last two engagements, and we now have 79 missiles remaining in inventory on that system."

"Something to consider," he said to Karpov. "We have a long way to go before we reach safe waters." He looked about, noting the time. "Helm—left fifteen degrees rudder and come to course 315."

"Left fifteen and stead on three-one-five" echoed the helmsman "Speed thirty knots, aye, sir."

"Walk with me, Captain." Fedorov had heard Admiral Volsky say and do this, when he wanted a private talk with an officer, and it seemed appropriate for the moment. Karpov grinned, but followed respectfully, and the two men entered the briefing room at the back of the citadel.

"I'm going to take us up to the Strait of Bonifacio," Fedorov began as he switched on the digital wall map and displayed the region. "At thirty knots we should be there by dawn, roughly six hours. It would be better if we could run the strait at night, but I don't want to linger in these waters any longer than I have to." He pointed to the map where the ship's current position was clearly indicated with a bright red dot, and there were several blue dots north and east of their position indicating other contacts already designated and tracked by their long range radar system. He tapped one of these contacts, well east of the ship.

"This is the heavy cruiser group," he said, "*Bolzano* and *Goriza*—both with 8 inch guns and better armor than the ships we just engaged. There will be another heavy cruiser here, *Trieste*, and each group will have destroyer escorts. This other group out of Naples will be another light cruiser. By steering 315 I'm taking the most direct route north to get us out of the Tyrrhenian Sea. These cruisers are fast, but I think we can stay well ahead of them at thirty knots and reach the strait before they can pose any threat. And my understanding of the Italians at this point in the war, I don't think the lighter surface action groups will attempt to engage us without support from more air units or heavier ships. There is considerable air power mustered near Cagliari, and we may remain in range of planes from those fields for some time on this route. But they have a mission against the British convoy as their first priority, and we may simply be an inconvenient barb in their side at the moment. They had a run at us, but with little more than twenty percent of the strength they might deploy in a well planned attack. At dawn, however, we will have to get past the naval base at La Maddalena. And we could also face some danger from German and Italian planes at Grosseto. That airfield would be here, very near the Island of Elba on the Italian mainland. The other route north around Corsica takes us very near the major Italian base at La Spezia. Thankfully, the really dangerous ships are at Taranto. They didn't move their battleships to La Spezia until later in 1942."

"No matter," said Karpov glibly. "If they were there, and they dared to send them against us those ships would get the same treatment."

Fedorov let that remark pass and simply said: "Well my hope is that we can avoid engagement whenever possible, Captain."

"Very well," said Karpov. "I agree that we must conserve our missile inventories, but what about this naval base?"

"There will not be much there, a few destroyers, perhaps a few swift boats and other auxiliaries. I think we can get by without much difficulty. But the strait is only 11 kilometers wide and there will be little room to maneuver in the channel. We can expect minefields, and possibly even enemy submarine activity."

Karpov's eyes darkened at this. If there was anything that he truly feared at sea, it was an enemy submarine. Yet these were not the fast, stealthy modern American attack subs he had drilled against so often in their training maneuvers. These were old WWII subs, and he took heart in that, his confidence still unflagging.

"The loss of one of our KA-40s was regrettable," he said. "And I am still concerned about the Horse Tail sonar. That said, I think we have more than enough capability to deal with these old boats."

"They are diesel, and can run on battery as well," Fedorov cautioned him. "I need not remind you that we were targeted earlier, and found these submarines difficult to find when they are simply hovering. So I want Tasarov on the sonar when we run the straits."

"He'll be there," said Karpov. "With the best ears in the fleet. And with your permission sir, I'll check on the status of systems repairs. We have trouble with radar sets, the aft Klinok systems, and the sonar there. Now that we are one helo short, we will need to be more deliberate in the event we encounter enemy forces, particularly undersea boats."

"You believed I waited too long to engage here?"

"I do, sir, with no offense intended."

Fedorov nodded. "None taken, Karpov. I know I have much to learn, and I will be relying on you and the other senior officers as well if we have to fight again."

"Every man will give you their best, sir," said Karpov. "With no doubt."

Fedorov paused for a moment, then said something else that had been in the air between them and harbored inwardly by both men. "I know this must be difficult for you, Captain—I mean, being reduced in rank and placed beneath me this way. I am not saying I have earned this position either. I know I have no real experience in combat, or even running the ship, though having been a navigator I can maneuver well enough."

"I understand your feelings, Fedorov, but I must shoulder my burden now as best I can. I asked the admiral for this post, and he was good enough to give it to me. I may have been wrong, even reckless before, and what I did should not be easily forgiven—not by the Admiral, or by you, or even by the junior officers. Yes, I admit it to you now. I had time enough to think about it in the brig these last ten days. You tried to warn me that the American carrier was no threat, but I had more on my head than I could hold at the time, and I acted... stupidly..."

"Alright, Captain," said Fedorov. "I'll make you a deal. You keep *me* from acting stupidly when it comes to fighting the ship, and I'll do my best to keep *you* from acting stupidly." He smiled, and Karpov clasped him on the shoulder.

"Done," he said.

An hour later the ship was again brought to action stations when yet another squadron of Italian bombers approached from the southwest. Karpov suggested they break up the formation early with one well placed S-300.

"If we throw a firecracker into their beehive they may just have second thoughts about attacking us," he said confidently, and he was correct. He had Gromenko fire a single long range SAM at the formation, and it was able to kill two planes and send the remaining eight scattering in all directions. Nikolin could hear the pilots chattering on the radio, clearly distressed by what had happened. Then, one by one, the planes broke off and turned southwest for Cagliari.

"That was just a probing attack," said Fedorov. "They have much bigger fish to fry later today when the British convoy approaches the Skerki Bank. The history records attacks by 20 aircraft at 08:00 hours, a major attack by 70 planes at noon, and then the real show before dusk with over 100 aircraft. Needless to say, I think we can feel fortunate that they are so preoccupied to the south. Tonight they will still be receiving aircraft from Sicily and the air crews will be getting the planes ready for those operations. They know where we are from that last abortive jab. My only hope is that they do not put us on their target list again in the morning."

He looked at Nikolin, a sly gleam in his eye. "Here is a job for *you* Nikolin."

"Sir?"

"I think it's time for a little ruse…"

Chapter 12

Hut Four at Bletchley Park was a nondescript extension off the main mansion complex, with plain pale green siding and a tar black roof. Its special purpose was decryption of naval signals intelligence and photo analysis, and one of its frequent denizens was Britain's top cryptographer Alan Turing, who was lounging at his desk a few minutes past midnight when the envelope first came in. Unlike all the other parcels received at Bletchley Park, it was delivered by a uniformed Navy courier, somewhat breathless as he clomped in with soiled boots, which immediately caught Turing's attention. Most everything else would come in at six in the morning, in a quiet, routine manner, the adjutant making the rounds, desk to desk, with a squeaky wheeled cart. For a courier to burst in at this ungodly hour meant something rather important had been caught in the intelligence nets.

"Lucky enough to find someone up at this hour," the man huffed.

Turing sat up, nodded perfunctorily as he signed the man's clipboard, and then eyed the package he was handed with interest and a good measure of curiosity. Of late the load of intercepts, reconnaissance film and photos wanting the attention of the boys in Hut Four had lightened somewhat. It was marked URGENT – TOP SECRET, as they all were, and he flicked a lock of dark hair from his brow as he looked more closely at the source.

Something out of the Med, he thought. It had come in by special overnight courier flight from Gibraltar, which led him to believe that someone there wanted to give it some rather pointed attention. My God, they put the rush on this one! Curious, he opened the clasps, and unsealed the envelope, not surprised to find a reel of video footage, typical gun camera film, and a few enlargements. He took one in hand, immediately turning it over to see the notation and date. It was very fresh, not a day old, which was again quite surprising. The date read 14:30 Hours, 11 AUG 42. Takali Airfield – MALTA – REQUEST ID. That raised an eyebrow, as he hadn't seen much out of Malta for some time, particularly with an ID request. Most every enemy ship and sub operating in those waters was well photographed and documented. What are they fussing over now, he thought? Probably some recent aerial photography over Taranto or La Spezia. Or perhaps some low level runs over the German U-Boat base at Salamis. Could Jerry have slipped a new U-Boat type into the Med? They had been operating with a handful of Type VIIs in their 29th Flotilla. What now?

He flipped the photo over, surprised again to see what looked like a capital ship at sea, awash in a hail of gunfire from an attacking plane, and very oddly exposed. Something about the light on the sea drew his eye, and the peculiar darkness of the ship itself, an ominous looking shadow. It was hard to see much detail in the grainy photo, so he decided to rack up the film reel and give it a spin in the video room. Moments later he was deeply absorbed in what he saw. He ran it through once, finding he had slowly leaned forward for a close look by the time the film ended, then he rewound the whole thing and ran it again. It was very curious, and something seemed to turn in his stomach as he watched it the second time, a thrum of anxiety mixed with a thimble full of adrenaline. When the reel ended he looked at the two photos he held in his hand.

"Request ID….Indeed," he said aloud. His eyes seemed searching, darkly bothered, and his brow was low and set with the focus of his mind. He got up and walked with a fast, deliberate pace to the file room at the back of the hut. When was it now? Some time ago. He went through several files before the date came to him again. Yes…That was it. The file…

He had called it simply that in discussion with a select handful of mates there at the hut. "The File." It had commanded their attention this very month, a year ago, and set the whole Royal Navy on its ears with the surprising emergence of a new German raider in the North Atlantic. The weapons the ship had deployed were awesome. Particularly the final blow that had been struck against the American Navy. It was a weapon of enormous power, frightening in its effect.

And it prompted the whole intelligence community to work overtime for the next six months. They had been frightened half out of their wits when the photos on that monster came in. Yet just as the Royal Navy and her American allies were closing in on this phantom ship, it disappeared, and was presumed sunk in that final action. The Americans put it out that their gallant destroyer flotilla had charged into close quarters with this sea faring goliath, and died to a man sending the dreadful ship to the bottom of the sea. Yet the matter was never fully set at ease insofar as British intelligence was concerned.

The public never knew about it, as the whole incident was a closely guarded secret, spun out instead as a dastardly combined German U-boat and surface raider attack on a neutral American naval task force. Few knew all the details of the encounter, and those that did lived with a terrible fear those next six months. They waited, eyes white with fear, every time a flight of German bombers would appear over London, thinking the next one would surely deliver another fatal and catastrophic blow with this horror weapon, but it never came.

Sailors who had been involved in the battle spread rumors in spite of warning to hush the matter, and the fleet soon came to believe that the Germans were developing fearsome new naval weapons to counter the Royal Navy's advantage at sea. But they were never seen again. Even in skirmishes with the last big German battleship, the *Tirpitz*, lurking in the cold icy water of the Norwegian Sea where this strange raider had first been spotted, there was no further deployment of the "wonder weapons" this ship has used with such deadly effect.

Weeks became months, and became a long year. All the information, Admiralty reports, interviews with senior officers in command and individual ship diaries, along with all their signals logs had been bundled, collected, classified, and coalesced under one file— "*the* file" as Turing had once called it—and a copy was still here, sitting right there in Hut Four with a plain white typewritten label on the box that read simply: "GERONIMO".

Something in the feeling that lodged in his gut sent Turing right to this very file, and he opened the box with some trepidation, reaching first for the sheaf of photo samples that had been obtained—all too few considering the resources that had been thrown at this raider. He took the best of them out, remembering how he had squinted and stared at it when he first saw the image a year ago, and how he had noted the shadow of a man standing there on the long foredeck to work out the scale and length of the ship. Now he held the photo in his left hand, and compared it to the new arrival in his right. He stared at them, for a very long time, his eyes darkening further as he studied them both under a magnifying glass. Then he sealed up the box and walked briskly back to his desk and picked up a telephone.

"Special line," he said tersely. "Admiralty."

"Right away, sir." A switchboard operator returned, and he was soon patched through on an encrypted channel. There was a brief delay, that seemed like long minutes to Turing, and in time a voice answered on the other end.

"Admiralty, special operations and intelligence."

He identified himself, saying simply "Turing, Hut Four. Geronimo. I repeat. Geronimo."

There was a pause, a very long pause it seemed. Then the voice said in quiet confirmation. *"Very good sir. Geronimo. I'll pass it on to the proper authority."*

In the early morning hours of August 12, 1942 a telephone rang in the personal quarters of Admiral and Commander-in Chief, Home Fleet, John Tovey. Its strident alarm roused him from much needed sleep, and he groped fitfully for the receiver on his nightstand, finally grasping it and muttering an irritated "yes?" that was clearly tinged with "how dare you." Yet he knew, on one level of his still sleep fogged mind, that he would not be receiving a call at this hour without real urgency behind it.

What could it possibly be this time, he groped? Home Fleet had no operations in progress. The Dieppe Operation was not yet teed up. Operation Pedestal was not in his purview. The only thing on his calendar was the laborious agony of hosting the Turkish Ambassador and Naval Attaché aboard *King George V* tomorrow. All Russian convoys were suspended after the disaster of convoy PQ 17 and also because of the transfer of Home Fleet units to the Mediterranean for Operation Pedestal. He had received the bad news concerning HMS *Eagle* before he turned in for the night. What more could have happened? Good God, he thought suddenly. Don't tell me they've put another carrier at the bottom of the sea—or even one of the battleships.

"Yes, John Tovey. What is it?" This time there was less irritation and more accommodation in his voice.

"Admiralty intelligence on the line sir. Please hold while we secure the connection." Tovey waited in the darkness of his quarters, dreading the inevitable bad news. It was far too early to hear any good news concerning the only major operation they had going now in the Med. So it had to be bad. What else?

The line cleared. He heard a low tone indicating an encrypted connection had been established. Then a voice came on the line with a single word, and his heart seemed to skip a beat when he heard it. *"Geronimo."*

There was a long silence while the other party waited, and Tovey realized the caller was needing his confirmation that the codeword was received and understood. "Very well," he said haltingly. "Geronimo.... Has First Sea Lord Admiral Pound been notified?"

"Yes sir, and Admiralty would like to request your participation in a meeting this morning at zero 8:00 hours, sir. The usual location. A Fleet Air Arm plane will be waiting for you at Hatston in...one hour, sir. I'm very sorry for the short notice, but we only just received this. Home Fleet staff has been advised that you have been taken ill and will not be able to receive the Turkish Ambassador this morning at Scapa Flow."

"I will confirm my attendance now—anything else?"

"No sir, that is all."

That was quite enough, thought Tovey as he hung up the receiver. It seems he would not have to suffer the boredom of formal protocols this afternoon after all. Instead it would be Sir Dudley Pound and all the other hatbands and cuff stripes at the Admiralty after a long, cold flight to London. Yet the nature of the call—that single word known to so very few—filled him with dread and foreboding. Intelligence has got their mitts on something new, he thought. What could it be?

He eased out of his bed, reaching for the light. There was very little time to waste if he was going to catch his plane at the appointed hour. God help us if there's been another 'incident,' he thought, thinking that word so completely inadequate for what he and his men had gone through in the North Atlantic...well...a year ago, wasn't it? Yes, a full year, almost to the day.

They put him on a fast Coastal Command Beaufighter, which was no surprise if they wanted to get him to the Admiralty in good time. The plane climbed through the typical shroud of low lying fog and up into a drab pre-dawn sky, the throttle opening up to near full power for most of the 500 mile run in. They landed at a little used RAF station, as close to Whitehall as possible, but one requiring a short drive to reach the Admiralty citadel. The grey dawn was breaking by the time Tovey's car reached his destination, and he was all of thirty minutes early, working his way in through security to eventually reach the citadel command center of the Admiralty, Special conference room 1. The door was plainly marked: MOST SECRET – AUTHORIZED PERSONNEL ONLY.

A solitary Marine guard stood to attention and saluted as he approached. When Tovey had returned the salute, the guard turned, knocked quietly on the door with a white gloved hand, then opened it for the admiral, standing stiffly to attention again as Tovey entered. The door was pulled quietly closed behind him, and he crossed the antechamber, opening the inner door to find four other men seated at the conference table. The guest list was not surprising. First Sea Lord, Sir Dudley Pound sat at the head of the table, flanked by his Second Sea Lord Sir William Whitworth and then Tovey's old friend Sir

Frederick Wake-Walker, now Third Sea Lord. The fourth man was not in uniform. He wore dark pressed trousers, white shirt under a fine knit vest and a grey tweed jacket. His tie looked over worn and ill tied, as though he threw it on as an afterthought. A dash of straight brown hair fell on his forehead above coal dark eyes, bright with fire.

The men stood to greet him, and Admiral Pound extended an arm as they exchanged handshakes. He made the introduction. "I can see you were surprised to see a man in civilian clothing in these chambers, Admiral," he said warmly. "May I introduce Professor Alan Turing, called in this morning from Bletchley Park."

"My pleasure," said Tovey as he shook the man's hand. "If I understand correctly, you led the decryption effort for German Navy Enigma traffic?"

"I did my part, sir," said Turing, his voice high and thin. "The chaps in Hut Eight had a good deal to do with sorting it all out."

"Well it's been a godsend, in more ways than you can imagine. First rate, but I'm inclined to think that we've just bit into a fairly salty cracker considering the number of stripes in this room."

Pound got right to the point, "Professor Turing received some gun camera footage taken by a Coastal Command Beaufighter at midday yesterday. Air Vice Marshall Park of the Malta Air Defense had a look at it and thought he better send in on to Gibraltar, where it was received at 17:00 hours and just happened to catch the last plane out an hour later. It's a miracle it got in to Bletchley Park as soon as it did. I'm to understand that Park also phoned ahead and set a watch on the parcel, putting the spurs to it, if you will. Just our good fortune that Professor Turing was also working very late last night, and round midnight he had a look at the footage and made a rather alarming deduction." The Admiral gestured to the chairs as all the men seated themselves.

Tovey's heart sank as he knew from the code word he had received what the general subject of this meeting was to be about. Admiral Pound settled in, and then extended a hand to Turing, inviting him to take the floor.

The young man cleared his throat. "Well gentlemen," he began, his eyes widening a bit as he spoke, "it was a simple enough request for identification of a vessel sighted in the Tyrrhenian Sea yesterday. There were two photos, he pushed a file over to Admiral Pound, "and I've taken the liberty of including photography taken of the *Geronimo* raider incident last August as well. I ran the footage and something about the look of this ship just set my stomach turning—considering the impact *Geronimo* had on our operations."

Pound had seen the photos and he passed them to Whitworth on his right, who studied them closely, a look of intense interest on his dignified features. He had been in the Royal Navy since the turn of the century and had commanded the Battlecruiser Squadron with its flagship HMS *Hood* in the first years of the war. No stranger to combat at sea, his flag was on the battlecruiser *Renown* when he mixed it up with the German raiders *Scharnhorst* and *Gneisenau* in the Norwegian Sea, besting both ships in the action and driving them off to lick their wounds. Just a few weeks before *Bismarck* sortied, he had been recalled from *Hood* to the Admiralty to take up a new post as Lord Commissioner of the Admiralty and Second Sea Lord. The loss of *Hood* days later was a shock to him, and he realized the change of command may have very well saved his own life, though he still regretted not being with his ship when she made her last desperate voyage. He ran a hand through his grey-white hair, high on his forehead now, but still full.

Whitworth passed the photos to Wake-Walker, a man who's career had been dogged with some misfortune, though it did not impede his steady rise in the ranks to his present position as Third Sea Lord. He had been found liable for mishandling his ship, then HMS *Dragon*, in 1934. Last year during the hunt for the *Bismarck* Admiral Pound had faulted him severely after the sinking of *Hood* for not re-engaging with *Norfolk*, *Suffolk* and *Prince of Wales*. In that incident Tovey had to come to his defense and threatened resignation if charges were brought forward, saying he would sit as a defense witness in any proceeding brought against Wake-Walker. The matter was eventually dropped. Then, scarcely a few months later, it had been Wake-Walker's carrier Force P that had first sighted, shadowed and engaged the *Geronimo* raider, which is why he took particular interest in the photos, staring at them a long time before he gave them over to Admiral Tovey.

"Please note the antennae situated on the secondary mast, on both photos," said Turing. "See how the panels are tilted at the same angle. Some thirty degrees off the vertical? That was one similarity that immediately caught my eye."

Tovey looked up, somewhat surprised. "You believe the Italians have mounted radar sets on their capital ships—perhaps technology given them by the Germans?"

"That was what I suggested," said Admiral Pound. "It's clear that this could not possibly be a German ship."

"My pardon, sir," said Turing, "But isn't that what we deduced a year ago—that the *Geronimo* raider could not have possibly been anything in the German inventory?" They had scoured every harbor, every shipyard, and came to the conclusion that the ship they had faced a year ago in the North Atlantic had been a pariah. Every other known ship in the German Navy that could have exhibited its speed, and characteristics had been accounted for. Yet this ship was a complete mystery. How it could have been built by the Germans without being seen and documented by Royal Navy Intelligence was a matter of lengthy discussion, and it had forced the Boys at Bletchley Park to review reams of signals traffic for months after. Yet they had found nothing whatsoever that in any way hinted at the existence of the ship, let alone the weaponry it deployed and used with such dramatic effect.

In the end they simply came to call the raider "*Geronimo*," after the renegade Indian chief that had been harried and pursued by the Americans, hunted down by a select group of Federal cavalry. The Royal Navy had its own select scout ships out in the hunt when this raider first appeared, followed by carriers under Wake-Walker and then Admiral Tovey's battleships from Home Fleet, but it did them no good. In the end they had acquiesced to the American line that the enemy ship had been sunk by the their own *Desron 7*, though none of the eight destroyers that formed that group survived the encounter to provide any real confirmation of that claim. Not a single survivor had been found, nor was there any sign whatsoever of wreckage on the sea, not even a drop of oil to mark the place where they must surely have fought the enemy to the death.

It left an uncomfortable feeling in the stomachs of men accustomed to much more certainty when it came to the intentions and capabilities of the enemy they were still facing. The intelligence failure had been profound. That was the way Churchill put it, and when the doughty Prime Minister stuck his umbrella in your gut it was sure to get your attention. Yet that was how they left it—a stinging black eye where the Abwehr had jabbed them blind. But Turing still had deep misgivings about the ship, and the weaponry it displayed. He kept it largely to himself, but inwardly never believed any of the official lines about the incident. He thought it useless to raise his suspicions with all the intensity of the brou-ha-ha then underway in the intelligence community. Yet he never gave them up or was able to put them to rest.

Pound looked at him, somewhat perturbed. "Would you say this is a cruiser? It looks to be something quite more."

"That is what struck me immediately," said Turing. "I can tell you definitively that this is not an Italian cruiser, sir. We have all those ships accounted for. Their battleships are very low on fuel, and they've taken to leaving them in port and using their oil to refuel smaller ships and submarines. Our operatives can verify that Taranto has not sent anything of this size out of in the last three days, and the same for La Spezia. Now we *do* know that Admiral Da Zara has sortied with his 3rd Cruiser Division out of Calabria—two light cruisers and three destroyers. And he is also moving the 7th Cruiser Division out of Messina and Naples with a couple of heavy cruisers and a handful of destroyers, but those ships were not anywhere near these coordinates when this photo was taken." He indicated the message decrypt record, also a part of the file, which listed the exact coordinates of the sighting.

"I can verify that," said Whitworth. "I had a look at the latest intercepts this morning. We've got all those ships under observation. But there's more to this sighting than these photographs. First off this ship was sighted alone, with no other escorts."

Pound shifted uncomfortably as Whitworth continued.

"We sent 248 Beaufighter Squadron from Gibraltar to Malta on the 10th of August. They were the planes responsible for this sighting, and I have Park's latest communiqué indicating this same group flew a strike mission on the afternoon of the 11th. They found the ship again, and, well...they were cut to pieces for their trouble. Four of six Beaus went down, and only two crews came out alive. And here's the rub—they were shot down by some sort of naval rocketry." He folded his arms gravely, looking at Wake-Walker and Tovey.

"Rocketry?" said Wake-Walker, the memory of his own squadrons off *Furious* and *Victorious* still an unhealed wound. "You mean to say the Italians have these weapons now?"

"Apparently so," said Pound quickly. "It's my belief that the Germans have brewed up a new lot of these fire sticks and they've shipped them to Regia Marina in an effort to tip the balance of the war in the Mediterranean theater. For that matter we might expect to find *Tirpitz* or their other heavy ships equipped with them in the near future as well. And should they be carrying anything more..." His implication was obvious to them all.

Turing had a strange look on his face, set and determined. He had not heard about this second strike mission or the use of rockets until just this moment. Now his very worst suspicions were confirmed, at least in his own mind, but how could he broach the subject with the cream of Admiralty? These men were no-nonsense naval royalty. They had centuries of combined experience between them and were accustomed to having things nailed down with brass tacks and well in order at all times. Yet he could not remain silent. He had to say something.

"Well sir," he said to Admiral Pound. "I must say that from my close examination of the photography in hand, I do not believe this ship is anything in the Italian naval inventory."

Pound gave him a hard look. It was enough that he had ventured to contradict the First Sea Lord, but even more that he would suggest…What *was* he suggesting? "See here," he began, somewhat perturbed. "Then you are telling me that this is *not* an Italian ship? It bloody well isn't a German ship. That leaves us with something out of Toulon, and it would be quite a stretch of the imagination to believe the French would be at sea, and even more so with weapons described in that last communiqué from Malta."

A remnant of the French Navy was still holed up in Toulon, and it included some rather formidable ships, including the battleships *Dunkerque, Strasbourg,* and *Provence,* and numerous cruisers and destroyers, some 57 surface ships and numerous subs, torpedo boats, sloops and auxiliaries.

Wake-Walker came in with another angle. "Could the Germans have gotten their hands on one of these French ships, and rigged her out with these new weapons? I dare say we haven't kept a very close watch on the French Navy since Aboukir Bay."

"Hut Four cannot confirm that," said Turing, "and I can say definitively that we have not seen anything in the Enigma coding that would in any way lead us to that conclusion over at Hut Eight."

Pound frowned at him. "I wish I could feel more reassured in hearing that, Professor Turing. After all, Bletchley Park had that same line concerning this *Geronimo* incident in the first place."

Turing ignored the obvious barb in the remark, feeling that the discussion was sliding away towards conclusions that would lead the Royal Navy to make a grave error. He had come to a far different conclusion about this ship when he first saw the gun camera footage and, as he tried to muster the courage to express his feelings, he realized that it was very likely that he would be scapegoated for any further intelligence failure here. Kill the messenger. It was all too common, even with all the apparent chin chin civility of these men. He girded himself, then finally began to speak his mind.

"Admiral Pound," he said flatly. "I have examined this photography very closely. The ship depicted is over eight hundred and twenty feet in length, and I estimate it to displace at least 30,000 tons or more. That is a hundred feet more than either *Dunkerque* or *Strasburg* from the French Navy, 60 feet longer than the Italian battleship *Littorio*, and the equal of our late departed HMS *Hood*. It has no visible armament above a few small deck guns, and yet it managed to bloody the nose of the entire Home Fleet: two carriers, three battleships, five cruisers and nine destroyers. Furthermore, it has demonstrated a speed in excess of thirty knots—faster than our most modern battleships of the line, and even some of our cruisers—yet it has *no visible stacks*, and has never been seen to be making steam of any kind, even in this latest photo…" He let that last bit dangle, his high voice somewhat strident as he realized he had let his passion for the point get the better of him.

Pound made no effort to suppress his anger now. "Preposterous!" he slapped his hand on the table, more than annoyed now with the truculence of this upstart professor. He had heard a few barbed rumors about the man—that he was eccentric, given to strange flights of fancy, and that he had other peculiar habits that Pound did not wish to entertain further in his mind. Now to have him make such statements in this room, before the highest ranking officers of the Royal Navy. Preposterous was not half a word for what he felt at the moment, and his face clearly exhibited his displeasure.

"Are you suggesting this latest photo is *identical* to the images we obtained a year ago—that the two ships are one and the same? Preposterous!"

Part V

The First Gate

"Through me you pass into the city of woe: Through me you pass into eternal pain… All hope abandon, ye who enter here."

The Inferno, Canto III
- Dante Alegeri

Chapter 13

When Karpov entered the officer's dining hall, the conversations seemed to hush, particularly at the far table where he saw the broad shoulders and telltale woolen cap of Orlov. The former Chief of Operations, now a mere Lieutenant in the Marine detachment, was seated with a clutch of young *Starshini*, one stripe Junior Lieutenants that been laughing together as the big man joked about something. Their sudden silence prompted Orlov to look over his shoulder, and as Karpov sat down, alone as always, he heard Orlov curse under his breath, *"Mudak..."* One of the other men at the table nudged him with a cautionary elbow, which prompted Orlov to say yet more—"Mne pohui!" he exclaimed, telling the man he didn't give a fuck.

Karpov ignored them, eating in the heavy silence that filled the room, and trying to keep his mind on Fedorov's last briefing, and what might lie ahead for them. But the awkward situation dragged him back to those last moments on the bridge as he struggled to complete the missile firing, and how Orlov had stood there in silence, doing and saying nothing when the bridge was compromised.

It felt so impossibly wrong now when he replayed the images in his mind. Orlov had agreed to back his decision, yet when it came to the moment, he let him drop into the stew without a second thought. On one level he felt betrayed, but even more ashamed that he had ever thought to enlist the allegiance of an oaf like Orlov. Yet as he tried to muster a kernel of anger over what had happened, another voice within him whispered that he had been the one who opened the hatch when the Marines arrived, stupidly thinking they had come in response to his own orders, and not thinking that Volsky might have already regained control of the ship.

You were an idiot, he thought. You knew it would only be a matter of time before someone tried the door at sick bay and the Admiral was freed. And you knew he would reassert his authority over the ship at once. That's why you locked yourself away in the bridge, and thought Orlov's presence there at your side would be enough to keep the other officers in line. You wanted to fire your damn missile, and that you did, blowing the Americans to hell where they belonged. But one day you will join them there. Yes, one day you will sit at the table with every man you have put under the sea in all this insanity. Forget Orlov, he concluded. Blame yourself, and yes you are every bit the bastard he calls you under his breath, that and more.

In time Orlov let out an audible burp and stood to leave, a cup of coffee in hand as he moved toward the exit behind Karpov. The Captain realized something was wrong immediately, as officers always left their dishes at the table and they would be collected and cleaned by the rankers in the galley, and no one ever took anything out of the dining room. The silence thickened when Orlov drifted near Karpov's table and then pretended to stumble.

"Watch your step!" Karpov said sharply, but it was obvious to everyone that Orlov had deliberately spilled his coffee on Karpov's right shoulder, and even more obvious that he was going to get away with it.

"Sorry, Captain," he said sarcastically. "I didn't see you there. It's these bandages," he said, holding up his hands. "Can't seem to hold on to anything, eh?" Orlov forced a strained smile that was more of a sneer, and Karpov waved him away, his eyes darkly on the far table where he could hear the muted, well restrained laughter of the junior Lieutenants. He could feel the heat on the back of his neck, and knew that Orlov had deliberately tried to humiliate and provoke him in front of the other men. He doused the stain on his jacket with a table linen as Orlov left, sullen and angry. Had it been any other man, he thought bitterly…

The junior officers finished, one by one, and a few were even bold enough now to drift Karpov's way as they left, some holding cups of coffee as well, though not one dared to do anything more. If they had, Karpov would have shouted them deaf, but as it was the scene had clearly demonstrated to them that Karpov was not man enough to stand up to Orlov, and not even his rank and authority as acting *Starpom* was enough to protect him now.

When they had all left, Karpov finished his stew, tired, angry, humiliated and wanting sleep. He stood up and saw where Orlov had set his stained coffee cup down on his table, right on its side, deliberately spilling the last remnant onto the table linen near his plate, and he swiped it angrily off the table, sending the cup clattering across the deck. His shoulders hunched, head low, he went through the door, immediately sensing a looming presence in the empty hall. It was Orlov.

"Oh, Captain," he said. "I just came back to say *excuse* me," he grinned balefully. "Did I soil your Captain's jacket?"

"Yob tvou mat' Orlov!" the Captain exclaimed, telling the big man what he thought he should do with his mother. "You want to act tough in front of the men, but when things came to a head how tough were you on the bridge?"

It was the first time the two men had ever spoken of their failed attempt to take command of the ship from Volsky, and the words tumbled out, with pent up anger on both sides.

"Fuck you," Karpov. "You duped me! You played me for an idiot with all your reasons and arguments, and I was stupid enough to go along, that was all."

"Come on, Orlov, just say you lost your nerve, and your backbone along with it. You like to push the men around, but not the Marines—not someone who can set you back on your heels if you get out of line."

Orlov lunged at him, seizing Karpov by the jacket in spite of the obvious pain with his hands, pulling the smaller man close to his face. He was easily fifty pounds heavier and a good head taller than Karpov, and he used his strength to dominate him. "Right, Karpov. What was all that bullshit when it came down to firing the missile, eh? You give your orders then stand there looking at me to give the last word! You dumped the whole pile of shit in *my* lap, because you wanted to set me up to take the fall if it all came apart. Yes?"

"Get your filthy hands off me!" The Captain's face was red with anger.

"Oh? What are you going to do now, Captain? No one is here. Where's Troyak, eh? Are you going to go whine to Volsky, or slink back to the bridge and tell Fedorov? *Piz-da!*"

The Captain tried to break loose, pushing hard, and then Orlov loosed one hand and buried a fist into Karpov's gut, doubling him over with the blow, though he grimaced with the pain to his own bandaged hand. Orlov pushed hard, shoving the Captain off his feet, and standing over him with a satisfied grin on his face.

"Na kaleni, *suka*," he hissed at him. "Go tell Fedorov, and just be glad I didn't put a knife in your belly instead." He turned and tromped off, his heavy soled boots clomping hard on the deck as he went.

The night deepened and the men aboard *Kirov* rotated in shifts, some snatching a few hours of fitful sleep while others manned battle stations. Still others started their shift in the mess hall, lining up for bowls of warm milk, cheese sandwiches, kasha and hot tea. Fedorov had decided to stand down from full alert, thinking his situational awareness was still solid enough in spite of the aberration he had discovered with the early sailing of the Italian 7th Cruiser Division. He had expected Da Zara's 3rd Division would be handled easily enough, but the other contacts still bearing on their heading were still some cause for concern. The Italian cruisers were fast, with each group capable of thirty knots, and so *Kirov* continued to sail north just shy of her best speed.

The ruse he had planned involved a fake distress call, sent out by Nikolin in Morse code with the intention of fooling the Italian Navy. Once decoded the message would read: *"Force K – Critical gun damage in engagement 23:45 hours - Aborting mission under Case B."* And to be certain it would be decoded he had dug up an old reference book he had on Royal Navy codes and deliberately used a version that he knew the Italians would be able to decipher. His intention was to convince Regia Marina that his ship now presented no immediate threat to their home bases or airfields, hoping they might call off the pursuit and simply return their ships to friendly ports, as they had decided historically during Operation Pedestal. In that campaign the Italian Navy had aborted its operations when the Germans refused to provide air cover over the Sicilian Narrows. Fedorov hoped that he could count on them to stand down here as well—but he was wrong.

Regia Marina had a bone to pick now. The fiery admiral Da Zara had escaped southeast to Cagliari with his battered task force, livid with anger that he did not get more air support during his sortie, and convinced that this was no mere British cruiser at large in the Tyrrhenian Sea, but a fast battlecruiser. He concluded that this ship must have slipped through north of the Skerki Bank before the submarine picket lines had been established a day earlier, and while most air recon missions had been focused much farther west. It obviously intended to disrupt Italian surface fleet operations aimed at attacking the convoy—and that it had accomplished well enough.

The arrogance of the British, he thought. They think to sail unchallenged into our home waters? On a secure phone line to Admiral Bergamini at La Spezia he was furious, demanding that the navy could not allow such an incursion into the Tyrrhenian Sea to go unpunished. What he heard in return gave him heart.

Bergamini claimed to have known about this ship for some time, since the submarine *Bronzo* had sighted it, on fire aft, a little before sunset on the previous day. *"Why do you think your Division was sent out in the first place?"* he said in a thin, distant voice over the phone. *"The Germans must have caught it during their ferry operations from Sicily to reinforce the air Squadrons at Cagliari. Furthermore, we have a new wire intercept concerning gun damage on this ship, and we believe it is now attempting to run for the Bonifacio Strait."*

He praised Da Zara, assuming it was his timely action that had inflicted this further damage on the enemy, and he told him that the ships of 7th Cruiser division were still in the hunt, chasing the impudent raider north at high speed even as they spoke.

"And there is more," he said quietly. *"We have a surprise or two prepared for this uninvited dinner guest. I cannot say more, Da Zara,*

but you will soon see that Regia Marina has more fight left in it than you may believe. I will encode details through normal channels. In the meantime. If any of your ships remain seaworthy, get them ready for action!"

"Seaworthy?" Da Zara said sharply. "Yes, they will float I suppose. But ready for action? I think not. It will take weeks, probably months to repair the damage we sustained."

"Then do not worry. We will handle the matter from La Spezia."

It was that very night, that Admiral Tovey had been awakened with that jarring coded message and sent on his way to a meeting with the Admiralty on the morning of August 12, just as *Kirov* was approaching the Strait of Bonifacio. Now he sat in the meeting with Admiral Pound and the other Sea Lords, and this curious Professor from Bletchley Park. In spite of Admiral Pound's reaction, Tovey could see more in those photographs than he wished, and it turned his stomach as well.

"The same ship?" Pound flailed at Turing. "May I remind you, Professor, that the final engagement with this raider occurred on the 8th of August, a full *year* ago. I'll admit that we've had our suspicions about the American story that this ship was sunk by their destroyer squadron, but for it to have survived for an entire year on its own in the Atlantic, and to have entered the Mediterranean undetected by our forces is absolute rubbish."

Tovey spoke up, wishing to clarify the situation. "Professor Turing," he began in a more civil tone. "The Admiral's point is well taken. Surely you don't suspect this is, in fact, the very same vessel we engaged a year ago. How can we possibly explain its presence in the middle of such a hotly contested war zone?"

Turing had his right hand at his temple, elbow on the table, thinking he had been foolish to express his suspicions in this room, at this time, before the weight of evidence might mount on his side of any argument. Now he thought how he might smooth this ruffle over without dampening the urgency he needed to communicate to these men. He was about to speak when there came a soft knock at the door, granting him a welcome respite.

Tovey looked over his shoulder and gestured to the Marine guard there, who held two neatly folded papers, decoded cable intercepts fresh from the cypher station. He took them, opening the first quickly to see it marked 'Most Urgent – ULTRA' and read it quietly before looking up with raised brows and a look on his face that conveyed his obvious concern.

"Well gentlemen," he said as he handed the intercept to Admiral Pound. "It appears that Regia Marina has found its backbone after all." He waited politely while Pound read the intercept, and Turing watched with some interest, the irony of the moment galling him. Here was a cable decoded as a direct result of his work, and the Navy was quick to embrace it as truth, yet he knew he would have to argue his point at some length to overcome their stalwart opposition to his suspicions about this ship.

Pound handed the cable off to Whitworth and spoke up. "The Italians got up steam on their heavy surface units six hours ago and sortied from La Spezia a little after midnight. It seems that Admiral Syfret may have somewhat more to deal with than we first anticipated. Battleships *Littorio* and *Veneto* were both confirmed as part of the task force."

"Battleships?" said Wake-Walker. "We thought they were laid up without adequate fuel for a major operation."

"Apparently not," said Pound. "Either they managed to obtain more fuel oil, or they've decided to make do with what they have. Either way it amounts to the same thing, and I must tell you gentlemen, that a move of this magnitude may mean they've decided to risk everything to stop this convoy to Malta."

"It's not surprising," said Tovey. "We've thrown fifty warships at this operation."

"Yes," said Pound. "Well it looks like *Rodney* and *Nelson* may have some work to do beyond blasting away at the Luftwaffe. What's this last bit in the cable?"

"Oh, excuse me, sir," said Tovey. "It refers to further movements of the Italian 7th Cruiser Division with ships based at Messina and Naples. They've put to sea as well, though they seem to be concentrating on the Italian Naval base at La Maddalena, which is somewhat surprising. Odd thing is this—the heavy units out of La Spezia haven't entered the Tyrrhenian Sea. They sailed *west*, on a course that might put them off the northwest coast of Corsica right about now." He looked at his watch, noting the time.

"The Bonifacio Strait?" asked Whitworth.

"Indeed," said Tovey.

"But why not just make a run down through the Tyrrhenian Sea and hit us north of the Skerki Bank? Their ships would be well covered by the airfields around Cagliari."

Tovey slowly opened the second intercept as Whitworth reasoned the situation out. "They may be thinking to swing down the western coast of Sardinia and get to the convoy that way."

"It doesn't make any sense," said Wake-Walker. "They would be much better positioned just west of Cagliari as Whitworth has it. They must know we've timed it to try and get round Cape Bon late tonight. If they're low on fuel they won't be making top speed, that's for sure. So even at twenty knots that's another twelve hours before they'd be anywhere near the convoy route by sailing west of Sardinia, and by that time our ships will be north of Bizerte. They'll find themselves well *behind* the action."

"Unless they mean to have a go at our covering force," Whitworth suggested.

"Engage *Rodney* and *Nelson*?" said Pound. "They'll regret that, I assure you."

"Well I can think of no other good reason for this La Spezia Squadron to be where it is," said Tovey. "In fact I can put forward no sound reasoning for it to be at sea at all!" Now he read the second cable intercept. "Hello," he said in a low voice. "Beaufighter Reconnaissance report out of Malta...It seems there was another engagement last night northeast of Cagliari. Malta reports no sorties, so none of our aircraft were involved, but the Italian 3rd Cruiser Division under Da Zara got shoved about rather rudely... All five ships are back at Cagliari this morning, and every single one appears to have sustained damage."

That news fell hard on the table and quieted the entire discussion. Then Turing spoke, his high voice clear and steady. He had been listening with some interest, and finally decided to throw another spanner in the works

"If I may, sir," he began, "and correct me if I am wrong, but I don't think we have any ships in the Tyrrhenian Sea at the moment— not northeast of Cagliari, which would be right about where 248 Squadron engaged and photographed this vessel yesterday afternoon, and got a fistful of *rocketry* for their trouble. I say the Italians have tangled with this very same ship! Now it's not ours, so it's quite evident, gentlemen," he said flatly, and then spoke the single word that had gathered them all round the table that morning. *"Geronimo..."*

Chapter 14

The dawn came in hues of scarlet and vermillion, brightening to pale rose as the skies lightened quickly. *Kirov* had raced northwest, a steel arrow aimed at the Strait of Bonifacio, and behind her a gaggle of Italian Cruisers and destroyers hurried in pursuit. Fedorov was back on the bridge after a brief two hours rest below when he gave over command to Rodenko coming off his leave at three in the morning. Now he studied the radar plots, satisfied that they were still well ahead in the race and would reach the Maddalena Archipelago in plenty of time to run the strait before these pursuing ships could interfere.

"I expect some more work for the deck guns," he said to Samsonov, also back at his station in the CIC.

"Good!" said Samsonov. "Gromenko's been boasting below decks and I've some catching up to do."

Fedorov didn't like the sound of that, but he let it pass. Then again, he thought, if they were going to have to fight again, why not do it without reservation? This is one thing Karpov had tried to impress upon him. He stared at the radar returns as daylight began to bathe the citadel in pale light. Another half hour, he thought, and by then we'll see what they have to throw at us from La Maddalena. His timing was just a little off.

Tasarov sat up quickly and sounded off at sonar. "New Contact – Undersea boat – Bearing 325 degrees, range 10.3 kilometers, depth forty feet, speed 5 knots. Designate Alpha One."

A diesel boat was creeping in on them from the northwest, very near the strait and obviously assuming a blocking position where it might get a shot at any passing ship. Fedorov went to Tasarov's station, encouraged. "It appears our sonar is operating well enough in spite of the loss of the towed array. Then again, I'm told you have the best ears in the fleet, Tasarov. Can you track this boat easily now?"

"As long as it continues to move, sir. If it stops and hovers, we may have to go to active sonar, but for now, I have a good location plot."

"Then you can kill this sub? Do you need one of the helicopters up?" Fedorov recalled the wild opening minutes when one of their first contacts had been a submarine. He remembered how the Admiral immediately sent up helicopters, and wondered if he should do the same. Tasarov's answer reassured him greatly.

"Sir, I can put a weapon on this target at any time. Our *Shkval* ASW system is in range now and can close this distance in a matter of seconds."

Again, the amazing technological leap that *Kirov* represented over its WWII naval adversaries was decisive. The creeping enemy sub was still far from the ideal range it needed to launch a torpedo at *Kirov*. For any chance of a hit it would want to be at no more than a 1000 to 2000 meters before firing. By contrast, *Kirov's* super cavitating *Shkval* rocket propelled torpedoes could strike targets at many times that range, and they would accelerate to incredible underwater speeds exceeding 200 knots by generating a gas bubble around the weapon that literally displaced the ocean water as the torpedo surged forward. In effect, the seawater was never touching the weapon to create drag. If launched at this target it would eat up the ten kilometer run to the enemy sub in just a minute and fifteen seconds.

"Just say the word, sir."

Fedorov thought for a moment. "What is our inventory on this system?"

"Sir, we have expended only one torpedo, and have nine remaining."

"And when they are gone?"

"We still have one KA-40 with sixteen standard torpedoes in the magazine. Normal load out is two per mission. Then we have the close-in UDAV-2 system, though it is far less effective than the *Shkval*."

"Very well," said Fedorov. "Make ready on your primary system, Mister Tasarov, but we will hold our fire momentarily."

"Aye, sir…But we are running at thirty knots and will be inside this sub's firing range in nine minutes."

"I understand," said Fedorov. "Helm, ahead two thirds."

"Ahead two thirds, sir and steady on 315."

"Come left fifteen degrees rudder to course three-zero-zero."

"Sir, my rudder is left on 300 degrees, aye."

He thought to buy himself just a few short minutes with the reduction of speed, as they were drawing very near the Maddalena Archipelago now, a cluster of rocky islands that harbored the Italian naval base. It was time to decide.

"Mister Samsonov, bring the ship to full battle stations. I'll want all systems manned with lookouts to both port and starboard to scan for mines. We may also face shore based guns."

The alarm sounded, and *Kirov* pushed on swiftly towards the first major bottleneck they would have to run if they were ever to find safe water again. Crews manned machine guns on both sides of the ship, and Samsonov also activated the AK-730 close in defense system to assist with floating mines.

The Maddalena Archipelago dominated the eastern approaches to the strait, a cluster of seven large islands with many more smaller islets. Their strategic position had seen them fortified during the days of the Roman empire, with old towers and bastions perched atop the rocky crags of the hills. In WWII these forts were improved with the addition of modern concrete gun casements in several areas, particularly on Caprera in the east, La Maddalena in the center of the archipelago and Spargi to the west. Both naval and anti-aircraft guns were placed in these sites, and they were elements Fedorov had failed to fully consider in his thinking. He knew they existed, but was not sure of their locations. The course change he had made would skirt the northern coastlines of the islands, and the first surprise came when battery Candero opened fire from Caprera Island just after dawn.

The sharp report and whine of the shell startled Fedorov, even though he had half expected it. *Kirov* was five kilometers off the coast, and well within the range of this battery.

"Samsonov," he said quickly. Can you locate that gun emplacement?

"Let them fire one more time and I can back-trace their approximate location from the arc of the shell on my weapons locating radar." The art of counter battery radar systems was highly advanced, and *Kirov* soon had a lock on the gun position.

Karpov rushed onto the bridge, clearly winded, just as the ship's forward 100mm deck gun began to fire. "I'm sorry Fedorov, the alarm caught me by surprise."

Fedorov looked to see that the Captain seemed to clutch his side, in some pain, but thought it was just the long climb up from the lower decks. He waved Karpov over to his side, and briefed him on the action as he pointed to the Tin Man display.

"There," he said. "Do you see it? That is the Candero shore battery on Caprera Island. They fired three rounds at us—all well off the mark—but I think Samsonov has a lock on them now." They watched the display as *Kirov's* forward deck gun put ten rounds on the target, enveloping the battery and surrounding hillside in a billow of smoke and dust.

"Sir, air contact, 150 kilometers, bearing 45 degrees northeast, altitude 7200 meters, speed 280kph." Rodenko's voice sounded the warning. He paused a moment, then continued. "Surface contacts, group of three vessels bearing 202 degrees southwest, speed thirty and closing on our position."

"Those are probably long range aircraft out of Grosseto," said Fedorov. "The surface contact will most likely be fast torpedo boats."

"I have them on my tracking radar," said Samsonov. "Permission to engage, sir?"

"Granted," said Fedorov. "Mister Karpov, will you plot an appropriate air defense with Rodenko?"

"At once!"

"Sir," said Tasarov, "Sub surface contact now at five kilometers."

"Submarine?" Karpov turned, his attention immediately focused on this threat.

"We have a good fix on their position," said Fedorov.

"Then I recommend we fire at once, sir." Karpov said quickly. "The *Shkval* system should easily neutralize this threat."

"I believe Tasarov has plotted this solution. You may engage, Mister Karpov." The sharp staccato of machine gun fire split the air, and Fedorov rushed to the port side view pane to see rounds churning up the sea. Fedorov immediately knew they had encountered a floating mine, and his great fear was that there were many more unseen threats ahead of them.

Kirov was now simultaneously engaging threats on land, sea and air, but Karpov was quick to put an end to the submarine threat. The super-cavitating *Shkval* fired, ejecting for a short run at 50 knots before the rocket motor ignited and sent it hurtling toward the unseen enemy submarine, a lethal underwater lance that they had no chance avoid. A minute later Tasarov verified a hit, and with it SS *Avorio*, which had been maneuvering to block the entrance of the strait, exploded and died a quick underwater death, its captain and crew never aware of what had hit them until they heard the screeching sound of the weapon just before contact.

Kirov's deck guns had already shifted targets to the *torpediniera* racing towards them from the gap between Caprera Island and La Maddalena. Three *Spica* class boats were out that morning, *Antares*, *Centauro* and *Lira*. When the 152mm shells began to range in on them, their astonished captains clutched their field glasses in a vain attempt see the enemy ship. *Kirov* was still well off shore, and firing at a range of over seven kilometers. How could the enemy have spotted his small boats so quickly? Now the *torpediniera* would have to run a gauntlet of fire to get within their 2000 meter firing range, and not one of the three boats would survive. Samsonov worked with his brutal efficiency, locking the guns in on the targets with radar and quickly bracketing the small flotilla with the fire from all three of the ship's 152mm batteries. *Centauro* died first, struck amidships and set on fire, the bridge shattered and the boat careening wildly about when helm control was lost. *Antares* exploded in a brilliant orange fireball when a round struck and ignited one of her torpedoes, and *Lira* died a slower death, peppered by five hits that riddled her hull and superstructure and sent her foundering, burning in three places. A total of thirty-six rounds had dispatched this threat with little difficulty.

The attack had been ill timed, as the air strike out of Grosseto was late, and it too would not get anywhere near the battle zone. *Kirov's* piercing radars could see and engage the squadrons of enemy planes well before they had any thought of making their attack runs. Karpov selected a barrage of six S-300 long range SAMs, firing them like a spread of aerial torpedoes at five second intervals. The first two missiles caught the lead formation of twelve JU-87s, blowing three planes away and sending the remainder diving with the shock of the attack. Behind them came a squadron of Do-217s, six planes, and two of these fell to the next two missiles, with shrapnel clawing through the wings of two others, and setting one engine afire, forcing them to abort their attack. The nine remaining Stukas found their evasive maneuvers provided them no respite from the attack, and watched in shocked amazement as the last two S-300s turned to seek them out, one shattering a sub flight of three planes before the pilots realized they had to completely break formation and scatter in all directions to save themselves from certain death.

In these engagements it was *Kirov's* incredible advantage in radar tracking that enabled her to see, target, and bring weapons to bear on all these simultaneous threats. The ship raced past the Maddalena Archipelago in the bright morning sun, up around Santa Maria and Razzoli Islands and turned into the Bonifacio Strait. Here they encountered a more devious passive threat when Tasarov's active mine countermeasures system indicated numerous undersea contacts, and very near the ship. Some were moored mines, anchored to the seafloor by a long chain, detected by the ship's forward looking high resolution sonar in the big bow dome.

Fedorov slowed the ship to just ten knots, clearly worried about the mine threat now. It was perhaps the cheapest weapon the enemy might deploy against them and, unlike the enemy ships and planes, which could be seen and engaged well before they posed a danger to the ship, the mines lurked in waters *Kirov* had to pass through in order to transit the strait. He seemed very anxious, knowing that much of the threat would not be visible on the surface and that they might face an array of minefields here: delayed-action, magnetic, acoustic, and older contact mines; moored, and floating mines. Snag lines might also connect a series of mines to set off numerous detonations. He was not sure what to do.

"It could take days to adequately sweep this channel and remove all threats," said Karpov. "We will have to take more expedient measures and use the UDAV-2 ASW system." Fedorov confessed he had no idea what the Captain was talking about, and Karpov explained.

"There," he pointed to a weapon system on the starboard side of the ship. "There is one on the bow as well. Think of it as a rocket launcher we can use against undersea threats." The unit did, in fact, look a bit like the old German nebelwerfers of WWII, with ten rocket tubes, five on each side in a semicircle arc. It was derived from the British use of the "Hedgehog," which was a kind of seaborne mortar system that could fire a pattern of twenty-four explosives out in front of an advancing ship. Russia's modern day equivalent could range out to 3 kilometers with salvos of rockets bearing 300mm warheads. Karpov aimed them much closer to the ship, trying to saturate areas where Tasarov's sonar detected heaver concentrations of mines. Minutes later the sea ahead in the windy channel seemed to erupt with explosions and geysers of white frothing seawater as the first salvos landed. *Kirov* was literally trying to blast her way through the minefields, slowing to five knots now as the ship slowly advanced through the turbulent waters.

They fired three salvos at varying ranges ahead, using UDAV batteries on both sides of the ship, and the large secondary explosions told them their plan was working. Some of the mines were packed with up to 1000 kilograms of explosive material, and the concussion shook the ship, sometimes setting off other mines rigged to explode via pressure or sound. They would fire a salvo, wait while Tasarov reacquired new contacts with his active ranging sonar, then fire again. To any landward observer, it looked as if the big battlecruiser was at war with the sea itself.

Soldiers of the 4th Coastal Defense Brigade stationed at Piazza La Maddalena and the northern coast of Sardinia gaped at the sight of the big ship out in the channel. If the British had such vessels, the war was lost for certain, some said. Others shook their fist at *Kirov's* grey silhouette and claimed that the Navy would soon arrive to deal with this ship. The intruder had batted aside the light 795 ton *torpediniera*, but the 7th Cruiser Division was still coming up fast now, it's lead elements just thirty kilometers from the scene with the heavy cruiser *Trieste*, light cruiser *Muzio Attendolo* and three destroyers. Behind them came heavy cruisers *Goriza* and *Bolzano* with three more destroyers, and the two groups were now coordinating their course and speed to join as one mailed fist and attack together.

Rodenko had a good fix on them with his long range radars, but Fedorov decided not to use any of the ship's precious anti-ship missiles, thinking they could push on through the Bonifacio Strait and out into the Mediterranean Sea beyond in another hour, and he did not think the pursuing ships would follow. He thought there would be nothing to oppose them at that point, and they might sail for the Balearic Islands as planned with only occasional observation by reconnaissance planes… But he was wrong again. As they reached the center of the channel, a new contact was sighted, not behind them in hot pursuit, but *ahead* of them, steaming towards the western exit of the Bonifacio Strait.

Commando Supremo had sprung its well planned trap.

Chapter 15

"Sighting ahead, sir. Surface contact. Five units at a range of twenty-five kilometers. Speed twenty knots, increasing, and closing on our position!"

Fedorov was surprised to hear this, coming quickly to Rodenko's side to look at his screen. "Five units?"

"It must have been hugging the coast of Corsica, and masked by this landform." He was pointing at the coastal signal returns, outlining the southern edge of Capo de Feno. The land rose steeply there to a height of over 200 meters, and this new enemy contact had been effectively hidden behind the cape. But what could it be, Fedorov wondered? There should be no further Italian warships in this sector. The last remaining threat should be behind them in the steady advance of the 7th Cruiser Division.

"Focus the Tin Man optronics on that contact and see if we can get an image. Use the highest resolution possible." Fedorov needed to know what he was dealing with. Could this be merchant traffic, or was it a threat? Minutes later he had his answer in the stalwart silhouettes of two very large warships on the far horizon. "My god," he breathed. "Those are battleships!"

"British? Up here?"

"No…Those two stacks amidships right behind the main mast …These are Italian—*Littorio* Class ships, but this isn't possible! All those ships were at Taranto! There is no way they could have reached this position from that distance, and they weren't moved to La Spezia until December of this year."

"Yes, in the history you *know*, Fedorov, but apparently things have changed, just like the early arrival of those cruisers at our backside." Karpov thumbed over his shoulder to the wake of the ship as they slowly crept through the straits. Then they heard the muted but prominent sound of a large detonation and the ship shuddered.

"What was that?" said the captain. "Tasarov? Rodenko?"

"I'm starting to see air contacts over land both north and south," said Rodenko, "small flights of three to six planes, and nothing close enough to pose a threat at the moment. Tasarov had a trace of some undersea movement just before the explosion, which prompted him to rip off his headset, started by the sudden sound. The news sent Karpov to a higher pitch.

"Another submarine? Ready on ASW systems!"

"I don't think so, sir. I think it was a moored mine, possibly jarred loose from its cable by our last UDAV barrage. I don't think we hit it, but it exploded off our port side."

Even as he finished Fedorov saw bright flashes and billowing smoke obscure the image of the oncoming ships on the Tin Man display. They were under fire, and this was not from the small six inch rounds of a light cruiser or shore battery. This time it was coming from the 15 inch batteries of the lead battleship.

"That is our main concern now," he pointed, noting how the big ships were turning, their dark silhouettes more prominent and threatening with the maneuver. Ahead of them a fan of three smaller destroyers were churning their way forward to make a torpedo attack. They heard the whine of oncoming shells, and a deep whoosh as the first rounds swooped well over the ship and plunged into the channel behind them. Fedorov realized that at five knots they were now an easy target.

"Very well," said Karpov, folding his arms. "We'll pepper them with our deck guns as before."

"That's won't be enough," said Fedorov quickly. "These are battleships, Karpov. Those rounds they just flung over our main mast were from the most powerful 15 inch guns ever mounted on a naval ship. Don't underestimate them, Captain." His tone warned of danger, his eyes carrying the seriousness of the moment. The ship was now in grave danger—a situation he had never thought to encounter. "They have 350mm belt armor and our 152 mm guns will not penetrate that," he continued. "Their main gun turrets are equally well protected. They will be able to stand with us in a gun fight indefinitely if they have the will to do so, and the constricted water here gives us no room for maneuver. I hope you understand what would happen if we were to take just one serious hit from a fifteen inch gun!"

"Then we will use the Moskit-IIs, as we did with the British."

"Yes, but you will need multiple hits to really harm these ships."

He shook his head, feeling that the history had played a cruel trick on him—but then again, he realized the very presence of *Kirov*, here and now, was a bald offense to this moment in time. They had already seen the catastrophic consequences of their actions on the future, the dark charred ruins of coastal cities still haunting them all. He realized now that the history of this period was also beginning to warp into a new shape. These battleships should not be here. For reasons he could not fathom, decisions had been made to move them to La Spezia three months early—three months…

In a flash he realized that the course of events must have changed by the early entry of the Americans in the war! *Kirov* had tempted fate and created an incident equal to the Pearl Harbor attack with that desperate engagement in the cold North Atlantic. The effects of that incident had apparently rippled through time, subtly altering the course of events. Much of the history was still running true, even down to things like specific attacks on individual ships, such as the loss of HMS *Eagle*. Far to the south the machinations of war were still grinding along in the attacks on Operation Pedestal. But *Kirov's* presence had caused a violent and increasingly escalating reaction by Regia Marina.

He shrugged, his hopes for a speedy transit here fading with each second. The safe waters he thought to find as they exited the strait were guarded by these two formidable ships, and now they were in a fight for their lives.

"Samsonov, activate Moskit-II system and spin up a full battery." Karpov turned to the young ex-navigator. "Shall I engage?"

There was no other way, thought Fedorov. Their only other course was either surrender or possible death. They were nearly through the channel, but still making only five knots. The range had fallen to 23 kilometers in just these few minutes and already he could hear the distant rumble of thunder as the big Italian ships fired their second salvo. They were obviously receiving position reports on his ship from observers on shore. The incoming roar of the shells was much louder, though the shots still fell in a widely dispersed pattern.

In one last agonizing minute Fedorov let his precious history go, let fate and responsibility for generations yet to come slip from his weary shoulders. Instead he embraced the most basic instinct for self preservation. Survival!

"Helm, ahead two thirds!" They were sitting ducks in the channel and he had to put on speed at once, in spite of the threat from the minefields. "Mister Karpov," he said, a deflated look on his face. "Engage at once!"

"Samsonov—fire!" Karpov ordered, and with a flick of a switch the missile launch warning sounded. The forward deck hatches sprung open and up leapt the sea sharks, sleek, deadly missiles, their gas jets precisely declining their sharp tips in the gleaming sun and the roar of their engines answering the distant boom of thunder ahead.

Aboard battleship *Veneto* Admiral Iachino squinted at the distant contact through his field glasses, a smile edging his lips. Regia Marina had been correct after all. Word that a fast British battlecruiser was at large in the Tyrrhenian Sea had set the telephone wires ablaze for the last twenty-four hours, particularly after Da Zara's ill fated sortie from Cagliari. Admiral Bergamini had pleaded with him to send out stronger forces, and join the 7th Cruiser Squadron in the hunt for this ship. Fuel was low, but the target invitingly close, and the northern squadron had been recently reinforced by the transfer of *Veneto* and *Littorio* from Taranto. Iachino decided on one more sortie. He had faced the British three times in the war, giving as good as he got from them, though many whispered that he had made mistakes at Cape Matapan that cost Regia Marina a much needed victory.

This time, he thought, the *British* have made a mistake. Da Zara's small force had been pummeled by the enemy, but now he sailed with his flag aboard *Vittorio Veneto*, one of Italy's newest ships, and her sister ship *Littorio* followed in his wake. If this was a British battlecruiser the odds looked very good for him now. He had been receiving radio reports of the enemy's position and speed for some time while his battleships worked their way down the western coast of Corsica, hidden by the prominent massif of Capo de Feno.

Reports soon came to him that the British ship had engaged shore batteries near La Maddalena and was now attempting to run the Bonifacio Strait. They had been firing an odd weapon system, churning up the waters around the ship to try and force a passage through the well laid minefields there. Rounding the cape with his battle force he was pleased to finally catch a glimpse of the ship's high main mast gleaming in the morning sun on the far horizon. He gave the order to increase speed to twenty-five knots and come right fifteen degrees so he could bring all his turrets to bear in an attempt to cross the enemy's T as it emerged from the strait. It was a sound maneuver, as the British ship was now committed to a westerly heading where it would have to run true for some time. If the enemy adjusted their course southwest to run parallel to his own, the ship would be forced into the Gulf of Asinara where the restricted waters near Capo del Falcone would again prove a major obstacle.

No, he thought. They will have to run due west and try to get up around Punta Caprara, the northernmost cape of the island of Asinara. If he aimed his own task force for that very same island, he would cut them off and cross the enemy's T. Already his opening salvo had announced his presence and thrown down the challenge to this upstart British intruder. And when I finish with you, he thought as he watched the ship take shape and form on the horizon, then perhaps I will run down and rain hell on this convoy to the south as well.

His first salvos were widely dispersed and well off the mark, which did not surprise him. Though his 15 inch guns were among the best in the world, they suffered from the same technical problem that often degraded the accuracy of the Italian cruisers—a lack of uniform consistency on the propellant charge bags. If he hit the enemy, he knew he could hurt her, as his guns could penetrate 450mm of armor at this range, and he doubted this ship was so well protected, particularly if this was a battlecruiser with its much lighter armor.

His second salvo was up and booming toward the enemy. Moments later he clenched his fist with excitement, seeing a bright flash and billowing smoke emanate from the foredeck of the British ship. Had they scored a hit there, or was this the first reply from their forward turrets?

His answer was not long in coming. Something rose up from the ship, a sleek barb that danced in the air for a moment, which led him to believe, in that fraction of a second, that he had struck a forward battery and smashed one of their guns. Then, to his utter amazement, the sleek fragment he took for a gun barrel surged into the sky with a fiery jet of flame! It moved with astounding speed! He saw another and another leaping up from the distant silhouette and streaking into the sky. A thin white contrail marked their deadly arc toward his ships and then he braced himself as the first came diving in with an awful roar and struck *Vittorio Veneto* amidships, some fifty feet behind the bridge, exploding with a violent fireball and immediately destroying three AA guns before penetrating at the base of the forward stack.

The second missile came in just shy of the bridge itself, yet low on the main deck where it blasted into the secondary 6 inch gun battery there with a thundering concussion and broiling fire. Fueled to fire at much longer ranges, the full load of missile fuel ignited massive fires at both locations,

Iachino was sent careening back against the binnacle, his field glasses flung madly on the deck as he struggled to stay on his feet. He was stunned by the suddenness of the attack and amazed by what he had seen. His eye fell on the navigation compass at the top of the binnacle and he was surprised to see the needle spinning about in wild circles. Now searing flame and coal black smoke erupted to completely obscure his view. What was this, a new British naval rocket of some type? He knew that the Germans and even Regia Aeronautica had been experimenting with radio controlled bombs, but these were to be delivered by aircraft. What was this? He had no time to think, as his ship was on fire and now he looked to see that *Littorio* had also been struck amidships, almost in the very same location as his own ship!

His main guns had not been damaged, and the ship still seemed to be making way well enough, but a call from below decks painted a grim picture. The fire was extensive, the number one stack fully involved and now partially collapsed and tilting to one side. The warhead from this new weapon had penetrated his relatively thin deck armor and bored deep into the ship sending a hideous hail of molten shrapnel in all directions. Yet all this damage was above his water line, and his ship remained seaworthy.

Veneto's third salvo fell closer in on the enemy ship, sending tall geysers of sea spray up into the crisp morning air. Close would not be nearly good enough, he realized. The enemy had also fired three times with far more deadly results. He squinted through the smoke, a red anger burning at the back of his neck as he caught sight of his adversary once more and saw the foredeck of the enemy ship erupt again with fire. One by one, three more rounds of this astonishing new rocket weapon burned their way toward his ships with roaring anger.

"Right full rudder!" he screamed out an evasive order, but to no avail. All three missiles were going to find their targets. There was no maneuver or trick of seamanship that could save them, no gun on his ship that could track them to shoot them down, and no hope in the long run for his gallant task force as long as *Kirov's* magazines still remained full.

Karpov watched the lethal Moskit-II missiles bore in mercilessly on the big enemy ships, two salvos of three each. NATO had called them "Sunburn," a good name for them, he thought. They were the fastest and most accurate anti-ship missiles ever developed, and there was virtually no way to defeat them once they were locked onto a target.

"That will give them something to think about," he said to Fedorov. "The lead ship is burning badly. The next is getting more of the same. We have them programmed to hit above the waterline to avoid their heavy armor. With a full load of fuel to feed those fires they are going to have their hands full, even if we haven't breached their hulls."

"These ships are also vulnerable to plunging fire," said Fedorov. Their laminated deck armor was not adequate, and its placement was questionable."

"The range is too short for that now, but we have hurt them just the same. Look at those fires!" Karpov pointed at the thick black smoke pouring from the lead ship. "Yes! They are turning away."

They saw the enemy task force wheel hard right, and the group of three destroyers matched the maneuver, all making smoke in a futile attempt to screen the bigger ships from further fire. Bright flashes of orange and yellow erupted from the battleships again as they both fired their big 15 inch guns in reprisal. They heard the drone of the heavy rounds coming in, and saw them plunge into the sea off the starboard bow, the geysers walking their way ominously towards the ship. A set fell very near, no more than half a kilometer off, and Fedorov held his breath as more rounds fell progressively closer.

"They've got our range now," he said, the last round falling near enough to send sea spray showering over *Kirov's* foredeck. They could feel something strike the ship's hull, undoubtedly splinter damage from the very near miss.

"Left fifteen degrees rudder," said Fedorov, "Ahead full!" They were out of the channel now, through the Bonifacio Strait, but it was still a risky maneuver to turn and put on speed. There could be hidden mines that Tasarov would not be able to detect with all the turmoil of shot and shell churning up the seas. *Kirov* came smartly around, and he gasped as one final shell from a late firing gun fell just where the ship might have been moments ago had they maintained their old course. This time they could feel the concussion of the heavy round as it plunged into the sea, so very close. The grating sound of something striking the hull again filled him with misgiving.

The Italians had fired that one last salvo, a defiant shake of their fist at an enemy they were clearly not prepared to face this day. Iachino elected to exercise the better part of valor—discretion. Both his battleships were on fire, but still seaworthy and without gun damage. Yet the fires were raging ever deeper into the guts of *Vittorio Veneto,* and he could clearly see that *Littorio* was in no better shape. Stunned and surprised by the powerful new weapons he had faced, he put on speed and ran north, hoping to find safe waters until the fires could be brought under control.

The billowing thick smoke was blinding, and the gunners would have a very difficult time re-sighting and ranging on the target. He might need another three or four salvos to find the mark again after his wild turn and change of course. Yet every weapon the enemy fired struck home with a vengeance. If they fired again... He did not want to think about the consequences. No, he would return to La Spezia, chastened and far less brazen than he had been when his proud ships set forth, but at least, he hoped, he *would* return to possibly fight again.

"Another day," he said to the watch officer at his side.

"Another day, sir?" The man stared at him blankly. "When the British have ships that can do this?"

Iachino glared at the man, but said nothing more.

Part VI

Decisions

"In a minute there is time for decisions and revisions which a minute will reverse."

~*T.S. Eliot.*

Chapter 16

They all stared at Turing—Pound with annoyance, but the others with grave apprehension and some bewilderment evident on their faces. The Marine guard interrupted them yet again, another folded message decrypt in his white gloved hand. Tovey took it, noting the source first.

"Signal intelligence through our network in the Med," he said. "Looks like one of the Twelve Apostles has come to supper." He was referring to a secret network of American OSS and British Special Operations agents that had been scattered throughout the French North African Colonies to gather intelligence prior to the planned Operation Torch landings this coming November. There were twelve agents in all, and one had been put ashore on Sardinia to scout out military buildup there and map coastal fortifications—more grist for the mills of the war planners. Apparently he had seen or heard something more, and thought it urgent enough to risk a direct transmission through the network. The Admiral read it aloud this time:

"Major Duffing tips his hat to Little Victor and his friend off Balham Tube... It seems this one is a bit of a Chinese box—code within a code."

"What's all that twaddle about now?" Pound complained. "Hasn't it been decrypted properly?"

"If I may, sir," Turing spoke up again cautiously. "Major Duffing is the Northern Med operations section code handle indicating an enemy vessel—a capital ship, sir. The tipping of his hat will mean there has been a surface engagement with this Little Victor—'Vittorio' in Italian. That would be the *Vittorio Veneto* to be precise. The mention of a friend would indicate a sister ship of *Veneto* was present, most likely the *Littorio*, as both these ships were recently moved to La Spezia. As for Balham Tube, that is not the underground rail station in London, sir, it is code for the Strait of Bonifacio."

Pound raised his eyebrows. "There's been a naval engagement involving two Italian battleships off the Bonifacio Strait?"

"You have it exactly, sir," said Turing with a smile.

"There's one more bit," said Tovey, reading: "Victor's off home by any road, and not the better man." He looked at Turing, suddenly appreciating the man in a new way.

"That would mean *Vittorio Veneto*, which I presume is the flagship, has broken off the engagement and is heading north for home." Any road was a colloquial expression from northern England often used instead of the more common "anyway," and it cleverly indicated the direction of the Italian withdrawal—north. "That would also mean that something has just engaged two of Regia Marina's heaviest surface units and beaten them off with some significant damage. *Vittorio Veneto* was not the better man, gentlemen. Now then…This was clearly not one of *our* ships up there. What in the world could face down two Italian battleships and come off the better man for it? A ship flinging aerial rockets at our 248 Squadron, I might add."

"Forgive me if I remain confused, Professor," said Pound, "but this *Geronimo*—isn't it a German ship? What's it doing taking pot shots at the Italian Navy? The last time I looked Italy and Germany were thick as thieves together."

Turing rubbed his hands nervously. The other officers all looked at him, obviously fielding the same objection in their own minds. He considered what to say, then realized he had no other course here. In for a penny, in for a pound, he thought, and spoke his mind. "No, Admiral Pound. I have come to the conclusion that if these two 'incidents' were caused by the same vessel, then this is *not* German ship—not a year ago, and clearly not now."

Pound was justifiably astonished. "Not German? My god, man, I suppose that you'll be telling me it belongs to the King of Swabia next! What do you mean not German? What other navy would attack us in the North Atlantic as this ship did?"

"I've given that considerable thought," said Turing. "Yes, it's very perplexing. It makes good sense to think this ship was a secret German raider in light of the North Atlantic incident, but the road we've been walking here has led us far afield of that comfortable path. If this *is* the same ship as before, as this photography leads me to believe, then it clearly could not belong to the Kriegsmarine."

"Then who?" Pound pressed him with growing irritation.

"Well sir, I thought it might be a Russian ship at one point, seeing as it was first sighted in the Arctic sea. Yet I had to discard that notion, considering the fact that Russia is our ally at the moment… "

"Very well," Pound harangued him. "Not German, not Russian, certainly not Italian…." He waited, like an irate school master dressing down a recalcitrant student.

"I must be frank and tell you I do not know what to make of all this just yet, gentlemen. Every line we take leads us into a corner. We're faced with one impossible circumstance after another, but the fact remains: something is flinging advanced rockets and weapons of unimaginable power at the Royal Navy, and now at the Italian Navy as well. This ship, these weapons—well it would take the resources of a major power to design and build these things. It could be that this ship is German after all, or even Russian, and that we have maverick sea captain out there, some kind of Captain Nemo, a rogue warrior at odds with Hitler or Stalin and with a very bad attitude towards anyone else who crosses his path. Impossible as it sounds, he's there, the ship is there, and we have to deal with this."

Whitworth spoke up, clearly trying to tether the boat before it slipped its moorings. "Well it seems to me that our confusion results entirely from the assumption that these two ships are indeed one and the same. Suppose that incident *was* a German ship last year, or even some renegade Russian captain as your suggest, though I find that a stretch. How it gets to the Med is quite a rabbit trick. I'm more inclined to think of these incidents as unrelated. Perhaps this ship in the Med is French, though it doesn't seem likely, or even possible, it makes more sense than anything else."

Pound folded his arms, frowning, but saying nothing more. Tovey tapped the table top with his finger and looked at Wake-Walker with a knowing eye. Whitworth seemed folded inward on some dark inner muse, then leaned forward, speaking softly yet firmly.

"Gentlemen, it's obvious that we need more information. Where is Force Z at the moment?" he asked, and the First Sea Lord replied.

"They should be somewhere between Bone on the Algerian coast and the southern tip of Sardinia. I have little doubt they're mixing it up the Luftwaffe and Regia Aeronautica by now."

"Then that would place them some 300 miles due south of this engagement—fifteen hours sailing, even at their best speed if *Rodney* and *Nelson* can still make twenty knots."

"Are you suggesting we should divert the covering force north based on this single report?"

"Not north," Whitworth said quickly, "West, gentlemen. West to Gibraltar. Respectfully, Admiral, it's not just this one report. 248 Squadron sights, and later attacks an unknown surface contact in the southern Tyrrhenian Sea at noon yesterday. We hear about it and then the Italians engage it at midnight and get a bloody nose for their trouble. The ship heads north for the Bonifacio Strait, and Iachino must have sent out his bully boys after it to settle the score—only he got handed his hat in the matter, if that latest intercept is correct, and there it is. This is obviously a job for the Royal Navy, but if we don't turn Force Z around quickly, this ship could make a run at the Rock before we could do anything about it."

There it was, yet these professional sea dogs still found it very uncomfortable to look at. What were they seeing here? There was no sense to it at all; no rhyme or reason. Something was happening that was clearly beyond their imagining, and it worried them all. Pound reacted with irritation and was all too eager to scapegoat Turing in the matter. Whitworth was dancing round the point, although willing to embrace it, if he only knew what he was about to grasp. Wake-Walker was darkly silent, a military stirring reflected in his usually placid features, eyes brightening above his thin nose.

"I agree with Admiral Whitworth," he offered, "I shouldn't think it wise to send the covering force north at this juncture. I should leave it right on track, but get word off to Admiral Syfret that he should be prepared to turn about quickly, upon our word, and head for Gibraltar with all speed."

Pound looked at him questioningly. "Have you lost your ardor for battle, sir? Shouldn't we get up north and sort this business out?"

"Lost my ardor?" Wake-Walker overlooked the insult, accustomed to this line from Pound, who has accused him of this very same thing in the engagement with *Bismarck*. Tovey shifted uncomfortably as Wake-Walker continued. "No, sir I haven't lost my ardor for battle, but I learned to keep my head on my shoulders and not run off half cocked until we know what we're dealing with here. Perhaps this is a French ship. Perhaps not. But if this is, indeed, *Geronimo*, as impossible as it may seem to us now, then we must ask ourselves what in the world this ship is about? How could it possibly be cruising in the Med, unseen for a year, but now suddenly here and inclined to duel with anything that comes within its compass rose? We may never answer these questions to our satisfaction, but if we are to believe these reports and sightings then we had damn well better be prepared. We don't have to go looking for this ship, Admiral. Something tells me it will soon come looking for us. Admiral Whitworth is correct. After all, there's only one way out of the bottle it now finds itself in, and that way leads to Gibraltar. Given the course it has been on, I believe this ship will soon be heading west, and I say we get Admiral Syfret and the whole of his Force Z back to the Rock as soon as they have discharged their task with the convoy. The sooner, the better."

Pound gave him a bemused look, but before he could say anything more Tovey spoke up, leaning forward on both elbows as he passed the latest intercept to Pound like a card dealer in a heated poker game. "And for my part," he exclaimed. "I think it would be wise to send word to Home Fleet at once and get up four hour steam on anything seaworthy. I'm afraid we'll have to inconvenience the

Turkish Ambassador, but I want *King George V, Prince of Wales,* and *Anson* out to sea by noon if possible."

"*Anson?*" Pound questioned. "But she's only just completed her gunnery trials. Raw as a baby's bum on a bad day."

"She's been working up with the fleet at Scapa Flow," Tovey replied. "May I remind you that *Prince of Wales* sailed under similar circumstances when *Bismarck* sortied."

"Yes, and with rather disastrous results," Pound admonished, casting a sidelong glance at Wake-Walker.

"Well it can't be helped. I want all the firepower we can muster if this ship is indeed this *Geronimo* raider we faced a year ago. As we've no further convoys to Russia planned at the moment, we might also bring *Duke of York* down from Hvalsfjord as well. We'll send out an oiler to top her off along the way. I don't think the Germans can bother us with *Tirpitz* at the moment."

"That leaves the cupboard fairly well empty if they do," Pound warned again.

"We'll leave *Renown* behind. She hasn't the armor for this fight. The loss of *Repulse* made that quite evident last time around."

"Yes, well she hasn't the armor to stand with *Tirpitz* either."

"*Tirpitz* is not our concern for the moment. She's been dry-docked at Trondheim for repairs. I don't think Jerry can do much of anything with her for weeks—possibly months. *Renown* can handle anything else they would dare to put to sea. You can get me on a plane to Holyhead on the west coast and have a cruiser pick me up to run me out to the fleet."

"Good show," said Wake-Walker. "It's fortunate we persuaded the Prime Minister not to send *Prince of Wales* to the far east last August. She's tangled with this *Geronimo*, and was in no shape for that long sea voyage in any case. Now she's patched up and fit as a fiddle. Home Fleet is stronger than ever, and throw in *Rodney* and *Nelson* at Gibraltar and we'll see who gets handed his hat this time around."

"Here, here!" said Tovey, seconding the matter as he tapped the table with his open palm.

The First Sea Lord sighed audibly, looking askance at Turing, then back at Tovey and Wake-Walker. "Well it seems as though you haven't lost your ardor for battle, Admiral." He smiled at Wake-Walker, mending fences. "Are you certain we can send the whole of Home Fleet's heavy guns south like this? You understand that this means the plans for Jubilee will have to be cancelled." He was refereeing to 'Operation Jubilee' the landing at Dieppe that was scheduled for 19 August, in just a few days time.

"I did have that in the back of my mind," said Tovey. "Well, it can't be helped. We won't have the ships to cover this Dieppe raid and run for Gibraltar as well. I shouldn't think we would want a division at sea in any wise until this *Geronimo* business is resolved."

"And if this *is* a French ship? It's going to be rather embarrassing when the Prime Minister returns and sees we've sortied with the whole of Home Fleet, cancelled major operations, and all this to run down a disaffected French sea captain."

"In a ship using advanced rocketry and capable of beating off two Italian battleships? If there's anything I've learned in this war, Admiral, it's that we must plan for the very worst case imaginable."

"I suppose you're correct," Pound put in one last time. "You say the Germans will not be able to sortie *Tirpitz*, but that may be the least of our worries. If this is *Geronimo*, let us not forget what happened to the Americans…"

He did not have to argue the point further.

The meeting was adjourned, and the Sea Lords soon scattered to their urgent duties. As they were led out, Tovey made it a point to nudge Turing's arm. "A brief word, professor?"

The two men were alone in the hallway now and Tovey spoke his mind. "Look here," he began. "This remark you made about Captain Nemo caught my attention. I read that story as a boy, and it always stayed with me. I wonder about Admiral Pound's theory on this.

We've been making overtures to the Vichy French with this Torch operation in the planning. Darlan has been trying to woo the fleet at Toulon to change sides. Might this be a French battleship, a rogue ship that has decided to join our side, or perhaps even trying to reach Vichy ports in their African Colonies?"

"That makes good sense on one level, sir. If it was a battlecruiser out of Toulon it might certainly explain these last two engagements with the Italians. But the rocketry, sir. That was your point, and the odd man out in all this."

Tovey nodded. "Well, I didn't want to press the matter, particularly with Admiral Pound, but I have the feeling you haven't quite fired a full broadside at us yet, professor Turing. Is there something else you haven't told us? Something you're holding back?"

Turing looked at him, appreciating the man's candor and glad to be spoken to with a measure of respect. He knew his arguments would likely do little to dispel the rumors circulating about him in higher circles, that he was a bit of a maverick himself, a madman at times, with wild theories and undisciplined habits. He did not wish to encourage that line further, fearing where it might eventually lead if the authorities got too curious about him, but Tovey's face was serious, receptive and wholly sincere. Was this his chance to truly speak his mind?

"I can't say as I've got my hand on the neck of this one entirely, sir," he compromised, "but I'll say this much, Admiral. You and I both know that it takes years to build a ship of that size—massive resources. The Germans have very few shipyards capable of building something that big. It simply isn't something that Germany, or any nation, could hide. Yes, we know the Japanese have been keeping a lid on a couple of monster ships of their own, but Rodgers and Bemis knew about those designs as early as 1938."

Captain Fred F. Rogers was a U.S. naval attaché in Tokyo, who had reported that 'Japan had designs for warships of 45,000 to 55,000 tons.' His successor, Harold M. Bemis, confirmed the report, the first clues that would eventually lead the American intelligence to the existence of the super battleships *Yamato* and *Musashi*. Turing continued.

"You see, sir. You just can't hide something like this. The Japanese have tried mightily, but we still know about their covert battleship program. If this was a German ship, we should have known about it. As for these rockets used against our ships and planes... They're graspable in our minds because we ourselves have similar projects in development, and we know the Germans have the same, but certainly not the French. I've been aware of Polish intelligence regarding development of a "flying torpedo" by the Germans, and there are other similar technologies they are working on. The Italians have been using air dropped torpedoes against this latest Malta convoy as well. But everything we have seen of these developments, *everything*, is far less advanced than the weapons used against us by this ship. Furthermore, we haven't seen a single peep from these weapons in a year. Why not? If the Germans could mount them on a ship, then they could also easily deploy them on land or even aircraft. Yet we've seen nothing."

"Yes," Tovey agreed. "I've thought this as well."

"I have come to the conclusion that the Germans simply do not have the capability, or the technology this ship has demonstrated. It saw your ships well before you ever knew it was there—so it must have very advanced radar, far beyond anything we have today. It targeted your vessels with amazing precision, and with weapons so lethal that I frankly believe they are beyond the means of any nation on this earth to produce..." he paused, a glint in his eye. "At least at this point in time." He knew he was running on now, and towards a very dangerous precipice, but here was a man willing to stand and listen to him. Perhaps he could lead him to the same conclusions he had drawn himself.

"I may have said too much here, admiral, so you can forgive me if I seem a young and foolish man, but I assure you, I am not."

Tovey looked at him, his eyes creased with a warm smile. "No, professor, the last thing I would take you for is a fool, nor I do consider this line of thought to be in any way preposterous, as Admiral Pound might put it. You forget that I have seen these weapons first hand—seen them thunder in against my very own ship. You say such technology is beyond our means at this time, but how long before we might have weapons like this ourselves if we put our minds to it? Have you considered that?"

Turing's mood seemed to darken with that, and there was a hint of hesitation, even fear in his eyes when he answered. "If you want my very best estimation, Admiral, it would take years of rigorous testing and development to reach this level of sophistication. You see it's not that the technology is beyond our thinking. We know the road, and where it might lead us, it's just that it will take us *time* to get there, perhaps decades. Where there's a will there's a way, right? It's all a matter of time, sir."

"I see," said Tovey, thinking deeply, his eyes betraying both uncertainty and concern, though he said nothing more on the matter, extending his hand. "Good work, Turing. Carry on, will you?"

"Thank you, sir. I shall."

Tovey walked off to find a fast plane to Holyhead and Turing ambled slowly down the long corridor, still thinking about what he had said, and wondering if the government would end up putting the thumbscrews to him for his rash ideas. I wonder if he got what I was really aiming at, he thought to himself. No, you can't come out with it plainly. That much is obvious given the reaction of men like Pound. No doubt there will be others very much like Pound and they would make your life a living hell if you push on this door too hard. But you've squeaked it open with Admiral Tovey, haven't you? He listened to what you had to say, and perhaps he'll come round to it on his own.

He looked at his wrist watch, realizing he had a plane to catch if he wanted to get back to Bletchley Park. *Time,* he said inwardly. Yes, that's the heart of the matter now. It is only a matter of time...

Chapter 17

By the time they passed Punta Caprara, the northernmost cape of the island of Asinara, it was well after 10:00 in the morning. They had fought their way past shore batteries, through minefields, torpedo boats, a submarine, an air strike, and a brief, violent surface engagement with two battleships. Fedorov counted his good fortune that the ship had come through it all with little more than splinter damage on the hull, but that was a testament to the amazing technological edge *Kirov* had over its adversaries. Yet one thing bothered him as they finished the damage control assessment. Tasarov was restless at his station, claiming that his systems were erratic, and he was losing signal processing integrity of the forward Horse Jaw sonar dome. With the towed array already damaged and still under repair, this was a matter of some concern.

Fedorov was troubled, but was hoping that the history would hold true for a time, as it indicated that most all available axis submarines were far to the south opposing Operation Pedestal. They watched the Italian 7th cruiser Squadron race towards the eastern approaches of the Bonifacio Strait, then slow to assume a defensive patrol there, guarding the waterway in the event this bold British raider might think to return.

"As I expected, they have no interest in trying to follow us, particularly after they must've learned what happened to their battleships."

For the moment he deemed their main threat to be further air strikes launched at them from bases in Sardinia, but again, he knew that the Axis air power would now be focused against Operation Pedestal, some 300 miles to the south. The situation presented them with an opportunity to get safely away from Sardinia and Corsica, and well out to sea. He set a course due west at twenty knots, wanting to put at least 150 miles between the ship and any potential land based enemy aircraft. Later he would slow to ten knots or less and put divers over the side to inspect the hull for splinter damage. He suspected something may have happened to the forward sonar dome as well, or the sensors along the outer rim of the hull. They would take whatever time was needed to effect repairs, perhaps near Menorca in the Balearic islands.

Rodenko reported that he could still see the Italian battleships on radar heading north, then northeast as they withdrew towards La Spezia. It had been an ill-fated sortie for them, perhaps the last gallant charge by the Italian Navy in the war.

The next item on his list was an assessment of their current weapons inventories. He took Karpov aside and the two of them hovered over Samsonov's CIC boards to see what was left in the cupboard. Two critical systems were beginning to run thin on ammunition. Their long range S–300 SAM system was now at sixty-four percent, with only forty-one missiles remaining. In like manner, the Klinok Gauntlet medium range SAM system was down to only seventy-nine missiles left in inventory. More serious than this, their primary anti-ship missile, the deadly Moskit-II Sunburns that had proved so effective against enemy shipping, was now at forty percent with only fourteen missiles left in the silos. They were lucky to have even these. A normal load-out would be twenty missiles, but they had taken on a complete set of twenty additional missiles before the live fire exercises that had first sent them on this strange saga, but all these were expended in the North Atlantic.

Beyond this they still had nine of the swift MOS–III Starfire missiles, which were extremely fast at mach 6 acceleration, but carried only a 300 kilogram warhead compared to the heavier 450 kg warhead on the sunburns. They still had a little more punch left with ten P-900 Sizzler cruise missiles, each with a 400kg warhead. All in all, the three systems left them with thirty-three anti ship missiles out of the sixty they began the voyage with.

As for their deck guns, the 152 millimeter batteries were presently at eighty-nine percent on the magazine, and they still had almost a full load for their smaller 100 millimeter forward deck gun. They had expended six percent of their close in defense rounds on the thirty millimeter Gatling guns, and two of the deadly *Shkval* anti-submarine torpedo rockets, with eight more remaining. Beside that they still had most of their UGST torpedoes, fifteen in stock, and there were additional load-outs available for their last remaining KA-40 helicopter. All in all, the ship still had a formidable array of firepower at its disposal, but the numerous engagements they had fought in the last day were beginning to slowly drain their weapons inventories.

"Now, more than ever, we are going to have to be judicious in the way we deploy our weapons," said Fedorov.

"What can we expect ahead on this course?" asked Karpov.

"For the time being we should have a little peace and quiet, enough to effect repairs and give the men some much needed rest. I intend to sail west to Menorca and into the Balearic Sea. That channel is between 160 to 200 kilometers wide for a good long while, and when we exit to the South will have at least a eighty kilometers of sea room between Spain and Santa Eulana Island. Then we enter the final bottleneck, the Alboran Sea. It's nearly 250 kilometers wide at the outset, but narrows to about150 kilometers as we approach Gibraltar. That's the last gate, about fifteen kilometers wide at its narrowest point. If we can get through that safely then we've got the whole Atlantic out there, and our speed can be a great advantage in that situation."

"And Gibraltar?" said Karpov. "What will the British have waiting for us there?"

"That remains to be seen," said Fedorov. "We will be all day getting out to sea, and I'll put divers over the side near dusk near Menorca. So we should be well into the Balearic sea by dawn tomorrow. I'm hoping our damage control situation can be easily resolved, but I would like to discuss this matter with Admiral Volsky, and come to some agreement on how we might handle the Strait of Gibraltar. Would you feel comfortable joining that conference Captain?"

"Of course," said Karpov. "We will need to know what we are facing, and let us hope the history settles down for a bit. Those two

Italian battleships were a bit of a surprise, I know, but our Moskit-IIs seemed more than a match for them."

"We used six missiles," Fedorov cautioned. "Yes, we drove them off, but my guess is that they will live to fight another day. Counting all three of our SSM systems, we now have only thirty-three anti-ship missiles remaining in inventory."

"No problem," said Karpov. "Six more to send this *Rodney* and *Nelson* packing, and plenty left over for any cruisers and destroyers they would care to throw at us."

"I wouldn't be so self-assured, Captain. The Royal Navy is a tough professional force. They'll learn from any mistakes they make, and they've had a lot of lessons in recent years. As for the *Nelson* Class battleships, yes they are old and slow, but with 16 inch guns and good protection. That aside, it's 1942 now, and once we get out into the Atlantic we'll find the British have added two more fast battleships to their home fleet with *Duke of York* and *Anson*. A third in this same class is scheduled to be commissioned in just a few weeks, HMS *Howe*. In short, their home fleet is twice as strong as it was when we first faced it, at least insofar as the big battleships are concerned."

"I think Volsky will want to head south, well away from the Royal Navy."

"True. Yet we'll first have to transit the Strait of Gibraltar much like we just fought our way through this last one. Very likely we will find ourselves in range of those heavy guns on *Nelson* and *Rodney* if they get there first. And Captain," he paused for emphasis. "We won't be deploying any nuclear weapons against the British this time out, at least not while I command the ship."

Karpov's eyes narrowed at that last statement, but he said nothing for a moment, then shifted to another topic. "If the landforms inhibit Rodenko's radar we can still deploy helicopters to enhance our over the horizon awareness. That may take the surprise factor out of the situation."

"That is a good plan, Captain." Fedorov concluded. "Very well, I'll go below and see how the Admiral is doing. You have the bridge for the moment. We'll send for you if Admiral Volsky is well enough to conference."

Fedorov started for the sick bay, a thousand things running through his mind. He had had very little sleep since this new saga unfolded. The ship had been pressed by unexpected adversaries, and sustained real damage for the first time. The constricted waters of the Mediterranean served to neutralize one of *Kirov*'s greatest technological edges—the ability to see the enemy at long range before they were even aware of the Russian battlecruiser. And what you could see, you could also target and kill. The landlocked sea here meant that they were surrounded by airfields on every side, and recon planes were almost certain to find them and report their position, speed and heading. To prevent that they would have to detect and shoot down virtually every airborne contact they encountered, and that was not going to be practical given their slowly dwindling SAM magazines.

This was going to give their adversaries much more situational awareness than they ever had before. They will know approximately where we are, he thought, and that was compounded by the fact that the ship had only three options if it wanted to exit these waters. Suez was not really a viable choice, and the Bosporus route, though appealing in one sense, would only leave them masters of the Black Sea, with the same long, grueling task of sailing to Gibraltar through an active war zone if they ever wanted to leave that place. This reason, and the circumstances that found them running straight for the chaos of Operation Pedestal, had prompted Fedorov to take this northern route. Now that the Bonifacio Strait was behind them they might at least have some time to think, rest and plan what they should or could do next.

Other thoughts plagued him, more ominous in his mind, and filled him with a nagging doubt. The ship's presence was like an irritating grain of salt in a clam shell here. What pearl would it produce in the history? Already both the British and Italians had used resources, men, ships and planes, that they might have otherwise deployed against each other. This was introducing more and more subtle changes in the history, and his great extra advantage of knowing the course of future events was no longer something he could rely on. He did not think his engagement with Da Zara's 3rd Cruiser Division, or the pursuit of the 7th Cruiser Division mattered much, as these forces had both been ordered to stand down. The 3rd Division sustained damage from *Kirov* that should not have occurred, but the 7th Division had been ordered to return to Messina historically, where it ran afoul of the British Submarine *Unbroken* and saw both heavy cruiser *Bolzano* and light cruiser *Muzio Attendolo* torpedoed. Now these ships were safely at the eastern approaches to the Bonifacio Strait. He thought the balance here was a wash.

The presence of the two Italian Battleships had been a dangerous surprise to him, shaking his confidence in the future course of events. They should not have been at La Spezia, or in any position to intervene here. He thought that the heavy Italian ships were all still at Taranto, which was another reason he had discarded the journey to the Black Sea.

Now, as he looked at the route ahead, he mused darkly over what the British may have learned about their battle in the Bonifacio Strait. They knew that none of their own ships were deployed in that region. Who would they think the Italians were engaging? This thought filled him with misgiving as he reached the sick bay and knocked lightly on the hatch.

"Mister Fedorov," Zolkin greeted him as he entered and removed his hat, smiling at the amiable doctor. The young navigator was also relieved to see Admiral Volsky awake and looking much more alert than the day before.

"I was hoping someone would come down here and tell me what all this shooting has been about. How is an old man to get any sleep?" The Admiral forced a smile, then asked the most important question on his mind. "Is the ship safe, Fedorov? What has happened? Zolkin has had me strapped to this cot and refused to let me go."

"Doctors give orders too, Leonid," said Zolkin, his brows lowering with admonition.

"Don't worry, Admiral, the worst is over and we should have safe waters for at least the next twenty-four hours or more." He gave Volsky a briefing on all they had been through, finishing up with an account of that surprise engagement with *Veneto* and *Littorio*.

"Battleships?" said Volsky. "So that is what was shaking things up down here. I thought it might be bombs from aircraft. The concussion was severe."

"A few big rounds fell a little closer than I would have liked," he explained. "We may have some splinter damage on the bow hull area, and Tasarov is having trouble with his sonar. We'll put divers over the side near dusk to have a look." He ran down the details of Byko's damage control report and then asked if he might summon Captain Karpov to discuss the route ahead in more detail. While they waited Volsky took a moment to sound out another matter.

"How are things on the bridge," he asked. "Have the men accepted Karpov? Do you feel comfortable with him there?"

"Yes sir," Fedorov did not hesitate. "In fact, his knowledge and ability to fight the ship in combat is invaluable. He can make quick decisions, put weapons on target, and the other officers seem to hold no grudge over what happened. I think Karpov is legitimately trying to rehabilitate himself. Yes, his pride is wounded, but he has lost that arrogance and argumentative edge, and frankly, he does not seem so obsessed with effecting some decisive blow, though I cannot say that has entirely left his thinking."

Zolkin spoke up: "You mean he won't be trying to fire of another nuclear bomb off any time soon. That is a relief."

"I have told him that option is out of the question, and he did not argue," said Fedorov.

"And you," said Volsky. "How do you feel at the helm, young man?"

"It's a great deal of responsibility, sir. I have much to learn, and I'm grateful for Karpov's assistance and the competency of the other officers. Now we have some hard decisions to make, and so I wanted you to guide us, and express your thoughts on what we should do."

"Not what we *must* do?" said Zolkin.

"I'm afraid we must consider both, my good Doctor."

Karpov arrived and stepped in to the room, looking as tired as Fedorov, and somewhat haggard. "Rodenko has the bridge," he said. "All is quiet for the moment. But Fedorov thinks we have some difficult hours ahead of us."

"Alright," said Volsky. "Let us hear your briefing Fedorov, and then we will decide."

Chapter 18

"**If the history** remains intact," said Fedorov, then Force Z should turn back for Gibraltar at 1855 hours, or just before sunset this evening. At most they can make twenty knots. That's all the speed the heart of that task force can muster, two battleships, *Rodney* and *Nelson*. They have 16 inch guns, and 16 inch armor on the belt, main turrets and barbettes. These are slow but durable ships. They may never be listed among the top battleships in the war, but they are dangerous and should not be underestimated. Captain Karpov drove off the Italian battle squadron with six Moskit-II hits above the waterline. I do not think the British will be moved so easily."

"You believe they will fight to the finish?" asked Volsky.

"I do, sir. For one thing, we will be threatening one of the most strategically important bases in the British Empire. Look at what they committed here to the defense of Malta. The British know they have to hold three places at this stage of the war: Suez, Malta, and Gibraltar. They will fight, sir. We cannot expect the them to break off, even if things go badly for them."

"What will they know about us?" Volsky's question was pointed and had been nagging at Fedorov for some time.

"I've been considering that, sir. If they learn of the engagement we just fought with the Italians then we may have created quite a conundrum for them."

"Yes, we're a big fish in this very small tank, and we've been nipping at the other fish. They will have to wonder who the Italians were slugging it out with just now, and why we can't seem to decide who's side we are on in this war."

"And remember, they had aircraft over us as well yesterday in the Tyrrhenian Sea. We could have been photographed. At that time they probably believed we were an Italian heavy cruiser, but after the engagement at Bonifacio, I don't know what they will think. Perhaps they might consider that we were a renegade French ship out of Toulon. That is my hope. There was a great deal of dissatisfaction in the French Navy about Vichy French cooperation with the Axis. Remember that the Allies are planning the Invasion of North Africa right now, and Eisenhower is urging the French fleet to join them. They will make an agreement with Admiral Darlan and use him as a standard to rally the fleet. Hitler was suspicious about all this, and he planned *Operation Lila* to attempt to seize that fleet intact and turn it over to the Italians. These events were to occur in just a few months time, but one thing I have noted is that things are happening sooner than they did historically. There has been a subtle shift in the course of events. Perhaps we could confuse British intelligence if Nikolin were to broadcast that we were a renegade French ship. They would have to overfly Toulon to verify that, and it might buy us some time."

"You think we could pose as a French vessel as we approach Gibraltar?"

"It's worth a try sir, though we have no real idea what the British may know about us now, and they may see through the ruse in time. Even if they do believe us, they will still send out ships to escort us, and then, well, the bear is out of his cave."

"We must assume as much," said Karpov. "They are not going to simply let us sail on through with the tip of a hat. What we need to know now is how they would plan to *defend* the Strait of Gibraltar."

"Our experience in the Bonifacio Strait will be your guide in that, Captain." Fedorov rubbed his brow, very weary. "Only it will be a much stronger defense. There's a hundred ton gun installation at Gibraltar, at Magdala battery over looking Rosia Bay. It's an old gun, but can still fire an 18 inch, two thousand pound shell to a range of five or six kilometers. It's not very accurate, but it we would be wise to sail south of that range line as a precaution. There may also be submarines, minefields, and the British will have planes at Gibraltar as well. Many more than we have encountered so far. We can avoid their coastal guns, but not the Royal Navy. We must assume that we'll be facing at least two battleships, three cruisers and many destroyers. If the history repeats itself, their best carrier, *Indomitable*, will take serious bomb damage tonight. This will still leave them with our old friends *Victorious, Furious,* and perhaps the smaller carrier *Argus.*"

Karpov shook his head sullenly. "I tried to sink them earlier, but no one would listen to me. Now we may have to finish the job."

"Anything more that we might face?" Volsky had a gloomy expression on his face already, clearly not happy with their situation.

"Well, sir," said Fedorov, "I doubt they could bring reinforcements down from Home Fleet. Those ships would have to be underway now to reach Gibraltar in time. I think we can safely say that Force Z, probably Force H again after it arrives at Gibraltar, will be our principle foe."

Volsky seemed to be weighing something in his mind. Then he spoke, suggesting another alternative. "Mister Fedorov, Captain Karpov… Might the British be receptive to negotiations concerning our safe passage of these waters?"

Karpov's brows raised with surprise. "Negotiations? I hardly think so. What would we tell them, that we were out on a pleasure cruise when suddenly one of their fighter planes attacked us and we were only defending ourselves?"

Fedorov's eyes brightened a bit at the prospect of negotiations, yet he knew that even this was a double edged sword. "I understand your point, Captain, but it still might be preferable to battle. If we fight, a great many men are going to die. We have already ripped a hole in the history of these events, and every ship and plane we destroy, every man that dies when our missiles strike, will be something that time will find missing from her balance sheets that day. There will be consequences—this we have seen."

"I don't think we could possibly make things any worse than the nightmare world we have just come from," said Volsky.

"And we might even change things for the better, Fedorov," Karpov put in. "Yes, I know my decisions and actions may have caused the Americans to enter the war early. So perhaps I am responsible, Vladimir Karpov, the man who destroyed the world.

Don't you think I've carried that in my gut ever since? So consider this—might we have a chance to correct this now?"

"How?" Volsky looked at him with a blank expression, yet open to his suggestion.

"Well… considering that our initial aim was to bring about post war conditions more favorable to Russia, my thought was to strike a decisive blow against the Allies."

"Yes," said Zolkin. "And if you had finished your dirty business you would have probably dropped another nuclear warhead on Roosevelt and Churchill!"

Karpov frowned, a flash of resentment in his eyes. "I'll admit that thought did cross my mind, Doctor. Such action may seem insane to you from the quiet of your infirmary here, but from the bridge of a fighting ship under attack things look a little different. That said, such drastic measures may not be necessary now. The mere *threat* of action can be as effective as the thing itself. If we do consider negotiation, as Admiral Volsky suggests, then I hope we will remember that we have power in our hands here—real power—and not simply to sink a few more British ships. The British need Gibraltar, yes? Tell them that unless they stand down we will flatten that rock and everything on it. This is negotiating with strength. Don't forget that." He folded his arms, his hand finding the pain in his side.

The Admiral rubbed the stubble on his chin, thinking. He could see that Fedorov seemed somewhat anxious now, and restless. "Something more, Mister Fedorov?"

The young man spoke, a tentative edge to his voice, as if he were still feeling his way through his argument. "I favor the idea of negotiation," he began, "but even that course is not without risk. I might point out that there are over 40 kilometers of tunnels under the rock at Gibraltar, a complete military city. That aside, if we communicate with these men, of this era and time, they will want to know who and what we are. Can we tell them? Remember that any information we divulge can also have an impact on the future course of events. Information was, in fact, one of the principle weapons of this war. We know a very great deal, and that is also power—real power, Captain—to change the future that may unfold from this encounter."

Volsky smiled inwardly. He had walked this same corridor in his own mind as he considered the prospect of negotiating with Churchill and Roosevelt earlier. In the end he realized that any such contact was fraught with as much peril as opportunity. "I don't think we can pass for a French battleship for very long," he said at last. "That ruse might buy us a little time, but the British will see through in due course. Then any negotiation we have with them must be tightly controlled. Perhaps we could simply ask for safe passage through the Strait in exchange for our pledge of neutrality for the duration of the war. We could tell them we will sail to the southern hemisphere, and stay as far as possible from forces on any side in this conflict."

"And when they demand to know who we are," said Karpov, a little too sharply. "Then what?"

"I don't know yet, Mister Karpov, but give me time and I will consider it—along with everything else we have discussed here. It may be that we will have no safe option."

"Particularly if the British are not so keen on negotiating. Remember they have a considerable score to settle, and I would not be surprised to find them intent on nothing other than our destruction."

"Everything we do involves risk, Captain. But tell me…Given the forces Fedorov has described, can we push through this last gate of hell and get back into the Atlantic?"

"Leave that to me, sir. Yes. We can get through."

"But at what cost?" asked Fedorov.

Karpov knew he was talking about British lives now, and he said as much. "If the enemy wishes to stand against us in battle, then they must carry the burden of the losses they sustain. Ours is to look to the safety of this ship and crew."

"That I understand," Volsky agreed with him. "It is all this talk about power and decisive blows aimed at changing the future that I do not yet grasp. We can never know what our actions here may lead to."

He paused, tired again and wanting to sleep without interruption by 15 inch gun salvos. "Very well, gentlemen," he continued. "I order the two of you to get some sleep, which is what I plan to do. Hopefully no one will shoot at us for the next five hours."

Fedorov thanked the admiral and slipped out of the hatch, longing for a few more hours in his bunk. Karpov stood with a grunt and started for the door.

"Mister Karpov," said Zolkin. "You seem to be favoring that ribcage. Is there something I can help you with?"

"It's nothing, Doctor." He rubbed his side where Orlov had buried his fist in their brief encounter. "I slipped on a wet deck and stumbled into a ladder. It's nothing. Just a bruise."

"Carry on then," said Volsky. "And Karpov…Thank you for what you have done to support that young man. He'll make a fine officer. Help him, yes?"

"I will, sir."

Aboard the cruiser *Norfolk* later that afternoon, **Admiral Tovey** was asking himself the same question that plagued Fedorov. What would it cost them this time? He had boarded a plane to Holyhead on the Irish Sea, where the intrepid cruiser was waiting for him at 14:00 hours. It had come all the way down from Scapa Flow, leading the charge of the Home Fleet. Behind it came three more fast cruisers and the light carrier *Avenger,* also new on the Home Fleet roster and still working up with 825 and 802 Squadrons. The battleships followed in a stately line, their sharp bows raking the light swells as they made way at twenty-four knots, four knots shy of their best speed. Even at that speed they would not get down to the warmer waters off the Spanish coast until late afternoon of August 14th. Destroyers escorted them on either side, though only a few of these ships would have the range make the long journey south. Tovey wondered if they would make it in time.

If this ship stays put in the Med, he thought, then we've got her, along with the answer to this mystery once and for all. If she moves now for Gibraltar, then God help Force Z. Syfret was an able man, his flag aboard HMS *Nelson*, and he would fight the good fight. His own second in command of Home Fleet, Admiral Bruce Fraser, was also there incognito aboard HMS *Rodney* to survey the whole of this Operation Pedestal and make a special report. Could *Rodney* and *Nelson* hold on until Home Fleet arrived? What might the cost be if he ordered Syfret to hold the Pillars of Hercules at all cost? He had seen the weapons this mysterious ship was capable of deploying. Was he merely sending these good men and ships to their doom? And if this unaccountable raider blasts its way through the strait and out into the Atlantic again, what then? Home Fleet will come charging up, tired and thirsty. His battleships were well gunned and armored, but with short legs. He could operate for a few more days, and then he would need to refuel. By that time this *Geronimo* could get well out to sea and leave them holding an empty bag again. Was he just burning up valuable fuel oil in another fruitless chase?

These and a hundred other questions turned in his mind, and he could still see the look in Professor Turing's eyes, almost pleading it seemed to him. What was he getting at in that last conversation they had had together? He had told him there was no nation on this earth that could have built and deployed a ship like *Geronimo*, or managed to perfect any of the weaponry they had seen her use with such deadly effect—that it would take years, decades to reach that level of sophistication. Yet Tovey had seen the flatly contradicting truth of the matter first hand, felt the shuddering impact of those infernal rockets against his armor plate, seen the proud bow of HMS *Repulse* slip beneath the angry sea and die....and that hideous mushroom of seawater! A chill shook him just to think of how the American task force had perished.

Years... Decades... he considered every implication of what Turing had said. What *was* this terror ship? Where had it come from? It wasn't German—not if it fought with the Italians at Bonifacio Strait—and it certainly wasn't French, not with this rocketry as its primary weapon. Could the Russians have built a ship like this?

Impossible! What then? The notion that there was some Captain Nemo out there building such a ship on a deserted island as Jules Verne had it *in Twenty Thousand Leagues Under The Sea* was also not one he could entertain for long. Yet this ship was indeed a profound riddle, as confounding as that *Mysterious Island* Verne wrote about in his sequel, and bent on picking a fight with the British Empire or anyone else, just as this Captain Nemo had in the novels Tovey had delighted to read in his youth.

Captain Nemo…Prince Dakkar, son of a Hindu Raja. Verne had said he discovered the lost civilization of Atlantis, and hinted that his wizardry had been derived from ancient knowledge he had uncovered. Tovey never forgot how he mused over the story, and especially when Nemo returned in *Mysterious Island,* old and gray after having sailed the oceans wide, the last survivor on the *Nautilus.* The odd thing there had been the strange incongruity with time, for the *Nautilus* escaped the maelstrom at the end of Verne's first book in June of 1868, then the ship strangely appears, with Nemo an old man, all his crew gone, and the captain dies in October of that same year on that mysterious "Lincoln" Island. He remembered thinking that perhaps his strange submarine had also traveled in back time during its many adventures, arriving at the end of its long journey right at the same place and time it had begun.

Traveling in time…He smiled, putting the story out of his mind and squinting at the gray horizon as *Norfolk* rose and fell in the gathering swell. The tang of the sea was in the air, and he felt at home again, his feet firmly rooted in the here and now. It wasn't possible, he thought. Jules Verne or H.G. Wells might have the liberty to delight themselves with such fanciful notions in their writings, but not the Admiral of the Home Fleet of the Royal Navy.

A flight of seabirds cruised by overhead, making for land, and his questions soared after them, seeking some comprehensible home in his mind. What was this ship? Who could have built it? The mystery drove his resolve, and he would move heaven and hell, and the considerable weight of Home Fleet to have his answer.

Part VII

The Enemy Below

"He who seeks vengeance must dig two graves:
one for his enemy and one for himself."

~ Old Proverb

Chapter 19

Dusk came after an uneventful voyage and a welcome interval of quiet. The ship had run out to sea at thirty knots to get well away from Sardinia and Corsica, cruising all day and into the fading light of sunset, and was now just off the largely deserted coast of Menorca Island. As the wan light faded, Fedorov was up from his bunk, feeling refreshed and well rested. He looked at the time: 19:thirty hours, just a few minutes before sunset. Menorca would be safe, he thought. There were no settlements of note there, particularly along this northern coast, and it was also neutral territory, officially a dominion of Spain.

He ate a brief meal and then went aft to find Byko and his damage control engineers. It was time to slow the ship, so he gave orders to make five knots and cruise in a wide circle so that Byko could put divers in the water to inspect the hull and forward sonar rims. Tasarov's passive reception was still no good, and they were going to need that equipment in good condition if they did have to face the Royal Navy again at Gibraltar.

While he was aft he encountered Orlov, sitting with his back to a half open hatch along with several Marines where they usually occupied bays near the helicopters. It seemed that Orlov made some deprecating joke when he saw Fedorov approaching, and the men laughed, settling down as he drew near. Orlov made a half hearted salute, with an odd grin on his face.

"Captain Fedorov," he said. The other men stood, a little more respectfully, but Orlov remained seated, his face a mask of derision.

"Mister Orlov," Fedorov returned. "I heard about your intervention during the fire. Admiral Volsky was particularly pleased. I hope you were not injured badly."

"What, these?" Orlov held out his still bandaged hands. "It's nothing. Healing up well. The burns were not severe."

"Good… Well, I would like the remaining KA-40 readied for operations. Rig for ASW. Byko may have to take the forward Horse Jaw sonar off line to complete his repairs. He tells me the aft towed array is also not ready for safe operation. That leaves us with this last KA-40. I'll want it rigged with dipping sonar and sonobuoys, two torpedoes, and also a full air-to-air defense capability."

"Yes sir, commander Fedorov, sir." Orlov was clearly mocking him now, and in front of the men, who fought to suppress grins. Fedorov turned to him, considering what to say, and how to deal with his truculent manner when he caught a shadow at the hatch behind Orlov's back. A man stepped through quickly, and took hold of Orlov's jersey at the shoulders, his fists bunched tightly on the cloth as he wrenched the big man from his seat and pulled him up onto his feet. The other Marines seemed to freeze stone cold, real fear in their eyes now, and when Orlov squirmed around he saw the steely face of Sergeant Kandemir Troyak glaring at him. Troyak released him with a shove and spoke in a low, threatening voice.

"Mister Orlov, you are now standing before the Captain of this ship, and you will come to attention in his presence and act accordingly. The next time I see you sitting on your ass like that, particularly in front of these other men, I will personally see that you regret it. Now, apologize to the Captain—*at once!*"

It was more than Fedorov had ever heard Troyak say at any one time, and that, along with his rock-like presence and impenetrable countenance was enough settle the matter. Orlov's neck reddened. He glared back at Troyak, but was of no mind to challenge him in this situation. He saluted, offering an apology in a low growl.

"I apologize, Captain—"

"What was that?" Troyak yelled. "None of us *heard* that, Mister Orlov!"

"Sir," Orlov raised his voice, clearly unhappy. "I apologize for my disrespect."

"Very well," said Fedorov. "As you were, and see that the KA-40 is ready in thirty minutes." He nodded to Troyak and moved on. He would make one more call to Dobrynin in engineering to make certain the reactors were in order, and it was not until he was well away from the scene that he allowed himself a smile.

U-73 was hovering in the still waters off Fornells Bay on the northern coast of Menorca Island and Kapitänleutnant Rosenbaum smiled as he peered through his periscope viewfinder, surprised to see a curious ship on his near horizon. Could this be the ship, he thought? What else could it be?

An hour ago one of his Funkegefreiten Telegram Operators had come to the con tower with a message from La Spezia. He was to look out for a fast British battlecruiser possibly heading his way, and last spotted on a heading of 245, cruising southwest towards the Island of Menorca, which was one of Rosenbaum's favorite haunts. After his triumphant sinking of HMS *Eagle*, he had been congratulated and given permission to head home. But to celebrate, he took his boat north to an old hideaway once used by the Barbary Coast pirates, Fornells Bay. There were a few fisherman in a tiny cluster of huts that almost passed for a village there, along with the remnants of old watch towers that once served as lookouts for the pirate ships—but they would never see this pirate coming.

U-73 was creeping along at barely three Kph, its bow perfectly positioned to slip through the narrow entrance to the bay where the depth was just 18 fathoms. It was dangerous to navigate in such waters, but his boat had a draft under five meters and he could even remain submerged in that depth as he snuck into the bay, then sit quietly on the weedy bottom with over thirty meters of water above him. Tonight he would surface briefly and put men ashore for some fresh water or perhaps even a little fresh fish to celebrate the occasion.

As was his habit, Rosenbaum was taking a last look over his shoulder as the light faded, to be certain nothing threatening was at hand. When he saw the silhouette of the big ship emerge from behind the massive bulk of Sa Mola Isthmus to the east, he was shocked. There, not four or five kilometers distant, was one of the most threatening looking ships he had ever seen. It was big, fully the size of a battlecruiser, though he could only vaguely discern its guns from this range. It was creeping along at no more than five knots, he guessed, a perfect target if ever there was one! Then he noticed a smaller craft in the water near the ship as well. Probably inspecting the hull for damage, he reasoned, or putting men ashore.

Something immediately struck him about this ship, jangling loose a distant memory, and setting his adrenaline to rush. This had to be the ship his cable had warned him about, and he now found himself in a perfect position to fire his single aft torpedo in the stern of the boat. He immediately lowered his periscope, giving orders for silent running, and to the other men it seemed that the Kapitän was very much on edge. His second in command, Horst Deckert was watching him closely, noting the distant look in his eyes and just the hint of a glaze of fear.

"What is wrong, Kapitän?" he asked.

Rosenbaum looked at him apprehensively. "I think I have seen this ship before," he said in a low voice, almost a whisper, as if the ship itself might overhear him and suddenly burst into action as he had seen it do earlier.

"A year ago," said Rosenbaum. "In the north Atlantic. Do you remember, Deckert?"

"Ah, that ship you took to be a target vessel southwest of Iceland?"

"Yes—that's the one!"

"The ship that killed Klaus Bargsten on U-563?"

Rosenbaum said nothing, nodding at young Hans Altmann, a watch officer who was surely listening to them out of the corner of his ear. He turned to the young man and gave an order. "See that that number five is pre-heated well."

"Ja Kapitän," said Altmann, and he passed the order back. For a long shot like this, they would get much better performance from a pre-heated torpedo. The boat had four tubes in the bow, and one aft in the stern, his number five tube, and there he was carrying one of the newer G7e model T2s, upgraded and designated T3 now to note that it was an improved torpedo. Heated to thirty degrees centigrade before launch, its battery would perform much better, running out to 7500 meters in trials. If he could get it to run true for four or five thousand meters he thought he stood a good chance to hit this ship. Then he planned to scoot into the bay and settled quietly on the silted floor for an hour in case this ship had a gaggle of destroyers in tow that he could not yet see.

"You're going to try a long shot?" Deckert whispered. "Remember what happened to Bargsten! You already got a big kill with that carrier back there, Kapitän. And you've already got your Knight's Cross waiting for you back home—if we can get there in one piece."

"Don't worry, Deckert, I have a good plan, you'll see."

He waited a few minutes consulting his chart for proper depth and angle on this shot while the torpedo was heated. A British battlecruiser, he thought. There were not many left, and this one did not look like anything he had ever seen before. His chart notes on HMS *Renown*, which sometimes operated in these waters, indicated her length at 242 meters and a draft of a little over eight meters. This ship was easily that long. If it were a cruiser, the length would be no more than 190 meters. Might this be a new ship? No matter. He would set his torpedo running depth at 8 meters and leave it at that. Word was soon passed that all was ready. He raised his periscope and took another look to be certain of the angle of his shot, leading the boat based on the running speed of the torpedo and that of the target. He had his solution.

The sun was gone now, but the gloaming light still sharply outlined the darker silhouette of the ship. All he had to do was nudge his boat gently to get the perfect angle. Gliding on battery, his boat was very quiet, and he could hear no sign of an Asdic signal indicating the enemy was suspicious of his presence. Once he had made his adjustment he clenched his jaw and gave the order.

"Feuer jetzt!"

The whoosh of the torpedo launch seemed the only sound in the boat at that moment, and he immediately lowered his periscope.

"Ahead two thirds," he whispered, wanting to get as far away from the track of his running fish as possible. There had been no need to rig it out with a Federapparat pattern running device, which was useful against convoys, but not in a situation like this. The last thing he wanted was for some enterprising seaman on deck to sight down the line of his incoming torpedo wake and get a fix on his periscope and location, so he went blind and nudged the boat ahead on battery power, content to slip behind the intervening mass of the Sa Mola Isthmus and then into Fornells Bay. Like a dangerous eel, he had taken a bite at the enemy, and now he would slink into his cave.

He looked to his man on the hydrophones, who was listening intently to the torpedo as it went. The man frowned, shaking his head. "It does not sound good, Kapitän. I think it is losing depth."

Rosenbaum clenched his fist with frustration. They had a surface runner! Now the weapon would strike too high, where most ships in this class would have a strong torpedo bulwark for protection. Ideally he wanted the torpedo to strike much closer to its assigned depth, where the hull would curve from the vertical towards the bilge of the ship, and the armor protection could be avoided. If he had fired a magnetic head, set to explode beneath the hull, it might have been worse, he thought. At least this one has whiskers, four metal spikes in the nose that would detonate the 273kg warhead on contact. It could still do significant damage, even if it was running shallow.

The entrance to the bay was a little over 500 meters wide here, but it opened quickly to two kilometers, and was all of five kilometers long, just deep enough near the little village to give him a place to hide on the bottom. They'll never find me here, he thought as he watched his wrist watch, counting down the seconds left in the long torpedo run. If he heard no detonation, indicating a miss, he would settle on the bottom and wait things out. The British would search for him in vain and, when he was ready, he would sneak out to have another look and begin the game again.

The second hand ticked away…

Byko was waiting on the fantail, watching the KA-40 slowly rise up from the flight deck, its twin rotors bronzed by the fading sunlight, its overhead engines roaring as the helo hovered, then slowly gained altitude. He was a big man, with good sea legs and burly shoulders and arms, sleeves rolled back and a spanner in one hand while he waited at the diving station. His features were raw, and weathered from years at sea, and his close cropped hair did little to conceal the prominent dome of his skull, with more hair on his short, thick neck than he seemed to have on his head.

The men had been in the water for two hours, coming and going from the small skiff where it hovered amidships. They had inspected the big forward bulge off the lower bow where the passive sonar array was installed and found it free of damage. The starboard hull was lightly dimpled by fragments of splintered metal, some still lodged there, and the men were removing them and filling the holes with a fast acting adhesive sealant. What little seawater they took had been confined to the inner void and was easily pumped out.

Now they were working the port side, and the divers had noted a large shrapnel fragment cutting cleanly across their underwater sonar rim. This was undoubtedly where the damage was, and after an initial assessment they had returned to the diving skiff to run round to the aft of the ship and use the side ladders and stair extension there to re-embark. They were going to need tools, and some replacement parts as well, including underwater Acetylene torches. A marine guard sat sullenly in the back of the skiff, standard procedure for security on any boat that was manned and away from the ship, no matter how close.

Andrey Siyanko had been with the 874th Naval Infantry Battalion for some years, and was excited to be included in the special detachment assigned to the new *Kirov* when she launched. Now he looked to the west, watching the last traces of sunlight fade and etch the distant islands of the Balearic chain in sharp relief. Then he caught something out of the corner of his left eye, and turned to squint at the placid sea. His eyes widened with shock when he saw it, the long thin trail of a fast moving torpedo aimed directly at the heart of the ship!

"Torpedo!" He shouted, and he instinctively unslung his automatic weapon, taking aim as the deadly undersea weapon bored in on them. He had little chance of hitting it, but reacted by sheer reflex as it came surging in, firing on full automatic.

With *Kirov's* sonar dark for this vital repair, no one saw the torpedo but this one man, and the sharp rattle of his weapon was the only reprisal the ship mustered against the attack. He was firing in sheer self defense, because the torpedo was now running up very near the surface of the water and aimed directly at his boat. Siyanko would not live to know what his reflexive, if futile, action had accomplished.

Chapter 20

The Torpedo ran true, right at the diving boat and struck it dead on, detonating and literally ripping the small boat to pieces. The fire from Siyanko's automatic rifle may have helped in that, but it could not save his life, or even spare *Kirov* from being hurt by the powerful explosion.

On the bridge, Karpov had just resumed his post while Fedorov remained below seeing to damage control. He was watching the launch of their last KA-40 on the aft Tin Man camera feed, pleased that they had some protection airborne against submarines. Yet no sooner had that thought come to him when he heard the violent explosion, and felt the ship lurch in response. His only thought in that wild moment was that they had struck an unseen mine.

He ran out the side hatch of the citadel to the watch deck, looking aft with shock to see that there was a huge explosive spray washing up over the ship there. The diving tender boat was obliterated, and parts of it had been flung against *Kirov's* hull. Then he saw it, the thin remnant of a torpedo wake dissipating on the water.

His heart pounded, eyes wide as he rushed into the citadel shouting at the top of his voice. "Torpedo! Submarine off the port quarter. Tasarov, do you hear anything? Go to active sonar!"

"Aye sir!" The sharp ping of the sonar resounded a second later. *Kirov's* passive systems had been shut down for the diving repair, but she could still shout at the unseen enemy below and listen for the telltale return of the sound waves.

"Samsonov, be ready on the *Shkval* system and get me an immediate firing solution."

But no solution came. Tasarov listened, and listened, and though he was one of the best sonar men in the fleet, he could hear nothing moving beneath the darkening still waters.

"We're too close to this island," he said. "I'm getting too many reflections from the coastal headlands. We need sea room, sir."

Karpov's mind raced ahead, trying to catch up with the unseen enemy. He noted the direction of the torpedo wake and resolved to immediately fire a salvo from the ship's UDAV system down that line at once. The sub had to be somewhere between the island and the ship, probably a few hundred meters left of right of that track, and trying to slink away. He squinted at the narrow mouth of an inlet, but could see little in the dark. It seemed entirely too small a channel there and he discarded it as a potential escape route. The sub would be diving now and maneuvering out to sea as quietly as it could.

"Activate UDAV ASW system! Fire in an arc toward that island, three kilometer range. Now!"

Samsonov was flipping switches to key the manual fire, as he had no data incoming from Tasarov's sonar. He quickly activated the UDAV-2 ASW system and fired two salvos sending a total of ten rockets out in a wide fan off the port side of the ship. They exploded with raging fury, generating a curtain of tumultuous seawater in the distance. If any submarine was lurking there, it would surely be shaken up by the sudden violence of the attack. *Kirov* had fired back, yet had not yet seen its foe. It was the first time they had fired without being able to precisely target their enemy, and with no real assurance of hitting or hurting him in the process. Even the frantic attempt by the young Siyanko had been directly aimed. This was no more than a random wall of fire intended to frighten their enemy and buy the ship some vital time while Karpov tried to better assess their situation and gain control of the engagement.

Karpov needed to move the ship now, but how bad was the damage? If he put on speed would he cause even more flooding? He decided to risk ten knots, feeling exposed and helpless at this slow speed. He could see the diving boat was gone, and they could come back for any man left in the water once he had found and destroyed this sinister enemy. But if they did not move soon they might all be in the sea.

The comm-link rang sharply and a watch stander answered. "It's Byko, sir. He has initial damage reports."

Karpov took the handset and heard what he had hoped. The torpedo had struck and destroyed the diving boat, which was five meters off the port side of the ship. The explosive concussion of the warhead was still enough to shake the ship and fling fragments of the destroyed boat against the hull, but learning lessons from the terrorist attack on the American Destroyer *Cole* in the port of Aden, *Kirov* had been reinforced amidships with a long 100mm anti explosive bulwark. It was enough to protect the watertight integrity of the hull, and Byko's men reported some minor buckling, but no flooding or damage below the waterline. That was exactly what Karpov had hoped to hear. Now they had their speed and maneuverability back, and he immediately ordered all ahead full, with a hard turn to starboard and the open sea just as Fedorov burst in through the hatch, breathless from his long run up to the bridge.

"Captain on the bridge!"

"As you were," Fedorov said quickly, seeking out Karpov, who quickly filled him in on what had occurred.

"What now?" asked Fedorov. "I think we should use the KA-40."

"Correct," said Karpov. "This sub must be very close. I used the ASW rockets as a kind of covering suppressive fire to keep his head down. These subs cannot fire when deeply submerged, yes?"

"Not at this stage of the war. They will need to be on the surface or at periscope depth to fire with any hope of hitting anything."

"Good," Karpov rubbed his hands together, the excitement of the battle animating him. "Now that we have full speed we will not be targeted again easily. How fast is this devil, Fedorov?"

"Slow. Perhaps no more than five knots submerged on battery power like it must be now. This is a diesel-electric boat, Captain. Where do you reckon it to be?"

"Do you have a chart?"

Fedorov motioned to his old navigation system and they had Tovarich call up the digital file for the Balearic Islands. "This is Menorca," Fedorov pointed. "And we are here, near this long inlet."

"Could he be there?" Karpov asked.

"I doubt it," said Fedorov. The entrance is narrow and the size of that bay is deceptive. The charts show enough depth for a boat to enter submerged, but half way into the bay it shoals quickly to a very shallow depth."

"Then I suspect this submarine is probably here." Karpov pointed off the coast to their east. "He would not run west for fear of being penned up against the headlands of that long cape. No, the bastard will run east, along this shoreline here, and try to get round that fat isthmus east of the bay. I will have Nikolin move the KA-40 off that coastline and we will soon find out. In the meantime, I have given him our backside and put on thirty knots. What is the range of his torpedoes?"

"5000 meters at best."

"Can they home on our wake?"

"No, they were largely straight runners after firing, unless fitted with a pattern running device, which would probably not be used here."

"Good. We will be outside his firing range in just a few minutes. Then we use the helicopter to make contact and prosecute. If their Captain survives another hour he will regret the day he set eyes on *this* ship, I assure you."

Karpov sighed heavily now, removing his cap and wiping the sheen of perspiration from his brow. He hated submarines—detested them—but now that he had *Kirov* safely away from the threat, moving at high speed, the foe did not seem so dangerous. It was slow, with old weapons that could not seek him out or follow his wake. He had little doubt that he would get this sub easily enough.

"Five knots?" he said. "Yes, they are slow. Compared to our training to go against those fast American attack subs, this will be no problem."

Minutes later the KA-40 had dropped three sonobuoys in a triangular pattern well east of the small inlet but perfectly positioned to cover the coastline. One would use active sonar to make the contact, the second to determine its bearing and the third would calculate the range. The helo could also use its dipping sonar, lowering a device into the water from above to refine the data and get a hard fix.

They waited while the KA-40 conducted its search and fed the telemetry directly to Tasarov's ASW board. Time passed, and the minutes stretched out without any sign of the enemy submarine, and Karpov began to pace, his boots hard on the deck as he walked back and forth, watching out the forward viewport.

"May I maneuver the ship?" He asked Fedorov, who nodded in the affirmative. "Very well, helm, reduce to two thirds and come right thirty degrees rudder to course 065 northeast."

"Thirty degrees rudder, aye sir. Coming around to course zero-six-five and steady at twenty knots."

Karpov was turning east to run parallel to the course he had expected the submarine to take, but as time passed and the KA-40 had no contact, he began to suspect they were up against a very wily U-boat captain.

"Come on, come on. Where *is* he?" he muttered as he paced.

Fedorov was still at the navigation station, studying the charts with Tovarich and missing his old post. What they needed now, he realized, was just a little time to complete repairs on their main sonar systems. They could just sail off at high speed to outrun this submarine. There would be no way the U-boat, if it was a German boat, would ever catch them, so he went over to consult with Karpov again.

"Captain, we are well out of range, and we can outrun this boat at any time. I suggest we use this interval to slow and complete our repairs. Take the ship back west and move the KA-40 between us and the island. We'll work round that long cape there and find some open sea to complete these repairs. The KA-40 can cover us all night if necessary."

"We'll lose the bastard," Karpov pointed at the sea, clearly unhappy.

"It doesn't matter. He's just too slow submerged to pose any further threat. Restoring full functionality on our sonar is more important now."

Karpov clenched his jaw, but relented. "Very well," he agreed. "The devil is most likely sitting on the bottom somewhere along that coast. If there are rocks there he would be hard to find in that kind of clutter. But if he so much as moves a rudder, I'll be on top of him with the helo in no time."

Karpov was angry that they had been caught sleeping like that. If this ship were in the Atlantic, he thought, we would not have a scratch on us. Nothing would have come within fifty miles of us to pose a threat. But here in these restricted waters we have seen one engagement after another, with damage to radar systems, sonar, the missile accident, hull damage, the loss of a KA-40, men dead and injured—even the Admiral. It was inexcusable.

"We lost men on that diver tender," said Fedorov. "I'm putting another boat in the water to recover anyone still alive out there. I'll notify Byko of our decision and have him get more men into wet suits, but this could take time. We have the aviation fuel to burn in this situation, so we'll have to use it."

That decided, they turned the ship and Fedorov ordered another boat launched for search and recovery. After an hour they had found only one survivor adrift at sea and clutching a floating spar of broken wood. Two other divers, the boat's pilot and the marine guard Siyanko were gone. All in all their casualties were not high, but now they had lost seven men to the sea, and Fedorov wondered how many more would die in the days ahead.

He spent some time next to Tovarich at the navigation station, accessing his database on German U-boat movements. What was this submarine doing up here, he mused? Was it Italian? It would definitely not be a British boat. Most of the Italian boats should be in the Sicilian Narrows opposing Operation Pedestal, and they would base out of Cagliari, Palermo, or other bases in Southern Italy. The

Germans were operating out of La Spezia, and he ran a search for this day trying to figure out who it might be.

U-205 was out and deployed against the British to the south, but it would not come this way, and returned to Pola on the Adriatic coast instead of La Spezia. U-83 was way off to the east near Alexandria, and U-331 had just departed La Spezia and was north of Corsica on this day. Unless that boat also left port early, then this contact had to be U-73 under Rosenbaum, the very same boat that had sunk its teeth into the carrier *Eagle* two days ago. He checked its daily reported track, noting that it should still be south along the line of the British convoy advance, but could he rely on the information any longer? The early movement of the Italian 7th cruiser Division, and the surprising sortie by those two battleships had shaken his faith in the history. It was clear that *Kirov's* unexpected presence in these waters was causing ripples of variation in all directions. Ships were moving out on missions they had never been assigned in the history he knew. Engagements were being fought that never should have happened.

What if this U-73 had been moved north, or had come north earlier than the history recorded? He noted that when it did return to La Spezia, it came very near this very island of Menorca along the way. Suddenly curious again, he took yet another look at his navigation charts, his eye suspiciously falling on that long inlet of Fornells Bay. If this U-boat was running on battery it would be very quiet, but three sonobuoys and active dipping sonar should have found it if it was hiding along the coastline where Karpov expected it. He wondered...

~~~

That night U-73 put out divers as well, a team of two skilled frogmen slipping away to scout the bay for prying eyes. He had learned the trick from another U-Boat captain who used it up on the Norwegian coast, slipping his boat into the many fiords there and then putting men ashore to give him eyes and ears on the situation, and watch for enemy destroyers. When the proverbial coast was clear, they could sneak out again.

Once ashore on the eastern side of the bay they made their way up a prominent hill, some hundred meters in elevation, and crouched atop its rocky ridge to search the seas to the north. Able seaman Heinrich Waldmann peered through his binoculars to the north , but saw nothing in the moonless night. Then he caught sight of something winking in the distance, and an odd sound came to him.

He did not know it then but he had glimpsed and heard the KA-40 helicopter where it now orbited *Kirov's* position, standing guard like a watchful sheep dog. Even so, he reasoned that must be the location of the enemy ship, and he and his mate slipped back down the craggy hill to get back to the U-boat and report. Sometime later the news gave Rosenbaum a chill, for it meant that this battlecruiser was still close at hand.

"Could you see any sign of fire? Smoke?"

"No sir, just an odd sound, almost like an aircraft, and a few running lights."

He clearly heard an explosion, and knew his torpedo had struck the target, but apparently the damage was not as great as he hoped. At least we've wounded him, he thought. He's probably cruising off shore with men in the water to survey the damage. It will be safe enough to surface here now for a quiet breath of fresh air. Then we can slip out of the bay and creep up on him again. They probably think I am long gone, and wishing to get as far away from this place as possible. But they are wrong. I'm going to get this ship, for Klaus, for U-73, and to beat my lucky number seven as well.

Chapter 21

Just before dawn on the 13th of August, 1942, *Kirov* was still hovering off the northern coast of Menorca, her sonar repairs and further hull inspections well underway, though it would be another six hours before they would finish. The KA-40 had good endurance and was able to stay up a full six hours before refueling. Though Fedorov regretted the loss of the aviation fuel, he kept the chopper aloft all that night and it kept a watchful eye and ear out for the enemy submarine, but saw nothing. Byko certified the aft Horse Tail towed array was now fully functional again and promised all would be ready on the forward dome by noon.

On his way back to the bridge he stopped briefly at sick bay, hoping to check up on Admiral Volsky. Zolkin was there with him, and the two men were chatting like the old friends they were, a bowl of good hot soup in the Admiral's lap where he sat up on the recovery cot.

"Mister Fedorov," Volsky smiled. "I was hoping to hear from you. What was it this time? Did we strike a mine?"

"No sir, the ship is well, but we had a very near engagement with a German U-boat."

"A U-boat? You sound very confident about that."

" I believe I know the boat, sir. And I think I know where it might be hiding as well."

"Your books tell you all this?"

"Not exactly, sir, but I have made some well informed assumptions. We put sonobuoys in the water where Karpov directed and yet did not find anything, so there is only one place this boat could be."

"Did you tell Karpov about it? The man is very edgy when it comes to submarines."

"I believe Captain Karpov has gone below, sir. Rodenko has the bridge for the moment, and I am heading there now. I just wanted to see how you were recovering and give you a report. Dobrynin says the reactors are stable, so the ship is stable as well."

"What do you mean?"

"Well sir, every time we have moved—experienced these odd effects and time displacement, there has been a strange flux in the reactor core. I think it happened several times after we first vanished from the scene of that last nuclear detonation. I found these odd references in the history to the sighting of a ship the allies believed to be a *Hipper* class cruiser, and on the very course we were making when we went down to investigate Halifax."

"Yes," said Volsky. "I remember you bringing this up. You are still ruminating on that?"

"It's just that I was considering that it might happen again, sir. It obviously *did* happen again, or why else do we find ourselves here, still stuck in the middle of this war?"

"Have you considered telling Dobrynin to fiddle with the reactors a bit more," Zolkin spoke up.

"What do you mean, Doctor?"

"Tell him to turn his dials, or whatever else he does down there, and maybe we will move again. Then we don't have this problem of Gibraltar in front of us and the British can relax, fight Germans and Italians, and leave us poor Russians alone."

Volsky got a laugh from that, but held up his soup spoon, a glint in his eye and said: "The Doctor makes a good point. Tell Dobrynin to plot a course for Severomorsk, the year 2021. Then we could all go ashore and forget this nightmare."

Fedorov smiled, still considering this for a moment. "I was thinking about something else," he said. "Perhaps it is only a coincidence, but it was twelve days from the day of Orel's accident until we eventually vanished into this odd green sea again. That was from July 28 through August 8, counting both days as bookends. Then we vanish again, and it is another twelve days sailing in that desolate world we discovered until 20 August—and we move again."

"You are suggesting there is an interval involved here, that we move every twelve days?"

"It was just a thought, sir. Perhaps it is mere coincidence. For that matter, we have never determined what sent us back in the first place."

"I thought it was all these nuclear explosions," said Zolkin.

"We all assumed as much," Fedorov agreed.

"Then if nobody tries to lock us up here in my sick bay and we can manage to keep our nuclear warheads in the magazine and not on the missiles, we should be fine," Zolkin concluded glibly. "We'll just sail about the Mediterranean until we run out of things to shoot at— or until we run out of missiles to fire at them."

"Not a very appealing prospect," said Volsky. "I would much rather find that deserted island in the South Pacific, but to do that we have to get there alive and in one piece. The longer we stay here, the more chance we have for these unhappy encounters with airplanes, battleships and submarines. Something tells me we have more trouble ahead of us than behind us if we are ever to get out into the Atlantic again."

"I have an idea," said Zolkin. "This submarine business aside, these waters are relatively safe, are they not? Wasn't Spain neutral in the war? Don't these islands belong to Spain? We could drop anchor here in neutral waters and wait another week or so to test Mister Fedorov's new theory. Maybe the ship will move again, on the twelfth day, and then we don't have to kill anybody else, and they don't have to kill us." He folded his arms, a satisfied look on his face.

Fedorov smiled, his thoughts returning to the problems in this moment. "Well, sir…We still have the KA-40 up and I could probably prosecute this submarine contact further, but repairs will be completed by noon and the ship is sound. However I am sorry to report the loss of four crewman in this last incident."

He told Volsky what had happened, and the luck that had saved them from a direct torpedo strike when the diving boat inadvertently shielded the ship and took the blow instead.

"Astounding," said Zolkin. "It could have been much worse."

"Very much worse, Doctor," said Volsky. "That torpedo would have probably caused severe damage, and flooding as well. We were very lucky."

"Sometimes fate does things like that," said Zolkin, his dark eyes wide. "We could have been hit, perhaps we *should* have been hit. Who knows how many we might have lost in that event? These four men died in their place, and that is all we have to console ourselves. It would be so much better if we were not sailing around here in these metal machines shooting at one another, but we are—until men come to their senses, I suppose, and realize that choosing life is better than death, even if it means you do not win the day or avenge a fallen foe."

Fedorov nodded. Then to Volsky he asked: "Do you want me to destroy this submarine, sir?"

The Admiral looked at him from beneath his heavy brows, then slurped another spoonful of his soup. He realized that the young captain was asking him to shoulder the burden of this next kill, to give him the order so that he would not have to pull the trigger himself, but he considered it best to leave this matter alone, and said as much.

"You are presently acting Captain of this ship, Mister Fedorov. The decision is yours. Protect the ship, that is all I ask, and also, I think when you are done with this submarine business it would be wise to recover all the sonobuoys before we depart this area. Leave nothing in the water that might be found and raise a lot of questions, yes?"

"Very Good, Sir… Will you be returning to duty soon?"

"Ask Zolkin here," Volsky inclined his head to his friend.

"Ask Zolkin, ask Zolkin. Everyone is always asking the doctor for advice. Well in this case, I think the Admiral is recovering nicely and should be back on his feet in little time. You may go chase your submarine, Mister Fedorov, but don't get too close. A few less explosions would help the Admiral sleep a bit better."

"Don't worry about me, Fedorov," said Volsky. "I'll be fine."

Fedorov left the sick bay, encouraged by the thought that the Admiral might soon recover to take the burden of command from him. He headed for the bridge, thinking what to do about this submarine. They had lost four men. He knew that the U-boat was still out there, and probably intent on stalking them further if they lingered here, yet he believed he knew what to do about it now. Moments later he stepped onto the bridge resumed command from Rodenko, sending him below for some rest.

Karpov had already gone below a few hours earlier, and would relieve him at dawn. Now he was ready to consider the matter of this submarine. The KA-40 was still up, though low on fuel, but he decided to follow his hunch and have a closer look at Fornells Bay. He had Nikolin radio the helo and ordered the pilot to overfly the inlet and use infrared cameras and sensors to have a look. Sure enough, when the telemetry was fed back to the ship he could see the knife like presence of a submerged submarine hovering in the shallow waters of the bay, very near the entrance. It was probably trying to sneak out at this very moment, he thought!

Returning to his navigation station he called up the reference to U-73 once more and clicked on the link to the boat's captain, Helmut Rosenbaum. There was Germany's newest recipient of the Knight's cross for the sinking of HMS *Eagle*, he thought. So there you are, you crafty little bandit. He looked at the first photo of Rosenbaum, smiling amiably beneath his captain's hat, a younger man in a better day. There was another photo of him arriving back at La Spezia after this very same patrol, a bouquet of flowers before him and his head turned left to the camera with a gritty smile, his beard unshaven and a jaunty look of pride in his eyes. He read the final notation on the man's fate:

"He left U-73 in October 1942 and became the commander of the 30th flotilla, which fought in the Black Sea. Helmut Rosenbaum was killed in an air crash on 10 May 1944."

As Fedorov stared at the photo he felt a strange connection to the man, and an eerie sensation in knowing his future like this. It was a heady, almost God-like feeling, and something that no man should ever have in his grasp, he thought.

"KA-40 reports it can put a weapon on the target at any time sir," said Nikolin, looking at Fedorov.

Roused from his muse, Fedorov looked at him for a moment and blinked. He could order the U-Boat destroyed in a heartbeat, snuffing out the lives of every man aboard as easily as he might blow out a match. In that event he suddenly realized the photo he was looking at would never even be taken!

Something in him revolted at that that. It was no longer a cold calculation of war or survival in the balance. *Kirov* was well off shore and safe from any harm this U-Boat might still wish upon them. It was his intention to sail west as soon as the helo was recovered, and even running at only twenty knots the ship would quickly leave Rosenbaum and his intrepid U-73 behind. He looked again at the photo, saw the pride in the man's eyes as he accepted his laurels, and then he made up his mind. Rosenbaum would die in that plane crash on 10 May, 1944. The man was living out the last brief years of his life, and Fedorov would give them to him, come what may.

He remembered what Doctor Zolkin had said just a few minutes earlier, and he knew he had chosen correctly: *"...choosing life is better than death, even if it means you do not win the day or avenge a fallen foe."*

"Mister Nikolin," he said. "Order the KA-40 to secure all weapons and return to the ship immediately. They are to recover all sonobuoys as well. Leave nothing in the water, is that clear? We are heading west at once."

Nikolin raised an eyebrow. "Very well, sir," he said, and he passed the orders on. When Karpov returned to the bridge an hour later *Kirov* had sailed and was off the western edge of Menorca. Heading into the channel between that island and the largest landform in the Balearic chain, Majorca. He gave a heading of 270 degrees due west, intending to move north of that larger island and then down through the wider channel to its west. There would be plenty of sea room there and the ship could stay well off shore and safe from prying eyes. He would use that channel to head due south before plotting his course for the Alboran Sea, the last great bottleneck that would lead them to the cork—Gibraltar.

Fedorov communicated his intentions to Karpov and made ready to leave the bridge. "I stand relieved, Mister Karpov."

"Aye, sir. Rest well."

Once alone Karpov inquired about the submarine with Tasarov just as he was about to hand over his shift to Velichko. "Any sign of that devil?"

"We spotted it in that inlet a little over an hour ago. The Captain had the KA-40 right on top of it, but he did not fire, and ordered the helo back to the ship."

Karpov's face registered real surprise. He started to say something, then stopped himself, thinking. *Fedorov had the U-boat in his crosshairs and let the damn thing live! He never said a word to me about it when I came up to relieve him.* He had half a mind to refuel the helicopter and send it back out to avenge its dastardly attack on his ship, and avenge the lives of the men that had died, but another voice spoke to him from within. *"He who seeks vengeance must dig two graves: one for his enemy and one for himself."* It was his headstrong obsession with righting perceived wrongs that had cause this trouble for them in the first place. He would let Fedorov's decision stand.

"Very well," he said at length, tapping Tasarov on the shoulder. "Get some sleep and wash the wax from those ears, Tasarov. We'll need you back in your chair when we sail for Gibraltar."

He let the matter go and turned to the helmsman: "Steady on two seven zero."

~~~

U-73 slipped quietly through the narrow mouth of the bay and out into the wide sea beyond that rocky shore. Rosenbaum immediately raised his periscope for a look in case his enemy was still nearby. He saw no ship, but spied a strange craft in the air, heading northwest, its running lights winking as it went.

A strange feeling came over him, and an involuntary shudder shook his frame as he watched the aircraft vanish in the grey dawn. It was as if the hand of death had been poised above his head, and stayed itself. He felt strangely alive, a vibrant sense of the moment keening up his senses as he scanned the horizon. It was empty, and the sun was casting its first golden rays on the rocky crest of Cape Caballería off to the northwest. He knew he could never catch up with that British ship again, and something told him that it would not be wise to try. So he decided to take his boat quietly out to sea and then turn northeast for La Spezia. He would not get his number seven kill on this patrol, and he would have to put aside the attack he had planned to avenge the loss of U-563 and Klaus Bargsten. Enough was enough, he thought.

He smiled, lowering his periscope and thinking of home. His patrol was over. He would go back to La Spezia and collect his medal, and then off to a new assignment in the Black Sea—commander of a new flotilla of six Type II boats!

Life was good.

Part VIII

The Best Laid Plans

"The best laid schemes of mice and men
Go often awry,
And leave us nothing but grief and pain,
For promised joy."

~ Robert Burns

"I say let the world go to hell, but I should always have my tea."

~ *Fyodor Dostoyevsky, Notes from Underground*

Chapter 22

Word came to Syfret in a brief respite in the middle of a very hard day on the 12th of August. It was marked highest priority, direct from the Admiralty, and he was to respond and confirm these new orders at once. It was more than he needed just then, as the Germans and Italians had been throwing everything they had at him. There was a relatively small attack that morning at 08:00 hours, easily beaten off with the substantial flak his escorts could put up. At noon, however, a stronger attack came, some seventy aircraft. It was just as the intelligence had indicated after intercepting and decoding orders sent to the Italian 77th Wing at Elmas, Sardinia. Yet there was also some odd chaff in that message about an engagement farther north, at Bonifacio Strait. What was that about? It was the only bright spot in his day, as it indicated that the Italian Naval units that had been gathering like a flock of black crows in the Tyrrhenian Sea had suddenly turned north, and were now well away from the planned convoy route.

It was clear from the intelligence that the whole operation was being taken in deadly earnest by the enemy. There were opinions expressed that the Germans now believed there was a direct threat to Benghazi, Tripoli or even to Crete, with the threat of Allied troop landings prompting them to reinforce all these areas with any available air and ground units.

Lord, he was having enough trouble simply trying to protect fourteen merchant vessels carrying supplies to Malta, let alone the notion of mounting an amphibious operation behind Rommel's back. He knew that was coming, but for the moment those plans were still hush, hush. Now he looked at his new orders, curious as to what might be so urgent in them.

'IMPERATIVE YOU WITHDRAW FORCE Z AT EARLIEST OPPORTUNITY - RETURN TO GIBRALTAR AT BEST SPEED - REPEAT - WITHDRAW IMMEDIATELY - ACKNOWLEDGE - END'

He frowned, noting how "at his earliest opportunity" had been duly strengthened by the addition "withdraw immediately." Here the Germans and Italians were doing everything possible to impede his progress—high level bombers, dive bombers, low level torpedo planes, submarines, minefields, some twist on a new aerial torpedo dropped from planes that would circle in the midst of the convoy to seek out targets. The Italians would call them 'motobombas.' He had even heard they had packed a seaplane full of high explosives and planned to fly it by radio control and crash it into one of his carriers. Thankfully the plane could not be controlled and flew harmlessly across the Mediterranean Sea to crash in the desert, leaving a large crater where it exploded but doing no other harm. The Italians, he thought, shaking his head.

Now the Admiralty simply wanted him to turn about with the heart of the surface escort fleet, and run off home to Gibraltar. For what? He knew he would have to turn back in any case, as they were very near the Skerki Bank now, and the channel narrowed there to make a transit by his battleships an unwise operation in these circumstances. It had always been planned that Force Z would turn back at this point. The question was merely how long to hold with the convoy before he turned it over to Admiral Burrough and Force X with his cruisers and destroyers.

They would have the worst of what was yet to come, he knew. He was taking the carriers, and both *Rodney* and *Nelson* home with him, and Burrows was left with whatever they could spare him.

"*Rodney* reports she's having difficulties with her steering, sir," said a watch stander. The ship had been having trouble that way for the last month, Syfret knew, and now it was all she could do to make just fifteen knots. If the Admiralty wanted them home directly, he had little choice in the matter. He had to turn back now.

"Very well," he said with a heavy heart, and gave an order to the midshipman at his side. "Signal Admiral Burrough Godspeed, and we'll turn about at once and head east for Gibraltar." He looked at his watch. It was 16:00 hours, some three hours before he was planning to make this turn.

So it was that the carrier *Indomitable*, which might have sailed on into the teeth of the enemy air attacks for another three hours, did not receive three critical bomb hits when the Axis air forces mounted a large and well coordinated attack with JU-88s, JU-87s, and Italian Cant 1007 torpedo bombers. *Rodney* was also spared three near misses and the crash of an Italian aircraft on her bow. The order from the Admiralty had changed the history—*Kirov* had changed the history by her very presence in this region, and by prompting those urgent orders.

Now Syfret sailed east chasing the setting sun, even as *Kirov* was beginning to put her first divers into the water north of Menorca Island. While Rosenbaum's U-73 was taking that long torpedo shot and prompting Karpov to churn up the sea with his ASW rockets and initiate his search with the KA-40, Syfret was receiving bad news over his shoulder and burdened with considerable regret. Burrough was under attack, and his cruisers *Nigeria* and *Cairo* had both taken torpedoes, along with the one ship he had dearly hoped to protect, the American oil tanker *Ohio*. He was inclined to split his force and send *Rodney* on home to satisfy this order from the Admiralty, while taking *Nelson* back east to cover the eventual withdrawal of Burrough's Force X. Yet he received further orders clarifying his options in no uncertain terms. He was to return to Gibraltar at his best speed, and with as much force as he could spare. At the very least he felt obliged to detach some of his escorts and send help to Force X, come what may. So he gave orders that cruiser *Charybdis* and destroyers *Eskimo* and *Somali* should be signaled by lantern to break off and return to the fray. It would end up doing little good.

In the next twenty-four hours the British would see two more cruisers torpedoed, *Kenya* and *Manchester*, and of the 14 ships they had mustered all this naval power to protect, only five would make it through the terrible gauntlet of fire and reach Malta. The *Ohio* was saved by a handful of dispossessed crewman who manned her AA guns while they watched the ship sink so low in the water that the waves were right at the height of the deck. Two British destroyers lashed themselves to either side of the beleaguered tanker and literally dragged her to port.

Five ships…only five made it through, but it was enough to keep the garrison and population of Malta from starvation, and the vital oil and fuel in *Ohio's* holds was pumped out in the nick of time before she finally settled on the bottom at her berth, a ruined wreck. She would never sail again.

As the haggard Royal Navy ships fell back on Gibraltar, Force Z would limp home with the two big battleships, carriers *Indomitable* and *Victorious*, two light cruisers and twelve more destroyers. The carrier *Furious* would be their rear guard with five more destroyers in escort. The weary crews would get little respite.

To his great surprise, Admiral Syfret soon learned that they were to prepare for a make or break defense of Gibraltar itself! He was to make immediate plans to close those straits to any and all ship traffic.

What in the world can have the Admiralty all rousted up like this, he thought? He was not one of the select few that had been briefed on the details of the engagements of a year past. Yes, rumors flew throughout the whole of the fleet of this new German raider with its wonder weapons and the terrible end it brought to the Americans there. And yes, he had seen the damage to *Prince of Wales* and *King George V* himself when they had returned to Scapa Flow, and knew that the venerable battlecruiser *Repulse* had not come home with them. But that was a year ago, and this enemy ship had been sunk, or so the official line had been put out. He knew nothing of the Admiralty's continued interest and preoccupation with the incident, and nothing of the code word "Geronimo" that had set these events in motion.

So what was all this bother about? Had the plans for Operation Torch been moved up? It was the only thing he could think of that made any sense, and so he made his plans for the fleet to refuel so his destroyers would to be ready to move out again on patrol in the straits of Gibraltar as soon as they reached that location. Perhaps he should invite Admiral Fraser over from *Rodney* and have a little chat. Maybe he knew something more and could explain matters to him.

~~~

Even as Syfret gave that reluctant order to turn about on the afternoon of August 12, Admiral Tovey was already aboard the cruiser *Norfolk* and well out to sea where he would soon transfer to the flagship, *King George V.*

While the KA-40 was searching in vain for U-73 on the night of August 12-13, Home Fleet had been pounding it sway south at twenty-four knots. While Fedorov had his last visit with the Admiral and Doctor, Tovey's battleships were already off the coast of Brest. There German reconnaissance planes spotted the fleet, and telephones were soon jangling as the Germans tried to surmise what this big fleet movement was all about. They had already been spooked by Operation Pedestal, with strong opinions that the British were planning an imminent amphibious operation on the coast of North Africa. These ships must be mustering for that operation, they now believed, and began to strengthen their defenses all along that coast.

Kirov lingered well north of Menorca while U-73 slipped quietly away to the northeast, heading home. At one point they saw the U-boat on their powerful surface radar sets, and Karpov had a second chance to think about killing it with a missile. He decided the boat was not worth the expense, and let Rosenbaum go. In his mind, however, there was no calculus of what may or may not happen at some future date, nor was there any musing over life and death. It was simply a matter of economics at that point. *Kirov* needed her anti-ship missiles for what lay ahead of them now, not what lay behind.

At noon Fedorov came off his rest shift and the two men were again together on the bridge for an hour before Karpov would take his rest. Fedorov now had one more weighty decision to make, and he decided to sound Karpov out on the matter.

"Here is the situation," he said quietly. "Force Z is now withdrawing towards Gibraltar. If we put on speed we might be able to beat them there, but I think it would be very close, and we would have to run at thirty knots from our present location to have any chance at all. I was going to turn south and run west of Palma, but I have now plotted another route southwest aimed at Cabo de Nao, Spain, and from there we would race down the Spanish coast past Cartagena and then enter the Alboran Sea south of Almeria. On the other hand, Force Z will be well west of Oran by that time, and if we are spotted, which is likely given the air traffic in this region, they will probably be vectored in to engage us."

"This means we fight these ships in the Alboran Sea, and not in the Straits of Gibraltar," said Karpov.

"Correct, but we could also take a more deliberate route at normal cruising speed and in this event they would reach Gibraltar ahead of us. We could then wait in the Alboran Sea and see what Admiral Volsky decides about these negotiations we spoke of earlier. It would then be his decision as to how we proceed."

Karpov thought for a moment. "From a military viewpoint, I would much rather fight this Force Z with good sea room, and in a situation where we can make the best use of our strengths—speed and ranged firepower. Yes, we may be spotted as we move south, but we will also see them easily enough, and I can engage at good range with our cruise missiles. Then perhaps we could have Nikolin order them to yield and if they have taken enough of a pounding, like the Italians, we could then transit the straits and leave them in our wake."

"I understand," said Fedorov, "but taking that course is almost certain to result in an engagement. It will not be easy to negotiate with them while we are hurling our missiles at their ships to keep them at bay. I think they will be slightly ahead of us, even if we run at top speed now."

"Then why waste time," said Karpov. "They may be ahead when we draw near, but from that moment our speed is decisive. We will overtake them and leave them in our wake, but to do this we need sea room if we are to stay outside the range of these sixteen inch guns you talk about all the time. Let's get the ship moving and see if we can win this race!"

"My inclination is to wait," said Fedorov, and he immediately saw Karpov's frustration increase a notch.

"Alright, Fedorov... I learned where our U-boat friend was after I came on duty. Hiding in that little bay, eh? And Nikolin told me you had the KA-40 right on top of the bastard and then just ordered it back to the ship. Alright," he held up a hand, head cocked to one side, "I let that pass. I understand why you decided to let him go. In fact, we saw the boat on radar later when it surfaced, and I could have finished it myself. I just didn't want to waste a missile. But *this*—this is something entirely different. If we have a chance to outrun these British ships, then we should take it. All we have to do is put enough damage on them to slow them down. They won't be able to touch us, and we'll win through. What are you waiting for?"

Fedorov looked at him trying to think his way through this. "But can we really use measured force here? It will be close, Captain. If we have any further difficulties—an air strike, another submarine, a mechanical problem, we will not get past them in the Alboran Sea."

"But we should at least try," said Karpov, though he could see the reluctance and hesitation in Fedorov's eyes. He pressed him further.

"What do you want to do—go to Volsky with this? How much time will that take, an hour? Two hours? And by then we will have lost our chance. *You* are captain of this ship now, Fedorov. I know this was the last thing you ever expected when that honor came to you, but Volsky is asleep in the sick bay and you are standing on the bridge. Now I have given you my best tactical advice, and I will follow and support any course you take here, but think carefully, Fedorov. Do you honestly think the British will negotiate with us? How much do we tell them? How many questions will they have before they are satisfied? You think they will just calmly agree to let us sail through the Straits of Gibraltar and go merrily on our way? *Think,* Fedorov. You know these men. You have studied them in your history books all your life. Look what they are doing this very moment to the south of us, risking half their fleet to save five merchant ships for Malta. That tells you everything you will ever need to know about them. What are they going to do when we come sailing up to Gibraltar with a white flag flying and ask them to kindly step aside? What did they do at Mers-el-Kebir? What did they do against *Bismarck?* Negotiate?"

Fedorov lowered his head, beset with what he knew to be the truth in the Captain's hard words. That was one thing about Karpov—he was a grim realist. Fedorov had indeed studied this war, and the men who fought it, for many, many years. They were an entirely different breed. He remembered how he had tried to explain this to Zolkin in the sick bay when he was hoping to prevent Karpov from attacking the American fleet. And now Karpov was making the very same argument—that these men were of a different mettle, they were exceptional, that they would not hesitate or equivocate or accept anything less than complete victory. They would stand, stalwart, implacable at Gibraltar and bar the way. They would become the very things they named their ships at sea: *Indomitable, Victorious, Furious.* This was the British Empire. This was the Royal Navy. These were men of character, backbone and unflinching courage. They would not give way in the niceties of discussion. They were going to want to know what *Kirov* was, where she came from, and so very much more, and they would not be satisfied until they had their answer. Karpov was right, but now that he stood at the edge of it, he could not decide what to do.

The captain saw his hesitation, and spoke one last time. "Fedorov, if we negotiate then *they* will decide our fate, but don't you understand? If we act now then the choice is ours—we become the very thing we hope to win from them with reasons and arguments— *we become fate itself,* Fedorov, and the future is ours to decide." He had given his last argument. Now he stood up straight, took a deep breath and looked Fedorov in the eye, as an equal this time, waiting.

Fedorov thought he knew what they had to do, what they *should* do. Karpov's words were a challenge, a gauntlet thrown down that could change everything from this moment forward. He had been so certain in his mind before, but now it was coming down to something else entirely. What *must* they do to save themselves, and save the future intact to have a world to live in again? Could he find a way to achieve both?

He decided.

Chapter 23

Orlov sulked in his quarters, still burning with the humiliation forced upon him by Troyak, and thinking how he might even the score one day. No one put their hands on him like that. No one! He was Gennadi Orlov, Chief of the Boat! At least he once was, after years and years of slogging up through the ranks. Now he was busted back to a stinking lieutenant, along with all the other stinking lieutenants, and his recent demotion still weighed heavily upon him. More than that, he hated the fact that Karpov still held forth in a command role on the bridge while he had been discarded to the aft maintenance bay, and put under Troyak with his Marine detachment. He wasn't used to taking orders from anyone junior to himself, either, and the thought that dog eared Fedorov was actually acting Captain of the ship galled him as well.

His only satisfaction since his release from the brig had been the brief measure of face he had won back by leading the effort to jettison the burning KA-40, though it had been short lived. His old habits of bullying and deriding the men in the ranks soon grew even worse now, almost as if he needed to have someone there in the pecking order below him to make him feel stronger, better, more privileged, even if he knew his career and life had gone to shit. The brief respect he had won from the other men that day had quickly been overshadowed by his innate bad temper and disagreeable disposition, and the others seemed to shun him now, seeing that everywhere Orlov went some kind of trouble eventually followed.

He still blamed Karpov for his misfortunes, and had some small gratification when he had eventually cornered the devious captain outside the mess hall and put a fist in his belly, but he doubted he would get away with anything like that again. He should have killed him, then and there, he thought.

Yes, I could have choked the living breath out of that weasel of a man, and left him dead right there outside the mess hall, he thought. No...That would have been another mistake, eh? Too many men saw what you did when you spilled that drink on his jacket. It would have come back to you too quickly, and you would be rotting in the brig again.

He was sitting at his small desk, thankful at least that they had not yet taken away his officer's quarters. On the desk before him he stared at a well oiled pistol he had been cleaning between swigs from a small flask of vodka that he had hidden away in his locker. His life was going to be one miserable step and fetch it after another now, with Troyak hovering over him like a shadow every minute of the day. He was not a trained soldier. He had never gone through combat drills. Why did Volsky stick him here with the Marines? He knew why, and it only soured his mood further as he ruminated. It only made him feel more useless when he was assigned to the engineering section, and issued a tool box instead of a rifle and helmet. Now he was supposed to become a dutiful grease monkey and rig out all the helicopters, and that was bullshit too.

What would he ever find again on this damn ship but the drudgery of daily work and menial servitude to skunks like Karpov and choir boys like Fedorov? And now any time he said anything there would be Troyak, that bastard Siberian, rock like, immovable, fearsome. He was going to have to do something about it, but he did not yet know what it was.

As he stared at the pistol in his hand he realized how stupid Volsky and the others had been. They never even bothered to search his cabin! What, did they think he was just going to fall in line with the *Mishmanny* and *Starshini* down here and eat shit for the rest of his life? Oh, no, he was going to do something, that much was certain, and as he slipped one bullet after another into the ammo clip, an idea came to him at last. It was as if his own wretched condition had brought him to the edge of a cliff in his mind, and his sorry, decrepit soul had finally thrown down a gauntlet, daring him to jump.... daring him to jump... Yes! That was it!

Yes! To hell with Troyak, and Karpov and Fedorov and fat Volsky too. To hell with them all. To hell with this damn ship and everyone on it! He pushed home the ammo clip with a hard snap, holding the pistol in one hand, and the vodka in the other. The loose ends of a dark and exciting idea were milling about in his head, like the ragged strips of the bandages on his hands, and he finally knew what to do.

~~~

Admiral Syfret looked out on the remnants of Force Z, still harried by reports coming in from the action he was leaving behind. It galled him to cut and run like this. Still, he held fast to the thought of those brave men fighting their way around Cape Bon, and down past Pantelleria with those infernal E-Boats nipping at them every step of the way and those vulture-like Stukas overhead, screeching in on them as they dove for the kill.

He looked at the time, weary already, and it was only noon. His haggard ships were already past Algiers, and dangerously close to the coast in his mind, but he had received further cables advising him to take the most direct route possible to Gibraltar, and make all haste. Thus far they had been snooped out by a few high flying reconnaissance planes, and no doubt they've had a look at my three aircraft carriers to give the buggers second thoughts about launching an air strike on his ships.

What in the world was going on back at the Rock, he still wondered? Did Fraser over on *Rodney* know anything about it? He had half a mind to get him on the wireless and have a talk, but as Fraser was the Deputy Commander of Home Fleet itself, and traveling incognito, he discarded that idea.

Nelson and *Rodney*, were the heart of his task force, making all the speed they could given *Rodney's* dodgy boilers and steering gear. He reckoned it at eighteen knots, which would put Force Z off Oran at 18:00 hours that evening. Thereafter the danger from enemy air strikes should diminish as he came within the patrol range of friendly aircraft from Gibraltar to augment the fighters he still had with his carriers. The Fleet Air Arm had lost twelve fighters in combat, and another sixteen went into the sea when HMS *Eagle* went down. Six more were on the *Argus*, which was already back in Gibraltar.

That left him with 36 Sea Harrier and Martlet fighters, and another 42 Albacore strike aircraft spread out among his three remaining carriers. *Victorious* had also been lucky today. The Italians slipped in a pair of fighters that were mistaken for British Sea Harriers and not fired upon as they approached the carrier. When they suddenly peeled off and dove to make bomb runs, one fighter scored a near miss, while the other planted a bomb square of the ship's forward armored flight deck. It took a good bounce, but did not go off, and so he was lucky to have these ships intact and ready for further operations.

He stared out the view screen, down the long ponderous foredeck of *Nelson*, her three big main batteries all mounted forward of the bridge. This was the only battleship class in the fleet where that was the case—all guns forward, no guns aft. You would think the designers thought to make this a pursuit ship, he mused, though they neglected to give her anything near the speed required for that.

He squinted at the hapless destroyer *Ithuriel* off his starboard quarter. Her captain had been a bit too rash when they encountered an Italian sub surfaced near the task force, and he went charging in to ram the damn thing, disabling the sub but also mangling his bow in the process. Syfret took a dim view of that. What? Don't these men realize that we've put deck guns on their destroyers? There had been two ramming incidents on this operation, and he was quite unhappy with both. He would have words with this Captain Crichton when they got back to Gibraltar.

The bridge phone rang and a midshipman indicated that there was a call from HMS *Rodney* on the wireless. That was odd, he thought as he went to the wireless room to see about it. To his great surprise, it was Deputy Commander of the Home Fleet, Admiral Fraser.

"Good day, Neville" came the voice. *"Sorry to interrupt lunch, but there's been a development."*

"I assumed as much," said Syfret.

"Yes, well I haven't got all the details yet, but Admiralty contacted me directly and asked me to brief you. Hush, hush and all. Now I won't say anything more on the wireless, but if you would be kind enough to let Rodney come up on your starboard side, I'll swim on over for tea and fill you in. And, oh yes, after this we're to lock everything down and go W/T silent."

Syfret raised an eyebrow at that. W/T stood for 'Wireless Transmission,' and apparently this would be the last authorized transmission until further notice.

"I'll put the word out, Admiral," he said. "And we'll fall off to 10 knots while you come aboard. It will be Earl Grey at 15:00. One lump or two?"

"Straight up for me, Admiral. I think we've already had our sugar on this outing. But more on that later. That's is all."

~~~

Fedorov was standing tensely on the bridge of *Kirov*, his mind finally set. The surge of adrenalin thrummed in his chest, and he pursed his lips tightly, jaw set. Karpov waited, holding his breath, and then Fedorov turned to the helm and gave an order.

"Helm. Come round to two-three-zero degrees southwest and ahead full," he said, a slight tremor in his voice.

"Aye, sir, my rudder is left and coming around for steady on two-three-zero. Speed thirty knots."

He turned to Karpov, noting a jaunty glint in his eye. "Captain, you have your race. We'll hold this course until about 17:thirty hours, then come left to 200 degrees and run past Cabo de la Nao and southwest to Cartagena. From there its back on 225 for the run into the Alboran Sea. Force Z has a good lead on us, and is probably near Algiers by now. By the time we make our next turn they should be approaching Oran. We might be able to pick them up on the long range radar, but if we can't see them, I think we should send up the scout helo to have a look south. I want to nail down their position, course and speed so I can calculate our best course from that point. And I'm saving those last two knots just to keep something in reserve if we need it." *Kirov* could make all of 32 knots if pressed to full battle speed.

Karpov smiled. "You have made the right decision, Captain." He said it proudly now, his eyes alight as he clasped Fedorov on the shoulder. "Now you know," he continued. "Now you know what it's like."

"We'll have some quiet for the next ten to twelve hours, I think," said Fedorov. "I've made my decision, but I think it best I inform the Admiral. Understand that if he countermands my order…"

Karpov shrugged. Volsky… There was yet one more hurtle they had to leap, as if the long race south to a near certain rendezvous with a British battle fleet was not enough. His first thought was to accompany Fedorov and put in his opinion on the matter, but then he realized that this was Fedorov's bone to chew. He had asked him to stand up and be Captain of the ship, and he did so. He would leave the matter to him.

"I think the Admiral will listen to your reasoning, Fedorov. He respects you, and that is worth a great deal. Give him your mind on this matter, and Volsky will do what he thinks best. I've come to a new understanding of the man. Yes, he may take the reins from your grasp again soon, but as you walk down to sick bay, feel them in your hands, Fedorov. You are riding the tiger's back now. Yes? And you will never forget it."

"Very well, Captain. Can you hold here for a few more minutes? I'll relieve you at zero-one-hundred hours."

"Aye, aye, sir."

Karpov raised two fingers in a brief salute. Then he turned to the *mishman* and said in a clear voice: "Captain off the bridge!"

The men saluted as he went, and yes, he never would forget how it felt—so very different this time. He *was* the Captain. Not just one of three or four officers on the ship who held varying degrees of that rank. He was the Captain of *Kirov*, flagship of the Northern Fleet, and it felt good.

He was not long reaching the sick bay, and found Admiral Volsky looking much better on the cot, his cheeks reddening up again, eyes brighter, and that look of agonizing pain gone from his face.

"Mister Fedorov!" The Admiral greeted him, "You have just missed another good meal."

"Something tells me he has a nose for good borscht," said Zolkin. "They made it right this time, cooked it up yesterday so all the flavors would blend correctly—carrots, parsnips, turnips, good cabbage and of course, the roasted beets!"

"It smells wonderful," said Fedorov. He removed his cap and took a deep breath.

"Sir," he began. "I have increased to thirty knots with the aim of trying to reach our objective before the British fleet can return to Gibraltar." He stood stiffly, hat tucked under his arm, waiting.

Volsky was still cleaning his hands with a white linen napkin. "I see," he said. "Go on, Mister Fedorov."

The young captain explained his reasoning, and Volsky listened quietly, saying nothing. "It will be close," he said. "Even at thirty knots we may not get by them in time, but I won't know that until I have an exact fix on their position, course and speed."

"And how close will we be to this Force Z? " He looked at Zolkin for a moment. "It sounds dangerous, eh Dmitri? Force Z."

"That will depend on a number of things," said Fedorov, "whether they have sighted us and marked our heading; their position, their orders, and perhaps even their curiosity may all figure in the mix. But I must be honest and say that there is not much room in the Alboran Sea. We will be in the bottle neck, but there is still much more room there than we will find at Gibraltar in the straits."

"Assuming we can get by them, we will of course outrun these ships?"

"Their big ships, yes. The battleships would have no chance to catch up with us if we take the lead in this race. They could pursue with their lighter ships, but not far, and they are much less a threat to us than those 16 inch guns. We have a number of factors in our favor sir. They have the lead at the moment, but I checked the service records on the battleships. HMS *Rodney* is having trouble with her boilers and steering mechanism. It has been an ongoing problem with the ship for the last several months and it was aggravated with all the maneuvering required when the convoy came under air attack. I would be surprised if she was capable of any more than fifteen knots, and we have twice her speed now. *Nelson* could probably get up twenty knots, but I think they would want to keep their battleships together."

"Agreed," said Volsky. "And what other cards do you see us holding?"

"We may have an advantage of surprise. They may not have a fix on us and our sudden appearance could hamper their response. Then we could try our ruse as a French ship and perhaps buy a few crucial minutes, or even hours. It is my intention to go in weapons tight unless we are immediately threatened. I want to use our speed, sir. That is our primary weapon now." He paused a moment, then nodded as he spoke.

"Of course I understand you were considering negotiations, Admiral. I must tell you that I have come round to the belief that they will be fruitless. I cannot see the British taking any less than days to sort this out with us, and one question will likely pile in on top of another. There will be no expedient solution for us in my opinion. If, however, you wish to countermand my decision, I will support you in any way I can during any negotiation you may choose to initiate. For now, I have chosen to act first, and talk later if we must. If I have made an error, sir we can reduce to twenty knots at any time."

Volsky looked at him, a smile brightening in his eyes. "No, Mister Fedorov. You have made no error. You have made a command decision, and I will support *you*. You have my approval to carry out your planned operation, but please keep me informed."

Fedorov stood just a little taller. "I will, sir. Thank you, sir." He smiled. "Then if you will excuse me, Admiral, I must check with Dobrynin and make certain we can run at high speed without any difficulties, and then I am scheduled to relieve Mister Karpov on the bridge."

Chapter 24

Admiral Fraser settled into his chair in the officer's wardroom aboard HMS *Nelson*, exhilarated by his recent transit to the ship, his cheeks and brow still red, the tang of the sea in his nose, and eyes alight. He took a moment to compose himself while the orderly brought in the afternoon tea. It was just as Admiral Syfret had promised him—Earl Grey, nice and hot.

Fraser was a fast rising star in the Royal Navy. He had served with distinction in the First World War, an expert in naval gunnery, and he supervised the internment of the German High Seas Fleet when that conflict concluded. His broad experience included a stint on the carrier *Glorious*, service as Chief of Staff for the Mediterranean Fleet, Third Sea Lord, and Knight Commander of the Order of the Bath. History would record that he would lead the British Battleship *Duke of York* and sink the German raider *Scharnhorst* in late 1943 before moving to a post in the Pacific Fleet, and he would one day sign the instrument of Japan's surrender on behalf of the British Empire aboard the battleship *Missouri* in Tokyo Bay. History, however, had a way of taking some very unexpected turns, though Fraser could not know that as he sat down for tea that afternoon.

"Well, Neville, it seems we've got a bit of a mystery on our hands. I know you were in the thickets back there, and had a mind to see it through just a little longer, but I received the same orders as you undoubtedly have, to turn about at once and make all speed for Gibraltar."

"I certainly hope you're going to tell me why, Sir Bruce," said Syfret. The two men had known each other for many years, and were accustomed to drop the formalities of rank and protocol when they met. They had shared many a toast and tea together, though seldom under circumstances such as these. "What, has there been a problem with this Operation Jubilee? I thought it was not to be mounted until this convoy was seen through to Malta and we could get Force H reconstituted at Gibraltar and in position to lend a hand if needed. You know we've been rather beaten up out there. They threw planes at us by the bushel, and God bless those boys in the carrier fighter squadrons, they were absolutely superb."

"Quite so," said Fraser, his sandy hair now white with his years, but his ruddy features still giving him an animated life and energy. He turned to the orderly, who was standing by the doorway in attendance. "That will be all, young man."

"Very good, sir." The man saluted, and quietly left the two men alone. When he had gone Fraser leaned forward and lowered his voice nonetheless, an air of caution about him now.

"No, it has nothing to do with Operation Jubilee—in fact that whole party has been cancelled. Sixty squadrons set back on their rumps at home, and the whole fleet up in a tither over something else."

"Something else? Do go on, Sir Bruce."

"Neville, I must first apologize that you will have no inkling of what I'm about to say here. Nobody knows everything, I suppose, and for that matter I only learned about this business when I assumed my post as Deputy Commander Home Fleet when Daddy Brind shipped over to the Admiralty as Assistant Chief of the Naval Staff. I'm just getting my feet wet, you see, and I never expected to hear very much more about the matter, but it concerns that incident a year ago south of Iceland. I'm sure you've heard something about it." He smiled politely.

"I knew *Repulse* never came home," Syfret said sullenly, "and we all saw the damage to *King George V* and *Prince of Wales*. I must say I made inquiries about it back then, but I'm old enough to know when a door's being closed in my face, and so I shut up and let the matter go."

"You heard the rumors, of course."

"The rocketry? Some new German raider raising hell out there. It was hard not hear about it. Word has spread round through every bar and brothel in the Kingdom by now. But sailors say a lot of things, don't they. We were told to squeeze the necks of any man we caught spreading such rumors, and I dare say I've squeezed quite a few."

Fraser nodded, taking a long sip of his tea and setting down the cup. "Well I'm to tell you that these rumors have more substance to them than we were first led to believe," he said. "In point of fact, most every last one was the gospel truth. There was a ship, a German ship we believe, and there was quite a row at sea when Home Fleet went hunting for it a year ago. As you know, the Americans were in on it as well, and they were hurt even worse. You've read the papers."

"Yes, that torpedo attack on the *Mississippi*. A stroke of good luck for us, if you want my mind on it. Brought the Yanks right in on our side just as Sir Winston was hoping."

"Yes…well there was no torpedo attack…"

Syfret raised an eyebrow, realizing that Fraser was now getting round to the front door on the matter. "No torpedo attack?"

"It was something else," said Fraser. "Bletchley Park says it was one of Herr Hitler's wonder weapons. You know he's got these rockets on the drawing boards, of all sorts. Well he's also got one bloody hell of a warhead to mount on them. Why do you think we've scattered command elements all over the Kingdom in the last year? What do you make of those underground bunkers they've been building in the Scottish Highlands?"

"I thought they were to be for munitions stores."

"So did I, until they started trucking in desks and telephone equipment, and all the other accouterments that clutter up the Admiralty offices. They've been spreading the butter and jam thin, Neville, because they don't want everything together if another of these rockets comes thundering in on Whitehall one day."

"I see… But what has this to do with our present orders, Sir Bruce? Why the rush home to Gibraltar?"

"Neville, this new General Montgomery is stiffening up the line at Al Alamein, and we think we can keep Rommel out of Alexandria for the time being. So that means Suez is safe—at least for the moment. Now, you've done your damndest to secure Malta, and in spite of the losses I think we got enough through to keep them running a few more months there. It's a pity it cost us so much, what with *Manchester, Nigeria, Cairo* and others all gutted, and losing *Eagle* was a hard blow. But Burrough will be turning west in about three hours with the remainder of his Force X, and Admiralty has indicated to me that Operation Pedestal is now of secondary importance." He tapped his finger on his tea cup as he spoke, his mind running on.

"Operation Jubilee is cancelled, and now all the plans for Operation Torch are up in the air as well. It's come down to this, Neville. The threat now is to Gibraltar…" he left that on the table for a moment, sipping his tea and noting Syfret's reaction.

"A threat to Gibraltar? Have the Spanish thrown in with Hitler after all?"

"No, Franco wants none of that. It's something else, a matter for the Royal Navy, which brings us round to our orders again. It seems there's another ship at large—right here in the Med. 248 Squadron got a look at it a few days ago. Park sent film through Gibraltar and it ran all the way into Bletchley Park. I'm not quite sure how just yet, but it apparently has something to do with this incident we had a year ago off Iceland. They've slapped a code word on it and we're to be ready to oppose any and all unauthorized sea traffic approaching Gibraltar. You're to go to full battle readiness at the first sign of any contact at sea, and they want your planes to begin searching north and northwest of our present position at once."

"I see," said Syfret, setting down his tea. "Forgive me if I seem a bit thick, sir, but what are we looking for?"

"A ship—a battlecruiser of sorts—the very same ship our 248 squadron took a nip at two days ago. We lost four of six Beaufighters, you know."

"I heard the report, but had more on my plate to worry about and dismissed it."

"Yes… well it was the *way* we lost these planes that got the Admiralty all rankled. They were shot down by rocketry, Neville. There's another ship out there, and it's heading our way. That first sighting was in the Tyrrhenian Sea, and apparently this ship ran up north and on through the Bonifacio Strait."

"An Italian ship?"

"That's what we thought at first, but there was an engagement off the western approaches to Bonifacio that set Admiralty on its head. This ship tangled with a couple of Italian battleships, and came off the better for it. I was only informed this morning."

"Then it must be a French ship," said Syfret. "They've been goading the Vichy Fleet to Join Admiral Darlan for some time."

"That was my opinion as well, but Admiralty isn't sure. A few things add up. If it was a Vichy French ship it might be likely to take a shot at anything that came in range. That much makes sense. Then again, it might be a renegade ship and crew making a run out of Toulon. Nobody knows for sure, but we do know one thing, this ship is heading our way, and we're to see that it gets nowhere near Gibraltar."

"Well if it drove off a pair of Italian battleships it would have to be the *Dunkerque, Strausbourg,* or perhaps even both. Then again, *Dunkerque* took quite a pounding at Mers-el Kebir. *Ark Royal* put a torpedo into her a few days later for good measure. It would have to be *Strasbourg.* She got clean away in that incident, and was still seaworthy. Probably the only ship the French still have that might have a chance against the Italians like that."

"This is what I suggested, but Admiralty isn't sure."

"What do you mean they aren't sure? What else could it be?"

"They haven't been able to get a long range reconnaissance flight over Toulon to see if all the eggs are still in the nest, and until they do, well, you know the routine."

"Too well, I'm afraid."

"Right then. They've given this ship, or ships, a codename— calling it *Geronimo.* That is to be kept close to your vest and not shared with anyone without this nice thick stripe on his cuff." He pointed to his own cuff insignia, the thick gold base braid that indicated Admiral. "This ship appears to be heading our way, and they want us to find it and say hello. We'll have company soon. Admiral Tovey is at sea this very moment with Home Fleet."

"I see…" That last bit surprised Syfret. "Do you think that is really necessary? I certainly hope we won't have another incident with the French, Sir Bruce. Wasn't Mers-el-Kebir enough of a thumb in their eye?"

"If it comes down to it, your orders are to stop this ship, by whatever means. It may be running for Dakar, but it is not to approach Gibraltar. Supposing it is a renegade French ship, we have yet to know who's side it might end up on. *Strausbourg* has eight big guns, all forward, and it seems to fit the general profile of this *Geronimo*—one main tower amidships, and a smaller one behind. I'd hate to see those 13 inch guns lobbing shells at Gibraltar. If we do have a disaffected captain out there, he may be looking to stick us one for Mers-el-Kebir."

Fraser was referring to the regrettable but necessary decision by Admiral Somerville to order the British Fleet, Force H out of Gibraltar in fact, to fire on the French fleet at Mers-el-Kebir on Aboukir Bay when they refused to surrender.

"Some feel that the French may have even gotten wind of this Operation Torch, and that this might be some sort of preemptive action against Gibraltar, or even an attempt to reinforce their forces in North Africa."

"I see, " said Syfret, thinking for a moment. "*Strausbourg* can run up near thirty knots, Sir Bruce. You're aware of the situation with *Rodney*. We've been lucky to make eighteen knots today."

"And it's likely we'll have to trim that to fifteen knots. Those boilers are insufferable, but we'll have to keep pushing on as best we can. It's imperative that we get the cork in the bottle before this ship breaks through to Gibraltar."

Fraser had put the best possible explanation to the mystery, and if he knew any more than he said, he wasn't prepared to share it at the moment. Yet he reinforced the one message he had come to deliver here, leaning in to emphasize his point. "We're to sink this ship if she won't heave to, Admiral." The added formality made it plain that this was an order.

"Very good, sir. If we get in front of them I think *Nelson* and *Rodney* can handle the matter."

"Right you are." Fraser's tea was cold and he stared listlessly at the half empty cup. He knew that Tovey was heading south as well with a lot more firepower to throw in, though he couldn't imagine why if this was, indeed, the *Strausbourg* as he suspected. It seemed entirely too much bother for a lone French battleship, but there it was. The Admiralty obviously knew, or at least believed, that this *Geronimo* was more of a threat than it seemed in his own mind. The fact that they cancelled Operation Jubilee was one surprise. Now he reasoned that the potential threat to the Operation Torch landing may be behind it all. If this French renegade were to add steel to the Vichy bastions on the North African coast it could become quite a problem. Still, this business about the rocketry was dangling like a badly tied shoe at inspection. He sighed heavily, sitting back in his chair.

"The world is going to hell, Neville. The whole bloody world is mixed up in this war now."

"Sadly so, sir Bruce," said Syfret, reaching for the tea pot to warm his friend's cup. "But at least we've got our tea."

Part IX

Desertion

*"Desperation is the raw material of drastic change.
Only those who can leave behind everything they have
ever believed in can hope to escape."*

~ *William S. Burroughs*

Chapter 25

At 18:00 hours Orlov got the word he had been waiting for. They wanted the KA-226 scout helo rigged for takeoff and mounted with the new *Oko 901-M* early warning radar panel. The *Oko*, or 'Eye,' was first deployed on the older KA-31 around the turn of the century, and the 901 model was a more compact panel that was mounted on the underside of the fuselage and could be deployed by the pilot to a assume a vertical position in flight. It would rotate slowly, and provided a 360° azimuthal coverage. The surveillance range against a fighter aircraft target was up to 150 kilometers, and for ships this range could extend to 200 kilometers.

Apparently someone on the bridge wanted to have a look around, he thought. When he heard the work order come down, he rushed to his quarters under the pretense that he was going to get the proper tools to rig the device, inwardly rubbing his hands together, and sure that this was his one last chance to do what he had planned.

Back in the helicopter bay below the flight deck he supervised the installation of the *Oko* panel, as he had many times in the past, occasionally taking a tool in hand and making adjustments. The two able seamen also assigned to his engineering detail pretty much wanted to stay out of his way, and no one said anything when he blustered about their sloppy work and claimed he was going to have to board the helo for the mission to make sure the damn thing deployed properly. He pointed a spanner at Ludvich, always finding a scapegoat first unless something really went wrong. Then he donned a flight jacket and helmet, muttering to himself as he boarded the helo. The pilot looked over his shoulder, surprised to see Orlov in the rear compartment.

"What are you doing, Lieutenant? There's supposed to be a Marine guard aboard."

"Don't call me Lieutenant, Pratkin, you stupid oaf. Haven't you heard? I'm in the Marines now, so get moving. Our baby faced Captain wanted this helo up ten minutes ago. If you want to make sure your damn radar panel deploys, be glad I'm here with my tools. Those idiots used the wrong control cables and I will have to work on it in flight. See?" He held up a fistful of tightly wound cabling, grinning balefully at the pilot, who just shook his head and radioed the aft helo con tower for permission to take off. Minutes later the KA-226 was aloft and heading south with orders to get some seventy to a hundred kilometers out and sweep the area for signs of a large enemy task force.

Fedorov was still on the bridge when Karpov arrived to begin his next shift. He was consulting with Kalinichev at radar and waved his first officer over.

"We turned on our planned heading of 200 degrees about thirty minutes ago, he said. The ship's radar might pick up Force Z soon, but I need information now. I've sent the KA-226 up with an *Oko* panel and we'll have a good look to the south. My best guess is that Force Z is some 225 kilometers southwest of our position now, and most likely approaching Oran. We should be getting some good signal returns from the helo in about twenty to thirty minutes."

"What about the enemy carriers," said Karpov. "Won't they have fighters up?"

"Probably, but they won't get a whiff of our KA-226. Remember, it's also got good jamming equipment, and I had it re-tuned to include British aerial radar bandwidths six hours ago. The game is on now, Mister Karpov. We want to find and mark their position as soon as possible, and keep them in the dark about our whereabouts at the same time. If they do happen to spot a British fighter, they can easily avoid it, and that failing, they will have to shoot it down."

The helo could mount interchangeable mission pods in the space that would normally be the rear cabin. This load out would include a thirty mm cannon and also air-to-air and light surface attack missiles. The *Oko* panel was mounted beneath this cabin and controlled by connecting utility cables. They waited while Nikolin monitored the routine signal feed from the helo, and routed it to the ship's main radar systems. Kalinichev was also watching the progress of the helo on his air search radar.

"Tell them it looks like they are a little too far west," he said over his shoulder, and Nikolin passed the message on a secure, encrypted radio channel. His voice was digitized, then encrypted for the transmission and decoded on the helo to play on the pilot's speakers. Anyone who might manage to intercept the signal would just hear garbage.

"Command one to KA-226. You are too far west. Resume heading of one-eight-zero and deploy your panel for radar sweep—over."

The helo was too far west for a good reason, or a bad one depending on whose perspective you took in the matter. Orlov had been sitting in the back compartment, and drinking from a flask as they moved south. He waited patiently, until the helo was about a hundred kilometers out, then took a long swig on his flask and pulled out his pistol.

"Are you ready back there, Lieutenant? It's time to deploy the radar panel."

"I told you *not* to call me Lieutenant," Orlov growled. "Am I ready?" Orlov grinned. "Oh yes, I'm ready. Are *you* ready, Pratkin?" And without a second thought he pulled the trigger and put a bullet right through Pratkin's head. The pilot slumped forward, and for a moment the helo danced wildly in the sky, but Orlov quickly scrambled into the co-pilot seat up front and seized the controls. He had taken some rudimentary flight training on the KA-226 years ago, as he often was tasked as a mission leader when the Marines would deploy on the chopper. Now he struggled to remember what he had to do to stabilize the helo and get it moving where he wanted it to go.

Orlov managed to gain control before the aircraft got a mind of its own, and he nudged it into a slow turn to the west, and put on speed. Then he picked up the auxiliary microphone from the flight instrument panel and sent Nikolin back a message of his own. "I'm sorry, sir, but I won't be deploying your damn radar today. You lose, Nikolin." He shut the system down, laughing. Then he looked over at the limp body of the pilot, saw the blood oozing from the bullet hole in his head, and laughed again. "What do you say we take a little vacation, Pratkin? Because that's the last either one of us are ever going to see of that stinking ship and crew."

He suddenly remembered something very important, and reached down to turn off his transponder and activate all his jamming gear at full power. The last thing he wanted now was a visit from one of *Kirov's* lethal surface to air missiles.

Back on the bridge Nikolin had a shocked expression on his face. He looked for Fedorov and reported. "Sir…that was Orlov on the radio just now, and he says they cannot deploy the radar panel."

"Orlov? He wasn't assigned to that mission. He was just supposed to lead the rigging and load out. What's he doing on that helo?" He shook his head, looking at Karpov and seeing his eyes narrow with suspicion.

"Tell them to report. What is the trouble with the radar panel?"

"I can't, sir. I've lost all telemetry. It looks like he switched off his transponder. The whole band is garbled now."

"Garbled?"

Kalinichev saw the telemetry feed terminate on his board and also immediately recognized the jamming signatures clouding his screen. "He switched on his jamming pods, sir, I can't see him any longer."

"What was his last recorded heading?" asked Fedorov quickly.

"It looked like he turned west sir. That's all I was able to get before the signal clouded over."

Fedorov looked at Karpov and saw that his suspicion had become a flash of anger now. "That bastard," he said. "What in God's name does he think he's doing?"

"Are you saying he did this deliberately?" Fedorov was stunned. He knew Orlov was an irascible and cantankerous officer, unruly and undisciplined, yes, and downright disrespectful at times, but this was more than he ever expected from him.

"If he's heading west he's making for the Spanish coast," said Karpov. "I should've known he was up to no good! Do you realize he actually assaulted me outside the officer's mess yesterday? The man is insane!"

"He assaulted you?"

"Yes, a good punch in the ribs. I suppose he thought I had it coming, and perhaps I did. He didn't like being stuck down there in the engineering bay. I think we have a renegade on our hands, Fedorov. I don't think he has any intention of returning to the ship."

"But… He *can't* take the helo like this! What in the world is he trying to do? Where could he possibly be going?"

"Spain," Karpov said flatly. "It's the only neutral land close enough, and with his jammers running full out like this he knows we can't see him or shoot him down. That lunatic is planning to take that helicopter and land there."

"That's crazy," said Fedorov, and his mind was awhirl with the consequences of what could happen if the helicopter were to be taken by the authorities there. "Do you realize what this means? We'll have to go after him, Karpov. We can't let him do this. That technology must not fall into the hands of any other living soul."

"I don't think we'll find him easily sir," said Karpov. "Not in the short run. Look at your map. That's fairly hilly country north and west of Cartagena. He could set down anywhere in those mountains, and it might take us days to find him. He's obviously planned this very well. Who knows what he is going to do? Perhaps the lunatic doesn't even know himself."

Fedorov was deeply concerned now. This was something totally unexpected, that one insane moment in the flow of events that could simply not be predicted no matter how carefully he had planned his course to the south. All he could think about was what effect this would have on all the history from this point forward. If Orlov survived, how might he changed things? He knew he was not an educated man, yet Orlov knew enough to cause real havoc if the information about days yet to come would ever be believed by anyone he encountered. Believed and acted upon...

Yet worse than this was the presence of the helicopter itself here in the middle of World War II. No matter how skillfully Orlov set it down, perhaps on some remote hilltop, one day it would be found and that discovery would have a dramatic and incalculable effect on the history. He lowered his head confused, angry, and frustrated. It was hard enough trying to learn how to command the ship when he had never been trained for such a position. He relied on the support of the Admiral, Captain Karpov, and his good officers here on the bridge. All it takes is one bad apple, he thought, and Orlov was as sour as they came. Why didn't he see it sooner? The man should've been left locked up in the brig. After the fire and incident with the KA-40 he thought Orlov might have a chance at redeeming himself, just as Karpov had. Now all that had gone to hell in one unpredictable moment, and how in the world could he possibly fix things this time? Where in all of his history books would you find a solution this time?

"I have an idea, sir." Kalinichev spoke up. "I'm very aware of the signatures his ECM pods are going to put out. I think I can follow them, sir."

"You mean you can still track him?"

"Not exactly sir, but what I can do is get a good estimate on the signal strength of this interference and isolate it to determine the source. I know what waveforms to look for because I helped program that system. I think I can get at least a general idea of his location."

"How close?" Karpov was at his side at once.

"I won't be able to pinpoint it but I can get it within... several hundred meters." Kalinichev was guessing, but neither Fedorov nor Karpov would know any different. Now Karpov turned and made a suggestion.

"Think submarine here, Mister Fedorov. We don't know exactly where he is, but we get enough of a signal to know approximately where he is. We know where he *won't* go, certainly not out to sea. And at this moment he is still in a range of our S-300 SAM system. If Kalinichev can get a close enough fix on his location, then a barrage of three or four missiles might have a chance of knocking him down before he reaches the coastline. If we can do that, then he goes into the sea and no one is likely to find it, or ever know about it."

Fedorov's eyes widened. He had to do something, and this was as good a plan as any he could've possibly devised. Then he remembered what he had told Karpov about the jammers just a few moments ago. "Kalinichev!" he said excitedly. "Can you isolate on the 150 to 176 MHz bands? Can you fine those wavelengths and home in on the source?"

"Well yes, sir, but we don't usually jam those wavelengths,"

"We do now! Find them if you can. Karpov! Get your missiles ready!" He didn't hesitate a moment. If there is any way possible that they could shoot this helicopter down, he had to act at once.

Karpov was only too happy to oblige. He gave orders to activate the S-300s and told Kalinichev to manually feed his best possible estimate of the helicopter's present and predicted position to the CIC. He knew they would be taking a long shot, like a destroyer lobbing depth charges into the sea where they thought a submarine might be hiding. They were going to take a proverbial shot in the dark, but the S-300s had a very wide shrapnel dispersion pattern. If he fired three to five missiles he might just saturate the area with enough metal to hit this target. He knew they had very few missiles to waste, but something in him also understood what had spooked Fedorov so deeply about this incident. Beyond that, something else want to throw a punch back at the man in a way that he never could do with his own fist. *Kirov* would punch back for him, and three tense minutes later he gave the order to fire.

They watched, their eyes transfixed by the phosphorescent glow of the radar screen which received the missile telemetry feedback and clearly tracked the outgoing salvo of five precious S-300 missiles. Their speed was incredible, and they quickly overtook the spot on the scope where Kalinichev had made his best guess as to the location of the jamming source. It was very near the coast, and Fedorov bit his lip, hating what they had to do, yet hoping against hope that it would work. Because if it didn't work, he thought; if that man vanishes into the midst of the Spanish countryside in 1942, then God only knows what kind of havoc the head and darkened heart of Gennadi Orlov might visit upon the world.

Chapter 26

Five missiles roared from the forward deck of *Kirov*, the deadly S-300s, capable of Mach 6 speed out to a range of 150 kilometers. They had been aimed at a location Kalinichev had selected at the most likely source of the intense radar jamming, with a focus on any signal emanating at 176MHz or lower as Fedorov suggested. As they fired Karpov realized they had yet another option and he shouted to the tactical officer over the deafening sound of the missile engines.

"Activate the secondary infrared terminal seekers on those missiles!" If they got anywhere near a good target, the missiles could also find it by other means. The five steel fingers reached out from the ship, like a mailed gauntlet clawing the sky as they went.

On the KA-226, Orlov saw the missile warning indicator and he knew he might have only seconds to live. "Bastards!" he shouted, and grabbed the safety parachute harness, knowing he had to get out of the helo at once if he was to survive. He had it on in fifteen seconds, frantically clawing at the release on the side hatch and grunting hard as he dragged it open. *Thirty seconds*—he was poised at the edge, feeling the hard wash of the overhead rotor and the cool evening air on his face. In that brief interval the missiles accelerated to their top speed and were already over thirty kilometers from the ship, closing fast.

His heart leapt with fear and adrenaline when he looked down. The helo might normally cruise at 1000 meters but they had climbed much higher for the planned radar sweep and were up over 4000 meters. He jumped, battered by the rushing wind, his big frame tumbling and soon falling all of sixty meters per second in freefall. Would he get far enough away before the missiles found their target? He prayed to all gods and demons that he would.

Karpov clenched his fist with jubilation when he saw the telemetry signal go white, indicating a hit. "Got him!" he shouted. The missiles had found their target. The jamming signatures Kalinichev had been monitoring immediately cut off, and now they could clearly see the detonation site of the attack on the radar scope, very close to the coast line northwest of Cartagena. "We got the bastard!"

He looked at Fedorov, who had a grim expression on his face, his eyes dark and searching. "Are you certain?" he asked.

"Of course," said Karpov. "Nothing could survive that. Five S-300s? It was a high price to pay for that scumbag, not to mention the loss of another helicopter."

Fedorov nodded, thinking for a moment, then quietly said: "Goodbye, Mister Orlov...." The others remained silent, something uncomfortable in the moment. They all knew the irascible Chief, and each one held some memory of their interaction with him. None among them had been close to the man, and many had felt his rude temperament and brutish ways, yet there was something in the way that Fedorov said that, and it pulled some undefined emotion from them, perhaps pity, perhaps regret, or a sense of waste, and in some way they felt diminished with his loss, and beset by a vague notion of dread, though no man would mourn him. But their emotion was misplaced...

Orlov fell a long kilometer before he groped for the parachute release, his unshielded eyes puckered near shut by the cold wind. He pulled hard, his body shaken when the chute deployed to brake his fall and he shouted, releasing the tension, ecstatic that he had managed to get out of the helo in one piece. Then he saw them, the five fingers of doom emerging from a low white cloud and moving at an impossible rate of speed towards his general location. The helo had flown on, cruising at 360 Kph for those last twenty seconds, moving two kilometers off. He had fallen over another kilometer and was now far enough away from the target to be relatively safe from the exploding shrapnel.

Four of the five missiles had locked on to the helo, the verdict of their infrared modules guiding them mercilessly in on its big heat signature. The last S-300 took passing note of another small heat signature hovering near and well below the target. In a few split seconds its missile mind considered what to do, then dismissed the object as a parachuting thermal decoy and joined its comrades, a majority opinion of five now. Seconds later the missiles ripped the evening sky apart with one explosion after another, and the KA-226 was obliterated.

Orlov winced at the sight, realizing how close he had come to death. It had seen him, reached for him, and he felt the cold brush of its steely hands as it nearly grasped him. But he was *not* dead—he was alive! He was a great laugh, a wild roar of elation, a bellowing shout of thanks to the heavens above as he fell through the cool evening air, vanishing into a low cloud. When he broke out through a gap in the clouds he gasped at the beauty of the last fading light on the stillness of the sea, tears streaking his face, his still bandaged hands gripping the harness of his parachute, oblivious to the pain.

He was alive, alive, *alive!* And in that jubilant singularity of this moment he realized that he was the only one who knew that. They would see the destruction of the helicopter and think he was dead. He was free, drifting in this sublime white mist, as if a second life had come to him. He was completely reborn—a demigod falling from the skies to a world unprepared for the power he might one day wield. Yes, he knew in that fleeting instant that he *was* like a god, for he had knowledge of all the days to come. Knowledge was power, and if there was one thing Orlov understood in this life, it was power.

He drifted down and down, and then he realized that he was still well out to sea and probably headed for a long slog in the water. This wasn't over yet. He pulled the tab on the life preserver embedded in his flight jacket and inflated it with a dry hiss. It would probably keep him afloat, but night was at hand and it would be much colder in the water. He had nothing to eat or drink, the pistol in his jacket pocket being the only other thing he had managed to hold onto in those wild moments before he leapt. Then he remembered that this parachute could be steered, and he began to work the harness, gliding it gently toward the land he could see to the west, wrapped in a purple haze of twilight.

As he descended he could suddenly see that the ocean was not empty below him. There was a flotilla of small fishing boats on the water, their bows pointed west toward the small ports and villages that undoubtedly dotted the coastline there, and he whispered thanks, hopeful that someone would see him go into the water and come to his aid.

That was what eventually happened, but it wasn't until he had been pulled from the sea like a big wet fish and was sprawled out on the wooden deck of the fishing boat that he felt that thrum of hope again, and realized his old life might really be behind him. He had been in the water for an hour before the boat drew near and saw his arms waving and heard his hoarse, deep shouts in the gloaming dark.

Now he sat, tired and drenched, his wool cap still pulled low on his forehead. He smiled and spoke to them gratefully. "Spasibo!" He said, thanking the three clueless brown eyed men staring at him. "Za druzhbu myezhdu narodami!—To friendship between nations!"

The men did not understand a word he said, of course, and Orlov spoke no other language but his native Russian, but his manner and the look on his face communicated his gratitude, and they all nodded, smiling. The heavy set man in the middle of the three spoke back to him. "Bienvenidos a bordo!"

The Spaniards had seen and heard the explosions in the sky, and saw the slow descent of his parachute. It was not all that unusual an event. There was a war on, though thankfully Spain had managed to stay out of it. They had seen Italian bombers flying in from their far bases to try and bomb Gibraltar in the past, and at first they presumed this was some hapless Italian pilot, but Orlov's appearance and language set them off that assumption. Perhaps German, or Eastern European, they thought. Polish soldiers sometimes fought for the British now. In any case, he was a man in need and they helped him below to get out of his wet clothes and get some welcome food into him. When they saw his pistol they gave it a second look, but then went about their business as normal, not wanting to provoke and trouble with this big man. Perhaps he was a commando, they thought. He certainly wore a uniform, and he looked threatening as well. The heavy set man was speaking to him, though Orlov simply nodded and smiled.

"Tenga cuidado, amigo mío. Si las autoridades descubren que eres un soldado, van a arrestar y detener a usted por la duración de la guerra. Tenga cuidado."

Orlov realized he was going to hear a lot of this unintelligible speech for a while, but for now the sound of another human voice was welcome, and he needed only one thing from these men—a little food, some dry clothing, and a few hours to sleep while the boat put in to shore. He was living in a new world now, and though he had nothing of value he could use for money, and little idea where he even was, he knew that he would have no trouble getting what he wanted, or where he wanted, in the long run.

Yes, he thought. This is going to be very interesting. There would be good food, and drink, and women. He knew that no one on *Kirov* would ever be able to find him now. He was safe, reborn, and free to live out a whole new life, if he just kept a good head on his shoulders. If this *was* 1942 he might make an awful lot of money with what he knew. He'd be living in a world where Karpov and Volsky and all the others were not even *born* yet, and he could settle more than a few scores if he wanted. How old was Karpov, he wondered? Somewhere in his forties? He would have to wait thirty odd years before he could pay him another visit, but it would be worth it. Then again…what would that rat Karpov do when I find his grandfather and strangle the man, eh? He smiled inwardly just to think about it.

~~~

Fedorov gave some fleeting consideration to sending out their remaining KA-40 to confirm the kill and see if Orlov might have survived, but Karpov convinced him it would be fruitless.

"We'll only waste more time and aviation fuel. It was bad enough that this incident cost so much as it is. Nothing could survive that barrage. All five missiles detonated on the target. He's gone, and I say good riddance. Now we must turn our attention to what lies ahead. If we send up the KA-40 it should be to find these British ships you are worried about."

Fedorov hesitated. He did not want to risk losing their last helicopter, and decided to just hold to their planned course. He had little doubt that they would soon see Force Z on their long range radar, and said as much.

"You have the bridge, Mister Karpov. I'll inform Admiral Volsky of what occurred and then take a few hours rest. Run steady on this course for another two hours, then come right to course two-two-five southwest."

He went below, his heart heavy, and reluctant to be the bearer of yet more gloomy news for the Admiral. When he reached sick bay he found that Volsky was asleep in the back room, and so he left the news with Doctor Zolkin.

"Don't take it too hard," said the Doctor. "Men like Orlov have a way of making their own fate, and their own misery. If it is any comfort to you, I will say you did the right thing. The Admiral gave a standing order that none of our weapons or equipment were to fall into enemy hands. You prevented that, at great cost, but it was wise to do so in any case."

"At first I thought Orlov might survive," he said, and then I felt even worse for wishing him dead."

"I know, I know. He was no friend of yours, but your conscience still bothers you. That is only because you are a good man, Fedorov. There was another man on that helicopter, Yes? I don't think Orlov was as kind to him. That makes nine now. Nine men dead in this business. At least I don't have to put these last two into the sea.

Remember that this was none of your doing, and look to what you must do now to keep us safe."

"Thank you, Doctor."

He left without much sense of consolation in spite of Zolkin's words. He still felt responsible for everything that had happened thus far, for all those nine dead men, even though he knew he was being hard on himself to do so. This was the dark shadow of command, he thought, the other side of the pride and excitement he felt that first time on the bridge. It weighed on him, every last ounce of it, and the responsibility seemed a crushing burden now, not just for the ship and crew, but for the history he had been stubbornly trying to defend. But how do you save tomorrow, he thought? Everything was once so certain; so predictable. Then those Italian battleships appeared from nowhere, and he could never feel safe or content with all the knowledge he had stuffed in his brain again.

As he walked to his cabin he was still harried by a strange, unaccountable feeling that something had gone terribly, terribly wrong. It was more than Orlov's betrayal and blind stupidity, and more than his death or the loss of the helicopter. It was something deeper, a great yawning uncertainty that overshadowed his every step now. It was a profound sense of misgiving and dread that he simply could not chase from his mind.

He reached his cabin and lay down on his bunk, staring up at the ceiling and trying to see just where it was that he had made some great but unseen mistake. He needed rest, but sleep would not come to him, and as he lay there the nagging question returned to his mind again.

What if he's alive, he thought to himself? Oh God, spare the world from this man if you will. Find a place in heaven for him and get him there soon. For if you do not he will surely find a place for himself in hell—for himself and how many others?

Chapter 27

When Fedorov returned to the Bridge three hours later Karpov reported all was well, and they now had a clear surface contact to their southwest.

"We are on course 225 now and the sea is calm. The ship is running smoothly at thirty knots and we've found your Force Z. You were correct. We spotted them about 150 nautical miles out. They are still well ahead of us on a heading of 255 degrees, but we've cut their lead and they just reduced speed to fifteen. If we increase to full battle speed that will give us another five knot edge to see if we can make up that distance."

"It won't be enough," said Fedorov, walking to his navigation board. His well trained eye took in the position, course and speed of the British task force relative to *Kirov's* and he knew at once that they had lost their race. "It's what I was afraid of," he explained. "If we had more sea room to the starboard side I could turn another fifteen or twenty degrees and then perhaps we could outrun them. Unfortunately, that course would send us right across Cabo de Gata— Cat's Cape here." He pointed to the prominent land mass southeast from Almiera. We can't sail on land and if they come any further to their starboard side, even a few points, then our situation is even worse. They just had too long a head start on us, but I can't see why. They seem to be several hours ahead of where I expected them."

Again, something was wrong. Something had changed. Unless *Rodney's* boiler problem was miraculously cured, they must have turned Force Z earlier. They were supposed to turn back at 18:55, but there is no way Force Z could be where it is now unless… He ran a hasty calculation.

"Damn," he breathed. "It's slipped again. They must have turned west as early as 16:00 hours! This means *Indomitable* wasn't exposed to that attack that put three bombs on her flight deck at 18:thirty hours, and they'll likely have her intact."

Karpov shrugged. "Three carriers now?"

"It seems so."

"And I could have taken out at least two of them if I had just had a free hand weeks ago. The cat you don't feed today will scratch your leg twice as hard tomorrow. Now we fight them again."

Fedorov seemed unsure of himself now. Their plan had failed. They would not be able to slip past Force Z tonight, and the prospect for a battle was looming on the far horizon, drawing ever closer with each turn of *Kirov's* powerful screws. He looked at the navigation plots, thinking.

"An hour before midnight, at 23:00 hours, they will be here if they stay on their present course. I doubt if they'll have planes up tonight, except perhaps to provide local air cover over the task force. We might be visited by some long range recon planes out of Gibraltar, but otherwise, I don't think they've seen us yet."

"And where will we be at that hour?"

"Here—about forty nautical miles off their starboard aft quarter." Then he saw it—one slim chance, but they would have to plan it very well, and it would be very risky. Karpov could see the new light in his eyes, and he probed him.

"What? Do you see another option?"

"Look... At 23:00 hours we'll also be about forty nautical miles due east of Cabo de Gata. Suppose we turn due west at that time and run directly for the cape. If they don't see us then we just might slip past them. If they do see us then they would have to turn fifteen degrees to starboard—but I think we could still out run them. The only thing is this: they won't catch us in this event, but they *will* spot us, and those guns range out to 36,000 meters, with an effective range of 32,000 meters for battle."

"We'll be inside that?"

"Unfortunately yes." He looked ahead in his mind, wondering. "We'll have no room to maneuver to starboard. We'll be right on the damn coast, so we'll just have to run the gauntlet."

"Let's try, Fedorov. When our first salvo of missiles hits home we'll give them a real surprise, just like the Italians. It will be a night action. We can jam any radar they may deploy. We have twice their speed, and plenty of firepower."

"Yes, but they have three carriers, and they'll launch everything they have at us. Gibraltar will get in the game soon after with their air squadrons."

"We still have thirty-five of our S-300s and seventy-nine more on the Klinok system, and we're going to hit anything we fire at."

"There may be submarines."

"Our sonar is now fully operational and we can use the *Shkval* rocket torpedoes to snuff them out like a match."

"And minefields in the straits…"

"You saw what we did at Bonifacio. We can get through, Fedorov! Don't lose your nerve now. Our only other choice is to drop anchor here and get Nikolin on the radio to Gibraltar." He pointed to the unseen base, somewhere to the west. "Do that and I guarantee you that this Force Z will come steaming up in any case, and then we'll have our battle right here. It will happen, sooner or later, Fedorov. But if we try to get by them we'll at least have a chance to win through."

Fedorov looked at it, and looked at it, and he knew that Karpov was right. "Very well," he said. "I suggest you get a few hours rest while you can, Captain, and a good meal. I'll want you back on the bridge with me at 23:00 hours, and we'll make our turn for Cabo de Gata, come what may. We'll call the whole plan Operation Gauntlet."

"Aye, sir. A good name for it."

Karpov had his battle.

~~~

At that very moment Admiral Tovey was also looking at his plotting board on *King George V*, in the chart room with his Chief of Staff, Michael Denny and the ship's Captain Patterson. They were passing Vigo, Spain and racing south for Lisbon, though they had many hours of sailing time ahead of them.

"As things stand," said Tovey, "we won't get into the western approaches to Gibraltar until 14:00 hours tomorrow."

"I'm astounded we moved this quickly," said Denny. "You would think the entire war effort was riding on this sortie."

A younger man at forty-six, he did not sport the gray mantle that many of the senior officers had. After service on the cruiser *Kenya* and carrier *Victorious*, he had been groomed to replace Daddy Brind as Tovey's Chief of Staff, and he brought all the sharpness and energy of his relative youth to the job. Still, Tovey was missing Brind at this moment, his grizzled wisdom and rock hard common sense was ever a touchstone for him.

"That may not be too far off the mark, gentlemen," said Tovey. "I hope I don't have to remind you what happened to the American fleet last year. I've sent word to Fraser and told him to offer Admiral Syfret a seat at the Round Table, so he's been briefed on this *Geronimo* business at long last. He's still of the mind that this is a French ship—*Strasbourg*. If that's the case then we'll all breathe easier and all we've lost in this little trip is the fuel oil."

"*Rodney* and *Nelson* will make quick work of *Strasbourg*," said Captain Patterson. "But if it isn't a French ship?" He had seen what *Geronimo* could do, felt the hard impact of those rockets on his ship's heavy armor.

"Then it comes down to guns and steel, gentlemen. Nothing more; nothing less." Tovey had a grim expression on his face. "What have we got at Gibraltar?"

Denny spoke up, referring to a clip board where he had the latest tally from the Rock. "Hudson bombers will be up from 233 squadron at first light. Campbell's 808 Squadron will give us strike capability with his Fulmar IIs. Hutchinson with have his Sea Harriers up with 813 Squadron, and then we'll have a few more Beaufighters from Coastal Command and a handful of fighters in 804 Squadron on the *Argus*. That's all of 48 planes. We darn near emptied the cupboard for Operation Pedestal, but Syfret still has three carriers with Force Z and they've got thirty-six Fighters, and another forty-two Albacore strike aircraft between them. We're bringing in 825 Squadron with sixteen Swordfish and 802 Squadron with twelve more Sea Harriers on the *Avenger*. That make s a total of 154 aircraft fit for duty."

"That's sounding much better," said Tovey. "Submarines?"

"We've got *Talisman* in Gibraltar and we're lucky to have even that boat in position now. She was mistakenly depth charged by a Sunderland in the Bay of Biscay and is docked at Gibraltar for repairs. *Traveler* is heading home as well, but has no torpedoes until she replenishes. Everything else is in the central and eastern Med."

"Not very promising, but *Talisman* will have to do." Tovey tapped his plotting pen on the map. "Gentlemen, here's the plan. Force Z is out looking for this *Geronimo* and with three carriers I expect to hear from them shortly. It's his job to bring them to heel, and that failing he's to hang on to their coat leg and buy us some time to get Home Fleet further south. If our aircraft, this single sub, and Force Z can do the job, all the better. But if things take a turn for the worse, then we're the goalie in this game. I'm not taking the fleet into the straits. Not enough sea room there, and we'll be bunched up like a row of fat geese. No, gentlemen, We'll fan out in a widely dispersed arc as I've drawn it here." He gestured to the western approaches to Gibraltar.

"We won't be forming a battle line either. All those tactics went down the drain the first time we tangled with this ship. So I plan to spread our four battleships out along this arc, each one within supporting fire range of the other three, but spaced far enough to force the enemy to disperse his fire. The cruisers and destroyers will deploy as a forward screen. We'll keep the carrier well back and to the north along the Spanish coast. *Avenger* can launch everything she has. I'll want all those Sea Harriers in her 802 Squadron armed with bombs. The Swordfish can go in low with the Harriers up topside. They, too, will fly in a widely dispersed approach. There will be no formation of squadrons and sub flights once aloft. It will be every man for himself. These rockets were taking out two and three planes at a time in the Atlantic. It won't happen here."

They looked at the plan, noting the careful dispersion of forces to cover any route of escape if the enemy exited the straits, and Tovey explained his reasoning further.

"If this ship is *Geronimo*, and they fling one of those blasted wonder weapons our way as they did with the Americans, they stand to hit no more than one of our capital ships in a single strike. It's a damn ruthless logic, but after what we saw a year ago, it's the only way to fight this engagement. If this ship breaks through Force Z, we had better be in position and ready for anything. As soon as they put their nose into the Straits of Gibraltar, I'll order Home Fleet to go into action. It will be the charge of the heavy cavalry, gentlemen. Every ship is to go in full out, and with all guns blazing. Just counting the two forward turrets on the four battleships, we'll have twenty four 14 inch guns in play. If any ship gets the range on the target and wishes to effect a turn to bring their rear X turret to bear, all the better, but I want you to close the range smartly, and get hits. You can expect hits as well if they fling those damn naval rockets at us again. As I said before, it will come down to the armor in the end—the armor, good gunfire, and a good measure of nerve. Now we've got *King George V, Prince of Wales, Duke Of York*, and *Anson*. One of us has to run this bastard through."

Part X

The Gauntlet

"*The soldiers in black uniforms stood in two rows, facing each other motionless, their guns at rest. Behind them stood the fifes and drums, incessantly repeating the same unpleasant tune.*
'What are they doing?' I asked the blacksmith, who halted at my side.
'A Tartar is being beaten through the ranks for his attempt to desert,' said the blacksmith in an angry tone, as he looked intently at the far end of the line."

~ Tolstoy ~ After the Ball

Chapter 28

It began a little after 23:00 hours the 13th of August, 1942. *Kirov* had raced south, undiscovered, and was now making the turn Fedorov had planned to run due west to Cabo de la Gata. They would take the 60 mile run in two hours. Reaching the cape by 1:00 AM. But as midnight approached they saw three planes coming up from the south flying obvious search patterns.

"These must be off the carriers," said Fedorov.

"Shall we shoot them down?" Karpov had returned to the bridge, rested and ready for action.

Fedorov thought a moment, and shook his head. "Why bother. If we do kill them, that act alone will give the British our approximate position, and immediately mark us as hostile. I want to see if we can try our ruse as a French ship. It might buy us just a little time."

So they watched the search planes grow ever closer, the nearest no more than four kilometers out before they all turned, heading south again. It was not long before Nikolin perked up, adjusting his headset and waving for Fedorov's attention.

"A radio message, sir. In English, and right in the clear."

Nikolin put it on the speakers and they listened, eyes drawn to the overhead grill, brows raised as Nikolin translated.

"Ship heading two-seven-zero, latitude thirty six degrees, forty two minutes, longitude negative two, please identify yourself."

Fedorov smiled. "Someone is ringing the door bell. They must have some good men in one of those planes. Those coordinates are very close to the mark."

"What shall I do, sir?" asked Nikolin. "Should I ignore them?"

"No, Mister Nikolin, now you get to practice your English a bit. But if you can sound more like a Frenchman, that would be even better! Tell them we are battlecruiser *Strasbourg*, and that we have broken out of Toulon, fought off two Italian battleships that tried to intercept us, and that we are running for Free French ports in Equatorial Africa to join Admiral Darlan."

"Very well, sir." Nikolin translated, his big brown eyes moving from his microphone to Fedorov and back again, excited. Time passed, and then they heard the reply Fedorov expected.

"Sir, they want us to reduce speed and come to a heading of 255 degrees. They say they will escort us to Gibraltar and that we may arrange passage south from there."

"Very well. Tell them we are coming around on that heading at twenty knots and will send up signal flares in thirty minutes."

"You're going to do what they say?" Karpov has a bemused look on his face.

"Of course not. Helm, steady on 270 and ahead full battle speed. Now we'll see how cagy the British are. If they wanted us on 255 then they should alter course to near zero degrees north to effect a rendezvous from their present position. Any course they take west of that will mean they aren't taking any chances and are maneuvering to make sure they can cut us off. Even if they do think we're *Strasbourg* they would know we can run up to thirty knots. Let's see what they do."

They had their answer shortly when Rodenko, now back on radar, indicated the contact had altered course to 302 degrees northwest and increased speed to near twenty knots.

"A careful breed, these British." Karpov seemed restless, arms clasped behind his back. "They made that course change before they even gave us a chance to come round on 255."

"They'll probably move something that direction, but I don't think they are buying our apples today. They didn't make the claim that Britannia rules the sea lightly," said Fedorov. "They know *Strasbourg* would not easily prevail over two Italian battleships. This is the one heading they should have taken if they wanted to intercept us on our old reported course and speed. Very well... we'll play the game a bit. In a few minutes I want a missile rigged with a star shell and fired right here, where we should be if we had turned on the heading they requested. They'll most likely loop those planes back to shadow us, but this may prove a distraction."

"We can just fire one of the UDAV batteries," said Karpov. "A single rocket timed to explode in the air should suffice."

They waited out the interval, and fired their rocket at maximum range. All the while Rodenko noted the steady approach of another aircraft. It was clear that the British were taking no chances with them at all. The plane diverted briefly to the location where they had fired their missile, then quickly turned northwest on a heading to intercept them.

"Are they seeing us on radar?" asked Karpov. "What's wrong with our jammers, Rodenko?"

"Nothing wrong, sir. I have the all their bandwidths snowed over."

"They are just experienced and efficient men," said Fedorov. "That man is flying by the seat of his pants out there, but he knows enough to get his plane northwest where we would be on our old heading."

"At his present speed they will re-acquire our position in approximately ten minutes," said Rodenko.

"Let them. They won't learn anything they don't already suspect. Our ruse is over, and now we run the gauntlet. Very well, rig the ship for black. We should reach the cape at zero one hundred hours. I'll want the ship at battle stations by then, and we'll alter course fifteen degrees to port to avoid the Almeria sea transit lanes. There are good thermals along the coast, and they make for excellent cruising stations for submarines. We'll avoid them if we can, but by 01:thirty we may be engaged. I suggest we take whatever time remaining to check the weapons systems. I don't want a repeat of that accident we had with the Klinok missiles. We'll need every round we have."

~~~

Aboard HMS *Nelson* Admiral Syfret had made the early assessment that this was a renegade French battlecruiser, on one side of the French coin or another, and nonetheless maneuvered to get his battleships in the best possible position to engage if they did not comply with his request. He had separated his force at 18:00 hours earlier that evening, sending the three carriers under Rear Admiral St. Lyster on *Victorious* some forty miles south on a parallel course to his own, along with his last remaining cruisers and an escort of five destroyers. It was also necessary to detach the wounded destroyer *Ithuriel*, and he sent her off south with DD *Quentin*. This left him with his two battleships and six more destroyers, more than enough, he reasoned, to run this *Geronimo* to ground. When they got within gun range, he would signal Captain Troubridge on the carrier *Indomitable* to launch his Albacore II torpedo bombers for good measure. He'd get his battleships right astride *Strasbourg's* line of advance and then have one last word before he let his 16 inch guns do the talking.

They were running W/T silent, but he imagined that Admiral Fraser had forsaken his role as an incognito observer on *Rodney* and was now on the bridge there. He signaled his intentions by lamp to his sister ship, asking her for her very best speed. When the lights winked back saying they would not be late for tea, he knew his hunch about Fraser on the bridge had been correct.

What was all this fuss and bother about, he thought. We'll have the matter in hand in two or three hours. No need to cancel major operations and send Home Fleet rushing off like a chicken with its head cut off. Yet what about this sighting report coming over from *Indomitable's* 827 squadron. He did not know what to make of it.

~~~

Sub Lt. William Walter Parsons, Fleet Air Arm Observer, 827 Albacore Squadron off *Indomitable* was the lucky man who spotted *Kirov* that day, and the sight of the ship gave him the willies. As fate would have it, he had been up north with Force P a year ago for the planned raid at Kirkenes with this very same 827 Squadron on *Victorious* at that time. The appearance of a strange new German raider had forced Wake-Walker to cancel the mission and enter that long, ill fated hunt. Oddly, the history once recorded that he was to be shot down over Kirkenes and captured by the Germans, but all that changed when this mysterious ship appeared in the Norwegian Sea, though he never knew it.

The cancellation of the Kirkenes mission meant that he would not spend those hard years in a cold German POW camp, or make that torturous long march from Sagan, forced to push a wheel barrel for several hundred miles on those frozen ice-gutted roads. His favorite ring would not be warped by his gripping the arms on that wheel barrel, and it still fit his finger snugly where he wore it every day—his lucky ring. Lucky indeed, for his squadron had been hit particularly hard chasing after that raider, losing some very good men. He was one of the very few that made back alive. He still remembered the faces of the men who died, McKendrick, Turnbull, Bond, Greenslade, Miles... And the awful memory of those rockets in the sky, like a wild pack of voracious sharks swerving and swooping in on the planes...awful...

One look at the ship below, knifing through the dark sea off the Spanish coast brought all this back with the sureness of an old memory that might be summoned up by a sound, or a smell. And with it came a sense of dread and foreboding. He was to shadow this ship, but something forced him to pull on the yoke and put the plane into a turn, and get himself as far away from this place as possible. He made his report and, some minutes later, he got hold of himself, realizing he would have to circle round and re-acquire the target.

"What's gotten into you?" he said aloud to himself. That ship, he knew, that's what's done it! I'll not be a shirker, but I'll be damned if that's a French battlecruiser. No sir. That looks all the world like... But it couldn't be here, could it? it couldn't be...

It was.

Thankfully the fuel gauge on Parson's plane allowed him to slip away with a little dignity, and he soon turned south for *Indomitable*. He had the odd feeling that he had been following a shadow, a nightmare, and the farther away from that demon he got the more he felt his old self again. When he landed on the carrier they would want him in the briefing room bang away. What should he tell them? He reported to his Squadron Leader, Lt. Commander Buchanon-Dunlop, and he spoke his mind.

"You weren't with us back then," he concluded, "and lucky for it. But this ship out there looks for all the world like the one we fought in the North Atlantic last August. Put most of my mates into the sea and stuck a fire bomb into *Victorious* as well."

~~~

Admiral Syfret eventually received the opinion through proper channels, but didn't weigh it too heavily. Men get spooked on these night operations, he knew. A case of the jitters before combat was normal. At least the man knew his duty, held on to his contact, and got a good read on her course and speed.

Parsons never knew that Fedorov had spared his life that night by declining to fire on his plane. So he would go on to survive the war, become a school teacher, and have grand children one day. Yet many in his 827 Squadron would not. They were already in the briefing room while the flight engineers worked the torpedoes onto the planes below decks. He would not be tasked to fly the strike mission, but would probably be up for battle damage assessment later on that night. So he caught one of his mates as he came out of the briefing room, tugging at his flight jacket.

"Have a care, Tom," he said in a low voice. "Don't bunch up on this one. Get down real low, and spread your flight out nice and wide. Stay down real low, and find any cover you can on the approach."

It was the best advice Thomas Wales was to receive in his life.

Force Z pushed on, their course aiming for a point some thirty nautical miles southwest of Cabo de la Gata. The latest sighting reported that his quarry was moving extremely fast. At midnight they were some thirty-two nautical miles apart, or sixty kilometers, and closing on that same distant point. He sounded battle stations and the ship was trimmed for action, her big guns loaded, the heavily armored turrets slowly turning toward the direction they expected their adversary.

It was time for one last effort at settling the matter amicably, and he had his radioman broadcast a demand to reduce speed at once and prepare to be boarded by a British liaison officer. There was no response, and so he folded his arms, shaking his head and had the signalman wink a message to Admiral Fraser: "Contact will not heave to. Will commence firing as soon as practicable. Please join in."

The men in the crow's nest with their high powered binoculars would have the next say, and it would be a difficult sighting. Radar seemed all fouled, and the operators reported they could get no signal returns from any ship in the formation. So it would come down to the old fashioned methods, he thought, a pair of sharp eyes behind the glass and well trained gun crews. So be it. He had his quarry just where he wanted it, penned up against the Spanish coastline and with little room to maneuver to their starboard side. He knew he would not have the speed to get much under 20,000 meters as they approached, but he could engage well before that. The target was fast, but it would have to run for nearly an hour under his guns. The crescent moon had set five hours earlier, so it was very dark. The French had picked a perfect time to make their run, but if they could spot the enemy, he was confident his gunners would do the rest.

He looked at his watch and gave an order. "Very well. W/T silence lifted. Time to get a couple of watch dogs out in front to look for this ship gentlemen. Send *Ashanti*, and *Tartar*. We'll hold the remaining escorts for the time being." He wanted a couple of fast destroyers to flush this rabbit out for his big guns, and the two ships soon broke formation off his starboard quarter and accelerated rapidly. It was a little after one in the morning when word came back that a ship had been sighted to their northeast. Range was well out, but it was clear that something big was sailing just southwest of Cat's Cape, and moving too fast to be commercial traffic. Syfret decided to send a more forceful message to this recalcitrant French ship. He knew his first salvo would be well off the mark, but it would serve him well as a proverbial shot across the bow before open hostilities ensued.

He selected A and B turrets, his foreword most guns, and opened fire with just the centermost barrel in each turret. There was something to be said for courtesy, even if this was war and deadly earnest business. And the thought that he was giving them his middle finger amused him as well. If the French returned his warning shots with a salvo of their own, then the bar fight was on, and he had little doubts as to who would come out the better. He noted that HMS *Rodney* had not fired, her dark shape tall and threatening some 5000 yards in his wake. He waited, calm and confident, until spotters on his lead destroyers caught the distant wash of white where his shells had fallen. They radioed back to report all shots wide off the bow and long by several thousand yards. It had begun.

~~~

Fedorov heard the first shells rushing overhead and their distant impact on the dark swells of the sea. He noted the time—01:10 hours in the early morning of August 14, 1942. A sea battle was about to be fought that never should have occurred. Men might die, perhaps on both sides, who might have lived. It was a maddening thought. The whole notion of war itself was a maddening thought, but here they were. His ship wanted sea lanes where another ship forbade him to pass. He briefly considered turning about and heading back to the Balearics, but knew that would only postpone this inevitable engagement. There was nothing left to do but fight.

In Karpov's mind the equation was simpler. One side or another must give way, and it would not be *Kirov*. He looked at Fedorov, saw him waiting, an anguished look on his face, and then said. "I believe we are under attack, Mister Fedorov. We've had our dance with Varenka and your Operation Gauntlet has now begun. Let's see what they have for us after the ball."

Fedorov caught the reference to the famous short story by Tolstoy where a man had been bemused at a ball by the beauty and charm of a lovely woman named Varenka. Later that evening he walked alone and stumbled upon a military discipline where an escaped Tartar was being forced to run the gauntlet, and the punishment was being administered by Varenka's father, a colonel in the army. It was cruel, and merciless as the soldiers were ordered to beat the man ever harder, and it shook his faith in human compassion so completely that he lost his ardor for the man's daughter. He claimed this chance encounter had changed his life forever, and something died in him with each withering blow on the poor renegade's shoulders and back.

Now *Kirov* was the renegade, a fugitive Tartar about to run the gauntlet of fire and steel. For the next hour the ship would be in the gravest danger, well within range of those lethal 16 inch guns. A chance encounter, a planned encounter, it mattered not which. In the end it was a madness at sea that would change the lives of every man present forever.

"Mister Fedorov?" Karpov prodded him again.

"That was just a warning shot," he said quietly.

"Yes, well it would be nice to reply in kind, but I don't think we can afford to waste the ammunition. I suggest we lock weapon systems on the target and give them a more direct warning. We have fourteen Moskit IIs remaining. Six should do the job."

"These are not the Italians," said Fedorov, deflated but coming round to the realization that this was a choice he had made hours and hours ago. Now the time was here, and they had to fight. He turned to Karpov and gave an order. "I want to put one P-900 on each of the two battleships immediately following their next salvo."

"P-900s? They are very slow."

"Yes, but I want them to *see* the missiles coming. See them clearly." He had asked for the sub-sonic cruise missiles instead of the more lethal supersonic Moskit Sunburns. The P-900s were slow, but still dangerous with a 400 kilogram warhead and pinpoint accuracy.

"Very well—Mister Samsonov, ready on the P-900 system, two missiles, target your primaries."

Samsonov could clearly read the positions of the two big battleships on his display. He moved a light pen, tapped each one, then selected his weapon system and keyed "ready."

"Sir, two P-900 missiles keyed to targets and ready."

They waited in the stillness. The satin of the moonless night seemed to flow in all around them, enveloping them with a suspended sense of profound uncertainty. Their faces were illuminated by the green luminescence of the radar screens, eyes searching the black silky night, as if they thought some horrible beast, a sleek panther, might leap upon them from the darkness at any moment. Then the distant horizon seemed to explode with fire and violence. Seconds later they heard a loud boom, thunder-like in the distance.

Nelson and *Rodney* had fired in earnest.

Fedorov shrugged, then looked at Karpov, a grim expression on his face. "Give them a little shove on the shoulder, Captain."

"Aye, sir."

Chapter 29

Syfret had never seen anything quite like it. The darkness lit up with distant flame and smoke, far off on the edge of the night. He could see something bright in the sky, arcing up, and then he heard a low, distant growl.

"What do you make of that?" he said to a Senior Lieutenant, pointing at the fiery light, which grew more prominent, and closer with each passing second. The slow approach had exactly the effect Fedorov wanted. Every man on the bridge seemed transfixed by the oncoming glow. They had seen burning planes plummeting into the sea at night, but this was nothing like that. It had a slow, purposeful movement, rising up and up, then leveling off to begin a gradual descent. Down it came, a bright burning tail behind it illuminating a trail of ghostly smoke. It was a plane, some thought—poor bloke going into the drink at last. Probably one of our search planes that got in too close.

But it wasn't a plane…It *wasn't* a plane! It suddenly seemed to leap at them with a mighty roar, a fiery dart aimed right at the heart of the ship. The P-900s had ignited their ramjet afterburners to make their final run into the target at mach three, but by that time every crewman with eyes out to sea had been transfixed by the spectacle.

In they came and Syfret to one step back, his hand reaching for a rail to steady himself as the fire in the sky came thundering in and crashed right below the tall armored conning tower of his ship. The concussion of the explosion shattered every window on the bridge, sending glass showering over the deck, but it had not struck high enough to cause any real damage there. Instead it came in low and rifled into the number three C turret where it had exploded with terrible flame and smoke.

It was all the Admiral could do to remain standing. Two midshipman were thrown to the deck. Black smoke poured in and choked every man among them and Syfret instinctively crouched on his haunches, as much to steady himself as to find better air.

"Mother of God!" he coughed. They hit us on the first bloody shot! But with what? Then all the rumors, and sailor's stories he had quashed as nonsense for the past year came home to him—*rockets*, lighting fast, with deadly precision. Rockets fired by a dark, dangerous ship that slipped through the night like a phantom.

It was here! This was nothing the French could have imagined or ever put to sea. *Strasbourg* had 13 inch guns, but this was something else entirely—no ripple of bright enemy fire in the distance; no sign of water splashes as her rounds came in. It was here! This was the ship Fraser had warned him of—the ship that put *Repulse* in her grave and blotted the side armor of both *King George V* and *Prince of Wales*. And now it had stuck its fist in his face and drawn first blood.

His amazement suddenly gave way to a new emotion. *Nelson* had been a proud but plodding ship in her years of service. She had foolishly run aground on Hamilton's Shoal in 1934, watched fast German cruisers and destroyers dance around her in the North Sea, ever beyond her grasp. She was nearly sunk by three German torpedoes near the Orkney's, but miraculously spared when all three failed to explode, then she blundered in to a mine off Loch Ewe. Most recently she had been laid up by an Italian torpedo, returning to service only in May of that very year. In all these actions her one great liability had been her ponderously slow speed and sluggish maneuverability. But never had any ship dared to put hands on her as this one just had.

Syfret stood up, no longer amazed, but angry now. He was standing in the heavily armored conning tower, with steel plate over a foot thick on every side, one of the most heavily protected citadels on any ship in the world. Yet he disdained his armored castle and rushed to the weather bridge to see if he could get a look at the damage.

C turret had been knocked about, and the concussion of the hit had probably killed or disabled men on one side of the turret. The barbette was black as tar and licked by flame, which had spread to engulf two lifeboats on the other side of the ship. The turrets leftmost gun of three was inclined upward like a metal finger, still pointing at the smoky contrail of the missile. But the turret was even more heavily armored than his own citadel, a full 16.5 inches thick, and by god, he saw the guns begin to slowly rotate to re-train on the target, its remaining two barrels adjusting their elevation, and he knew there were men still alive and fighting in there, though the heat from the flames that still broiled on one side of the massive turret must be unbearable. He looked astern to see that *Rodney* had also been struck, a little lower amidships where much of the blow had been taken by her heavy side armor. There was a fire, but it did not look serious and all her guns appeared to be in good order.

"Damn you, sir!" he shouted at the distant, unseen foe, and rushed back into the citadel with an order. "Get the range, by God. Ready on A and B Turrets."

Down in the guts of the ship men were feverishly receiving optical sighting reports and working the fire control boxes, or FCBs as they were called. They were cranking levers to set elevation, gun deflection, range, gun training, and also sliding precision rulers over tables to calculate wind deflection. There were dials to set the estimated target speed and bearing, gyros to read variations in the roll of the ship, measures to calculate the ballistic height of the target and a line of sight transmitter. Within the box, wires and cables connected all these dials, gauges and levers to try and make sense, though to any untrained eye the contents of the box looked more like the workings of a Swiss watch. There were metal plates etched with millimeter hash marks, azimuth conversion gears, oil motors whirring to move levers and flanges, speed governors spinning, fuze clocks for firing intervals, and even heating elements to dissipate moisture and keep the system dry.

Other men were sighting from their gun director posts and shouting information through voice pipes to the men who worked at the FCBs. The controlling officer manned a telephone to the bridge. Still others were squinting through telescopes and slowly turning hand wheels to fine tune their settings. While it all seemed very precise, it was basically a mechanical guessing machine. It was a team effort, with range takers, line of sight finders, elevation directors, heightfinders, a collective synergy of human eyes, heads and mechanical elements which took a long minute to reach a solution while the crews in the gun turrets were seeing to the loading of the massive shells and propellant charges. It made very well educated guesses in the end, but was wrong more often than not, and by a wide measure.

When *Nelson's* sister ship HMS *Rodney* engaged the *Bismarck*, she had taken three salvos and fifteen minutes to get her first hit, and that was at dawn, with a range of about 20,000 yards. Here the range was greater, and it was a night action with Syfret's ships initially relying on forward spotters in his two sheep dogs, *Ashanti* and *Tartar*. He knew it would take at least five salvos before they got the range, and perhaps even more, and he hoped he had the time before this demon slipped from his grasp.

"Give them bloody hell!" Syfret yelled at the top of his voice, commanding the whole process from the bridge. "Shoot!"

Seconds later the whole ship shook with the kick of the massive guns. Anything on the bridge that was not riveted down went clattering across plotting tables and rattling to the deck. The last loose shards of glass in the viewports were shaken free and the binnacle rattled and vibrated with the concussion, which was basically just a controlled explosion gripped in the tight steel cylinder of the gun barrel. It did indeed look like hell when the fire and smoke belched from the yawning muzzles of the guns, and the scream of the heavy shells as they went wailing away towards the enemy was frighteningly loud. Now he could just make their adversary out on the far horizon, lit by the fire of their own rocketry as the range slowly diminished.

They wanted a fight, with the Royal Navy, he thought. By God, I'll give them one!

~~~

The salvo that had sent *Kirov's* P-900 missiles flying was again long, but frightening as the shells whooshed overhead and fell into the sea, sending tall white plumes of seawater up into the air. Karpov saw the missiles strike home, smiling when each one ignited in a fireball, dead amidships.

"Two hits!" he said.

"Come right, fifteen," said Fedorov. "Begin evasive maneuvers."

"That will take us right into their last salvo," said Karpov.

"Exactly," said Fedorov excitedly. "We have the speed and maneuverability to chase salvos here. They'll be correcting that long shot based on their read on our heading and speed. Their next shots should fall off our port side and short."

He wanted to use *Kirov's* great advantage in speed to make it more difficult for the British battleships to accurately range on the ship. They saw the night ripped apart by another salvo, a second ship behind it firing as well, and the thought that there were now at least twelve, and possibly eighteen massive shells heading their way gave him a chill. *Kirov* was a middleweight champion with a merciless jab, a strong right arm, and terrible speed. The ships she was facing were big, bruising heavyweights, lumbering slow but with tree trunk arms and hammers in their fists. They only needed one punch to connect to stagger their opponent and possibly decide the bout.

Karpov's words returned to him again. What did they have for us after the ball? No, thought Fedorov, the dance is not yet over. We have to move, maneuver, and one glance at his navigation plot told him they needed to do everything possible to get out of range of these guns.

The two salvoes fell in a long line off the port side as he had predicted, better placed now, and ranging nearer. He changed heading quickly, turning into the salvos, the ship's powerful turbines frothing the sea in her wake as *Kirov* ran at full battle speed, all of 32 knots.

"Shall I finish them?" Karpov asked, the elation of battle in his eyes. He was leaning over Samsonov, waiting to make his next missile selection.

"Finish them?" said Fedorov. "They're just getting started, Captain. I'm afraid we only angered those two monsters out there. Speed is what we need now. Speed and a quick hand on the helm."

"Yes, well I suggest we hit them again, and this time with the Moskit-IIs."

"Fight your battle," Karpov. "I will maneuver the ship."

Karpov nodded, glad to have a freer hand, and turned to Victor Samsonov. "Give me a salvo of four Moskit IIs..." He had suddenly noticed two the secondary contacts edging closer to the ship on Samsonov's screen. "Those must be destroyers," he said quickly. "They are at 15,000 meters. Engage them with the 152mm deck guns. Then put two missiles on each primary."

"Aye, sir!" Samsonov went to work, feeding commands to the ship's weapons systems. In contrast to the labor of the British at their gun directors and FCBs, *Kirov*'s systems were lighting fast computers integrated with their 3D radar. Seconds later they saw the forward 152mm battery rotate, its twin gun barrels elevate slightly, and then a crack, crack, crack, as the guns fired, both barrels recoiling in perfect unison with every salvo. One of the two aft batteries joined the fray as Samsonov targeted each of the two advancing destroyers with one battery.

Then the forward deck hatches flipped open and up leapt the Sunburns. They would fire at three second intervals at a range of 28,000 meters. In a matter of six seconds they would accelerate rapidly to mach three, over 3500 kilometers per hour or about 1000 meters per second. They would strike their targets in just twenty-eight seconds! By comparison the muzzle velocity of the British 16 inch guns was 766 meters per second. The missiles were actually faster, designed to defeat the lighting reflexes of American Aegis class cruisers, and they were a hundred times more accurate than *Nelson's* guns. They were going to hit whatever they were aimed at, almost without fail, and they were going to hit hard.

While the British heavyweights swung their heavy arms, sending metal haymakers *Kirov's* way in wide arcs, it was as if the Russian ship calmly reached out one hand to steady their foe's chin, then rammed a strong right hand right to the face with thunderous speed. And the only way they were going to knock these ships out was by a head shot. Their armor was simply too thick to give them body shots. Karpov was again targeting the ship to be hit well above the water line, hoping to strike the superstructure. The Moskit-IIs each carried a 450KG semi-armor penetrating warhead, and tons of fuel for their propulsion system which would ignite when they exploded. The whole missile weighed over four tons. They were basically a hypersonic armor piercing fire bomb, and fire had been the nemesis of ships at sea for centuries.

Syfret had ordered *Nelson* and *Rodney* to give their enemy hell, and seconds later it came rebounding back at them with a fury. The missiles flashed in on the battleships and blasted into the center of the ships with terrific force. They exploded in huge massive fireballs of broiling heat and molten shrapnel, almost as if two miniature suns had ignited their angry fire at the heart of each vessel. One warhead smashed into the armor plating at the base of *Nelson's* citadel but was frustrated by twelve inches of hardened armor there. Seconds later the second hammered against C turret again, this time immolating the guns with its terrible impact and fire. The armor withstood the impact, but not the men inside, who were killed almost instantly by the terrible concussive force generated by the velocity of the missile.

A column of torrid fire and smoke mushroomed up from the ship, and this time Admiral Syfret was thrown from his feet, his head striking the bulkhead and knocking him unconscious. For her part, *Rodney* suffered equal harm, struck slightly aft of the main conning tower where the range finders, gun directors and FCB controllers were feverishly working up their next salvo. They had fired just as the first missile came in, however, and the second Moskit was caught in the tremendous blast of six huge guns, adding its exploding fury to their tumult and shock, which rocked the ship violently. Pipes burst all over the ship. Chairs went flying in the mess halls, hand rails quavered, equipment was shaken loose from its bolted moorings and, aft of the citadel where the armor was thinner, the warhead came on through the outer bulkheads and blasted into the metal chambers beyond.

Had these been modern ships, those hits would have utterly destroyed both targets. But here, though rocked and damaged, burning fiercely and shaken almost senseless, neither *Nelson* nor *Rodney* had been dealt a fatal blow. Men scrambled up from below, some aghast to see the hard pine wood main deck planks contorted and bent by the concussion of their own guns alone. Dazed and tired, they reacted by reflex, fetching fire hoses, grabbing crowbars to move loosened shards of mangled steel, and then set about fighting the terrible fires. Some tried to get to the back hatch on *Nelson's* stricken C turret but were amazed to find the hatch wheel was melting when they fought their way to the scene with fire hoses!

From *Kirov's* perspective the scale and violence of the explosions seemed decisive. Karpov folded his arms, satisfied that he had smashed their enemy, and that the ship would now be free to sail on, but he was wrong. He was looking at Fedorov, a smile on his face when he caught the young Captain's eye, and just as he was about to crow they heard yet another explosive salvo fire in the distance. Karpov thought it was a secondary explosion from his missile strike at first, until they heard the dreadful wail of the shells overhead, mostly long this time, though one fell short, no more than a thousand meters off their starboard bow.

"Con – Air radar contact. Multiple readings at one-eight-zero degrees. Range forty kilometers and closing on our position at 200kph. Altitude 15,000." Rodenko has spotted the squadrons of Albacore II torpedo bombers off the British carriers. There were nine each from 827 and 831 Squadrons off *Indomitable*, and another twelve with the whole of 832 Squadron off *Victorious*. A flight of six Sea Harriers from 800 Squadron escorted them in, some thirty-six planes in all.

"Those will be torpedo bombers," said Fedorov. "They are biplanes like the ones we faced earlier. Helm, come hard left twenty degrees."

"Aye, sir. Coming left full rudder on a heading of two-six-zero."

"I can see the carrier task force on radar," said Rodenko, looking at Karpov.

"Let's discourage any further air strikes. Give me one Moskit-II, Mister Samsonov. Put it in the center of that task force." He knew there were three carriers south of him, but did not want to commit three missiles. Perhaps if he lit a fire on one carrier the others might relent, or scramble to recover her aircraft, which would disrupt further offensive operations. It was thinking that failed to consider the measure and mettle of his opponent, but he soon turned his attention to the Klinok SAM system, ordering both forward and aft silos activated to deal with the incoming tide of planes. The 152mm batteries stopped firing, and he clutched his field glasses, seeing the two smaller British destroyers that had been rushing at them both burning and nearly swamped. *Ashanti* was listing to port, and *Tartar* was a burning wreck. But he was soon surprised to see four more ships on his port side. The British had released the hounds.

They want to make a coordinated air/sea torpedo attack, he knew at once. Four destroyers and thirty six planes! He rushed to Samsonov, noting the inventory readouts on his missile panel. The missile he had ordered against the carriers fired and surged away to the south, and the readout on his Moskit-II inventory now reduced to nine missiles available. He also had eight more of the slower P-900 cruise missiles and nine more MOS-III Starfire missiles, blistering fast, yet with slightly smaller warheads. *Kirov* had just twenty-six ship killers left. He had put three missiles into each of the British battleships and still he saw their guns booming in the distance, the range still agonizingly close for a ship accustomed to firing at adversaries up to a hundred kilometers or more away.

"Fedorov! What is the range of the torpedoes on these ships and planes?"

"A maximum range of about 11,000 meters, but they will probably try to fire much closer. Remember the torpedoes will not track us. They run true as aimed. The destroyers may fire at long range just to harass us, but I don't think the planes will fire much beyond three or four thousand meters."

That was welcome news to Karpov. His Klinok's would deal fiery hell to this air strike, and now he ordered all three 152mm batteries to engage the destroyers.

Some 15,000 meters to the south, on came the British hound dogs. *Lookout* was leading the way, *Lightning* just a five hundred meters off her starboard quarter. Behind them came *Intrepid* and *Matchless.* As Karpov stared at them he had bad memories of those final hectic moments on the bridge when the American *Desron 7* had come charging in while he struggled to fire that devastating MOS-III missile with its powerful nuclear warhead. With a flash he remembered how he had ordered Martinov to also mount a warhead on the number ten cruise missile as well! Was it still there, he wondered, or had the missile crews replaced it with a conventional warhead? That did not matter. He had no missile key around his neck, and he was not the same man now. Those frantic memories seemed to come to him from another life, but the heat of battle was on him, and his adrenaline rushed. They had been engaged for over thirty minutes now, much more time than he thought it would take to stop the British battle force. He had wanted this fight, and the British were giving it to him.

"Aircraft descending rapidly," said Rodenko. "They are dropping down low and dispersing on a wide front."

The crack of *Kirov's* deck guns shuddered in the air, a sharp head-pounding staccato. Fedorov again maneuvered the ship, even as the distant battleships blasted yet another salvo. How could they have weathered those missile hits? The heavy rounds came wailing in, much closer, and then one fell terribly close off *Kirov's* port side, exploding in a violent upheaval of seawater and shaking the ship so hard that he could feel it roll from the force. The concussion was enough to buckle the hull slightly, but it did not break. Yet splinters of metal had showered that side of the ship near the impact, and there were many men down, blood staining their bright yellow life preservers where they manned their posts.

"Come right, twenty degrees hard!" shouted Fedorov, still maneuvering the ship in fast evasive turns. *Nelson* had found the range on them at long last, but *Rodney's* salvo fell well off their port side. That was close he thought. That was oh, so very close. Then he heard Karpov shout the orders to engage the incoming air strike, and *Kirov's* decks were soon awash with fuming white smoke as one missile after another popped up from the decks, like wet barracudas, and then went streaking off to the south. This time there were no misfires.

Chapter 30

The four destroyers raced forward, their sharp bows cutting smartly through the calm seas, their commander's eyes riveted on the distant silhouette of the enemy ship ahead. *Lookout* made the grievous mistake of trying to illuminate their adversary with its searchlights, and was soon given the primary attention of *Kirov*'s deck guns. The armor piercing rounds piled into the ship and riddled her with five successive hits and one near miss. She was burning forward and aft, with two of her four 4.7 inch guns now blazing wrecks.

As the other ships fanned out to set up for their torpedo runs their crews could hear the distant drone of the Albacore IIs, right on cue. Then they saw the alarming missile fire from *Kirov*, gaping at the wild rush of black darts in the sky, driven by fire and steam. The missiles rose and veered in swift jerking motions, like a school of angry fish seeking prey. And they found the lumbering Albacores with little difficulty, blasting one after another from the sky as they descended to make their torpedo runs.

Aboard the destroyer *Intrepid*, Lieutenant Commander Colin Douglas Maud stood squarely on the bridge, his stout frame and thick black beard making him look for all the world like an old pirate captain of old. All he needed was an eye patch and scarf, but instead he wore a woolen black beret in place of his hat, one hand grasping a long blackthorn walking stick which he tapped on the deck as they made their torpedo run, almost as if to urge his ship on just a little faster.

He had joined the Royal Navy in 1921, with two years on the old *Iron Duke* before eventually coming to serve with the destroyers. He had killed two U-boats earlier in the war, and was out with several other destroyers in the hunt for the *Bismarck*, over a year ago. It was his ship, *Icarus*, that had first come upon the flotsam of HMS *Hood's* tragic sinking, ropes rigged on her sides and ready to pull men out of the water, but they found only three souls alive that day.

He had also been out with Tovey's fleet a year ago, screening Home Fleet as it closed on another fast German raider in the North Atlantic. His was one of two ships that suffered badly when the enemy used rockets to strike the fleet at long range, and Maud's luck ran out when his destroyer, *Icarus*, was struck amidships and sunk. Thankfully, he was pulled out of the water and saved, but lost many shipmates, and his beloved bulldog Winnie as well. The loss of his ship was a shock that took some time to get over, but he recovered, steeled himself, and immediately asked Home Fleet for another destroyer. They gave him the *Intrepid*.

The Malta convoys had been his lot of late, but this was something different, and he growled out commands to the bridge crews, full of pluck and vigor as the ships sped forward. He had seen the rockets that struck the battleships, his mind frozen with the memory of those awful moments in the North Atlantic, the terrible explosion and fire, the bone chilling cold when he went into the sea. Yet this was what a destroyer leader lived for, he thought, not the slogging drudgery of escort duty, nor even the prowling measured hunt for enemy U-boats. It was the mad dash he loved most, even if it meant he might rush again into fire and death. That was the thing that gave its name to these ships—*Lighting*, *Intrepid*, and as he urged his men on his heart also burned with the thought that he was now bringing vengeance to the ship that had taken *Icarus* from him. He would get in close and fire his torpedoes at the monster, or he would die trying.

"Come on, lads," he shouted at the torpedomen as they worked to get the tubes ready on both sides of his ship. "Get yer backs into it!" He was well lined up on the enemy ship, some 9000 yards out and cruising at his top speed. By god, this ship was fast! It was running over thirty knots and his 36 knot destroyer was laboring to close the range. He would have to come left to lead the ship by a good measure if he was to have any chance of hitting it, and that would make his ship a fine target when he turned.

Above them the black night was being ripped open with blazing fireballs and the hideous streaks of the enemy rockets. As he stared at the enemy ship it seem a seething medusa, with each missile contrail a winding, hissing snake with venomous death in its fangs. *Lookout* was swamped and on fire, falling off to their stern, *Lightning* was battered by enemy gunfire, straddled and hit amidships, where one of her torpedoes exploded, breaking the ship near in two, yet *Intrepid* plowed on. And when the enemy guns began to range on him, the first round blackening the forecastle off the starboard side, he bellowed out the order to fire. He would bloody well get his torpedoes in the water, come what may.

The other three destroyers had been pounded into submission by the incredible rate of deadly accurate fire from the enemy deck guns. They were turning away, some making smoke, others burning so badly that that would have been a needless afterthought. It was *Intrepid* that still carried the charge forward the only ship that got her fish into the sea.

Captain Maud watched the torpedoes go, looking to see a subflight of three Albacores come right up the wakes of the destroyers, roaring in over the wave tops on his starboard side as they veered to attack. He raised his blackthorn and shook it at his comrades with a hearty cheer. "Go on and get the bastard," he shouted. "Get your bloody teeth in 'em, boys!"

It was Tom Wales of 827 Squadron and two of his mates. They had put their planes right on the deck, just feet above the water and came roaring down the wakes of the four destroyers, shielded by the ships until they came under that deadly shell fire.

"Stay down real low, and find any cover you can…" That was what Parsons had told him outside the briefing room.

As *Kirov's* shells found their marks on the destroyers, several Klinoks did not see the three Albacores running up behind the destroyers, and they selected other targets at higher elevation. The planes veered at the last minute, emerging from behind the ships and roared on past, like flying fish that had come up from under the sea, their fuselages and wings wet with spray. It was the most daring thing Maud had ever seen, and he continued to wave his blackthorn walking stick high overhead, his deep voice urging the planes on. Then he saw a burst of fire from the dark enemy ahead, and heard a grinding rattle.

Samsonov had seen the planes at the last minute, so close now on his targeting radar, and he immediately activated the ship's close in defense Gatling guns. There were three guns on each side of the ship, with six rotating barrels and sinister looking housings that looked like looked like soldier's helmets. The barrels whirled and bright fire burst from the guns, sending a hail of steel toward the oncoming planes. Two were hit, riddled with shells and careening wildly, end over end, as they hit the water, but Tommy Wales pulled hard on his torpedo release and he got his fish in the water. Immediately veering behind the burning mass of *Lightning* just ahead on his left, he was shielded from the withering fire of the Gatling gun that had targeted his plane.

He would be the only man that would return from 827 squadron that night. The rest had all been taken by the SAMs. Three of nine men survived in 831 Squadron. They had pulled their levers early and then dove for the deck, but their fish were not well aimed and they went wildly astray. 832 Squadron off *Victorious* lost eight of her twelve planes, and only because *Kirov's* missiles had broken up the squadron as it descended and scattered it so badly that the remaining four pilots bugged out. They had never seen anything like the terrible fireworks this ship had flung at them, and they hoped they never would again. They had flown bravely through enemy flak, dodging the mindless rounds as they puffed and exploded in the sky around them. But these things came at you as if they knew your name. They were death in a steel cased shell with wings on it, and frightening beyond belief.

~~~

"Torpedoes in the water!" shouted Tasarov on sonar. His system immediately went to active rapid pulse detection mode, beeping in ever shortening intervals to indicate the closing range of the oncoming threat. "I have three contacts."

"Come right, thirty degrees hard!" shouted Fedorov.

The ship heeled over with the high speed turn, but Karpov could see that they would easily avoid the barbs *Intrepid* had hurled at them on this course, yet that turn would put them dangerously close to the last torpedo, the fish that had fallen from Tom Wales Albacore II.

"*Shkval!*" said Karpov reflexively.

The fast rocket torpedo was fired, acquiring a target in seconds and racing with impossible speed to destroy it. Karpov looked back out the port view panes and saw the explosive dome of seawater slowly subside, and the threatening streaks of two more torpedoes leaving cold white wakes behind them. Then the scene grew quiet again, and there was only *Kirov's* churning wake, and the distant glow of fire on the heavy British ships. Tasarov signaled that all was well.

The ship had turned on a heading of 292 degrees northwest now, still running at full battle speed. They had raced past the Almeria bay in the last forty minutes, coming around past another flat headland that jutted south into the Alboran Sea. Ahead Fedorov could see the wrinkled shadowy highlands rising from a rocky coastline and climbing steeply to heights up over 1800 meters. The ship was heading straight for them on this course, in spite of the danger posed by submarines that might be lurking near the coast. It was the only sea room they would find off their starboard quarter for a while, and he knew he would soon have to come left again to get round Cabo Sacratif looming in the distance. Yet they had finally pulled well ahead of the British battleships, and the range was now increasing with each passing minute.

They saw one last bright orange belch of fire from their pursuers, and then the British guns fell silent. *Nelson* was still burning badly, with her smoke so thick that the entire conning tower was engulfed in the black plume and the ship had to turn to get the prevailing wind off angle so the weary bridge crew could get air and function. *Rodney* had hurled one last vengeful salvo at them, and now the rounds came soaring in from her A turret and fell in a tight spread so close to the aft section of the ship that they could feel their rump jostled by the near impact. She would not find the range again.

The British ships knew that the sea devil they had been chasing would now escape them. *Kirov* was opening her lead steadily, and there was no way they could possibly catch up. The intercept course they had wisely chosen allowed them only this brief window for engagement. So now they turned thirty points to port, the command of the battle squadron falling to Admiral Fraser on *Rodney*. Syfret had been hustled off the bridge of *Nelson*, alive but still unconscious below decks. Fraser also got word from Admiral St. Lyster that *Indomitable* had been hit by one of these rockets, and took some heavy damage below the fight deck amidships. They couldn't stand to lose any more carriers. *Eagle* was enough, so he wisely decided to turn his battered ships southward to cover the carrier force. Most of the destroyers were fairly well beaten up, except for *Intrepid*, who came out remarkably unscathed, though she had gotten in closer to this devil than any other ship.

Slowly the rumble of guns and roar of the missiles subsided, and the night once again settled heavily over the scene. The 'Battle of Almeria Bay' had been fought for well over an hour and was now concluded. Though *Rodney* and *Nelson* had clearly taken the harder blows, they would say that they were not the first to turn from the heat of battle, and that their enemy had fled into the night, breaking off with her superior speed to escape the grasp of their 16 inch guns. It was an old story for the *Nelson* class battleships. *Scharnhorst* and *Gneisenau* had escaped them in the past, and they were not fast enough to chase either *Bismarck* or *Tirpitz* until the former was stopped by planes off the *Ark Royal* so *Rodney* could catch up. Their day had come and gone, and they survived to be eventually folded into laborious convoy escort duty later in the war, still a stalwart threat, but well past their hour of glory.

When the destroyer attack failed and the air strike suffered such grievous losses, Fraser knew his men had suffered enough for one night. They had all done their best, and a good many DSOs would be awarded for this action—but too many of them posthumously. As destroyer *Intrepid* led the remnant of the flotilla south, he gave the order to turn and effect a rendezvous with the carriers. Then he tramped listlessly into the wireless room to get a message off to Tovey. It was just three short words, and they would carry the whole of what his men and ships had striven for and failed to win in the end.

'Geronimo...Geronimo...Geronimo...'

~~~

Submarine *Talisman* had been lying quietly in the cool still waters off the coast of Adra, her Asdic operator listening to the churning sea battle above. Lieutenant Commander Michael Willmott had drifted the boat up to periscope depth. He had come to this boat in time to get in on some exciting North Atlantic patrols. His boat had hunted for the cruiser *Prince Eugen* and was also engaged in the hunt for *Scharnhorst* and *Gneisenau,* and thought he had them in his sights on March 12, diving to begin his attack. But as he lined up on the targets he suddenly realized he was looking at HMS *Rodney* and *King George V!* He made the best of an embarrassing moment and used the situation as a drill for a practice attack before surfacing and signaling his presence to the battleships.

Now he was listening to the rumble of *Rodney's* guns off to the southeast, their massive report still audible at this shallow depth, a dull boom resounding through the sea. The old girl still has a temper when she wants to, he thought. He was glad he had not stupidly fired on her those months ago. It seemed his boat had been fated to run afoul of his own side far too often in this war. A year ago he had fired on what he thought was an enemy submarine and later learned it was Favell's boat, HMS *Otus*. Thankfully all his torpedoes missed. Most recently he had been stalking a U-Boat in the Bay of Biscay, and when he surfaced to get up some speed he was quickly pounced upon by a British Sunderland and depth charged!

Talisman was knocked about quite a bit, and put in to Gibraltar for repairs on the morning of 13th of August. Operation Pedestal was in full gear and he was gratefully spared that duty while the engineers worked feverishly on his boat at the docks—a little too feverishly, he thought. He remembered pulling a mate aside and asking him what all the haste was about.

"Can't say as I know, Lieutenant," the man said. "We were just to have this boat seaworthy by sunset, and that's all I know."

"By tonight? Well look at her—look at that hull buckling there."

"Don't worry none sir, we'll patch her up nice and good…But I'd keep to shallow water if I was you, sir. None of that deep diving and such."

Willmott was flabbergasted, but he had orders in hand by 15:00 hours that afternoon and was told to get out into the Alboran Sea and lurk in the coastal waters off Spain to look for a renegade French battlecruiser. And here he was, at a little before 04:00 hours on the morning of August 14th.

At least it was a little excitement. He could be stuck in an office in the bowels of the Rock answering a raft of tedious questions about that Sunderland incident. Now he had a shot at another fast capital ship, and by god, there the bugger was! He spied the threatening silhouette of what looked like a battlecruiser, the ship his Asdic operator had been listening to for the last half hour, and she was running fast and furious right in his direction. All he had to do now was fire.

"Down scope! Load tubes one and four. On the double quick!"

The crews rushed to battle stations and he had his fish ready to fry in record time. He raised the periscope again to check his alignment. There it was, still barreling in at high speed, some 3000 meters out. He could take a long shot, or he could wait silently in the shallows until it came just a little closer, he thought. While he was considering his options his luck ran out. Something came out of the murky depths with lightning speed and found his boat first. He felt a massive explosion well aft, the terrible sound of metal wrenching apart, then the rush of seawater raging in. The tail of the sub had been blown clean away.

In one last moment of life he looked at his dazed Executive Officer, eyes wide and said: "My God, Johnny. I think they've buggered us!"

They were the last words spoken by any man on the boat.

~~~

An interval of uneasy calm ensued, and the men aboard *Kirov* eased back in their posts, breathing a little more calmly after the *Shkval* had killed the sub. Tasarov again signaled all clear and Karpov visibly relaxed, his shoulders slumping, face drawn with fatigue. They had been running the gauntlet for the last three hours, evading the heavy blows of the enemy with everything their skill and the amazing technological advantages of their ship could deliver.

Fedorov looked at the position of the enemy surface action groups on radar and he knew they had broken through. He consulted his navigation board and settled on a course of 250 degrees southwest. They were still 240 miles east of Gibraltar, and when Byko called and asked him to slow the ship down so he could check on some possible damage aft, he reduced to twenty knots for a time and changed his heading slightly west to an area where he thought the thermals would not provide any acoustic cover for another lurking submarine.

At the time he knew nothing of the codeword that had been flashed from Fraser to Tovey indicating that he had escaped the grasp of Force Z and was headed west. He knew nothing of Home Fleet as it made its steady approach, now well past Lisbon and churning its way south. His only thought was that they were now out in front of Force Z, out of range of those terrible 16 inch guns, and not likely to be caught again. He intended to get back up near thirty knots at his earliest opportunity, and to make Gibraltar by nine or ten in the morning for the slog through the straits.

But the best laid plans of mice and men, have oft gone awry.

Part XI

The Eleventh Hour

"It takes something more than intelligence to act intelligently."

~ *Fyodor Dostoyevsky, Crime and Punishment*

Chapter 31

There was one more attack just before dawn out of Gibraltar. A well coordinated strike from both land based aircraft and the remaining strike aircraft from Force Z's Carriers. As before, the planes and pilots were gallant, but they were seen from the every moment they took off and assumed their formations to begin their approach, and they were targeted by *Kirov*'s deadly SAM systems long before they could pose any threat. Yet it cost them another eighteen Klinok missiles before Rodenko reported the remaining flights were breaking off and turning away. They had already expended twenty-four Klinoks earlier that morning to repel the first carrier strike.

"What is our magazine still holding?" Fedorov asked, concerned.

Samsonov took note, a look on his face like a poker player who was slowly watching his chips diminishing as he pushed one stack after another out onto the table, winning hand after hand, but getting nothing in return. "Sir," he began, "this last action has reduced our Klinok SAM inventory to thirty-seven missiles, and we still have thirty-five S-300s remaining—seventy-two total SAMs."

"What about our primaries?"

"Nine missiles each on the Moskit-II system and MOS-III Starfires. Eight P-900 cruise missiles remaining."

That was now a matter of some concern. He looked at Karpov, his eyes clearly carrying the message he was trying to convey. "Twenty six missiles," he said slowly. "That's all we have left in the way of anything that can seriously damage a ship. When they are gone this invincible battlecruiser becomes a big, fast anti-aircraft cruiser, and little more. When the SAMs are expended, then we have only the Gatling Guns remaining against air strikes, and when *they* run out of ammunition, we will be more vulnerable to enemy air attacks than a tramp steamer. I note from Rodenko's screen that we did not sink either of the two British battleships, though we undoubtedly hurt them badly. Force Z will still be behind us now, though I would think they would be more than cautious about engaging us again, even if they could. That said, they will soon be reinforced by Admiral Burrough's detachment, Force X. He was escorting the surviving merchant ships on their final leg to Malta, and his force took some significant damage, but he will have destroyers to reinforce Force Z and a couple of damaged cruisers, *Nigeria* and *Kenya*. My guess is that they will reform as one new task force to block the route east again if the Straits of Gibraltar prove a major obstacle for us. They will put out the fires on those battleships and still be a dangerous force coming up on us from behind."

"Not if we race for the straits now," said Karpov. "What else might they throw at us? Are there more ships at Gibraltar?"

"I cannot be certain," said Fedorov. "The reference material I have is not comprehensive, and things are already in a jumble. Destroyers have been shuffled about from one task force to another and the history is starting to look like well stirred cream in a cup of hot tea—hard to see my tea leaves now. I think we are fortunate that they dispatched so many ships east to support Operation Pedestal, but anything they do have in Gibraltar will be deployed to block the straits. Given the situation with our missile inventory, we must be very judicious in how we employ them."

"Will there be large capital ships?"

"No, I think we can safely rule that out."

"Then the deck guns should be sufficient. Our rate of fire and accuracy is so superior that we can handle their destroyers and cruisers easily enough, and our ammunition there is still solid, is it not Samsonov?"

"Sir, we have expended a total of 434 of 3000 rounds on the 152mm batteries."

"Good. That leaves us well over 2500 rounds. I have a suggestion, Fedorov. What about the KA-40? We could send it ahead to survey the area and report back. With its jammers they will not be able to see it on radar, and it can defend itself from anything that might happen to spot or attack it. In fact, it can even drop a few sonobuoys to see if any more submarines have been deployed in the straits. This way we will know what cards the enemy is holding and can make better tactical decisions on how to best employ our remaining weapon systems."

Fedorov thought for a moment. "This is our last helo," he said. "Yet I suppose it does us no good to leave it sitting in the hanger as though it were already gone. Alright, Karpov, we'll risk it. We certainly have plenty of aviation fuel left for it with the other two helicopters gone. You can make the arrangements. I must go and inform Admiral Volsky of our situation and see if he has any orders for us. The next stage is crucial and I want to keep him in the soup."

"Certainly, Fedorov. Certainly." Karpov nodded, but inwardly wished they could handle the matter themselves. Volsky was an experienced and wise commander, but Karpov thought the Admiral was too cautious, and believed himself to be the superior tactician. Thus far they had come over a thousand miles through hostile seas and the ship had been fought well. He was proud of himself, and confident they could complete the last leg of their marathon and get safely out into the Atlantic.

Two messages were to change all that. The first was from damage control Chief Byko, calling on the ship's comm-system to report a matter of some concern. He had been below decks in the aft of the ship where those two near misses had fallen close off the stern. Now he reported that they were taking seawater below decks near the vital machinery that would run the ship's drive shafts.

"It is a slow leak, sir. Nothing the pumps cannot handle for the moment, but it could get worse, particularly as we continue to run the engines near full like this. If you could give me some time, a few hours, I might get a better look at the damage. I can't get men in there when the ship is at thirty knots."

This weighed heavily on Fedorov. They could not afford to lose the great advantage of speed. Still wary of Force Z at his back, he told Byko that they would have to maintain this speed for another two hours, but when they had put more distance between the ship and their pursuers, he would cut power to any speed he advised. As long as

Rodenko could still see the enemy behind them, they could take any action necessary before a threat closed the range. This was the one great advantage *Kirov* still had at her disposal. She could both see and fight her enemies at very long rage range, like an aircraft carrier might do in WWII. Her only problem was that when she sent out her missiles to attack, they never returned.

That matter settled, he was about to exit the bridge when the second message came in, this time from Nikolin at communications. The young Lieutenant was sitting at his station, weary, but dutiful nonetheless as he waited for his shift to end. Then he heard something odd in his headset, and it drew his attention, a steady beeping which he soon realized was old Morse code. At first he thought to ignore it as simple signals traffic from the many ships and bases in the region around them. But being curious, he decided to listen in. The message seemed to be repeating itself, over and over. He began to decode it, writing the letters down on a note pad he had been doodling on, but it made no sense when he assumed the language was English. Perhaps it was being sent by a Spanish operator, or even French. Then something in his innately Russian head heard a *Russian* Morse code, with its unique melodies that would be used to convey their special alphabet. He immediately began to make sense of the signal, writing the letters down in large capital letters. The signal faded slightly, but repeated. *Dash—dash—dash...dot—dash—dot—dot...* He had written that last set of letters below the first, and then put them together, staring at them, quite surprised: НИКОЛИН. It repeated three times, and two short words followed.

"Captain..." he said tentatively. "I have just received an odd message." Both Fedorov and Karpov turned, waiting.

"Well don't just sit there with that stupid look on your face, Nikolin," said Karpov. "What is it?"

"Well sir...It's in Morse code and I've written down the letters, but it's Russian Morse, sir, and look what they spell!"

Karpov walked over to his station, somewhat annoyed, but when he looked at what Nikolin had written he turned for Fedorov, clearly bothered by what he had seen.

Half way out the aft hatch Fedorov waited. "Well, what is it?"

"My *name*," said Nikolin. It repeats three times and then sends two more words: 'you lose.' It repeated three times, sir. Then I lost the signal."

"*Russian* Morse code? Your name?"

"My surname, sir—Nikolin. Everyone calls me that. No one ever uses my given name. But sir…" he bit his lip, and then launched his missile. "I was playing cards with Orlov below decks on my last leave after dining yesterday. I thought I had a winning hand, sir, two pair, but then Orlov drew one last card and…Well, that was all he said to me: Nikolin, Nikolin, Nikolin—*you lose.* Then he laid down his cards and there were five spades…"

~~~

An hour later both Fedorov and Karpov were with Volsky in the sick bay, their faces grim and worried.

"I thought I had a headache before," said Volsky. "Then the missiles and gunfire started again. Now this! Why didn't you report this Orlov business to me earlier?"

"I'm sorry, Admiral," Doctor Zolkin spoke up. "That was my doing. Fedorov gave me the news while you were sleeping. I thought it could wait."

"Then what does this mean? Orlov is alive? Nikolin believes that *he* sent this Morse code?"

"He does, sir," said Karpov. "And I tell you it would be just like Orlov to do such a thing. He must have bailed out before we targeted the KA-226, and now he's goading us. We got the helicopter, so you have nothing to worry about on that account."

"Yes, we got the helicopter, now all I have to worry about is Orlov! The man may not be a historian like Mister Fedorov here, but he knows enough to cause real problems if he opens his mouth."

"Who would believe anything he said? Besides that, he's in Spain, and speaks only Russian. No one could even understand him. Yes, he'll cause a little trouble. He'll need food, and money, and he'll have to find new clothes. So he may hurt a few people until he gets what he wants, and then he's more than likely to just get himself drunk in a bar, and attract the attention of the local authorities. They'll arrest him and he'll be detained for the duration of the war. Perhaps it will do him some good."

"We might hope so," said Volsky, "but I have read the file on this man when I took command of the ship. He was mixed up with some very shady characters before he came to the navy. He is cagy, and ruthless. Look how he planned his escape. We may have much more to fear in this situation than we realize. It would not be surprised if he evaded capture, and then what might he do? I can tell you one thing. He will not stay in Spain. He will try to make his way to Russia if he can, and then we get real trouble."

"He's a long way from Russia, through a lot of enemy occupied countries."

"Even if he is captured and detained, what happens after the war ends and they release him?"

Karpov frowned. "We just sent the last KA-40 out an hour ago to scout the straits. It's due back soon, and we could send a detachment of Marines to look for Orlov. Send Troyak after him. He'll get the job done."

"That may not be as easy as it first sounds," said Fedorov. "Where would they look? Orlov could be anywhere along that coast east of Cartagena now, or well inland if he made it to shore. The signal we received was too brief to get a fix on his location. Finding him may be impossible. It is not like we can simply send Troyak over to make discrete inquiries. None of the Marines speak the language either, and for that matter that whole scenario is simply not practical. I had a bad feeling about this the moment we fired those S-300s. This may have implications we can scarcely imagine now."

Admiral Volsky shook his head. "I have the same feeling. The man will cause nothing but misery and trouble. Perhaps there is nothing we can do about it beyond hoping that his bad temperament gets him jailed as Karpov suggests, or even killed. I know that is a hard thing to say or wish on one of our own, but there is little more we can do now."

He looked at them, a weariness in his eyes. "Now for the rest of your bad news. What does Byko say?"

"Flooding below the waterline near the propulsion shafts." Fedorov was blunt and to the point. "He wants us to reduce revolutions so he can get men inside near the shafts, and put out divers to seal the leak on the hull again. It must have been splinter and concussion damage from those near misses. It aggravated the initial damage there when the helicopter was jettisoned."

"Can we make these repairs safely?"

"We have been running at thirty knots since midnight. In that time we fought our battle and moved well west. We are now ninety nautical miles from the Straits of Gibraltar. Force Z is sixty nautical miles southeast of our present position, and making fifteen knots in a slow circle. They are gathering all their remaining ships and covering the carriers. Even if they turned to try and engage us again, that gives us at least three hours for Byko to get men in the water and effect repairs before we would have to move again...Unless they release their cruisers and destroyers to pursue us."

"If they head in our direction we can discourage them at long range if need be," said Karpov. "Remember, our deck guns can range out to 50,000 meters if need be with radar guided round tracking. That long range ammunition is very limited, but we have a couple hundred rounds in the magazines."

"Very well," said Volsky. "Tell Byko to get started."

"His men should be in the water in ten minutes, sir."

"And what does our helicopter report? We must have received telemetry by now."

Karpov looked at Fedorov, clearly uneasy. Then the young Captain spoke up, his manner somewhat discouraged, and almost apologetic. He had been surprised by the Italian battleships earlier, but this was an even harder blow.

"I'm afraid we have more trouble ahead than we do behind us. Our KA-40 had a good look west of Gibraltar and reports another large British fleet at sea off Lagos, Portugal, and moving south at about twenty-five knots."

"I would like to think that is just another convoy heading for Gibraltar," said Volsky, "but not at that speed."

"True, sir." Fedorov was looking at his shoes, clearly bothered.

"Then this is a battle fleet?"

"We spotted four capital ships in a long battle line, a carrier, at least four cruisers and a handful of destroyers. It can only be Home Fleet, sir. How they could have learned of us and moved south so quickly is amazing."

"But they did," said Volsky, his eyes dark with concern. "So now it is our turn to be astounded by the sudden appearance of an unexpected enemy at sea. Lagos… How far away are they?"

"Some 200 miles, sir. If they keep to their present course and speed they would arrive at the western approaches to the straits in another eight hours, right around 16:00."

"We are ninety miles from Gibraltar now. Yes? Then let me do some mathematics. If we give Byko two hours, and can then run again at thirty knots for three more, it will take us five hours to reach the eastern approaches to these straits. That is a slim margin to slip through. I imagine we may have minefields to contend with?"

"Very likely, sir."

"We used the UDAV-2 missile system to blast our way through at Bonifacio," Karpov put in quickly.

"Yes, and that was very clever, Captain, but how long did it take you to transit the strait?"

"Two hours," said Fedorov.

"Two, plus three, plus two makes seven. If this British Fleet hurries they can probably trim another hour's sailing time from their run as well. Gentlemen, the numbers do not add up very favorably." The admiral was not happy.

"Our choices are clear," said Karpov. "We must now decide whether to forego these repairs Byko wishes to make, and run for the straits at once, or to wait and risk another major battle if we are late."

"You say four capital ships, Fedorov?"

"Yes, sir. Probably all four *King George V* class battleships. We fought the first two earlier in the Atlantic and, though we damaged them, it took three hits to force *Prince of Wales* to drop out of their battle line, and all from our best missile, the Moskit-IIs."

"Yes, I have been listening to them launch all night. I lost count. How many are left?"

"Nine, sir."

"And another nine Mos-IIIs, with eight more P-900 cruise missiles," said Karpov. "It is enough, sir. I can get us through."

"Who is commanding this British fleet?" The Admiral looked to Fedorov now.

"We cannot know for certain, sir, but my best estimate would be the fleet commander himself, Admiral John Tovey."

"What kind of man is he?"

"Experienced, highly disciplined, an excellent military planner, well respected by his peers and all who serve under him. He can be a single minded and determined foe, sir. His pursuit of the *Bismarck* was typical of his style at sea."

"This is the same man we encountered earlier?"

"Yes, sir. After the Captain struck him at range, he fell off, linked up with additional forces, called for the support of Force H, and then continued his pursuit."

"You fought this man, Mister Karpov. What is your military opinion?"

"He was determined, that much is clear. But outmatched, sir. *Kirov* can do the job, I assure you."

"Oh? Then why did you have to resort to tactical nuclear weapons?"

Karpov was silent. "I have answered this, Admiral. In my mind I saw no reason why the ship should not use the full measure of our real power."

"Yet I have spoken with the other officers on the bridge that day, and they tell me the tactical situation was not favorable. We were confronted by four separate task forces, and to engage them all would have most likely depleted our entire missile inventory."

"Which is why I elected to let one missile do the work of many."

"Yes, we noticed," said Zolkin.

"I am well aware of your opinion in the matter, Doctor," Karpov said sharply.

"There is no need to go over all that again," said Volsky. "What was done, was done. Karpov knows what he did, and why. He has asked to serve and redeem himself, and he has done that."

Karpov raised his chin, sniffing. "Thank you, Admiral. While I believe I can win the battle with our conventional weapons, it is also my duty to state that we still have our nuclear option should it become necessary."

"I am well aware of that, Mister Karpov, but this consideration is a cold logic. It asks me to trade the ammunition we save for the lives of hundreds, perhaps thousands of men. Believe me, I do not relish that thought. What I wish to know now is how this Admiral Tovey will fight us if it comes to that?"

"He will be a tenacious and dangerous opponent in battle sir. If you want my opinion he will not like his tactical situation at dusk this evening , and may wish to wait and fight his battle tomorrow. We will be arriving near sunset, and his ships will all be starkly silhouetted by the sun."

"That makes no difference," said Volsky. "We can see them as easily at midnight."

"Yes, sir, but he does not know that. Remember that he will think tactically like a man of his era. If our striking power was as limited in range as his own, I do not think he would hesitate to close and engage. As it is, however, I believe he will have learned from his experience in the North Atlantic. He will think we fight more like an aircraft carrier than a battleship. He knows we are capable of scouting his forces out and striking at very long ranges, and this is, in fact, our great advantage. The key to battling a strong enemy carrier has always been air power, but our tremendous SAM defense has neutralized this option. Every time they throw an air strike at us it gets cut to pieces. If he uses his planes again, it will simply be to harass us, or distract us."

"You agree, Karpov?"

"I do, sir. Their air power is not a concern for the moment. At least not in this engagement. We have enough missiles to keep it at bay and neutralize it."

"Then how do you attack a strong carrier, Captain. One that can neutralize your air power?"

"Sir? You saturate it with missiles, a minimum eight, and preferably sixteen or more if you have them."

"How could the British replicate such a tactic against us?"

"They would have to come at us with more targets than we can neutralize." Karpov did not like the direction this was heading.

"Do they have enough planes to do this, Fedorov?"

"Probably forty to fifty at Gibraltar, perhaps twenty four on the carrier they have with them. We hurt the air squadrons in Force Z badly, but they could throw in another twenty or thirty aircraft as well, mostly fighters, but they can still carry bombs."

"Mostly fighters….We have seen what just one of those did when it got in close. I have not forgotten why I have spent the last three days with Doctor Zolkin. That is enough planes to seriously deplete our remaining SAM inventory. I am not liking what I am hearing, gentlemen. Now, what about his surface ships? How will he fight?"

Fedorov spoke again. "After what happened to the Americans Admiral Tovey will also be wary of concentrating his force in any one central task force. For this reason I believe he will not enter the Straits of Gibraltar tonight, even if he does get there first. No, sir. He will wait for us in the western approaches, and he will disperse whatever force he has in a web there, which we will have to penetrate. Then, once we commit ourselves to a breakout heading, he will make one mad dash and engage us with everything he has—all his ships and every plane they can put into the air. His dilemma is how to close the range on us as quickly as possible so the fourteen inch guns on his battleships can have a chance at getting some hits. And it would only take one hit from a shell of that caliber to decisively shift the battle in his favor. Yet, there have been engagements where as many as a hundred rounds are fired with no hits obtained. Last night the darkness, their inability to use radar, and our tremendous speed helped us a great deal. That said, they put rounds so close to us that it damaged our aft hull. We have been lucky thus far against the Italians and Force Z."

"Will we also have to also watch our back?"

"Force Z will certainly move up behind us and block the straits, particularly if we are engaged with the British Home Fleet."

"Volsky took that in, his eyes distant, and focused on his inner muse. "Karpov?" he said at last.

"I agree with Fedorov's assessment."

"Then how will we proceed?"

"If they disperse their forces as Fedorov suggests, then we must pick one point in the line for our breakthrough, preferably at one of the extreme flanks. We will attack this point in his defense and neutralize it quickly. We do not have enough missiles left to engage all the battleships decisively at one time in this option. But we can hit one very hard, and then simply run through the gap at high speed. I suggest we focus on a route to the southwest, and hit them on their left flank."

"How many missiles will it take us to do this?"

"We will target the most dangerous ship along our route of advance and use perhaps three missiles—five if necessary. If cruisers are deployed there, then a single missile should be sufficient to stop a ship in that class. For their destroyers, I will simply use the cannon."

"Those tactics did not stop those other battleships in Force Z."

"It slowed them down sufficiently to allow us to use our speed and break through, sir. It jarred them and limited their gunnery effort as well. We can fight this battle exactly as we did at Bonifacio or against this Force Z"

Volsky nodded. "Unless our luck finally runs out and we take a serious hit. What if this Admiral Tovey places his battleships close enough to one another for supporting fire? These big guns have a long range, correct Fedorov?"

"They do sir. With good light for sighting we can expect fire from as far away as 28,000 meters, even 32,000."

"So even if we do saturate and neutralize one of these big ships the others may very well still have the range on us. This is not a very satisfactory situation, Karpov. And I must tell you that this business aft with Byko is most disturbing now. If our speed is affected…" He did not have to say anything more.

"I have another strategic option," said Karpov. "And no, Doctor, it will not involve nuclear weapons." He gave Zolkin a sidelong glance.

"Very well, let me hear it," Volsky folded his arms, waiting.

"Fedorov's remark about the night action is very true, sir. The darkness prevented their optical sighting and allowed us to use our speed to evade their gunnery efforts. If possible, it would be better to run the strait at night as well. We should not wait until dawn. Let Byko have all the time he needs to assure we'll have no trouble with speed. Then move for Gibraltar so as to arrive there after sunset."

"That will give us better odds, I suppose," said Volsky. "But I am still not entirely convinced we can face four battleships and run through their defense without taking even one hit."

"I was not finished, sir, begging your pardon, Admiral."

"Continue, Mister Karpov."

"We arrive after sunset, and if Fedorov is correct they will be deploying in the western approaches. We use the KA-40 to scout their position on the other side of the straits and feed us targeting information, and then we hit them with the cruise missiles before we even enter the straits. Fedorov suggested I begin the last engagement with a P-900 simply because it was slow, and he wanted them to see it coming. That was clever, because I believe this had a strong psychological impact on them. We must break their will as much as the steel in their ships. So consider this… Darkness falls. We linger near the eastern entrance to the strait and target two P-900s on each of the four battleships. The missiles make quite a shocking display at night. They will see them arc over the headlands, from a completely unseen enemy, and when they hit home it will shake their morale considerably. This Admiral Tovey will look at his well laid trap and see all four of his precious King class battleships on fire, and yet he will not have any inkling of where we are, and will be powerless to strike back at us."

"They will see us firing the missiles from Gibraltar, and radio our position" said Fedorov.

"All the better. The fact remains that they will not be able to do anything about it. Not without entering the straits and coming for us. We will be well out of the range of his guns in that position."

"Very dramatic," said Volsky. He looked at Zolkin now and said: "I told you this man was one of the best tactical officers in the fleet, Doctor."

"Yes," said Zolkin. "He has the bravery of being out of range. It's very comfortable—but just a little a bit devious at the same time."

Karpov rolled his eyes, but was not willing to get into a missile war with Zolkin at the moment. "Consider it…Now the British have all four of their best ships hit and burning, and then we make our demand that they stand down or we will rain hell upon them. They will not know we are low on missiles. Tell them if they do not give way we will sink their ships before they ever lay eyes on us. We need never come within range of their guns, because they will be at the bottom of the sea before we transit the Strait of Gibraltar. If they do not yield, then we send over the Moskit-IIs, only this time there will be sufficient range to program them for a plunging attack angle. One on each battleship could have very good results."

Volsky scratched his head, looking from one to the other, and then came to a conclusion. "Well here we are at the eleventh hour, gentlemen. I have heard your analysis, and yet there is one other weapon we have not discussed that we might try using here."

"Sir? I thought you did not wish to consider our nuclear option."

"Oh, I considered it, Mister Karpov, and I have discarded it. The weapon I am thinking of now is intelligence. We have looked at two options here. The first has considerable risk. We make a run at this man, give him a shove as we go and hope to slip by him in the dark. It might work if our luck holds out. Now you suggest that we punch this man in the face first, and then threaten him with further harm if he does not stand aside. Yes, it is a strong tactic. Something our old friend Orlov might do. But I will propose another solution. Suppose we talk to this man *before* we punch him in the nose, eh? I think he might be more inclined to hear us."

"Negotiate first? Before we've shown him what we can do to him if he persists?"

"Exactly. Mister Karpov, I believe he has already seen what we are capable of—weeks ago in the North Atlantic. He already knows we can hurt him before he even catches a glimpse of us. This is why he will position his ships to be within range from the moment we first exit the strait. Yes, he knows how dangerous we are. He knows we can hurt him severely, and yet here he comes. That is a different sort of bravery, is it not." He glanced at Zolkin.

The Admiral's eyes gleamed with a sudden inner fire. "I want to talk to this man—face to face. I want to look him in the eye and see if we can reach an understanding *before* any more men or ships die—on either side."

He smiled, looking at the Doctor. "Dmitri, it has been a wonderful stay, but now I feel sufficiently recovered to re-assume my duties. Mister Fedorov, Mister Karpov, you have served well. I commend you both, but as of this moment I am formally re-assuming command of the ship. Fedorov will continue as *Starpom*, and you will remain on the bridge as Executive Tactical Officer, Karpov. Now, gentlemen. Let us get the ship in order and I will tell you what we are going to do."

~~~

Aboard *King George V* the wireless operator got a most unusual message, just before sunset, and in plain English. It was directed to Admiral John Tovey, coming as a great surprise to him when he heard it. He listened to it carefully, repeating quietly over and over, and thinking about it as he listened. Considering the gravity of the situation, Tovey found it welcome. He had to hurry on if he was to get a good blocking position in the western approaches. He was nearly there, but all reports out of Gibraltar indicated the enemy was now in a very good location to make a run for the straits, heading south of the Rock, just outside the range of their shore batteries. These circumstances were going to see him arriving there just before sunset, a most unfavorable situation, with all his ships nicely silhouetted on the horizon.

When he finally caught up with *Bismarck*, he wisely elected to refuse battle at dusk and fight in the morning. If at all possible he wanted to fight at sunrise, with his enemy well silhouetted instead of his own ships. That may not matter to the enemy, he thought, but it would certainly help his own gunners. This message gave him just what he needed now—time—and he agreed to it at once, smiling at his flag officer of the watch.

"Get a message off immediately," he said. "Send it in the clear." He folded his arms.

"What shall we send, sir?"

"Las Palomas. Just that. Nothing more."

Chapter 32

The island of Las Palomas is the southernmost point in all of Spain, poised at the edge of the Straits of Gibraltar and marking the boundary between the Atlantic Ocean and Mediterranean Sea. It dangles like a pendant from the Spanish mainland, a small heart-shaped spit of land no more than 1800 feet wide, with an equal length. Layers of history can be found there, from yawning caves where Paleolithic petroglyph drawings of horses grace the stony walls, to ruins of ancient Roman sites, and on through the centuries. Its strategic position at the entrance to the Straits of Gibraltar had seen it fortified by many empires. The nearby Spanish town of Tarifa just north of the island on the mainland was named after the Moorish general Tarif Ben Malik, who spearheaded the invasion in the year 711. Some said that the word "tariff" was derived from his name when the island became one of the first ports in the region to levy fees on ships seeking an anchorage. Remnants of castle walls and towers can still be found there, some built by the famous Abdul Ar Raman, a prominent Caliph of the Moors who invaded southern Europe until he was eventually stopped by Charles Martel at the Battle of Tours.

Given the island's location, it had seen many desperate battles over the years. The Spanish fought to reclaim their land from the Moors for centuries, and the island had also been noted for a few famous last stands, one in the year 1292 when the Spanish Lord Guzman El Bueno was holed up in a fortress there and besieged by 5000 Moorish warriors. A treacherous rival, the Lord Don Juan had kidnapped Guzman's son and thought to force his surrender with the threat of the boy's execution. Yet stalwart to the end, Guzman refused, standing on the high walls and even throwing down his own knife so his antagonists might use it to kill his son.

In 1812 it was the British who joined the Spanish there to make a gallant defense against the invading Armies of Napoleon. Jean Francois Leval sent 15,000 French soldiers against Tarifa and was stopped by the tenacious defense of the 3000 man garrison. In the end the miserable and incessant rains had as much to do with the outcome of the battle as anything else. The French army slogged away, wet and beset with illness, leaving many of their siege guns stuck in the thickening mud. Now it would see warriors meet again, for a delicate negotiation on the razor's edge of war.

Just after 17:00 hours on August 14, 1942 the ominous shadow of *Kirov* stretched in the wake of that imposing ship where it waited in the eastern approaches to the narrow Straits of Gibraltar. Her active sonar was pinging audibly, to make certain no undersea threat could come anywhere near them. Her radars rotated to scan the airspace all around them equally alert. To the northwest they could see the stark angles of the Rock itself, one of Great Britain's most important and strategic bases in all the world.

A small motor craft had been launched from the ship, and it made its way under a flag of truce slowly through the straits toward the rocky eastern shore of Las Palomas. Admiral Volsky sat proudly in the center of the boat, flanked by five other men. They could have made a much more dramatic appearance by landing on the island with the KA-40, but Volsky had decided not to create a spectacle that would simply lead to more uncomfortable questions. The less these men knew about them, the better.

He knew, however, that what he was attempting now was dangerous, perhaps more dangerous than anything the ship itself had faced in these last few harrowing days. Soon the Admiral's party made landfall and worked their way ashore. Now they stood beneath one of the old coastal ramparts, a beautiful castle ruin built in Neo-Renaissance fashion, smooth walls of amber sandstone with crenulated tops and styled parapets where the swarthy Moorish archers once stood their vigilant watch. Beneath it sat the squat rounded shapes of heavy stone encasements where old naval guns cast off from Spanish WWI Dreadnaughts had been installed as shore batteries in 1941. Their stark steel barrels jutted from the recessed gun ports, cold and threatening, and shadowed Volsky with the thought that war seemed to have no end, persisting through every generation throughout the whole of human history. The ruins and fortifications of one epoch after another were all folded together here on this tiny sentinel outpost, yet here he was, an outcast from another era, fighting in a war where he was never meant to be.

In the distance he could see the whitewashed stone lighthouse that marked the entrance to the straits. Built in the 1800s, it sat on a high cliff and towered over the rocky coastline below, where squadrons of sea birds soared in from the restless ocean, gliding over the stony shore. The wind was up, whipping the wave tops out in the straits, and he could look across and see the hazy silhouette of Jebel Musa rising on the coast of Spanish Morocco in the distance.

Volsky's boat had come in on the Mediterranean side of the island with his small detachment that included Fedorov, Nikolin as translator, and the redoubtable Kandemir Troyak with two of his best Marines. Admiral Tovey's launch had landed on the Atlantic coast on far side of the islands, and they would meet here, men of two different eras standing in the shadow of all this history, the legacy of mariners, sailors and soldiers that had occupied this tiny demarcation point in the long stream of time.

They saw Admiral Tovey's detachment approaching from the northwest, making their way slowly along the rocky shore. The Admiral stood tall in his dark navy blue uniform, his deportment clearly marking him as much as his uniform and cap as a man of authority. Admiral Volsky waited for him at a point he deemed to be the thin borderline between the ocean and the inland sea, a fitting place, he thought, for the meeting of two minds. There were six men in the British party as well, one clearly come from the Admiral's staff, his uniform crisp and proper, then another seaman in common dungarees and sweats, with three more men at arms to match his own. As they approached Volsky heard one of his Marines shift his automatic weapon to a ready position, and he turned, gesturing with his palm for the man to stand down. Troyak glared at the Marine, who quickly assumed a position at ease, lowering his weapon.

The British party came up, stopping about thirty paces off, a mixture of curiosity and caution in their eyes. Tovey indicated that his armed escorts should stand where they were, and he tapped the shoulder of his Chief of Staff Denny and the Able Seaman who would serve as their translator, leading them forward with a steady, measured pace. For his part, Volsky turned to Fedorov and Nikolin with a wink, and then stepped forward to greet the British, a noticeable limp still evident as he favored his bandaged right leg. He stopped, taking in the man before him now, noting Tovey's thin nose and narrow eyes beneath his well grayed hair.

Fedorov stood just a pace behind him, his eyes filled with awe and admiration as he stared at Tovey, a man with whom he had spent many long hours in his mind, within the history books he so loved. It was as if a living legend was before him now, yet flesh and blood, not the small black and white photos he would stare at to try and see into the man's mind. Here he was, Admiral of the Home Fleet!

Volsky extended his hand, his eyes warming as he greeted this fellow officer and denizen of the high seas. Tovey took the man's big hand, listening as Volsky spoke first, with Nikolin quickly translating what he said.

"My admiral says that, as it is impossible to get any sleep with all these guns and rockets and torpedoes flying off, he thought it might be best to have a little talk and see if we could calm things down before dinner."

The remark brought a smile to Tovey's face, softening the hard lines of his taught cheeks and easing the tension inherent in the situation. So here was his modern day Captain Nemo, human after all, he thought to himself, a hundred questions in his mind. But which to ask first? Politeness was always best, and he introduced himself with a tip of his cap. "I heartily agree, sir. I am Admiral John Tovey, Commander of the British Home Fleet, Royal Navy." The Able Seaman translated slowly, and Volsky nodded. Nikolin was to speak up if he heard anything mistranslated, but all was well.

"You will forgive me, Admiral, if I do not introduce myself beyond saying that I, too, am a commander of a proud fleet, and so we stand as equals here, at the edge of these two seas, and hopefully to find a better way to resolve our differences without further bloodshed. As you can see, I have a bit of a limp today, from a fragment of shrapnel that found me while I was climbing a ladder and decided to bite my leg. So I know only too well what can happen when men speak first with the weapons they command, and not their wits instead." Nikolin's voice echoed Volsky's, the Able Seaman listening, and satisfied that all was translated correctly.

"My apologies, Admiral," said Tovey. "It's just that your ship has made its way into a war zone, and has been taken as hostile from the moment it was first encountered. The attacks made on numerous Royal Navy ships did little to dissuade us from that conclusion."

"That is understandable," said Volsky. "But wrong. I must tell you that it was never my intention to involve my ship or my crew in battle with your navy. Yet one thing leads to another, does it not? Particularly at sea, when faced with uncertainty and driven by the need to defend your ship, and your country, from all harm."

"Then I'm to understand that you now wish to claim that everything that has transpired these last days had been an exercise of self defense?"

"That is so," said Volsky, his eyes trying to convey his sincerity.

"In defense of what country, may I ask?"

"You may not. The answer would not mean anything, and it would not help us resolve the issue before us now."

That confused more than it helped, but Tovey pressed on, edging out on a limb he had been climbing for so very many long months, ever since those first rockets branded his ship, and he saw that awful mushroom cloud of sea water towering over the cold North Atlantic.

"May I ask the Admiral if it is true that our ships and planes have met once before in this war, a year ago to be more precise, in the waters southwest of Iceland?"

Volsky shrugged. "Yes, you may ask it, and you may know it as well without the question. But I think it best we confine our chat to what lies ahead now, Admiral, and not what we have left behind us. Nothing that has happened can be undone—or at least that is something I once believed. I am not so sure any longer. But I will tell you that what we decide here today may have a grave impact on days that lie ahead, and more than either you or I can fathom at this moment."

Was the man being deliberately evasive, Tovey wondered? Yet he seems sincere. I can see it in his eyes, and hear it in his tone of voice. Yet who is he? Where has he come from? What is this dreadful *Nautilus* of a ship he commands with weapons the like of which this world has never seen?

"Then it *was* your ship that engaged the Royal Navy a year ago? Well now it is I who must ask your forbearance sir, but this is incomprehensible to us. How is it possible that we now find you here, in these waters, and yet have not had the ghost of a whisper of you, your ship, or these terrible weapons you possess, not in all the world for a whole long year? Your ship is not a submarine like the German U-Boats which use the swift currents in these straits to drift silently into the inland sea, unseen. You could not have passed Gibraltar without our knowing about it, and for that matter unchallenged. Nor could you have entered via the Suez Canal. Your presence here is therefore a matter of grave concern, and utterly confounding."

"Believe me when I say this, Admiral, but I am as much bewildered by these questions as you are. Yet I must be frank with you, sir. I do not wish to speak of who and what we are, or where we have come from, or how we came to be here. Yes, I know these questions beg answers, but the less that is said about them, the better. You may come to your own conclusions, I suppose. First off, you have found a young Able Seaman here who speaks our mother tongue." He let his eye rest on Tovey's, noting the man's reaction as he continued. "And from this you may surmise that we are a Russian ship and crew, but I must tell you that Joseph Stalin back in Moscow will have no inkling of us either—no knowledge whatsoever of our presence here, and he would have these very same questions for us if this were Murmansk and we were standing at the edge of the Kara Sea. We do not now sail in his name or serve the interests of the Soviet state he commands."

He paused, letting Nikolin catch up in his translation, but could see Tovey's frustration, and the confusion that must surely be plaguing him. Yet he noted how the man composed himself, inclining his head and asking another question.

"Was your ship built by the Soviet Union? And are you telling me you are at sea without orders, and against the wishes of the Soviet government? You are a renegade ship out of the Black Sea?"

"Admiral...You know very well that Soviet Russia could not build a ship that can do what you have witnessed my vessel do in battle, at least not today. We have just fought a long night engagement with two of your battleships. What were they called, Fedorov?"

"*Nelson* and *Rodney*, sir."

Volsky nodded, repeating the names as best he could. "*Nelson* and *Rodney*. More a admirals. It was an unfortunate engagement, and one I hope we do not have to repeat. It was our intention to outrun these ships and avoid combat. At least that is what my young Captain here, who commanded that action, tells me. But your ships fought well. I will express my regret to you now for any loss of life, but to secure the safety of my own ship, this engagement became an unfortunate necessity. Suppose I were to tell you that my ship *was* built in Russia. Could you believe that? I do not think so. What ship in Stalin's navy could stand with your *Nelson* and *Rodney* and come away from that battle unscathed? No. The Soviet government does not know that we even exist."

"I see..." Tovey was silent for a moment, thinking. "These weapons you deploy...They are certainly beyond our own means for the moment, unlike anything we have ever seen. Oh, I must tell you that rocketry is as old as gunpowder, but yet you seem to have perfected the art in a manner that is… rather frightening, at least to the men who have faced your weapons, and died…"

"For that I am truly sorry. I will tell you that I, too, have put men into the sea that I would rather see standing at their posts this evening. What more can be said of that? I will weep for them in my own time."

"Then *do* you serve a nation, Admiral? You are not German as we first thought; not Italian, not French as you wished us to believe. You clearly *are* Russian, but claim you bear no allegiance to the Soviet Union, our ally in this war at the moment, as I hope you must know."

"At the moment," said Volsky, thinking he had said just a little too much with that. "Admiral Tovey," he settled his voice, intent on forcing some new line in the discussion. "None of this matters, and there is no point in discussing these details. We are here, you are there. This thin boundary separates us, this line between the ocean and the sea at our feet, and yet it is a gulf that may seem impossible for either of us to ever cross. Still we must try to do so as best we can."

Tovey considered that, his eyes narrowed under his thin brows, lips taut. "I must tell you, Admiral, that I have brought my fleet here to make an end of your ship, and to put it at the bottom of the sea if I can do so. The oceans wide may appear to be the province of God, and God alone, but at this moment, as I stand here now before you, they are in point of fact the domain of the Royal Navy, and the British Empire that built it."

"And there is a difference between us now," said Volsky. "For I will not lay claim to God's great seas, nor did I bring my ship here to quarrel with you or your nation. I will admit that there are officers aboard my vessel who wished you no good once our battle was joined. Yet I do not sail here to throw down a gauntlet before your British Empire, or to contest these waters for any hope of gain. Your ships gave challenge. We defended ourselves. Men have died on both sides, and I am seeking a way to end this nightmare and go home. Yes, if you must know the truth, Admiral, I am simply trying to find my way home again."

"And yet you cannot even say where that is? Where in blazes did you come from?"

Nikolin had a little difficulty translating that last line, but knew enough to indicate that Admiral Tovey was expressing some anger. "He wants to know where we have come from, and I believe he getting a little angry about it, sir."

"You might say: where the hell you've come from?" The Able Seaman at Tovey's side put in.

Volsky nodded his understanding. "For the third time, I cannot answer that," he said. "For both our sakes. You will not know what I mean just yet, but perhaps you will in time." Then he spied the high promontory of the fortress wall on the hillside above them, and noted the gun casements that had been built for shore batteries at the foot of the walls. "Look there," he pointed. "My young officer Fedorov here tells me those walls were built by the Moors in the twelfth century. And below them there are casements and gun positions to be manned by men guarding these waters today. Years ago the Caliph of Morocco was master of these straits. Today it is your ships and guns who guard the way. And what if you were to sail here in your flagship one day, Admiral, and find those gun casements missing, seeing only the walls of that castle in their place? What if you were to meet the Moorish swordsmen and archers there, and they boldly told you that all you could see, on every quarter, was the domain of Abdul Ar Rahman?" Volsky glanced at Fedorov, a quiet smile on his lips, then continued.

"Things change, Admiral Tovey. Things change. I cannot answer your questions any more than you could explain your existence to the men who built that fortress. I can only say this: If you wish to try and put my ship at the bottom of the sea, then I must prevent you from doing so. Yes, your Royal Navy is here, and no doubt with all your finest ships, but they will not be enough, Admiral. They will not be enough. I must tell you that I did not wish to see the destruction that occurred when last we met at sea. There was great disagreement among my senior officers as to what should be done, and how much force should be used. Unfortunately, I was indisposed when it came to battle, and my ship was under the command of another officer, with another mind as to how the matter should have been dealt with. And yet, while I am reluctant to act in that same manner, I must tell you that I have the power to do so—that my ship has the power to sail on though these narrow straits, and find the open sea by force of arms if necessary, and you have not seen even a small measure of what we are truly capable of doing in battle."

Tovey frowned, a grave expression on his face, but Volsky continued, his tone changing now, more human, and with no hint of bravado in his voice. "There," he said. "We have both thumped our chests like a pair of old fools, and now we must decide what happens next. We can decide as Admirals in a sea of war, or we can decide as men, eye to eye, and face to face, and find another solution. We can use our warships to settle the matter, or our intelligence, and perhaps a little more. There was a great Russian writer who put it this way: 'It takes something more than intelligence to act intelligently.' We must find what that is, you and I, or I'm afraid a great many more men will pay the price of our stupidity."

Tovey took that in, considering. Yes, it made all the sense in the world now to find a way to settle this amicably, and without more loss of life, or ships for that matter. If he fought here, as he had hastened south with so much might to do, what would be left of his fleet at battle's end, even if he did prevail? Yet how could he allow a ship with such power to sail out into the Atlantic where the life blood of the Empire now moved in big fat convoys, guarded by ships of war— convoys like the one they had just risked so much to fight through to Malta. If he let this ship pass it could pose the gravest threat to those sea lanes. The outcome of the entire war effort could depend on their security. He had this mysterious ship before him now, and wondered if he would ever have such an opportunity again. He cleared his voice and spoke his mind.

"I am charged with the security of these sea lanes, sir. Surely you must understand that."

"Well, Admiral, it has come to the eleventh hour, and fearing what might happen if we let the time slip by to midnight without reason having a seat at the table, let me make a proposal. I seek an armistice in our private little war within a war here. You are busy enough with the Germans and Italians. Yes? So I ask you to leave my ship alone now and grant us safe passage through these straits and to give us the open sea you claim to rule. You may wish to know my intentions, and I will tell you that I have no hostile aim, nor do I wish to engage in any further combat, or even *contact* with your navy or that of any other nation. As to the security of your convoys, I must leave that to you, but I will give you my pledge that my ship will not fire on any merchant vessel we encounter, on any side in this war. We will give them a wide berth and do no harm. This is my word to you." He paused briefly, allowing Nikolin to catch up, and noting Tovey's facial expressions to read his response.

"All I wish is to find a nice peaceful island somewhere out of the stream of this war and consider how I can get my men and ship home again. To put this formally, I ask you now for safe passage in exchange for a pledge of armistice and neutrality. It would be my intention to get as far away from your war as my ship can possibly take me. Yes, I know it is a world war, and that may prove difficult, but there must be some island out there where I can get some sleep and find some peace and quiet to think. And if I never see another man die at sea, particularly as a result of my commands, then I will be a happier man for it. So that is my offer. That is all I desire, Admiral." He nodded his head. "And perhaps a nice bowl of borscht and a bottle of good vodka once in a while." He smiled, seeing his last remark well taken by Tovey.

Then the British Admiral's eyes hardened for a moment. Tovey clasped his hands behind his back, thinking as he gazed up at the tawny sundrenched walls of the Moorish fortifications. This Captain Nemo had said a good bit with that business about the castle, he realized. Perhaps he said more than he might have wished.

His eyes seemed to see far now, as if he were suddenly aware of distant events, a future time unseen, when this war was long over…when the British Empire itself was long gone, and when other men might walk the rocky shores of this island with no thought of conflict and war in their minds. Was that ever possible? He knew what the Admiralty would advise him here—what they would in fact order him to do. Somerville had faced it at Mers-el Kebir when he had asked the French fleet to join the Empire, and that failing, to scuttle their ships. They refused, of course, even as he himself would in the same situation. Yes, pride goeth before the fall, but pride could be as much a virtue as a vice, and he had little doubt that this Admiral before him would be found a proud and willful man if put to the test.

The man wanted to find an island, he thought, a mysterious island where he could rest and think. Well, we moved heaven and earth to put Napoleon on one. Here he is looking to make a graceful bow and drop anchor on his own St. Helena. The man's earnest desire to avoid further conflict was both obvious and admirable. Might he consider another proposal? It was worth the offer, and he spoke his mind.

"Admiral, I am inclined to believe you when you state your wish to avoid further hostilities. You have asked me to consider the question of armistice. May I ask you if you would consider the question of alliance? Might we two become friends instead of the witless enemies we have been up until now?"

Volsky smiled, as he had thought long and hard about this possible meeting, and knew this question would inevitably arise. The matter was coming to a head, and he knew his response now would be critical. He looked Tovey squarely in the eye. "If you had lightning in a bottle, would you pour it in your friend's glass, or your enemies?" He smiled. "I think to make either choice would end up killing them both. No, Admiral. I cannot join your war. We fought only because we had to—fought Italians ships and German planes, and you British as well. For a long time I think you believed we were a German ship. And the Italians and Germans may now think we are British. But if it is all the same to you, I think we would be most unwise to take any side in this war. We have done enough harm as it stands."

"I see," said Tovey, not surprised by the answer. The question was now starkly before him. There would be no alliance, but would there be war or peace with this man and his mysterious and terrible ship of war? With four battleships at hand Tovey still believed he had the means to prevail if it came to further conflict, but he was under no illusion that the task would be easy, or that he would even live to see it to a successful completion. He was going to lose ships and men if he fought now, that much was certain. Then an idea came to him. He knew it might cost his command, and even his rank and position in the Royal Navy itself, but somehow neither of those things seem to weigh in the balance.

"We faced this same dilemma with the French fleet, on more than one occasion," he began. "Now they are sitting comfortably at Toulon, though we did have word that the *Strasbourg* had been heading this way." He gave Volsky a knowing smile. "That said, might you consider sailing to a neutral country, under Royal Navy escort, and accept internment for the duration of the war?"

Again, this was not unexpected, but Volsky shook his head, smiling. "Admiral, do you think this ship would be left in peace under such circumstances? In what port, on any shore, could we drop anchor without fear that there would be men who would be very, very curious about us, men who would want to ask the same questions that remain in your mind? No. Such questions must remain unanswered, and it would be better if they were never asked. We must have freedom of movement to assure ourselves that this would be the case."

"But surely, you'll need fuel, water, food and supplies for your crew."

"We carry all the fuel we will ever need, and then some." He realized that Tovey would not comprehend that, so he manufactured a little white lie, a little *vranyo* to smooth the matter over. "We have a way to convert seawater to steam, so fuel is never a concern. As for food and water, these things we will find on our own, and with as little interference with others as possible."

"Then you don't see any further room for compromise?"

"I have compromised, Admiral. I did not have to ask for this conference, but yet I found it a wiser course than the one I was sailing at the time. I know the issue foremost in your mind now is trust. I suppose your Mister Churchill is thinking the same thing at this very moment as he sits down to dinner with Joseph Stalin in his *dacha* at Moscow." He saw Tovey raise an eyebrow at that, and pressed his point home. "Perhaps that is the one thing a man really needs to act intelligently—a little trust, a little faith, and a good heart. I know that you are driven to find answers to the questions in your mind about all of this, but I must caution that you stand to lose very much more than you gain should you do so."

Tovey breathed deeply, struck by that last remark. There was something more in the what the Admiral said just now. Something very much more. The conference in Moscow was held as a state secret and a matter of high security. Only very few knew it was taking place, even within the highest circles of the British government. For this man to know of it, and speak of it so casually…He regarded this Admiral with a knowing eye.

"Very well, Admiral. I will consider what you have said and asked here, but I think it best that I return to my ship for the moment, and you to yours. I will contact you at Midnight with an answer to this dilemma."

Volsky reached and again shook the man's hand. "Consider well, John Tovey. I will await your message."

Tovey spent those last hours considering the careful logic of his war plan, and wondering about all the subtle clues he had taken from this extraordinary encounter. *Russian*, he thought. They were clearly Russians, but yet they denied any affiliation with Stalin or the Soviet state. But how could they know of Churchill's meeting with Stalin in Moscow? Were they lying? The man's candor was clearly apparent, but more than that it was the logic of his argument that weighed more heavily on the issue. When I mentioned that Russia was our ally, the man's remark was rather telling ... 'At the moment...'

He said it as though he knew something to the contrary. *Could* this ship be a new Russian model, one they managed to build in the Black Sea, perhaps? Is that how it came to be in the Med—sneaking out through the Bosporus? Was it trying to get out into the Atlantic to strike at our convoys? Was Russia about to switch sides in this war? Then what about that business a year ago. The man clearly led me to believe that this ship was the same we encountered earlier. Was it? Could it have come out of Murmansk a year ago, and was it sunk by the Americans? This could be a sister ship, perhaps launched from Odessa or Sevastopol...But could the Russians build something like this, and without our knowing about it?

One question after another ranged through his mind, and he ticked them off, discarding each as utterly impossible. The Russians could not have built this ship any more than the Germans could have built it. Even if they did, how would it have escaped our notice? How could it have passed our coast watchers along the Dardanelles unseen, sailed through the Aegean like a phantom and then right past Vian's cruisers in the Eastern Med, let alone the Italians at Taranto? Impossible! No nation on this earth could have built it, unless there *was* some mysterious island out there where a consortium of renegade mad scientists had built this ship. The mystery was profound.

And what did this man mean when he pointed to those old fortifications like that, saying I would have a good deal of trouble explaining the presence of my fleet here to the Moors. There was clearly something there that kept tugging at the edge of his thinking, all wrapped up with his muse about Jules Verne and his strange story of Captain Nemo, and again, with the odd look in Professor Turing's eye in that hallway back at the Admiralty.

Why was this man being so blasted evasive? He refused to account for his presence, either here or in the North Atlantic a year ago, and it was as if the disclosure would cause some irreparable harm. He chided himself for not being more insistent, more forceful. By God, he had all the muscle and sinew of Home Fleet with him here. Syfret and Fraser had a couple of old, slow inter war battleships, their keels laid down in the early 1920s. He had four of Britain's newest dreadnoughts, fast, well protected, well gunned. He could force the issue and have an answer to these nagging questions once and for all, but the Admiral's remark still haunted him: *"I know that you are driven to find answers to the questions in your mind about all of this, but I must caution that you stand to lose very much more than you gain should you do so."* Was that simply another veiled threat should it come to battle here, or was there some darker implication in the Admiral's warning?

The damage reports from Fraser on *Rodney* finally reached him. There were over 200 casualties, yet the fires had finally been put out. Neither ship could make more than twelve knots, and *Nelson's* C turret was out of commission. But beyond that they were both still sea worthy, and their remaining guns were in good order. It would take them some time to come up behind this enemy ship again, but eventually they could throw in with his own fleet and he could squeeze this *Geronimo* between his fingertips like a bug.

Or could he… Memories of that awful mushroom of seawater and the capsized hull of the American battleship *Mississippi* glistening in the angry sea like a dead whale still haunted him, and told him that this bug might not be so easily squashed, and might as yet have some considerable bite.

Damn it then, Jack, he anguished. What's it to be? Did you sail here with the whole of Home Fleet to bandy about like this? The man wanted an island, he said. He just wanted to be left in peace and find his way home. And where was that?

He thought of Nemo coming at last to that Mysterious Island to die an old man, his vengeful sorties against navies of the world now ended. He would not accept internment at a neutral port…Then he thought of Napoleon again and had his answer. Yes! St. Helena! Suppose he offered this man safe passage and escort to St. Helena, a place far enough away from the curious eyes of anyone, to be sure. Yet his ships were already low on fuel and St. Helena was another thousand sea miles to the south. Yet he could transfer fuel to *Norfolk* and *Sheffield*, topping them off. That accomplished those two ships would have both the range to serve as escorts, and the speed to serve as a shadow if this ship attempted to slip away.

That thought was a foil opposing his hope in this alternative. If he needed every battleship the Royal Navy could spare here just to have an even chance with this demon, then *Norfolk* and *Sheffield* would be no match. They could not prevent this ship from sailing off if it wished. Then he realized it all came down to that one thing this Admiral had argued—trust. He had looked in this man's eyes and the mysterious and impenetrable riddle had become a human being, just another ordinary man and not a wizard from heaven or a monster from hell. His ship and its weapons might be monstrous, but so were the guns on *King George V*. Men build these monsters, and it is men who decide whether or not they will be used.

He folded his arms, staring at his battle plots in the chart room, seeing the action unfold in his mind's eye, wondering which ships would be stricken by those deadly sea rockets, or if the ocean would again be seared and boiled away by another of those terrible atomic weapons. He could probably sink this ship, but a very great many men would die tomorrow if he tried.

He decided.

Epilogue

"**Ship ahead!**" A watch stander called from the weather bridge, pointing off his starboard bow. Captain Clark stood on the flag bridge of the cruiser *Sheffield*, field glasses at his eyes as he peered at the distant ship.

The word was flashed quickly by lantern and signal flag to their companion, the heavy cruiser *Norfolk*, steaming a few hundred meters in their wake. From there it was passed again to the distant gray silhouettes of the big battleships farther out to sea. It was here…It was coming through the straits even now. Clark could see it—the white bow wave kicked up by the long, sharp prow, the dark mass behind it, her superstructure climbing up and up, bristling with strange antennae and pale metal domes. The sight of it gave him a chill, for every line and cut of her jib spoke of power, massive and threatening power. He had heard all the rumors about this ship; that it bloodied the noses of both *Nelson* and *Rodney* combined!

"Hal-o Mate," he said aloud to the distant ship. "What are we to do with these six inch popguns if *Nelson's* sixteen incher's weren't enough?"

He passed the word on to the Signals Lieutenant where he would let Captain Wilson on *Norfolk* worry about it with his eight inch guns. He was just told to get out in front of the fleet with Shiny Sheff and keep a sharp eye out for this ship at all times, and that is what he would do.

Sheffield had been selected for a very special mission. His ship was called 'Old Shiny' in the navy, because all the fittings that were normally crafted in brass on the other ships in this class had been machined in stainless steel on *Sheffield*. All her railings, stanchions, horns and even the ship's bells, were made of steel, and the ship sometimes glimmered in the light as she rolled in the heavy seas. But that had little to do with her mission here today. It was more her speed, good endurance, and most of all her advanced radar that made her the perfect scout ship.

The radar was mounted well up on the foremast, which came to be called the "cuckoo's nest" when sailors finally got a look at the odd antenna mounted there. The ship he was looking at now had even more wizardry about it. He could see the slowly rotating antennae on her aft mast and it gave him the chills to think of how far it might see, through weather and darkness, and even the smoke and fire of battle. By comparison the antennae rigged out in the cuckoo's nest on *Sheffield* seemed feeble.

Clark watched, spellbound, as the ship emerged from the mouth of the straits, like some evil sea beast being spewed from the belly of a whale. He looked over his shoulder again at the heart of Home Fleet, glad the stalwart battleships were there, spread out behind him in an arc of steel. They were cruising at wide intervals, their huge guns gleaming in the morning sun.

The strange interloper loomed ever nearer, then he saw the phantom ship turn fifteen points to port on a heading to take it quickly past the sharp rocky headlands of Cape Spartel west of Tangier. Its mass and size were even more evident now at this angle, and he found himself admiring the hard, yet elegant beauty of the ship, an amazing synthesis of artistry, power and speed. Yet, peering through his field glasses, the gun turrets he could make out at this range seemed no bigger than his own. He had heard about the rocketry, all the rumors, and had even seen some of the damage himself, but it was still hard to believe.

After a hard and costly journey through the cauldron of fire of the Mediterranean Sea, *Kirov* was finally back in the Atlantic. Admiral Tovey had sent word three hours ago that if this ship would accept an escort of two British cruisers and sail to the Island of St. Helena in the South Atlantic, then he would accept the offer of armistice in exchange for neutrality for the duration of the war. Admiral Volsky was grateful that he did not have to order the ship to fight again that morning, and that no one else would have to die. And he would have his island in the bargain as well! So he had agreed to sail on a course that would have him skirt Funchal Island, then to Palma in the

Canaries and finally Ribeira Grande in the Cape Verde Islands where coast watchers could also mark their progress south. From there it would be southeast to St. Helena, the island where England buried its monsters and the place where Napoleon Bonaparte had lived out his final days in captivity.

Fedorov had impressed the significance of this upon Admiral Volsky, urging him to accept Tovey's offer, but the Admiral needed no convincing. He got what he had asked for, a grudging peace, but peace nonetheless, and an island where he and his crew could rest, far from prying, curious eyes to have some time to decide their fate. Volsky had agreed to sail at no more than twenty knots speed at all times, and not to jam the British radar, as long as the two British ships would come no closer to his own vessel than five kilometers. He knew that range was nearly point blank for a well sighted naval gun, but trusted to the integrity of the men who had made their pledge in this negotiation. He wanted *Kirov's* war on the world to be over, but like the wishes of so many others that have gone unfulfilled, the world would not yet give that to him.

It was the fifth day since the ship had first arrived in the Tyrrhenian Sea of 1942, and *Kirov* sailed on through the Straits of Gibraltar on the 15th of August, cruising boldly past the long baleful line of Tovey's Home Fleet, the squat metal shapes of four identical battleships watching in silence. High overhead they saw fitful flights of British aircraft off the carrier *Avenger*, circling with watchful eyes.

Kirov turned south with *Sheffield* and *Norfolk* in her wake, starting the long sea cruise that would last all of seven more days. They followed the route as planned, through calm seas and past the exotic islands off the coast of Africa. And on the seventh day, a day when God himself was said to have rested, they saw a heavy shroud of fog lying low on the seas around a distant island peak.

They had agreed to heave to off the southern shores of St. Helena, anchoring at Sandy Bay off Powell's Gut at the base of a high ridge of tawny brown hills that rose 600 meters above the sea. There they would wait beneath the folded ravines and auburn cliffs known as the Gates of Chaos, or so it had been agreed. Volsky watched the distant island looming on the near horizon with rising curiosity. Karpov brooded, unhappy over the agreement but resigned. Fedorov seemed to be fidgeting nervously, his eyes glancing at the ship's chronometer as they approached the low haze laced island, the fog thickening around them as they went.

Five kilometers to either side of them, the watch officers on both *Sheffield* and *Norfolk* were relieved that the long sea journey was finally over, their charge nearly delivered. The strange ship would soon come under the observation of a special Royal Navy team that had been flown in ahead of them to Jamestown on St Helena. Soon the cruisers could finally turn and head north again.

The watchmen peered through their field glasses one last time, seeing the sleek battlecruiser pass slowly into the thickening fog. The land based observers were to call them from the top of High Ridge above the Gates of Chaos to report the ship's anchorage. In the meantime *Norfolk* and *Sheffield* would sail round either side of the island themselves, with each captain bound to log and report that the ship had been duly delivered to its place of internment, and obtain photographic evidence of such.

The Royal Navy was taking no chances that their new ward and visitor would slip away unseen. There were already three planes up from Jamestown with watchful eyes on every side of the island. The seaplane tender *Pegasus* would also make the long journey south to anchor at Jamestown with six more search planes for good measure.

And so it was that twelve days after she had again been pulled through time to the year 1942, *Kirov* sailed into the low bank of fog off the Island of St. Helena… and never sailed out. The observers on High Ridge would wait for her in vain, and would never see her arrive at Sandy Bay. For other Gates of Chaos had opened for her again that morning, and she was gone, lost, vanished from that day and year.

Norfolk and *Sheffield* searched in vain all that day, as did every plane available on the island, but not a trace or a whisper of the ship was seen or heard. In desperation the ships put divers in the water to look for any sign that the *Kirov* might have foundered and sunk while approaching the island through that heavy morning fog. Nothing was found…

Days later a car drove quickly up the lane towards a stately estate, its buildings clustered one against another in an odd mingling of architectural styles. Bletchley Park, or 'Station X' as it was called, was one of ten special operations facilities set up by MI6, where 'Captain Ridley's Shooting Party' was supposed to be enjoying afternoons on the adjoining sixty acre estate, with shotguns and hounds to hunt down quail. Yet its real purpose was derived from the feverish activity of the Government Code and Cypher School, England's code breakers, a collection of brilliant and dedicated men and women who would generate the vital intelligence information needed to prosecute the war.

Here there were walls of colored code wheels, strange devices like the Enigma machines and odd looking equipment fed by long coiled paper tape, dimpled with a series of small black dots of varying sizes. The minds of Bletchley Park were already in the first stages of digitizing the analog world into forms their nascent computing machines could digest and ruminate upon. A year later the estate would see the installation of the first "Colossus" machine, a rudimentary computer housing all of 1500 vacuum tubes to power its mechanical brain.

The car stopped, its door opening quickly as Admiral Tovey stepped out, a thick parcel under his right arm. He did not approach the styled mansions up the main walkway, but veered left towards a green sided extension—Hut 4, the heart of naval intelligence. A year ago the men who worked there had been reveling in their first breakthrough, the deciphering of the German Enigma code. Then came the unaccountable appearance of a strange ship in the Northern Seas, and it set the whole community back on its heels.

Tovey walked past the row of white trimmed windows and entered through a plain unsigned door. He was immediately greeted by a Marine guard, who saluted crisply and led him down the narrow hall to the office of Professor Alan Turing, who had been reading a volume of Byron's poetry as he waited for the Admiral.

"Good day, Professor," said Tovey as he walked briskly in, his hand extended. Turing set his poetry down and rose to greet him, his dark eyes alight with a smile.

"I've brought you a little something more for your file boxes," said Tovey.

"Ah," said Turing, "The photography!"

"Indeed. Two reels of film here with photos, and a full report. I've collected the logs of all ships involved, so you'll have a good time sorting it all through before it gets filed away with everything else on this *Geronimo* business."

"Very good, sir," said Turing, his curiosity immediately aroused. "I wonder, Admiral. Might I persuade you to allow me to fly out to St. Helena one of these days and have a look for myself?"

Tovey raised an eyebrow, his face suddenly serious, and seated himself, his eye falling on the open volume of Byron's poetry. He scanned the lines, reading inwardly:

> *"On the sea the boldest steer but where their ports invite;*
> *But there are wanderers o'er Eternity*
> *Whose bark drives on and on,*
> *and anchor'd ne'er shall be."*

With a heavy sigh he looked at Turing, and all the unanswered questions in his mind took a seat there with him, waiting to have their say. "I'm afraid I have some rather interesting news for you, Professor," he said quietly. "And I think it's high time that you and I have a very frank chat."

The Saga Continues...

Kirov *III* - *Pacific Storm, By John Schettler*

Admiral Tovey's visit to Bletchley Park soon reaches an astounding conclusion when Tovey reveals that, reaching the island of St Helena, the battlecruiser *Kirov* has vanished without a trace. Gone from that day and year and lost again in a desolate future, they sail east, round the Cape of Good Hope and into the Indian Ocean, hoping to find some sign of human life in the southern hemisphere. Reaching the Pacific they soon learn that *Kirov* has once again moved in time, seemingly trapped in a strange cycle that displaces the ship every twelve days.

Now First Officer, Anton Fedorov is shocked to finally discover the true source of the great variation in time that has led to a devastated future they have come from and the demise of civilization itself. The chronology of the war at sea in the Pacific has been radically changed, and nothing in his history books can help them navigate the dangerous waters of the Coral Sea.

Discovered by the Japanese fleet poised to invade Port Darwin, the ship now faces its most dangerous and determined challenge ever when they are stalked by the powerful Japanese 5th Carrier Division and are eventually confronted by a powerful enemy task force led by the battleship *Yamato* and an admiral determined to sink this phantom ship, or die trying.

In this amazing conclusion to the popular *Kirov* trilogy, the most powerful ships ever conceived by two different eras clash in a titanic final battle that will decide the fate of nations and the world itself.

Please visit www.writingshop.ws for final publication date

~ OTHER BOOKS BY JOHN SCHETTLER ~

The Meridian Series

Book I: *Meridian – A Novel In Time*
ForeWord Magazine's "Book of the Year"
2002 Silver Medal Winner for Science Fiction
The adventure begins on the eve of the greatest experiment ever attempted—Time travel. As the project team meets for their final mission briefing, the last member, arriving late, brings startling news. Catastrophe threatens and the fate of the Western World hangs in the balance. But a visitor from another time arrives bearing clues that will carry the hope of countless generations yet to be born.

Book II: *Nexus Point*
The project team members slowly come to the realization that a "Time War" is being waged by unseen adversaries in the future. The quest for an ancient fossil leads to an amazing discovery hidden in the Jordanian desert. A mysterious group of assassins plot to decide the future course of history, just one battle in a devious campaign that will span the Meridians of time, both future and past.

Book III: *Touchstone*
When Nordhausen follows a hunch and launches a secret time jump mission on his own, he uncovers an operation being run by unknown adversaries from the future. The incident has dramatic repercussions for Kelly Ramer, his place in the time line again threatened by paradox. Kelly's fate is somehow linked to an ancient Egyptian artifact, once famous the world over, and now a forgotten slab of stone. The result is a harrowing mission to Egypt during the time frame of Napoleon's 1799 invasion.

Book IV: *Anvil of Fate*

The cryptic ending of Touchstone dovetails perfectly into this next volume as Paul insists that Kelly has survived, and is determined to bring him safely home. Only now is the true meaning of the stela unearthed at Rosetta made apparent—a grand scheme to work a catastrophic transformation of the Meridians, so dramatic and profound in its effect that the disaster at Palma was only a precursor.

Book V: *Golem 7*

Nordhausen is back with new research and his hand on the neck of the new terrorist behind the Palma Event. Now the project team struggles to discover how and where the Assassins have intervened to restore the chaos of Palma, and their search leads them on one of the greatest naval sagas of modern history—the hunt for the battleship *Bismarck.*

Alternate Military History (Naval)

Kirov

The battlecruiser *Kirov*, is the most power surface combatant that ever put to sea. Built from the bones of all four prior *Kirov* Class battlecruisers, she is updated with Russia's most lethal weapons, given back her old name, and commissioned in the year 2020. A year later, with tensions rising to the breaking point between Russia and the West, *Kirov* is completing her final missile trials in the Arctic Sea when a strange accident transports her to another time. With power no ship in the world can match, much less comprehend, she must decide the fate of nations in the most titanic conflict the world has ever seen—WWII.

Historical Fiction

Taklamakan ~ *The Land Of No Return*
It was one of those moments on the cusp of time, when Tando Ghazi Khan, a simple trader of tea and spice, leads a caravan to the edge of the great desert, and becomes embroiled in the struggle that will decide the fate of an empire and shake all under heaven and earth. A novel of the Silk Road. (Print and eBook) Note: Print version contains the original parts I and II in a single volume. eBook versions present parts I and II as separate files (each over 300 pages) and part II, *Khan Tengri*, is extended and revised.

Khan Tengri ~ *Volume II of Taklamakan*
Learn the fate of Tando, Drekk, and the others in this revised version of Part II of Taklamakan, with a 30,000 word, 7 chapter addition! (eBook Only)

Science Fiction

Wild Zone ~ *Classic Science Fiction*
A shadow has fallen over earth's latest and most promising colony prospect in the Dharma system. When a convulsive solar flux event disables communications with the Safe Zone, special agent Timothy Scott Ryan is rushed to the system on a Navy frigate to investigate. He soon becomes embroiled in a mystery that threatens the course of evolution itself as a virulent new organism has targeted mankind as a new host.

Mother Heart ~ *Sequel to Wild Zone*
Ensign Lydia Gates is the most important human being alive, for her blood holds the key to synthesizing a vaccine against the awful mutations spawned by the Colony Virus. Ryan and Caruso return to the Wild Zone to find her, discovering more than they bargained for,

and the ancient entity at the heart of the mystery of life on Dharma VI. (eBook Only)

Dream Reaper ~ *A Mythic Mystery/Horror Novel*
There was something under the ice at Steamboat Slough, something lost, buried in the frozen wreckage where the children feared to play. For Daniel Edwards, returning to the old mission site near the Yukon where he taught school a decade past, the wreck of an old steamboat becomes more than a tale told by the village elders. In a mystery weaving the shifting imagery of a dream with modern psychology and ancient myth, Daniel struggles to solve the riddle of the old wreck and free himself from the haunting embrace of a nightmare older than history itself.

For more information visit:
http://www.writingshop.ws
http://www.dharma6.com